PENGUIN BOOKS

'A great insight into how hard it is to be an intern at a music television company' – Trevor Nelson (BBC Radio 1, 1Xtra)

'A brilliant insight into a world I know all too well. A real page-turner' – Reggie Yates (BBC Radio 1)

'A blast from the past. Takes me back to the good old days' – Lisa Snowdon (Capital FM)

'An amazing read. It's a brilliantly told story about getting ahead in the media world' – Rickie H-Williams and Melvin Odoom (Kiss FM and T4)

'A revealing and engaging account of taking those first steps into music television. *The Devil Wears Prada* meets *Entourage*' – Laura Whitmore (MTV)

'The way Dillon has brought [this] era back to life . . . is amazing. After reading *The Intern* I wish I'd partied even more' – Nihal (BBC Radio 1)

Dillon Khan was born in London, a city that gave him a rich music education. After graduating from university, he spent eight years as a journalist and producer, making shows about music, lifestyle and youth culture at MTV. In his collection he has 4,786 CDs, 3,669 tape cassettes, 6 vinyl records, one 8-track and counting. *The Intern* is his first novel.

For advice on internships, more information and extras, go to
www.theintern.co.uk

the INTERN

Dillon Khan

PENGUIN BOOKS

PENGUIN BOOKS

Published by the Penguin Group
Penguin Books Ltd, 80 Strand, London WC2R ORL, England
Penguin Group (USA) Inc., 375 Hudson Street, New York, New York 10014, USA
Penguin Group (Canada), 90 Eglinton Avenue East, Suite 700, Toronto, Ontario, Canada M4P 2Y3
(a division of Pearson Penguin Canada Inc.)
Penguin Ireland, 25 St Stephen's Green, Dublin 2, Ireland (a division of Penguin Books Ltd)
Penguin Group (Australia), 250 Camberwell Road, Camberwell, Victoria 3124, Australia
(a division of Pearson Australia Group Pty Ltd)
Penguin Books India Pvt Ltd, 11 Community Centre, Panchsheel Park, New Delhi – 110 017, India
Penguin Group (NZ), 67 Apollo Drive, Rosedale, Auckland 0632, New Zealand
(a division of Pearson New Zealand Ltd)
Penguin Books (South Africa) (Pty) Ltd, Block D, Rosebank Office Park,
181 Jan Smuts Avenue, Parktown North, Gauteng 2193, South Africa

Penguin Books Ltd, Registered Offices: 80 Strand, London WC2R ORL, England

penguin.com

First published 2012
001 – 10 9 8 7 6 5 4 3 2 1

Set in Sabon LT Std
Typeset by Palimpsest Book Production Limited, Falkirk, Stirlingshire
Printed in Great Britain by Clays Ltd, St Ives plc

British Library Cataloguing in Publication Data
A CIP catalogue record for this book is available from the British Library

ISBN: 978-0141-33804-0

www.greenpenguin.co.uk

MIX
Paper from
responsible sources
FSC   FSC™ C018179
www.fsc.org

Penguin Books is committed to a sustainable
future for our business, our readers and our planet.
This book is made from Forest Stewardship
Council™ certified paper.

ALWAYS LEARNING   **PEARSON**

Dedicated to my nieces
and interns (past, present and future)

'Your attitude determines your latitude.'

CONTENTS

1
THE IMPOSSIBLE DREAM

'Single to Notting Hill,' I said hurriedly, no time to buy a weekly or monthly pass. I looked at my watch, compared it to my phone, then the clock above the turnstiles and, out of the corner of my eye, quadruple-checked the watch of the cute girl waiting behind me in line. My desperation was a sorry-ass attempt to reclaim some wasted minutes that I had lost somewhere between getting ready early and walking out of the door late. This particular morning I was blaming *The Big Breakfast* and a mesmerizing feature about a skateboarding dog.

My journey became a DVD 'forward skip' moment, where I hopped on to the Tube, got squashed inside the carriage under someone's armpit, saw the cute girl reading her *Heat* magazine and bored myself silly re-reading the onboard adverts for the umpteenth time as the train slowly meandered from east to west London.

Apart from the renowned carnival and the film starring Julia Roberts, Notting Hill was famous for being a melting pot. Some of the capital's elite rich inhabited the Victorian townhouses, while a stone's throw away were the poor working classes living in squalid social housing. From the posh yummy mummies and the whispering drug dealers, to the antique-shop owners and backpack tourists, everyone mixed like a canteen in the UN building. It was cool, creative and 'edgy': read – prone to the odd drug-related stabbing.

It was 9.55 a.m. as I surfaced from the underground on to the busy street. Opposite the station people jockeyed for position to get on the approaching bus like marathon runners before the sound of the starter's gun. I ignored the man screaming 'Big Issue!' and ducked past the group of nursery-school kids out on a day trip, getting into a sprint of my own. Ten minutes later, I arrived in a sweat at my destination not far from the trendy Portobello Road.

The building in front of me was so ugly the Broadwater Farm council estate in the 1980s looked more welcoming. Even after the riots. Its front stretched down the street, the two-storey walls covered in pigeon shit, unattractive graffiti, puke and urine. You wouldn't think it, but it housed American media giant Gibaidem Corporation's best-known business, The Beat. It was an unrivalled youth channel spanning the globe that played music videos and irreverent TV shows and it was synonymous with all things cutting edge and 'cool'. They'd only moved in a few weeks earlier because the previous office had become too small. From here the iconic channel broadcast all across Europe, with its corporate headquarters still based in the best spot on the Monopoly board: Mayfair.

As I stepped on to the huge forecourt beyond the security barriers, I passed the only colourful thing in sight. I tell a lie: two colourful things. They were identical except one was ruby red and the other arctic blue, but the latest BMWs certainly added some bling to an otherwise dull place. To the side of the main entrance was the only clue that gave away what was inside this monstrosity of a building. A small fifteen-centimetre by fifteen-centimetre silver plaque with black writing that read 'THE BEAT' in Helvetica typeface.

I pressed the stop button on my Sony Walkman and took my headphones off, resting them round my neck. I headed through the revolving glass door, coming out the other side to a cacophony of ringing phones, shouting voices and lots of different music. And this was just Reception. In a small room to my right was Security, with a host of CCTV screens manned by three uniformed men who were staring intently at them like they were showing porn. Further on, the small passage opened into a larger area where a receptionist sat behind a long desk as the huge plasma screen behind her showed the Red Hot Chili Peppers painted in metallic silver. As I walked towards her, the post room on the left blasted out its own music, setting a tempo for the packages and letters that were being flung into pigeonholes. This morning's track was Adam F's 'Circles'. The walls were covered in posters saluting Arsenal FC and some voluptuous *FHM* beauties alongside fire-escape plans and various DHL courier forms.

As I stood in front of the receptionist, who was on the phone, nerves and a sense of anticipation tingled through my body, visible only in the goofy smile plastered on my face. I looked around at the visitors waiting on the big red beanbags next to the water cooler. A middle-aged man in an expensive-looking suit clearly felt out of place. He sat uncomfortably low down and would definitely need a hand getting up. Even more amusing to me was his early-twenties female colleague sitting on the beanbag next to him. Obviously all dressed up, trying to be cool and trendy for the occasion, she looked even more awkward than the man as her skirt rode dangerously high up her legs. As hard as she tried to hide them, her knickers were blatantly pink.

'Hi, I'm here to see Maximilian Miller, producer of *Total BEATS*,' I said to the receptionist once she got off the phone.

I stood in front of her in my dweebie clothes and within a split-second she had given me a full up-and-down glance from my waist to my hair. If the desk wasn't in her way it would have been a complete scan, quicker than you could say the word 'pervert'.

'You mean Max. Who may I say is calling for him?' she said in a posh accent.

'Jay Merchant. I'm his new intern,' I replied proudly.

She picked up the phone and after a brief chat that seemed more about the must-see TV shows that weekend than about me she put the phone down. Exhaling through her nose, she gave me the same look I got when I failed my first driving test.

'Max said you weren't starting today but next week. I think there's been a mix-up,' she said quietly, almost whispering.

I smiled. 'April Fools' is a few days away yet,' I joked.

The muscles on her face didn't flinch.

My smile dropped and the excitement became short-lived. 'Oh . . . OK,' I said in shock, not knowing what I should do next. I instinctively reached for the letter in my pocket, opened it up and there in bold was my start date: 27 March

2000. I hadn't got it wrong. But I couldn't wait another week – I wasn't just broke, I was in the red thanks to my student loans. I'd already cancelled the shifts at Foot Locker and told them to stick their job because I had a new one. *I can't eat humble pie and go back*, I thought. It would taste of double choc shit.

'Max said to say hello before you go,' she added.

'Oh, OK,' I mumbled, still feeling sorry for myself.

'He said to meet him in the Greenhouse,' she said, pointing into the main part of the building.

I followed her directions and stood at the entrance to the huge break-out space, marvelling at its mish-mash design from left to right. It was filled with huge green plants, funky and futuristic-looking furniture, an arcade area, laptop stations, a pool table, weird sculptures and paintings in a gallery space with white lino on the floor, perfect if you fancied a bit of breaking on it. It looked tempting. One wall was covered in graffiti art like an iconic 1980s New York subway train while another had autographs from famous visitors. There was a stage with a permanent backline including DJ decks. Above it was a banner proclaiming The Beat's mantra: Doin' it for the Kids! Was this an office or a weird youth centre?

I answered my question by looking up at the next floor where the actual offices were. That had a traffic flow all of its own, as people passed each other hurriedly, notebooks in one hand and spilling coffee with the other.

All of a sudden a gaggle of people brushed past me into the Greenhouse, like a rugby scrum with a woman in a hat and shades in the middle. Was that Mariah Carey? I wasn't sure as in no time she was rushed through a door and the quiet returned. As I stood soaking it all in, my nerves were momentarily replaced by a rush of excitement: I was at the heartbeat of music.

2
THE WORLD IS YOURS

As I waited for Max, I plonked myself into a beanbag in the Greenhouse next to a well-dressed bloke about my age, a fellow recent graduate perhaps. We sized each other up and saw a familiar look of nerves running through the other. After a head nod and introductions, Leon and I began making small talk as there were no magazines on a coffee table to occupy us. Eventually I asked 'So, what you in for?' like we'd come to court for a misdemeanour.

'I'm here to drop my CV off to someone in HR. Hoping they've got some entry-level jobs. What about you?' asked Leon.

'Starting my internship,' I replied, although I was still unsure when that would be.

His eyes lit up as he sat up straight – hard to do in a beanbag. 'Niiiice. It's so hard trying to get a look in anywhere. How did you manage it?'

'Long or short version?' I asked.

He looked around. 'I've been waiting for fifteen minutes already so you can go with the long one.'

'Well, I left Birmingham University with a degree in Classical Literature and Civilization but without a clue about what I wanted to do with my life. I'd kept putting off addressing it for years.'

'You and me both!' he said, our camaraderie cemented.

'I sent CVs out to marketing and advertising firms and kept getting rejected. With a huge student loan to pay off and no job in sight, I was in the doldrums for months and unable to do anything except watch daytime soaps.'

'*Sunset Beach* was my guilty pleasure,' he said, causing us both to chuckle.

'Oh no, not you as well. So anyway, one day I was watching *Total BEATS* and it hit me: *I want to work on that show*. I knew it inside out as we all watched it religiously at university and it became the centre point for most of our discussions, several heated arguments and one small punch-up.'

'About?' Leon enquired.

'Who was better, Tupac or Biggie?'

He laughed and then asked, 'So you wrote to The Beat for a job?'

'Yeah, but I decided to hunt down the producer, Max, first,' I said, hesitating before being remarkably honest to a stranger. 'You could say I stalked him.'

'Nice!'

'I didn't want to be just another letter. Luckily for me a few weeks later Max was a panellist at a talk on the impact of technology on the music industry to three hundred students. As soon as it was done, two hundred and ninety-nine kids bum-rushed the stage to talk to people from the record labels as he slipped away round the back. Believe me, I wouldn't normally do this but I found myself giving chase after him like he was a pair of limited-edition Superstars in the sales.'

'You chased Max?'

'Yep. I shouted down a darkened corridor behind him and harassed him into taking my CV before Security escorted me away.'

'Didn't he think you were a bit weird?' he said, looking astonished.

'Course he did, but I had to show him I was serious. He didn't call for two weeks so I went about tracking him down. At first he never picked up except once in a blue moon for a few seconds saying, "I'm busy, call back next week." But I soon realized Friday was the best day to get a proper chat out of him and that's when I showered him with ideas I had for the show.'

'And how long did this courting period last for?' asked Leon cheekily.

'Several months but I persisted.'

'And then you got the internship?'

'No,' I responded.

Leon suddenly became distracted and looked over my shoulder at someone official walking down the stairs, but when she went into the toilets he realized it wasn't someone from HR coming to collect him. I continued my tale of how I got through to the Production department's Rottweiler-like PA who was answering his calls. Her response to a request for Max's email address was: 'Don't call him, he'll call you.'

'So I got her name and decided to go old school on her ass. I wrote her a poem. That's right, a poem. Dedicated to her, her greatness and begging for an appointment to see Max.'

'And?' Leon said in anticipation.

'Three years of studying literature finally proved useful in getting me coffee with him two days later.'

'And then he offered you an internship?'

'No. He said there was no paid work but I could come in and do work experience. So I juggled shifts at Foot Locker and went to The Beat's other offices and helped out part-time.'

Leon fidgeted in his seat as though his legs were going numb having been sat in the same position for so long. 'So then what happened?' he asked.

'Well, I thought I'd be going on shoots, edits and learning. Instead I sat logging tape after tape of artists' interviews and Max's footage from the BRITs and the GRAMMYs, basically watching him have fun. Mind-numbingly boring and hardly an opportunity to make an impression. But I didn't have anywhere else. Then after a few months Max gave me another box of tapes and told me to go see some bloke called Robert Johns.'

'For more logging? You should have said something!' said Leon, exasperated on my behalf.

'Well, the words formed a jumbled queue in my head. "You" and "piss-taker" wanted to get to the front but were being held back by "I", "don't", "want", "to", "sound", "ungrateful" and "but".'

'You chickened out?'

'I had to and in the end the most pathetic word managed to get bumped to the front of the queue – "OK".'

Annie Ferguson, one of The Beat presenters I recognized,

distracted us both this time, walking past with bouncy blonde hair and flashing us her distinctive smile.

'So who was Robert Johns?'

I described the meeting with the blond dreadlocked chap sat in a lotus position on his sofa in a corner office, who turned out to be a senior producer and Max's boss.

'He didn't want me to log anything for him but started asking me questions about what I studied and where. It was turning out to be a job interview. My facial expression stayed neutral like a gear stick until he said, "To be honest, if it was up to me, you'd be a girl. They work harder and look a lot better. But if you're good enough for Max then you're good enough for me. Besides, if you're not I'm sure you'll leave of your own accord!"'

'Harsh,' said Leon.

'Yeah, but it was only then I realized how lucky I was. He showed me a huge pile of what must have been a thousand CVs to fill six intern spots.'

'A thousand! No way,' Leon said in disbelief.

'He told me kids from all over applied. Rich, poor, connected, unconnected. Apparently people were even offering bribes to get in.'

'And you got a job because you stalked Max.' He laughed.

'No, it was talent, perseverance . . .' I hesitated and then admitted, 'and logging a million bloody tapes for six months!'

'Fina-bloody-ly,' said Leon, letting out a sigh. I wasn't sure if he was happy my story had come to an end or that I finally got something for my tenacity.

'He told me, like any job, this was a stepping-stone not

the end point of my career. "The Beat's like the university of the TV world",' I recalled.

'Sign me up for three years, please,' said Leon excitedly.

'At the end he says, "Ray, getting a job is all about luck. Being at the right place, right time. Do you know how I avoid employing unlucky people? I throw half of the CVs in the bin without reading them."'

Leon's face dropped at the prospect he might be wasting time handing in his CV. Seeing this, I continued quickly, 'I'm still not entirely sure what was true and what was a "joke" in that interview. The wage was definitely the latter and the six-month contract the former.'

Suddenly there was a voice behind me. 'Dude, I'm so sorry for the mix-up, I should have called you.' It was Max.

He was dressed in baggy designer jeans and a white T-shirt showing an image of a man about to destroy a guitar on the floor. I knew he was heavily into martial arts and had learnt Calinda, Krav Maga and Taekwondo, which kept him in great shape. Added to this his arms were inked in Japanese tattoos that made him look hard as hell to men and sexy as hell to women. Dude's whole ensemble was fucking cool and made him look like he was the business.

I stood up. 'It's OK,' I said, happy to shoulder the inconvenience.

'The department's up in the air since we moved in. There's been some major goings-on at the top so HR still hasn't signed you off yet,' he said, frustrated.

'No worries. Sounds quite manic,' I obliged, doing my best to smile.

I said goodbye to Leon, who looked like he was re-evaluating just blindly handing in the CV he was holding.

'C'mon, let's go for a coffee, I need to get out of this mayhem,' said Max, leading the way and flashing a grin at Miss Pink Knickers as we passed Reception.

3
BREAK ON THROUGH (TO THE OTHER SIDE)

A week after the mix-up Max was meeting me in the Greenhouse again, but this time all systems were go. Each step we took up to the first floor filled me with excitement. Once at the top of the stairs, I finally got to see above the parapet. In front of me lay an open-plan office, just desks with computer screens and TVs playing music videos as far as the eye could see. And people. Not just people but good-looking people. Some sat on the desks with their feet up, others were looking over papers in a huddle or eagerly recounting tales from the weekend. It felt like a cool school common room, like the one from *Beverly Hills, 90210*.

The tour of the building was conducted in The Beat way. Max and I hopped on two push scooters and wheeled around the building like it was a playground. He pointed out all the different departments and graded them for their drinking prowess, along with where all the hot girls sat. By the end of it, my mind was buzzing with both excitement and information overload of names and faces, functions and places. But I knew I was about to get a whole lot more as he dropped me off at a room known as The Sixties. Every meeting room was filled with images highlighting musical icons from a particular decade, ensuring music subliminally remained at the front of everyone's minds when in discussion.

On the door was an A4 piece of paper with felt-tip handwriting reading 'intern induction'. There seemed to be a lot of A4 pieces of paper dotted around the building as makeshift signs. I'd already spotted one on a viewing machine ('dubbing'), on a chair ('director/part-time DJ'), on rubbish ('to be collected') and on someone's back ('I love Vanilla Ice').

For once I was on time, yet I was surprised to see so many people had arrived early. They were gathered in a tight cluster around a small table, holding paper cups in one hand and chocolate digestives in the other. A PowerPoint presentation was set up on a laptop as the projector next to it shone an infinity symbol, The Beat's iconic logo, on to the wall.

As I walked in, everyone turned to look at me. It was a communal look of nerves. I hesitated for a moment then walked up to them sheepishly. At that point everyone realized I too was part of the flock and not the shepherd that they were all expecting.

'Am I late? Sorry, I'm Jay, intern for *Total BEATS*.'

The group opened up and let me in. A hand came out towards me and I reached forward and shook it.

'No, bang on time. Hi, I'm Sonya, intern for *iWant*, the video request show.' She was petite, cute and blonde with beautiful blue eyes. Kind of like Smurfette, but with an Antipodean accent.

'Hi,' I replied, doing my best to look friendly.

'How are you? I'm Cara, intern for *D.A.N.C.E.*,' said another voice, this time Irish, followed up by a very firm handshake. She was tall, had huge breasts and looked gothic, like a young Morticia from the Addams Family.

Next up was Tola, intern for *The News Feed*. She was a smartly dressed Nigerian American chick. She was carefully co-ordinated, from the earrings and nail varnish to the shoes and handbag. She looked like Vanessa Williams in her prime, when Digital Underground put her name in their rhyme for 'Doowutchyalike'.

The next hand came out with a biscuit, then went to a mouth, popped the whole biscuit in, wiped the crumbs on a jeans leg then came back to mine, and an accompanying voice said, 'Hooy, mammesmaamurrd, mimtemvoormoovovovy.'

A couple of quick munches later it came out clearer.

'Sorry . . . James the Third, intern for *Musosophy*.' He spoke in a Yorkshire accent, was tall and built like one of those rugby player-cum-volleyball spiker-cum-water polo toffs. It was ego-bruising to stand next to an Abercrombie and Fitch-like model.

'The Third?' I asked, thinking, *Do they have posh boys up north?*

'Yeah, there's two Jameses already in the office. So I'm the third.'

'Ah, makes sense,' I replied as the introductions continued.

'Hi, I'm the intern for the hip-hop show *Rap Beat*,' said the final girl, who was Scottish. 'I'm Samina, but you can call me Sam.' She was pretty, with a tomboy look about her. No make-up, hair scraped back in a ponytail, big earrings and a hoodie.

They all looked like they should be on the front cover of *i-D* magazine as the 'new cool kids on the block'. Was that how I looked to them too, in my scruffy clothes? It was like the first day at school. Everyone was bright-eyed and bushy-tailed but with a look of fear as they headed into the unknown.

'So we're the ones who made it,' I said. I knew *I* had a story, so I asked, 'How did you guys get in?'

'I slept with the head of Production,' said Cara, getting in first.

The room paused as we stared at her, her face straight from the poker tables of Vegas. It turned into a wry smile.

'I made a short docu-film about Irish protest music with my dad's camera that got shown at the London Film Festival,' she said with a casual tone that downplayed the accomplishment. 'One of the heads at The Beat saw it, recommended me and I was offered a role. I don't really want to work here, but, hey, it's a bit quiet in Cork.'

Shit, I hadn't made a film. I hadn't even picked up a camera. Jesus, this girl must be good. I suddenly felt out of place. There was still hope. Maybe the next person got in without a short film or a bloody BAFTA.

'What about you, Sonya?' asked Cara.

'Oh, I used to be a runner at one of the edit houses The Beat uses in Soho. For a whole year I was getting meals for clients and cleaning out the rubbish but I did get to watch and learn some editing techniques. One day an editor called in sick with the runs and there was no one else about so I seized the moment and edited for one of The Beat's executive producers. It allowed me to sneak my CV to her at the end of the day. A few months later I got the call,' she said, smiling like she'd won the lottery.

'You can edit?' I asked in shock.

'Just the basics on the Avids,' she said humbly.

Er, what the hell's an Avid? I thought.

We continued round the room to hear everyone's remarkable stories. Sam had started her own free urban magazine at the age of seventeen. Her referral came from the head of marketing at Arista Records who said Sam was pivotal in breaking acts on the underground. And no wonder, she had interviewed everyone in the UK hip-hop scene and was a respected aficionado.

Tola had graduated from Columbia University in New York, having majored in Economics. Straight after, she had an unpaid job with UNICEF's press department where she went with camera crews into some of the poorest areas of the world to highlight the suffering. From there she saw the power the media had to change things and wanted to pursue a career in it. She had been put forward by someone 'high up' at UNICEF who'd gone to school with a member of The Beat's senior management.

A self-published magazine and working for UNICEF. It was up to James III to make me feel better. Turned out he had sent a Kit Kat and his CV to the head of HR with a covering letter that simply read 'Gimme a break, Have a Kit Kat'. Maybe the moon was aligned with the sun at just the right angle with Jupiter in the correct quadrant with Venus, but it worked in grabbing her attention. James III landed an interview where he used his boyish northern charms to make him a must-have.

I went over the shorthand version of my way in and it seemed I had jumped through a few more hoops than they had. But, instead of feeling like I deserved to be here the most, I felt boring in comparison to their stories of creativity and talent.

All of a sudden the door opened and a woman in a tight grey trouser suit walked in with a man who looked like her father. He was dressed in jeans, a scruffy T-shirt, a scarf and a plastic Casio watch on his wrist. I stared at him like I'd seen his face before. Was he famous? Just then I realized who he reminded me of: Willy Wonka, without the hat.

The woman with him spoke up. 'Hello, everyone, I'm Kim Smith, from HR. Please take a seat so we can get started. Apologies for the delay but I was just getting all your induction booklets.' She dropped them on to a chair by the door with a thump while we all sat down like we were in class and she counted our heads.

'Looks like you're all here, but before I get going with the booklet, I'd like to introduce Dr David Hewson, the head of The Beat in the UK. He'd like to say a few words to welcome you.'

The Doc's the head honcho? I thought to myself.

'Thanks, Kim. Hey, guys and gals, welcome to The Beat,' he said in an American accent. 'I just wanted to meet you for a few minutes to congratulate you on making it and to say how happy I am to have you here. As you're aware, the media is a major influence on people's lives, giving access to a world of entertainment, politics and social commentary as it charts the next step in our evolution. We're recording history as it happens.'

As he spoke and gesticulated with his hands, the entire room sat captivated.

'With a new century comes a new challenge as The Beat itself sheds its old skin and grows a new one. Embracing new technologies and fresh ideas is the way forward. Now, with that said, can anyone tell me who the most important person in this building is?'

Everyone sat quietly for a moment, not wanting to be the kid who said the stupid thing in class.

Eventually James III spoke up like it was a trick question. 'Is it you?'

The Doc laughed. 'No, I'm not that important at all,' he said, although no one in the room quite believed him. 'The most important person in this house of opportunity is you.' He pointed at James III. Then, shuffling slightly, 'It's you,' he added, pointing at Sonya, going on to repeat it for all of us.

'You're not just interns, you're the inspiration for us all. Your views, your thoughts, your ideas are what will continue to make us a successful and relevant youth brand. Equally the internship will open your eyes to so much and you'll experience what other people wish they could.'

Without any notes or prompting, he addressed each of us individually, referencing from our CVs and those who'd recommended us. 'James,' he finished, 'I liked the Kit Kat approach. That's the kind of out-of-the-box thinking we need in this place.'

'I've got my last Rolo for you, if you like,' James III responded. The room giggled.

Wow, how the hell did he remember all that stuff about

us? He'd even wanted Sam to show her DJing skills on the 1210s he had in his office. Everyone was impressed.

'What would the world be without music?' asked the Doc. Everyone pondered for a moment and, before James III could answer what was a rhetorical question, he continued. 'The thing that links us all together is our passion for music. Music is what makes the world go round. Music can make you feel good listening to James Brown, sad listening to Coldplay, hyper listening to Prodigy, lifted listening to the Lighthouse Family or simply help you to reminisce by listening to Pete Rock & C. L. Smooth. It's more powerful than any drug in the world. It's the secret to life. It's the secret to peace. It's the secret to love. It's the secret to youth.' He paused and let it all sink in to us. 'Peace.'

And with that he smiled at us, nodded goodbye to Kim and was out of the door with a bounce in his step. Kim had probably heard this many times before but she seemed as enthused as we were. Sure, dude was old enough to be our dad but he talked, walked and acted like us.

I looked round at the others and saw the electricity running through them. They were fully charged now and ready to go. The Doc's personal touch on the pulpit had left us inspired. We had each been lucky enough to get one of Willy Wonka's golden tickets and were now officially inside his factory of delights.

4
DON'T LET ME BE MISUNDERSTOOD

I stood outside the quiet pub that evening in the warm April drizzle, looking up at the sky. Summer was knocking on the door trying to let itself in early. The rain was soothing and refreshing and reminded me of waiting for the bus after a school cricket match.

I was waiting for my girlfriend, Sophia, who I hadn't seen since Saturday. She had just got back to London for the Easter break from Manchester University, where she was in her first year of Politics. We had one week together before she went skiing with her family for a fortnight, so I had to make the most of seeing her. And if there was anyone who was more thrilled about my internship than me, it was Sophia. She would want to know every detail of my first day.

We first met when she was watching her then-boyfriend play football against my team on a wet and dreary August morning. She was standing on the sidelines as a spectator and one of the clearances I made hit her plumb on the leg and nearly swept her off her feet. I went over to apologize to her while her boyfriend and his team continued to play on with me out of position and scored a goal.

By sheer coincidence, a couple of months later, in Emporium

nightclub in central London, I spotted her from the other side of the bar. I asked the barman for a champagne tub of ice and a sponge, marched over to her and asked her if she needed any medical attention for her leg injury. She recognized me instantly and laughed while her mates looked on, thinking I was a nut. I introduced myself properly and we spent the night talking and drinking. It turned out she was single again and I offered her further physio if she needed it. It sounds cheesy now, but a year and a half ago it was a game-winning line, though I'm sure the alcohol had something to do with it.

As soon as she spotted me this evening, she raced over in her Burberry check jacket, brolly in hand, and hugged me. Wow. I hadn't realized how much I needed it. I held on for longer than normal. I squeezed her slim frame tightly and her familiar smell made me relax that bit more. She had big brown eyes, beautiful soft clear skin, full rosy lips, short black hair and looked like Winona Ryder. Sophia was naturally beautiful and didn't need layers of make-up. I never understood why blokes liked girls who did. Why would you want to wake up next to someone the next morning and find the Joker's make-up on the pillow and the Joker without hers next to you?

'Sorry, LV,' I said as I held her.

'What for, RV?' she asked, her head resting on my chest.

LV and RV were initials she had given us. She was the left ventricle and I was the right, of the same heart. Sappy? Perhaps, but it was OK just between us.

'Rearranging to meet you four times in one night. I didn't expect to be getting out of work at ten o'clock.'

'It's OK, babe, it's not going to be a regular thing. Your first day was always going to be hectic.'

'True story,' I said.

'So, how much do you love me?' she asked.

'Oh much-much,' I replied, smiling at her.

'Even with all the hot women in the office, huh?' she asked with a raised eyebrow and a mischievous smile.

'Like I said, much-much,' I promised, emphasizing it the second time as we headed inside. We found a seat in a quiet corner by the window and began the post mortem of the first day.

'So, how was it?' she asked excitedly, grabbing my hand tightly once I'd put our drinks on the table.

'Wow. Where do I start? Hectic. Crazy. Scary . . .' I said, reflecting.

'Oh, come on, it couldn't have been that bad. Surely it was fun? It's The Beat.'

I told her how I'd struggled to get my head round all the departments in the building and what they did. The next thing that had had me scratching my head were the details in the induction like PAYE, health cover, depression counselling and pensions.

'Depression? Pension? I'm twenty-two, not sixty-two,' I said in a panic.

She laughed at my reaction to it all. 'All very grown-up and official.'

I showed her what looked like a forged attempt at a staff pass. A flimsy card, the size of a credit card, with The Beat stamp, displayed an out-of-focus headshot of me from

Blackpool Pleasure Beach, my details scribbled in the hand-writing of a twelve-year-old.

She ran her fingers over it and stared at The Beat logo. 'So what will you be doing?'

I inhaled deeply and let out my anxiety. 'We have two shows to produce every week. *Total BEATS*, the weekly entertainment round-up show, and *Defm8*,' I said, spelling the latter out.

'Your English teacher will be so proud,' she said, smiling. 'What's it about?'

'Third-party deprecation. All the week's gossip is ripped into by a different celeb guest every week alongside the presenter, PJ,' I told her, a look of worry on my face about the pending responsibility.

Everything I said seemed an exciting opportunity to Sophia, but to me it was a potential way to drown and fail. To illustrate this to her, I opened up a black A4 diary Max had given me to make notes of all my daily duties. I briefly smiled, remembering what he had said before handing it over: 'This isn't for your "dear diary" moments or to note your girlfriend's menstrual cycle so you calculate when you can giddy up.'

Looking on the first page, I'd copied down the first sentence verbatim, after which it was all shorthand and illegible scribbles.

On Monday we research both shows and finalize scripts for the record the next day. Research newspapers, Internet, magazines (VIBE, MOJO, NME, Blues & Soul, allmusic.com, et al.) & record labels. Get biogs on guests to interview. Roll-ins, movie EPKs. Watch & timecode. Get NEW music videos. Finish off scripts.

<u>Tuesday</u>: Studio record shows (x2). Floor manager (me) director (M). Sort out admin. Send Defm8 to TX a PA logsheet & forms. Defm8 transmits on Weds p.m.

<u>Wednesday</u>: research more news, roll-ins & new vids. Sort admin & chase leads. Check Billboard and Music Week mags. End of day, go edit M. Show tape to The Beat. TXs on Thurs p.m.

<u>Thursday</u>: Keep researching & admin. Catch up emails. Do artist interviews and poss. edits. (Support M). Filing systems. Pull library tapes. Logging. Sort legal docs.

<u>Friday</u>: Get all content for both shows. More research. Give M vids & research so far. Make show running order (x2). Speak to lawyer. Liaise with edit. Updates.

I just about managed to decipher my own notes, stuttering throughout like it was in a foreign language. But the words sure did paint a clear picture: one of long days and late nights. Even Sophia's face dropped at the workload.

'The stuff I'd been doing for work experience was basic. I had no responsibility. Within the first few hours today, I felt like I had everything on my shoulders and that Max was counting on me not to screw it up,' I said, all flustered.

She tried to bring back some positivity. 'Yeah, but this is about music. It's about what you love. Or would you rather be doing something else?'

I paused. The alternatives were bleak. Wearing a suit? Working nine to five? No, far too boring and adult.

'It's just a lot, that's all. Any small mistake could have

massive effects. I just don't want to fail . . . or let Max down,' I said, looking apprehensive.

'You'll be fine. Max wouldn't have chosen you if he felt you weren't capable.'

Sophia would have made a lousy politician because she made good sense.

'So will you get to direct stuff?' she asked quickly, changing the subject.

'No way, that takes years of experience. I've just got through the door and you want me piloting the shuttle.' I laughed as she gave me a look that said *Why not?*

I carried on filling her in on every minute detail as she listened intently. Anyone else would have been bored as soon as I said 'caching form', but not her.

'So what was the work like?' she asked.

'Forget about getting any actual work done, you end up spending most of your time deleting and answering heaps of emails,' I complained. 'I did attempt one piece of work. Max wrote *Total BEATS*, and told me to look at old scripts as a guide to writing for *Defm8*. But, no matter what I wrote, he said it was wrong and I had to start all over. It was like waxing an armpit with Sellotape,' I said, clearly frustrated.

'Sounds like tough love.'

'More like barmy love,' I replied. 'I spent six hours rewriting twelve links till he called it a day on busting my balls and told me to finish it tomorrow morning. It's why I had to keep changing the time to meet you,' I said, feeling worn out as I said it.

'Babe, you've taken some wobbly steps for your first ever

script. Be patient; you'll be walking, then running in no time. I believe in you,' she encouraged.

'I know,' I replied, still not satisfied and ready to keep complaining.

Sophia tried to shift the focus. 'What are the other interns like?'

It worked as I perked up describing the other people in the same boat. 'Pretty cool. Some are quirkier than others, like James III who inexplicably likes to whistle Christmas carols. You have to admit, hearing "Away in a Manger" in spring's a bit weird.'

'I wonder how long till it goes from quirky to annoying?'

'Well, that could be in my favour. Cara's already heard rumours that there's one permanent contract up for grabs at the end of the six months.'

'Wow, that's amazing,' said Sophia, with a shot of excitement.

'There's no way I'm going to get it. The others are much better than me,' I replied, reverting to being downbeat about it all.

'Forget about the others. First things first, your work will be on TV. On The Beat! It's what you've always wanted. Look how long it's taken you to get here. Be proud of yourself.' She grabbed my hand again, placed her fingers in between mine and squeezed.

No matter what I said, my pessimism was being beaten back by her optimism like Rocky. She was a great cheerleader and my best friend. Sophia knew that thinking positively wasn't my natural habit. Some people deal with life's ups and downs through religion, friends, counsellors, watching *Oprah*. Not really for me. My coping mechanism was music, and Sophia knew how important it, and now The Beat, was to me.

Music had played a big part in my life from my earliest memories. Mum said she played it to me all the time when she was pregnant, to nurture me for the nine months I was in her womb. As a little kid it became a distraction for me when my parents would shut me away in my bedroom while they argued. To block out the screaming and violence next door, I focused on the music they left playing on the radio or the record player. I still remember that the louder they yelled, the tighter I squeezed my eyes and concentrated. Soon, I didn't hear them, just the music.

I spent so much time in this state that, after a while, I didn't just hear the music: I saw, felt, smelt and tasted it too. Stevie Wonder literally tickled the tips of my fingers; Wham! fooled my tongue into tasting a hint of Coke; Beastie Boys made myriad colours seem to bounce off the walls; I'd smell grass when The Beatles' *White Album* played. It was hard to explain and the closest I'd come to understanding it was when I read an article about a person with synesthesia. They experienced music similarly to me, but not quite the same, and turned out to be a world-class concert pianist.

As time went by, I found further practical uses for music. Dad walked out on us when I was eleven, suffering from chronic depression, and we never heard from him again. As a result, Mum was hardly at home, working two jobs to make ends meet and so lyrics became my parental guidance through life. Marvin Gaye's 'I Heard It Through the Grapevine' rang true when a girlfriend cheated on me; REM's

'Everybody Hurts' played for months when I was feeling aimless and down, having left uni jobless with what seemed like a useless piece of paper.

Some kids play with their imaginary friends, eventually getting rid of them when they get some sense and grow up. Without any siblings, I turned to my equivalent, but it was usually in the guise of a singer or sometimes an entire band. I'd have actual conversations with the artists in my head and sometimes – only sometimes – I'd see them in front of me. It was a natural, if freaky, occurrence that allowed me to function, especially in traumatic times. Even Sophia didn't know about these bizarre conversations. I hadn't told anyone for fear of them thinking I was loopy like the kid in *The Sixth Sense*.

Sophia slipped her fingers out of my grip and went to the Ladies as I closed my eyes and tried to focus my panicked thoughts. Music entertained, inspired, educated and somehow gave me confidence. It didn't judge, betray, nag or lie to me. It was the only constant and true thing in my life. So here I was working at The Beat, the highest church of music. And I was pissing on my own parade having made it to the Promised Land.

Sophia was right; I had got what I asked for. I had been given an opportunity most people don't get to see on their first day but have to earn over months or sometimes years. Max had believed and The Beat had given me a chance; it was up to me how far I'd take it.

Warmth began to radiate from my chest and circulate around me like the Ready Brek kid as I loosened up. The voice of optimism, confidence and belief that was normally shackled behind bars in solitary confinement was out. Well, being allowed to exercise in the yard at least. I wasn't foolishly letting down my guard and thinking everything was going to be OK, but I had at least removed one hand from my knackers.

5
IT'S THE HARD KNOCK LIFE

I awoke to the door slamming as my flatmate went to work. I lifted my head off the pillow but my body didn't move an inch. I slumped back down.

By the time Sophia and I finished catching up over drinks, headed back to mine for a Pot Noodle and the first non phone-sex in weeks, it was late – 2.24 a.m. late. I had to be up at six o'clock to get to the office for seven. My scripts weren't good enough for Max so I wanted to have another go before he came in. He'd look over them ahead of us going to the studio and I really wanted to nail it this time.

I kept dreaming I was late and woke up nearly every half hour checking the bedside clock. But, despite the paranoid interrupted sleep and the slamming door, the irony was that it was now 6.14 a.m. and I *was* now running late.

My flatmate, Pritesh 'Pritz' Shah, worked as a trader for Lehman Brothers in the City, which meant he had to be at work by six a.m. sharp. He tried explaining what he did to me on several occasions – it boiled down to 'playing with other people's money' – but I'd glaze over and think of paint drying on walls. Pritz had been my best friend since nursery and the closest thing I had to a sibling. What he lacked in good looks he made up for with confidence and the gift of the gab. He was that average bloke you see walking down the street with a really hot girl.

Pritz was part of a classic two-point-four kids family, with a father who was a dentist, a mother who was a part-time dentist and housewife, and an older sister who was a trainee dentist. The Shah's were part of the North London Hindu community, which was aghast when Pritz didn't follow in the career footsteps of the family.

He was part of the new generation of Brit-Asian kids who didn't want to be stereotypical doctors, dentists or accountants. The new profession was banking. The aim? To get filthy rich. ('Look at the huge rims on my limited-edition Porsche; I own a house next door to Kate Moss; I can buy a date with and shag a model/Bollywood or Hollywood actress/ Virgin stewardess/aristocrat/all of the above; I want a helicopter, a yacht and a submarine; I want to retire to the South of France and be divorced at least twice by the time I'm ~~sixty, fifty, forty,~~ thirty-five.')

As a new member of the Lehman Brothers graduate training scheme, Pritz wasn't yet earning the six- or seven-figure amounts that the experienced traders took home. Confidence was high as everyone realized the Y2K bug was about as dangerous as a ladybird, and Pritz was hoping for a bumper bonus even though the bubble of the dotcom boom had just burst.

'Don't worry, mate, I won't leave you behind. You can live above the garage of my mansion once I've made it,' he once told me. But for now we lived in a two-bedroom apartment in Angel above Kemal's Kebab Shop. Pritz's favourite was a number-six chicken shish, even though his mother raised him as a strict vegetarian. But once he got hooked on hamburgers and sausages in primary school, meat-eating became the first of his many dirty secrets that he kept from his mother.

Pritz was happily paying a bigger share of the rent as he knew I couldn't afford to live on my Foot Locker salary or The Beat intern's wage. I got the food shopping in when I could and sent him a direct debit every month that he probably spent in one night entertaining clients at the 'Holborn Bar & Grill', which was the official name of the establishment on his receipts after a night out at a strip club. He wasn't shy of flashing his cash. Whenever I'd say he was wasting money on an ugly lamp/shirt/shoes/watch, he'd respond, 'Don't be such a tightwad. You're thinking short term. This market is going up and up. I can spend all my cash for the next few years knowing that when I'm thirty I'll still be a millionaire.'

However, it would be unfair to not highlight the fact he was at work at six a.m. Monday to Friday and didn't get home till eight p.m. or, if he was entertaining clients, three in the morning. He barely slept but somehow used the power of money to help wake him up. Literally. He had a stack of fifty-pound notes by his alarm clock so that when it went off he was reminded why he was getting up.

Right now, at 6.14 a.m., I didn't have the same money-motivation. My motivation was to not royally screw things up and embarrass myself. I had a nervous energy inside that was hitting panic buttons every five seconds saying, 'You're late, you'll never make it, oh shit!'

In a bid to prove my mind wrong, my body jumped out

of bed and headed to the shower, stubbing my toe on the door on the way. I screamed in silence so as to not wake Sophia. I fell into the shower and turned it on, not waiting for the hot water to start flowing. The cold hit me and jolted my body like a defibrillator.

Once dressed, I felt my bowels churning and a big weight began to pull me down, like gravity on Newton's apple. But I didn't have time to give in to it. I grabbed my rucksack and went to the kitchen for breakfast: a banana on the run. Pritz had left a note for me on the fridge next to the Premier League fixtures, which were a constant reminder that his team, Manchester United, were dominating once again, having controversially dropped out of the FA Cup. The note read 'Yo, Ndugu Bwana, we out on the chirps tonight?'

Heading out I noticed the light on in Pritz's room so I stuck my hand in and hit the switch to turn off the light. Yet there was still a slight glow. It was probably his bedside lamp. I opened the door fully to find a girl lying asleep in his bed. Not wanting to disturb her, I quickly grabbed the door to close it, scanning the room for clues to establish who it was. Judging by the see-through high-heeled stilettos on the floor and her perfectly upright breasts as she lay on her back, Pritz had brought a stripper back the previous night. As I left, I smirked, thinking, *What would his mother say?*

6
SPACE ODDITY

As I entered through the revolving door of The Beat offices, my insides were turning at the prospect of having to rewrite the script for *Defm8*. The TV screen in Reception was on mute and it was so quiet in the building you could hear the sound of silence. I was eager to flash my spanking-new but crappy ID card, only to find both the security guards sleeping in their chairs. In fairness, it was a pretty boring twelve-hour shift protecting a bunch of videotapes and some flashy Apple Macs. Max had joked that the closest these guys got to action was once chasing a dog around the building after it had crept in one night trying to find shelter from the rain.

Once behind my desk, I began amending my script. I read over what I'd done so far and still couldn't find what was wrong. The sentences were well constructed with tantalizing information, subtle wit and the right splashing of youthful slang. *What's wrong with it?* I thought.

I'd been at it for an hour and a half and I could now hear crew from the studios gathered round one of the tables in the Greenhouse, slouched on beanbags eating breakfast while reading the papers. As my eyes scanned the rest of the ground floor I saw Max running up the stairs, balancing a coffee in one hand and a plate of toast in the other. He came over to my desk and plonked his stuff down.

'So, how did you get on?' he asked, getting his breath back.

'I went over it again this morning. I think it's better,' I said confidently, with a touch of cockiness, moving my chair over so he could see my computer screen.

'Right, let's have a look then.' He bit into his toast.

No 'good morning', then. Just straight into it like the last ten hours and wardrobe change didn't happen, I thought.

He began to mumble as he read the first link. Then he went silent. I stared at the computer screen, too anxious to look at him. Moments later he came to life as though the script was taking time to settle in his mind this early in the morning.

'OK, I see you've tried to make changes. Good. This is a good script for you.'

'Thanks, I did –'

'No, I mean it's a good script if you were the presenter. Are you the presenter?' he asked condescendingly.

'No,' I said, taken aback.

'Well, why haven't you listened to what I said to you yesterday? You've got to think like you're PJ. And the links are too long. Kids today just don't have the attention span,' he said.

I felt patronized on behalf of the entire youth population. He continued before I could get a word in.

'The intonation is non-existent and your research seems patchy at best.'

Good job it was so early in the morning and none of the others were here to see my first dressing-down from Max. The last time someone spoke to me like this was my mother when I was ten and I forgot to leave the toilet seat down.

Max carried on scanning through all the links, correcting and deleting big chunks. If this was an essay marked by a teacher, there would be question marks and 'see me' all over it in red biro. As much as it pained me, his detailed critique was right. I'd tried my best for hours with several rewrites. I'd come in early to get it spot on and I wasn't even close. My first attempt at writing and I was a total loser. My ego was shrinking faster than a buffet at the hands of Homer Simpson. This wasn't like writing my dissertation; it was a whole different ball game.

Max must have seen the discomfort written on my face.

'Don't worry, we've all been through it. My boss, Robert, did the same to me when I got here and I'd written for national newspapers and magazines. It's a good start but there's still a long way for you to go, so be sure you learn from this. Take my feedback and apply it to next week's script.'

'What about this week's script? We're in the studio in an hour,' I said with a worried look on my face. I stared at my near-blank computer screen where my script had resided only a short moment ago.

He quickly opened another document from the shared server. 'We can use the one I wrote.'

I sat there in silence as he continued.

'I got a call yesterday from our Talent & Artists department that there's an artist flying into the UK today. In fact,' he said, looking at his watch, 'he's coming straight to The Beat from Heathrow right now to be a guest presenter on *Defm8*.'

'Yesterday? When was the call?' I asked.

'About three-ish,' he replied, unashamedly straight-faced.

What? So he'd known my script was for nothing? And all the work I'd put in had been a total waste. I felt increasingly frustrated the more it sank in. I stayed silent.

Max realized why instantly. 'Don't worry, your work wasn't in vain. I had to see what level you're at. Success comes before work only in the dictionary. You learnt from it, didn't you?' he asked as he cut what good was left of my script and pasted it to his.

This was a fucking test? It just happened to last the same time it had taken for me to sit *all* my A-level exams! But I had to be professional and not show my true feelings. Instead of what was going through my head, I said, 'Yes.'

'Aren't you interested in who the guest is?' Max asked.

Yeah right. No guest could make up for the last twenty-four hours of pain. 'Who is it?' I asked begrudgingly.

'Jay-Z,' he said, as cool as you like, while typing and staring at the screen.

I couldn't hide my surprise. The angst of being ridiculed, shot down like I was the Luftwaffe in the summer of '44, and being made to run a pointless errand was all forgotten in an instant. The biggest rapper in the game was in town and appearing on my first show.

I stopped sulking. Instead I gathered tapes, collected scripts and fan mail and followed Max down to the studios like Sonic the Hedgehog's hyperactive sidekick. It was a dream come true. But I was nervous too. This was the first time I'd see a show recorded in the studio, the first time I'd meet a star and the first time I'd meet PJ.

After showing me around the gallery, introducing me to the staff and telling me what I'd be doing on the studio floor, Max took me to the dressing room. PJ was sitting in the corner with his shades on, clearly nursing a hangover as the make-up lady fussed over him, covering up the evidence of his excesses from the night before.

As soon as he saw Max he pleaded, 'Please, nothing hard today, dude!'

Max laughed. 'Is it ever?'

'Course it is, otherwise they'd have you doing it,' PJ quipped.

The mood for the studio banter was set.

PJ, who was barely a few years older than me, was a chancer, a blagger, a Del-Boy, who came to The Beat by pure fluke. He hadn't gone to university but his life experiences thus far included owning a fifth of a gardening business, selling time-shares in the Middle East and artist management of some unsuccessful groups, like the twins called 'Double Trouble'.

He'd come to The Beat one day to drop off their music video when an overly eager intern took him in error straight to the studios to do a presenter audition. It was an easy mistake to make: when you see someone good-looking in Reception, with a designer mohawk, trendy clothes and wearing shades indoors, you assume they're auditioning for something. Realizing a cock-up was in progress, PJ kept quiet and did the screen test as a laugh. Weeks later he was contacted about the video for Double Trouble and informed it was the worst thing that had ever been submitted to The Beat. However, his audition got the opposite reaction. He charmed his way through the next set of screen tests and landed a contract.

His laissez-faire approach made him a natural, flirting with the camera as others fluffed their lines under the pressure. But what sealed his position as a mainstay was his photographic memory and phenomenal knowledge of music trivia. He was a musical Norris McWhirter, who was famous for recalling facts from the *Guinness Book of Records* off the top of his head. PJ's on-screen exposure was matched off it, as he was always pictured falling out of clubs with his celebrity friends on drunken nights out.

As Max introduced me, I stuck my hand out to shake PJ's. He didn't move. My hand stayed hanging for several seconds till I moved it back into my pocket and looked at Max, confused and embarrassed. He sat in one of the make-up chairs next to PJ without flinching.

'So you want to be part of the gang, do you?' PJ said in a Clint Eastwood style growl.

Not sure of what to say, I looked back at Max. He sat straight-faced, offering no help.

'Er, yes?' I said, unsure.

'Well, do you have what it takes?' he continued.

'Er, yes?' I repeated. *Was this guy for real?*

Then he took his shades off and began to fire music questions at me. At first I was daunted by the challenge, but soon began to hit everything he threw at me out of the park. The cockier I got, the more agitated he got. He kept going till I finally got one wrong.

'I knew you'd slip up on The Doors. Rookie mistake. I'm not sure he's a keeper,' he said, shaking his head at Max.

I looked to Max for some back-up but he raised his hands, not wanting to get involved. 'Hey, there are no friends in this game. Each man for himself.'

For the next hour PJ kept referring to me as 'rookie'. Now it was my turn to get agitated as he got cocky. We recorded *Total BEATS* first, waiting for Jay-Z's arrival to film *Defm8*. I stood nervously with my floor manager's headphones on. It was my role to cue PJ before each link, and his frosty attitude became colder as I fluffed counting down from five to one.

'Max, why have you got someone in the gang who can't even count?' he asked, staring into the camera. He then looked at me and signalled with his fingers. 'Rookie, after the number threeeee comes the number twooooo. Not one!'

By now everyone on the studio floor and in the gallery was laughing at me. I tried to laugh it off with them, but I was in agony on the inside. Was humiliation the weapon of choice?

I concentrated hard on doing the next count. The words were right but this time I got the countdown on my fingers wrong. Cue more ridicule. PJ's cockiness was limitless and he didn't bother listening to my instructions to practise reading through each link before we recorded it to tape. I prayed for him to mess up, but he was too good. We flew through the recording, getting to the penultimate link and that week's best fan mail. I had several to choose from but couldn't decide which one to go for. My hesitation brought another jibe.

'Where's the letter, rookie?' PJ asked impatiently.

I shuffled through all the papers trying to choose one, dropping pages on the floor like a dithering idiot.

'While we're still young,' he added.

Max was barking similar orders in my headphones as he'd heard Jay-Z was minutes away.

'Couldn't we have got a hot female intern?' PJ said to Max.

Agreeable laughter came through my headphones. I finally chose the best mail and gave the accompanying picture to Max to roll in. I handed PJ the letter that was written on pink paper. Snapping it from my hands, he said, 'C'mon, let's roll to record,' and began reading it to camera as soon as I cued him in.

'"*Dear PJ, I love watching the show*",' he began.

'Of course you do,' he said, looking back up at the camera and winking.

'"*I can't go a week without watching you do your thing on TV. I love all the interviews and videos.*"'

Looking back up at the camera, he said, 'Why thank you, my dear,' brushing imaginary dirt from his shoulder.

'"*You're so sexy! I'm your number-one fan and I have a poster of you above my bed that I look at every night before I go to sleep. I can't wait to come to The Beat to meet you in person.*"'

'Well, you can if you're over eighteen!' he joked, winking again. The letter went on sycophantically, and getting to the end of it, he read, '"*P.S. I've enclosed my picture.*"'

'Max, put the picture up onscreen,' PJ demanded eagerly. He turned the letter over and finished reading it.

'"*You make me TOTALLY hard, from . . . Steve*"?' The name came out of his mouth as a near whisper.

Max had done as he was told and split the TV screen, with PJ on the left looking shocked and on the right the picture of a teenage boy grabbing his crotch with a poster of PJ above his bed.

PJ squirmed, uncomfortably lost for words as the screen dipped to black.

Seconds later he could hear the laughter coming from the gallery through my headphones as everyone pissed themselves laughing.

'And end of link,' I said.

'Fuck off! No way! We're not using that. Max?' he shouted.

'Sorry, PJ, we have to, we don't have time to re-record it,' said Max over the tannoy system to the studio. 'Besides, gay fan mail means you've arrived.'

I felt a sense of satisfaction as I walked over to PJ to collect the letter from him but I didn't let it show on my face. I stuck out my hand to take it from him, but he didn't move.

Shit, I've just majorly pissed him off, I thought. I was hoping he'd see the funny side to it, not react like this. I groaned inwardly. There would definitely be fall-out from my stitch-up and I was regretting it already.

Just as I was about to put my hand back down, PJ grabbed it firmly, shook it and smiled charismatically. 'You're definitely one of us, kid. Welcome to the gang.'

Initiation was over.

7
CHINA WHITE

Pritz and I sat in Pizza Hut eating from the buffet, seeing who could knock back the most slices. It's weird how blokes can make a competition out of anything, from the credible 'Who can run the fastest 100m?' to the not-so-credible 'How many peanut M&Ms can you throw in the air and catch in your mouth in one go, while leaning back on your chair?' We'd been playing this current pizza-eating game since we were kids and it was a sheer miracle that neither of us was the shape of the legendary wrestler Big Daddy and his arch nemesis Giant Haystacks. Pritz held the lead of 2,356 victories to my 2,331 – approximately.

The thing with Pizza Hut buffets, and any other all-you-can-eat buffets for that matter, is that the idea sounds good value for money. Your greed gets one step ahead of your stomach, and when you do start to eat you can barely polish off a few slices. However, we were veterans and knew how to get past the psychology of it all. Patience really was a virtue, along with some visits to the toilet. The average customer sat for forty minutes in the restaurant while we sat for double that. We were possibly the only loss-making customers for the corporation as we didn't even order any drinks. Instead we settled for tap water with ice and lemon to keep the extra space in our stomachs for food and not over-priced fizzy cola. Another trick was to not eat anything too spicy that required extra gulps of water, and we varied the pizzas so we didn't get bored of the taste.

Pritz was on his fourteenth slice and I was on my eleventh when I got a text from Max:

Outside Chinas. Air Street. 11:30pm. Don't be late!!!

It was 11.15 p.m. now, so we paid up and scrambled out. Soon we were heading down Regent Street in the rain, virtually hugging the shops, hoping the buildings would offer us some cover. Groups of girls clustered under umbrellas were tottering their way to the clubs and bars located within a stone's throw of Piccadilly Circus. Any girl who walked past would get an instant look back over the shoulder from Pritz. He was getting his female radar in check before the night began.

'So the Quant made you write that script for nothing?' Pritz recapped. 'He deserves a first-class ticket to Quantville. Population: Max. But I have to admit the studio stuff sounds fun. That's not a job, that's Mickey Mouse stuff,' he said.

I laughed. 'Quant' was Pritz's version of the C-word. It had been made up by one of Pritz's workmates to highlight the geeks in their research department and we'd adopted it as our own. 'Yeah, yeah, yeah. And I suppose getting your boss's coffee is hard work,' I replied.

'Hey, it's the price I have to pay to make sure he stays sweet and gives me a hefty bonus at the end of the year. So what was Jay-Zed like? Did you get your picture with him?' asked Pritz.

46

'No. It felt a bit cheesy,' I said, scrunching my face up.

'Who cares? Imagine if the boys back at school saw it? How else you going to prove it?' said Pritz.

'I don't need to prove it. Besides, do you want me to carry a Polaroid in my back pocket?' I said in defiance.

'Oooh, look at yooouuu, maaaam. C'mon, it would be good to see that twat Michael Four Eyes' face when he finds out you met his idol.'

I imagined the look on the face of the neighbourhood bully from our childhood and it made me contemplate it for a second. Then I realized he'd most likely thump me, mug me and rip up any picture.

We got to Air Street on time to find it in chaos as traffic had come to a halt. Just by the entrance to the road, people were shouting at big burly men dressed in suits, as long queues snaked out behind them along Regent Street. The only female standing with them was holding a clipboard in one hand, smoking a cigarette with the other and ignoring the people talking to her. They were outside a single plain and unsigned doorway that lead to London's hottest club, Chinawhite. Cameramen with powerful lenses were standing on the opposite side of the road, talking among themselves, fingers twitching and ready to snap at the first sign of anyone remotely famous.

We stood on the corner waiting for Max, spending our time looking at the two queues, which were moving painfully slowly. The drama that was ensuing with revellers and the traffic was a great advert for the place, giving the impression that this was a hotspot and very exclusive. The longer people waited, the more exclusive it was – treat them mean, keep them keen. The same people would turn up week after week to be treated the same way. Everyone in the queue probably wondered if it was really worth it, but looked around to see others clamouring to get in and figured surely all these people can't be wrong, there *must* be something wonderful inside.

The smaller of the two queues was for the guest list. It was mainly made up of businessmen and models. The club's PR company would email invites to all the top modelling agencies, and they'd send their girls (and boys) down for free. The girls inevitably got treated to free drinks and were discreetly provided with drugs all night, courtesy of the businessmen. In return the suits got to feel big among the other alpha males, getting the girls drunk enough to flirt with. And the club made sure there were beautiful girls and boys inside to be gawped at by the average folks. In this *ménage à trois* everyone was happy. If you had a club like this with dog-ugly people inside, it would be empty the following week and you'd be closed for good the week after.

In the other, less-exclusive, queue, similar agreements were being made. There was a mixture of average folk ranging from wannabe singers and dancers to tourists and students, all desperate to be at the hottest VIP spot in town. Groups of girls in the queue were fine, but groups of guys were not. So the boys would end up having to try to persuade girls to go in with them. The uglier they were, the more the girls negotiated on the amount of drinks they'd have to buy them later.

Annoyingly for everyone waiting outside, there was a third invisible queue. It consisted of people who had the velvet rope lifted for them and walked straight through, without paying, and to whom the restriction of 'no hats, no trainers' did not apply. Famous people, friends of staff and rich regulars would hug the bouncer or kiss the doorgirl before disappearing inside.

It was approaching midnight and after my long day I was tired and fading fast. I wanted to call to see where Max was but didn't want to seem like I couldn't wait without panicking. But the never-ending rain and Pritz's complaints made me realize it wasn't so unreasonable. I dialled Max's number.

He picked up and it sounded like he was still in his car, but then the line went dead.

'Where is he?' asked Pritz.

'I think he's still driving,' I said, unsure.

'Driving? That means by the time he parks up and gets here, it could be another twenty or thirty minutes.'

'Yeah, I suppose . . .' I said.

'Let's try and get in ourselves. I'll blag us in. Once we're downstairs, text him.'

I didn't fancy standing in the cold and rain another minute so was open to 'Plan P' – sending in Pritz as last resort. He always rose to any challenge, thinking he could accomplish it with ease like he was The Wolf from *Pulp Fiction*. But his calm assurance now left me more worried than reassured.

We headed in the direction of the small guest-list queue, which was currently empty. Pritz walked with an air of confidence like his dad owned the club and not two dental practices in north-west London. I walked in his shadow like I was a fraudster going to claim benefits while working cash-in-hand.

The doorgirl with the clipboard had her back to us as we got there.

'Hi there, we're on the guest list,' said Pritz in an unwavering and steely voice.

She turned around, looked him up and down. 'What list?' she bellowed for the street to hear.

'Lehman Brothers. We've got a table here,' Pritz said equally loudly, whipping out his business card.

She looked on her clipboard, turned several pages over and scanned up and down it. 'Nope, nothing here,' she replied as people started to look round at us.

'Really, can you check one more time? My boss definitely got a table today. Short fat guy, laughs a lot, mainly at his own jokes. You must have seen him?'

'There've been lots of those types today,' she said, unimpressed.

'Of course.' Pritz laughed nervously, realizing he wasn't getting through to her. The silence between them was deafening.

My hands got sweaty and I knew she was going to turf us humiliatingly from the queue. I was about to turn around and disappear into the shadows when Pritz got another idea.

'OK, can you look for The Beat please?'

What the hell was he doing? Stop, stop! I thought. Too late.

'The Beat? You said you worked at Lehman Brothers,' she pointed out with obvious suspicion.

'Yeah, I do, but my boy here works at The Beat,' he said, like he'd just played his trump card.

By now the paparazzi were looking at us too. I couldn't

believe it, we could have all walked away from this perfectly unharmed yet Pritz had to go out in a blaze of glory. That's the risk you take with a 'Plan P' – on the trading floor or outside, he just didn't know when to stop gambling.

The woman peered around Pritz as he moved to the side so she could get a better look at me. I had my hands in my pockets and stood hunched, wearing the liquorice allsorts outfit I had hurriedly thrown on in a rush that morning.

She looked me up and down and sniggered, 'I don't think so.'

'Yes, he does.' Pritz turned to me. 'Go on, show her your pass.'

I froze.

'Go on,' he egged me on again.

Eventually I went to my back pocket. *This really isn't going to make a difference to this woman*, I thought to myself but I didn't want to get in the way of Pritz's persistence. I got my multicoloured Benetton acrylic wallet out and undid the Velcro strap, which opened with the loudest noise, taking about ten years off my age. The paps were nudging each other and now we had an audience ready to laugh at our failed attempt to get in. Horror gripped me like I was watching *The Blair Witch Project*. I couldn't find my pass.

I searched frantically then looked up at Pritz, holding out the wallet in despair, horrified I'd let him down. He stared back with a look that said: *You had one line in this play, and you just fluffed it.*

The doorgirl had a look of happiness on her face like she'd solved the crime of the century. But, before she could even throw us shamefully out of the queue, the paps were clicking and their flashes engulfed the street.

Everyone was looking towards the club as two people carriers with tinted windows pulled up in front. Paps jockeyed for position and ran on to the road to slow the vehicles down so they could get ready for whoever stepped out. There were enough flashes to cause an epileptic fit as the door slid open on the first Mercedes.

Seconds later a big bouncer wearing a XXXL Rocawear T-shirt stepped out, towering over everyone at the door. He quickly huddled Jay-Z past the lifted velvet rope and straight in, followed by his entourage and several girls with short skirts, all trying to avoid the falling rain.

Pritz turned round to me as I looked on equally energized.

'We've definitely gotta get in now. I wanna party with S Dot Carter.' He began to sing the incorrect words to a Jay-Z song and jig without a beat.

The other Mercedes was offloading the rest of Jay-Z's entourage and some more girls. Among them I saw two figures I recognized. One was the TV promotions plugger for Jay-Z's record label who I'd met in The Beat studios earlier that day, and the other was Max. So that's where the cheeky bugger had been – in a car full of girls. They stepped out and I smiled at them, but, with the flashing cameras going off and all the bouncers in front of me, they didn't see me. Before I could even call out his name he had gone inside.

I turned to Pritz. 'That was Max at the end.'

'Really? Max, your boss at The Beat?' Pritz asked, straight-faced.

'Yes,' I replied.

'Well, what are we still doing outside then? I see you're both *reeeal* tight. He's gone in and left you out here?'

'He probably didn't see me,' I said, trying to defend him.

'Call him then,' Pritz challenged.

'OK, I will.' I got my phone out and dialled. It went straight to the answer machine. I was so embarrassed at being forgotten. I'd waited for what seemed like hours, standing in the rain with my friend who was now questioning if I really worked at The Beat or not. I was wet and wanted to get out of there. I turned to leave and started walking when a voice behind me shouted out.

'Oi, where do you think you're going, holmes?' I turned round. It was Max. 'I told you to wait, didn't I?'

'Yeah, but I –'

'No buts, get in here. It's about to go down,' he said with a wry smile. 'Bring your girlfriend too.' He ushered Pritz over, who for once wisely kept his mouth shut but couldn't resist flashing a wink at the clipboard queen on his way in.

Max put his arm round my shoulder and squeezed. 'Laura darlin', this is Jay. He's part of The Beat family.'

After years of waiting in queues, not getting in because we didn't have any girls with us, not knowing the head of security and generally being unknowns on the outside, the velvet rope had been lifted for us.

8
BICYCLE RACE

I felt like shit. In the last seventy-two hours I had slept a total of twelve hours and every minute of those was restless. Either I was anxious about my first day, paranoid about getting scripts completed or so drunk that I slept one eye up. I went to bed at four a.m. and had to be at work by eight to ensure Max's edit was ready and that he had everything he needed. The flat I left behind increasingly resembled a squat.

I got to the office still slightly drunk and with a headache from hell. The first floor was as empty as Harrods on Christmas Day. As I walked over to my desk, I passed a brand-new BMX parked neatly next to someone's desk. I turned back round and took a closer look at the bike. There was a Post-it note on the saddle, which said 'c/o Mr Brian Haw, competition prize'. It was the kind of bike I'd wanted as a child but could never afford. It was the kind of bike I'd seen on cereal boxes and wanted to win but needed a thousand coupons to enter. It was the kind of bike I fell in love with having seen ET wheelie away from the FBI in a hoodie.

I walked towards my desk with a nagging voice in my head as I sat down and logged in.

Go on, you know you want to, said the voice in my head. It was Robbie Williams.

No, I can't, I'm at work, I replied.

No one's here! he exclaimed.

Yeah, but still . . .

Oh, go on. You have free run of the entire track.

No, I have a script to write in less than an hour.

This will take a few minutes. One quick lap! Ride or die!

I can't.

It will relax you and put you in a creative mood, like a five-knuckle shuffle.

I can't.

Perhaps the five-knuckle shuffle then? Robbie-in-my-head laughed.

I can't.

Pussy!

His final argument was conclusive. I got up, walked over to the bike and got on. I gripped the handlebars tight, pushed the bike back and forth to check the brakes and then pushed off with my feet. Smooth. The floorboards shifted and thudded underneath the carpet as I rode over them. I peddled past the meeting rooms to the land of folders that was Ad Sales, the merchandise heaven of Marketing, finally taking a right towards the CD-loaded Talent & Artist department, a.k.a. T.A.D. A quick left and I was at full pelt as I went past the office of the head of The Beat Europe – otherwise known as Darth Vader – past all the flashy Apple Macs of On-Air Graphics, round the back towards the toilets and down to the hush of ER – European Regions. Some carpet tiles came loose as I took the hairpin to the left past the music programmers' neat desks and back towards the mess of the UK Production department. Looking at my watch, it had taken me one minute and fifteen seconds.

Beat it, said Robbie Williams, all excited.

We agreed one lap though, I replied internally.

Yeah, but I didn't expect you to be that quick, he said, egging me on.

I was quick, wasn't I? I wasn't even trying. Even though I knew the conversation wasn't real, I actually felt proud.

This time go faster and get it to sub one minute, said Robbie Williams.

Yeah, why not, no one's here. Sub one? No problem, I thought.

This time I knew the route and could peg it much quicker, so I really went for it. Soon I was on the final straight and moving the bike side to side to get extra speed, emulating the Tour de France sprints of Lance Armstrong in my head. Except I was less talented. The front wheel clipped the edge of a cardboard box, pushing me and the bike into carefully stacked tapes on someone's desk. They fell everywhere like a deck of cards, the noise of which echoed across the top floor. I lay still for a second.

'Oh shit,' I said aloud.

Luckily no one was around to see my embarrassing drop. I got up, took a sigh of relief that the bike was unharmed. I rested the BMX back against the desk, crouched down and began to pick up the tapes from the floor. I heard footsteps approaching and quickly gathered as many as possible and began stacking them.

'Impressive,' said a German voice as it went past my

shoulder and continued walking. I stood up and saw Darth Vader heading towards his office.

I sobered up in an instant. *Fuck. I'm fired*, I thought.

No you're not, said Robbie Williams, rejoining the conversation in my mind. *It was just a few tapes.*

That's not the point. This isn't a playground, I responded angrily, imagining the words HR would use.

Oh relax, it's fine. More importantly, was that an impressed 'impressive' or an unimpressed 'impressive'? Maybe the former. It was hard to tell, said Robbie Williams.

Who cares? That's the last time I listen to you, I said.

(Pause.)

Do you wish you'd gone for that five-knuckle shuffle instead? he said, before departing.

At the cafeteria I ordered an extra-strong coffee and grabbed a packet of Jaffa Cakes. I didn't know why, but they always made a hangover a lot less painful. I struggled to get back up the stairs and wondered how great it would be if we had Oompa-Loompas to carry us up instead, or at least an escalator.

By ten a.m. the Production department, the self-appointed 'centre of the universe', was in full swing and the infectious energy of the place had me up and running. The department contained most of the creativity of the company, and deserved its lofty title. We had talented film-makers, aspiring musicians, inebriated writers, wannabe artists, failed actors, nerdy graphics bods and everything in between.

Max called from his edit with instructions to 'be ready by the phone if I need you, and go and speak to the different departments about content for the shows'. I felt awkward at the prospect. All these important people working on important things with me interrupting them. Great. Approaching people unannounced wasn't my forte, and I felt as fearful as Oliver going to ask for more.

Clutching my coffee, Jaffa Cakes and diary, I ventured out, using a tip Max had given the day before on how to find my way around the place. 'Do what every man in an office does. Use the fit women as markers for each department. For example, wanna get to the toilets from Production? Easy, take a left by the hot blonde in Ad Sales, straight past the busty brunette in Programme Scheduling, a right past the ginger in Marketing and you're there,' he'd said in a matter-of-fact way.

Problem was there were lots of fit women; which one went where?

For a while I walked around aimlessly, unsure of who I should be speaking to. It soon became apparent that the Jaffa Cakes were coming in handy not just for my splitting hangover but for making friends, as various people called me over with bulging eyes.

The T.A.D. girls, who were responsible for dealing with all the record labels, showered me with CDs and concert tickets in exchange for half a packet. A three-minute report about the latest fashions from the hot girls at The Beat Italy, who produced *The Style Guide*, cost me four cakes. Bargain! I'd run out by the time I finished meeting the team from *The Beat Movies*, who provided me with premiere tickets to see John Cusack in *High Fidelity*.

It wasn't the conventional way of making friends and

influencing people, but I'd figured out a way in – food. More importantly, chocolate! It was available in the canteen on the floor below but a combination of guilt and laziness stopped people from going after it. So back to the canteen I went for more Beat currency. Holding a fresh box of Jaffa Cakes, I continued working through lunch in my search for new friends and suppliers of content for the shows. I was like a fiend, sniffing out my supply lines.

Time had flown when I made it back to my desk and I still had lots to do. At this rate, I wouldn't make it back home before midnight. I'd miss watching my first show of *Defm8*. My work phone rang as I sat down for a split second to catch my breath.

'Yello, Jay here,' I said joyfully.

'Why are you handing out Jaffa Cakes?' asked Max.

'What?' I said, sitting up and looking round for him.

'You're making us look stupid,' he barked.

'What? No, I was just making friends like you told me to . . .' I said.

'No, I said to get content for next week's show. If you want to make friends, do it in the pub, not while you're meant to be working,' he snapped.

'Yeah but –' I wanted to tell him I'd got two weeks' worth of content.

'The show's almost made, get down here now,' he said.

'OK. Do you need –'

'*Chop-chop, yalla-yalla*,' he said as he put the phone down and introduced me to his friend Tone. Dial Tone.

Before leaving, I quickly went through my emails checking for anything important and saw a heap of messages from the people I'd met, with various subject lines, from 'Bienvenido!' and 'Where my Jaffa Cakes at, biatch?' to 'Hanover Grand tonight?' and 'Party invite for Saturday'. Finally I had some recognizable names in my inbox and not just random group emails with subject matter like 'Clear away rubbish' or 'Flat to rent'. The office seemed a little less intimidating now my circle of friends had grown, along with my confidence about getting things done in such a huge organization. But most importantly I needed the emails because I had forgotten how to spell some of the names, especially the European lot. No way I could remember Rochefoucauld or De Cerventes! I finally felt like the next six months might be as fun as I'd always envisaged. I had five months, three weeks and two more days to find out.

9

THE CHOICE IS YOURS

The formation in the seven-seater cab was based on senior-ity, with Max up front. I'd met 'Max's mates' during my work experience and had got to know them when they sat at the logging machine next to me, nicking my Jelly Baby sweets.

In the seat behind Max was Stuart 'Stuey' Johns, producer of *The News Feed*. He was a North London boy, well spoken but often combining the odd bit of street talk for comic effect and irony. He was a real camera whizz and had directed several short films.

Next to him was Oliver 'Oli' Horwood, assistant producer for *D.A.N.C.E.* I wasn't sure where he was from but he was known for his huge tongue, small mouth and resulting lisp. Which didn't stop him from being a right gobby git.

Next to Oli was his partner in crime, Hugh Williams, assistant producer on *iWant*. A posh boy from Newcastle, he'd played three instruments to Grade Eight by the age of eleven. Eclipsing that success, he was now the '99/'00 holder of the golden beer mug for being the best drinker in the department.

Finally, squeezed at the back with me, was the assistant producer for *Life & Rhymes*, Milly Brown. Born in the UK, she had moved around Europe with her hippie parents and returned as an adult, speaking four languages fluently. I don't know if this contributed to the fact that her voice sounded like she was permanently turned on.

It was Thursday, just after six p.m. and we were late. We meandered slowly through Soho in rush-hour traffic in our Addison Lee cab. It was affectionately known by some as 'Uncle Lee' because The Beat had an account with the taxi service and it came in useful particularly for those needing rescue in moments of 'emergency' – most often drink- or shopping-related.

We were heading to 10 Room nightclub for a showcase party to celebrate Craig David's new single 'Fill Me In' and his upcoming album *Born to Do It*. Leaving the office was a nightmare. There was always something pulling one of us back in like an invisible bungee cord. We'd get round the corner and someone had left the mic cube, a wallet or their house keys behind.

The official aim was to film a two-minute report for *Total BEATS* and the news team. Unofficially, it would be a great opportunity for a free piss-up, as one of the crew would pass it off as their birthday to other people in the industry in attendance. Apparently between them they'd already had thirteen birthdays that year.

The driver had the radio tuned to Capital FM and Dr Fox on the drive-time shift, playing the hits that were moving London that week. Everyone in the cab was drowning out Westlife with their rendition of 'Fools Again'.

'Eddie Murphy all day for me. Stuey, what you sayin'?' Max asked, shouting over the singing.

'Oh, that's a close one. But Richard Pryor was like a baby drinking vodka and milk. Sick!' he said.

'What?' Max said in shock.

'But did he have two top-selling shows?' Oli interjected with his Mike Tyson-like lisp.

'Yeah, but what about all the audio recordings Pryor had? Fuck Eddie's two shows,' Hugh countered.

'But Eddie crossed over and went on to do bigger and better things . . .' said Max.

'But Pryor was the father to his style. If there was no Richard Pryor, there would be no Eddie Murphy. Even Eddie admits it,' replied Hugh.

'He might admit the influence, but it doesn't mean he was inferior. Philip was father to Alexander but he wasn't known as Philip the Great,' Oli shot back.

'En Vogue were mothers to Destiny's Child,' said Milly from the back.

'Exactly, they learnt from those that came before them and moved it on a little,' agreed Oli.

'It's that classic struggle for supremacy between Generation Now and Generation Then, innit,' said the driver in his wide-boy accent, his contribution going unnoticed.

'If we're talking who's hot today you have to include Chris Rock,' I yelped from the back.

'Oh, please! That jheri-curl joker from *CB4*?' said Max.

Stuey piped up. 'Rudeboy, I have to agree, Chris is funny in *Bigger & Blacker*. C'mon, don't hate, congratulate.'

'Bah humbug,' said Oli.

'I quite like Chubby Brown personally,' said the driver as he tried to get into the conversation once more.

The cab went quiet for a split second. All you could hear were the wiper blades going back and forth. Just at that moment Dr Fox intervened and the song changed on the radio. There was a big ironic cheer from all as 'Fill Me In' played in the car.

At the steps of the club Max shouted out the key instructions for the night, with The Chemical Brothers' 'Hey Boy Hey Girl' playing in the background.

'Right, lads, you go to the bar. Milly and Jay go set up and I'll find someone from Wildstar. Let's get filming, pronto.'

It was hard to breathe in the small club. A gigantic fan was set up as the solution but it added to the suffocating atmosphere, sending hot air and cigarette smoke swirling around the room, which was definitely over capacity. But so long as the drinks flowed people would grin and bear it. Anyone who was anyone had to be seen at this party or risk not being considered an industry player.

Once set up, Milly pointed out the movers and shakers who spoke to the record-buying public in their own unique way. From the all-powerful producers of kids' TV and the major talk shows, to the radio programmers from national, regional and pirate stations. All forms of print media and the supermarket stockists were crammed in alongside the video programmers from the music channels. There might have been the odd competition winner inside, but on the whole this party was strictly private and members of the public weren't invited. Only the hypnotists and suppliers were allowed in.

Max came over, carrying a few drinks and some food, with a girl from the record label who he introduced as

Regina Simonson. I sipped on the Coke, realizing it was more like a glass of Jack Daniel's with a dash of Coke. I was meeting Sophia at the flat later to cook dinner and watch my first show on VHS. I didn't want to turn up drunk, so I took small sips, allowing the ice to dilute its strength a little.

'Right, guys, let's get some vox-pops going,' Max commanded. 'We'll do Craig in about fifteen minutes, so get cutaways of people partying and a few of the performances. Then cameras down and let's have some fun.' He glanced over at Regina, who looked back at him all gooey-eyed.

'Yeah, that's fine,' she replied.

'And, Jay, I know you've got to leave, so you can head off at seven-ish once everything's done. You guys wait here and I'll send some punters over for interviews.' Then he was off again, working the room, waving to people across the club and kissing women on both cheeks as he squeezed through the tightly packed crowd. Regina trailed off behind him.

'OK, so I'll ask the questions and you can shoot?' suggested Milly.

'What? I can't shoot. I've never held a camera before.'

'Max's not shown you? Don't worry, it's not that hard. Just point it in their direction, hold it steady and make sure you can hear their answers in the headphones.'

She continued the on-the-job training but it was hard to focus when there was a party happening two feet away. Over the noise, she spoke about framing, zooming, focusing, white balance, gains, DBs and zebras. I didn't have a Scooby Doo what she was saying, but I just nodded. It was too late to hesitate as TV personalities and industry heads stepped up to talk to us.

Eventually I sat down in the corner with Milly, anxiously looking at my watch while sipping another JD and Coke. It was already twenty past seven and Craig hadn't arrived. I'd have to leave soon. I didn't know what to do. Should I just go? Should I wait for Max? He was nowhere to be seen. I didn't want to leave till the job was done – it was my responsibility – but I had to get back for Sophia. Everyone in the club was merry and I was on to my third drink by the time Max finally came back with Regina.

'OK, good news is he's coming shortly.' He looked over at Regina again and she gave him the same doey-eyed expression as before.

'Yeah, that's right,' she said.

Do I say something to Max now? I looked at him while he flirted with Regina, thinking of how I could word it to him that I needed to go. He'd understand, wouldn't he? It was all done anyway, just Craig's interview and a minute of performance. Surely he could do that with Milly?

'Max, could I have a quick word, please?' I squeaked like a mouse.

'Yeah, make it quick. I gotta go get a drink, I'm parched.' He looked around at the talent.

'Er, do you still need me? It's just that –'

'Of course I do,' he snapped. 'Who else is gonna help Milly with the filming? I can't, I gotta keep the label happy.'

I looked across at Regina again. *You mean you've got to schmooze with her*, I thought. She would have been happy watching Max peel potatoes.

'You got somewhere better to be than this?' he asked,

looking at everyone from the industry enjoying themselves. 'Welcome to your new working life. At any given time we may have to cover an interview or a party.'

'OK,' I said, in a flat dumb-ass tone. I'd bottled it. I just hoped Sophia hadn't left home yet. I reached for my pocket to send a text message but I had no reception. As I went to the stairs to try to call her a human tsunami of minders, management, label and hangers-on, with Craig David somewhere in the middle, swept towards me. I quickly ducked back into the club as they headed backstage.

The room was buzzing now in more ways than one. Rumours were circulating that some of the kids from the royal family were coming to see Craig perform – and that the alcohol was running out. Both had the audience in quite a stir. I stood waiting to film, wondering if I should step out quickly and text Sophia, but each time I tried the tiniest bit of crowd noise would stop me in my tracks. It would always turn out to be a false start to Craig's arrival on stage, but I couldn't take the risk.

It was eight p.m. when he finally came on and the restless crowd were easily won over by his apology and flattering words. Women of all ages shuffled to the front of the stage, swooning at his fast lyrical wordplay as he seemed to perform directly to each and every one of them.

As we waited to interview him, Milly lit up a cigarette and took the weight off her feet. She was enjoying the buzz of the alcohol she'd knocked back and was happy for the downtime. It was now half-past eight and I was having nightmare visions of Sophia sitting in the smelly kebab shop below the flat waiting for me.

'So, you got a girlfriend then?' Milly asked in a drunken, forthright manner.

'Yep,' I replied.

'How's it going?' she asked, perking up.

'Good,' I said, unsure if it would be by the end of tonight. 'How about you?'

'Nah. Was in a relationship until a few months ago.'

'Why, what happened?'

'Ah, mixture of things. We both worked long hours. In fact I worked the long hours, he sat at my place waiting for me. He eventually ran off with my flatmate.' Despite the depressing news she was delivering, her voice still made her sound as turned on as ever. Suddenly I thought, *Oh God, am I setting up Pritz and Sophia*? Moments later a voice in my head burst into laughter.

I looked around to see people dancing and having fun. People would have killed to be in this club. Yet I couldn't enjoy it with my mind on Sophia. Just as I was about to dash for the exit to text her, Max returned with his shadow, Regina, who led us backstage for the interview.

'I bet you didn't have this grade of women at uni,' he said, tilting his head to the right and admiring Regina's pert back-side. He pointed towards the crowd, leant in and whispered, 'Once the interview's done, get involved.'

'I've got a girlfriend,' I responded, wondering if he'd forgotten.

He grinned. 'Not in here, you don't.'

As soon as the interview was over, Craig was whisked out of the club with his massive entourage, and that signalled the end of the party. A few stragglers stayed on for the remaining free booze but there was a mass exodus, as though someone had let off a stink bomb.

Stuey, Oli and Hugh surfaced from the different corners of the club with stories of what they'd been up to, regurgitating the industry gossip of who was sleeping with who. I just wanted to get out and call Sophia, ready to say sorry at least a hundred times while on my knees. But Max had already lined up our next party and, crucially, filming mission: Puff Daddy's bash at Rock on the Embankment. I couldn't get out of that either.

'But do we have supplies for it? Did anyone pick up any Daz?' asked Hugh in a panic.

I knew from meeting these guys before that Daz was their code name for cocaine. It was called many names but this particular one took off with everyone after Oli explained his first encounter with it at the age of sixteen. He'd gone out clubbing and bought some off a dealer in the club, then went to the toilets to snort it with his mates. After a strange reaction, he panicked and went to the hospital, only to spend the next few hours in A&E trying to explain to the nurse how he'd lost the ability to smell from his right nostril. She then spent a matter of seconds explaining he'd been snorting Daz washing powder.

Oli went to his back pocket and pulled out several small envelopes made from the front cover of a *GQ* magazine, distributing them to the others. It wasn't my thing so I dived into a camera bag pretending to check the equipment to avoid Oli's outstretched hand.

Hugh's face lit up. 'That's just don-ter-coo,' he said, which I'd learnt to interpret as meaning 'Sweeeet!'

The excitement of going to a legendary Puff Daddy party was put on hold by the guilt that not only had I stood up my girlfriend but I hadn't even called her yet. I should have told Max then that I had to leave, but I didn't. He'd made it clear this sort of impromptu thing was now part of my job and I didn't want to let him down or face his wrath again.

Before I knew it, I was in the back of an Uncle Lee heading towards the Embankment with my head being filled with the wonders of what the party ahead would be like. It could have been Lucifer in my ear but instead it was Max: 'Ain't no party like a Puff Daddy party, cos a Puff Daddy party don't stop.'

As corny as the line was, I fell for it.

10
GIRLS ON FILM

It was mid morning the next day when I walked over to the photocopier by the window for some privacy. Some of the boys were making a racket, having a remote-control car race in the department. I pressed number two on my speed dial and waited for Sophia to pick up. 'I thought I'd see how you were doing.'

'If you hadn't rung I could have carried on dreaming about flashing lights and sparklers coming out of champagne bottles.'

I laughed. 'Well, it really happened.'

'It's all really foggy,' she said, yawning, clearly having just woken up.

En route to the Embankment, I had begged Max if he could save my bacon with Sophia and get her into the Puff Daddy party. He'd looked at me confused, like he was trying to solve a theorem, but eventually took pity on me. As Sophia's Uncle Lee pulled up outside the club, he wasn't too happy when my other girlfriend, Pritz, also arrived in tow, not wanting to miss out on all the fun. I gave Max a pathetic look that said, *Please don't make me skank my annoying friend?*

'I've never known what it's like to be in the VIP section, let alone be treated like one,' said Sophia, trying to remember the details of the night before.

'Hey, I treat you like one,' I said, feigning insult.

'You know what I mean,' she laughed. 'It was like a zoo, although I'm not sure who was looking out and who was looking in.'

'So, I forgot to ask you, what did you think of Max?'

She paused. 'Honestly, he's nice but I have to admit he's a bit intimidating.'

A smile grew across my face. I was glad she'd met Max and had a better understanding of what my boss was like in person.

'I was so underdressed compared to the girls you introduced me to.'

'Not at all. In fact, I'm sure most of them were wearing the same outfit they'd been to work in,' I said, trying to recall who'd been wearing what in the office the day before.

'Wow, well I didn't know who was a model and who was just a girl from your office. They were all equally good-looking.'

'They're not *that* nice,' I said, trying to reassure her. I wasn't sure if I'd pulled it off though. 'OK, I'd better go. I'll see you tonight for a full debrief and this time I'll call you at home when I'm actually done so you're not left waiting.' I laid it on thick for effect.

'Not too late, I hope.'

'Who knows with this job? Maybe Puffy will throw a sequel tonight. You in?'

'Defo!' she said as her voice picked up with excitement,

also signalling that she was now fully awake. 'I'm going to call Mia. She won't believe last night!'

'Even I don't believe last night.'

As I put the phone down, I could only imagine the level of girly detail they'd go into and, for just this once, I couldn't blame them! Back at my desk, people were throwing things across the department to one another: frisbees, paper balls and aeroplanes, tennis balls, a mini American football and anything else that could float or fly through the air. Music was blaring once more from all corners. Ad Sales weren't fans of our noise and had complained several times in Senior Management meetings to the Doc, who in secret probably welcomed the atmosphere. This was The Beat; it was expected.

In today's sound clash, the rock boys were playing Limp Bizkit, the dance crew blasting out Armand Van Helden, and the hip-hop heads had on DMX. But Stuey trumped them all with some good old-fashioned pop that everyone could get into. Next thing, everyone was singing Ronan Keating's 'Life Is a Rollercoaster'. Other departments across the building stood up to see what the crazies were doing.

As the singing stopped, Terry 'the Minister' Perkins, the head of Production, walked past on his way to a meeting. He was nicknamed the Minister because he was tall and inadvertently walked a bit like John Cleese's character in Monty Python's 'Ministry of Silly Walks' sketch. Made all the more stupid as he wore professional running shoes to work thinking they were cool trainers. He generally kept his distance from the department, perhaps to keep an air of mystery and thus control. There was no reason as mere interns we'd cross his path but he was the one who ultimately held our future fate at the company in his hands.

Seeing him bob past, everyone jumped back into their seats and pretended to be working away furiously. 'If I don't have it in the next fifteen minutes there will be hell to pay,' screamed Oli with his loud lisp.

Hugh was more blasé and carried on reading the papers, looking at the gossip sections to see if any of us were in the background of a celebrity shot from the previous night's parties. There was a support pillar in the middle of the department by Max's desk that housed these pictures. If any part of your body featured – even just an elbow or a knee – you would take pride of place on the 'Pillar of Fame/ Infamy'.

While the producers were larking about, us interns were running around as usual. I was knee-deep in research when Max came over to my desk in a hurry, looking flustered, as if the events of the night before had made him forget about the events of today.

'Stop what you're doing. I want you to get a camera and set it up in the Sixties room,' he said in a panic.

'What for?' I guessed a surprise artist had just turned up.

'Didn't I mention I've got some presenters coming down today to audition as roving reporter for The Beat parties?'

'Er, no,' I said, looking at my diary for confirmation.

'Well, I'm mentioning it now,' he snapped, trying to hide the fact he'd forgotten. 'Pamela in Reception will call you to collect them and bring them up.'

'OK. When?'

'Now. The first one is waiting for you downstairs. Giddy

up!' he said with a sense of urgency as if it were me who'd cocked up.

I ran around the department looking for equipment, rummaging through cupboards and under people's desks. Once I'd managed to set up, I went downstairs to get the first presenter for the audition. Pamela the receptionist pointed to a girl standing by the mirror checking out her make-up. It couldn't be right. I looked back at her and she confirmed with a nod. I walked up behind the girl and said, 'Regina?'

'Hey, Jay,' she chirped back.

'Are you here for the audition?' I asked as if there had been a mistake.

'Yeah. It is now, isn't it? Have I come too early?' she said, looking at her watch.

'No, not at all. Come with me.' I continued with the small talk as we walked up the stairs. 'So have you done any presenting before?'

'No, but Max said I was a natural for it and I thought why not?' she giggled.

I bet he did, I thought to myself, holding back from smirking.

Once at the top of the staircase I could see all the men in the surrounding departments standing up like they were meerkats on the lookout. To the untrained eye it would seem like they were all going about their daily business, conversing by the water cooler, speaking on the phone, playing with radio-controlled cars, but I knew what they were up to, as did the women in the building. They'd seen it many times: the communal hot-girl radar was on. It was as though a silent alarm had been tripped, alerting all the men. They were like hunting dogs that had caught the sniff of a fox.

Regina took a seat in the Sixties room as I went to get Max. As I closed the door I saw him coming towards me flanked by the other two Marx brothers, Hugh and Oli.

'It's Regina,' I said, still not sure it was right.

'Yes, thanks, Einstein. You can carry on researching those news stories now,' Max said, like I was a pesky little brother who'd served his purpose.

'Don't you want me to film?' I asked, like I was missing out on all the fun, even though I didn't know what the 'fun' was.

'No, I think we've got it from here.' All three smiled at each other as though they were invisibly high-fiving, walked in and shut the door behind them. As I turned to leave, Max came back out. I thought he'd had a change of heart. Instead he put up an A4 sign on the door:

DO NOT DISTURB – AUDITIONS

The rest of the day was taken up flying between researching the shows and acting as centurion on the lookout for more girls at reception. The auditionees had come from far and wide and were all shapes and sizes. From modelling agencies, presenter agencies, friends of friends, girls the boys had met out in clubs and, on a handful of occasions, people who had sent in presenter showreels.

The Beat got dozens of VHS tapes every day, letters pleading for a chance attached, and they'd be put in a box by the Pillar of Fame/Infamy. Some sent knickers (unwashed), some sent money in foreign currency and one sent a spliff with a Post-it note that read: 'Sit back, relax, roll up a phat one and let me blow you away.' When one of the producers needed a laugh after a long, hard day in the office they'd watch the reels with a nice cup of tea and some biscuits. In fact, there was a Fox's biscuit tin especially stored in the showreel box.

The production of some of the tapes was so poor you could barely see the wannabe presenters' faces. It was as if they'd got their arthritic grandmother to hold the camera as unsteadily as possible. Some were so nervous they would stumble on saying their own name. Others would be connected to someone famous in the music industry and would interview them thinking it would help them look like a real presenter. And age didn't matter even though The Beat was for kids. Some forty-year-olds tried to get away with being a cool older brother but failed instantly, most looking like an uncool uncle, some unfortunates seeming like sex offenders instead.

If getting a 'normal' job at The Beat was hard, it was a doddle compared to becoming a presenter. This was the Holy Grail and was as good as . . . no, it was better than finding the cup of Christ. It was a VIP pass to everything exclusive in life – meeting the stars, flying first class, a good wage, going to all the exclusive parties and concerts and getting complimentary alcohol and drugs, screwing the stars (if you knew what you were doing), invitations to exclusive holiday resorts, being 'cool famous' not 'D-list famous', rubbing shoulders with the rich and powerful, getting bags of free stuff from clothes to gadgets. It was like getting the keys to a penthouse apartment overlooking Central Park in New York when you'd been living in a Third World village in which you shared a tiny room with twelve others. Only Forbes could calculate the true value of this experience and lifestyle.

The number of girls coming through that afternoon could easily have filled a class register. With my research for both shows done, Pamela called me to collect the next contestant, Isabel Ripolli.

She looked confident and was miles more charming than any of the others. The look in her eye was quite mesmerizing, how I imagined Helen of Troy. We spoke briefly in Reception and I prepped her with as much generic information as I could: 'Look straight down the camera . . . Be yourself . . . Have fun . . . Smile . . .'

I led her to the Sixties room where the Marx Brothers sat smugly. As I went to leave, I heard her ask, 'Oh, isn't Jay staying?' She was looking at Max with big puppy-dog eyes.

I was shocked enough, but Max was completely on the back foot and his mouth spoke before he could think clearly, 'Er . . . yes, he can stay if you want him to.'

She smiled at me. 'If you're not busy?'

'Not at all. I've just finished all my research actually.' The look on my face as I peered over at Max could have been accompanied by a Nelson-Muntz laugh. Isabel's timing was better than Michael Schumacher's at a corner in Monaco. I quickly joined Oli behind the camera before Max could change his mind.

By the time I returned from showing her back down to Reception, the judges were in the middle of their deliberations.

'I liked her,' said Hugh as I stood over his shoulder and peeked at his notes. Next to all the names of the girls he had doodled, drawn pornographic pictures, written some remarks like 'Can't present' and marked them out of ten. So far no one had scored over six. Next to Isabel's name he had written 'wheelbarrow – good potential – eight.'

'What are the pluses?' asked Max.

'A – she knows her stuff and B – she gave me a rise in my Levi's,' said Oli cheekily.

'She's never presented before, so it would be good to uncover a new gem,' said Hugh.

'She doesn't have an agent which means she can't be a diva . . .' Oli went on with his wet lisp.

'. . . which means, we all have an even chance of nailing her,' finished Hugh.

'Not all of us,' said Max.

'Oh yeah, I forgot Jay's in here,' said Hugh, and they all laughed.

Yeah, hilarious, I thought.

The banter continued as I nipped out to deliver the next sacrificial lamb to the slaughter. Some of the girls were straight twelve out of tens and full of confidence, but as soon as the little light on the camera started flashing red in front of them, they just froze. They became too self-conscious, didn't know where to look and acted unnaturally. Result? The camera didn't like them.

At the end of the day Max offered Isabel the unpaid job, which required her to be The Beat party reporter, as the main presenters were sick and tired of talking to drunk kids. However, if she did well and the producers liked her, it would be a foot through the pearly gates. I was pleased that she'd made it. She was hot, but she had real talent too. Even Max knew that a bad presenter would make his show look amateur, no matter how big her cleavage was.

After I had de-rigged the equipment, I returned to my desk to see the building was empty. It was eight p.m. Max, Hugh and Oli had already split like Bros. Even my fellow interns had all scampered, leaving a Post-it note that said 'Gone to Notting Hill Arts Club to see a new band'. As I looked across the empty office all I could see were computer monitors with screensavers of The Beat's infinity logo bouncing around, and TVs on mute. There was an envelope on my keyboard with my name on it. Inside was a pair of tickets to Wembley Arena to see Puff Daddy & the Family that weekend from the girls in T.A.D. My inbox was full of unread mail, but it would have to wait till next week. For now I texted Sophia to come and meet me and the intern crew for a drink and a bitching session about our first week.

As I walked down the stairs and out of the building, one thing was sure: I'd been thrown in. The deep end was exactly that but I had managed to keep my head above water, even if I was now paddling furiously to stay afloat. The scary question at the back of my mind was, *Would I sink or swim?*

11
ALPHABET ST.

Sophia woke me up the next morning in the middle of a dream. I was scoring a goal for England thanks to an assist from David Beckham and then kissing Posh in the changing rooms afterwards. It was a weird dream but better that way round, as I knew Posh didn't have the ability to play a thirty-yard ball over the defence perfectly into my stride for me to volley into the top corner.

Having seen *Football Focus* and eaten breakfast (four Weetabix with lots of sugar), Sophia finally persuaded me to get out of bed. She suggested a Saturday afternoon hang-out session in Camden Market to bond after my chaotic first week. Despite plenty of phone sex, a long-distance relation-ship was testing. We only saw each other every other weekend, alternating the trip on the M1 between us. Although she'd finished university for Easter break, she was off skiing next week with her folks so I needed a dose of her before she left. Even if it involved bustling through the throng of backpacker tourists in search of trinkets and second-hand designer gear.

Time flew by and soon we parted ways with a long embrace. Sophia had to get back for dinner with her parents and I had to go to Soho for a mate from uni's birthday.

'You sure you can't come tonight?'

'I'd love to but I better head back or Mum's going to hit the roof that I'm missing dinner for a third night.'

'You're sure?' I said, trying to tempt her again.

She laughed at my efforts. 'Maybe we can meet tomorrow if I get my packing done early,' she said as we separated. 'Say hi to Sara D at the party and apologize that I can't make it.'

Sara D had sat next to me in lectures and we'd occasionally enjoyed throwing paper aeroplanes from the top of the auditorium and watching them glide a distance then crash against the board, narrowly missing the lecturer. Those of us who lived in London had lost touch as everyone started working and no one's schedules matched. So this was a good chance to catch up after several months. After that I'd promised the other interns I'd see them at Monica and Alyssa's party, the girls from The Beat Italy.

I arrived at Alphabet Bar and opened the door, where a blast of heat, smoke and noise hit me in the face. My head moved round like a surveillance camera till it landed on a drunken-looking face. It was Sara D. She came over and greeted me with a 'Whassup?' as her tongue extended out fully and flailed about for a bit. I didn't want to be the one to tell her she couldn't pull it off, especially as it was her birthday. I wondered how long it would be till the phrase from the new Budweiser advert got annoying. Judging by the reaction in the bar, it was still pretty new to them all.

Cue lots of hugging and back-patting as everyone from uni shared news of conquering our respective fields. I found myself centre of attention in a small group as the others listened on fully absorbed. I suddenly felt quite proud that one week as an intern had been worth the praise of my peers. But it was short-lived – they soon turned me into a low-grade tout to get them concert tickets. I broke off and headed for the bar and started speaking to one of the girls in the group I didn't know, who seemed bored on her own.

'Hi, I'm Jay,' I said, smiling.

'Hi,' she replied without much warmth.

'So, what's your name?' I continued.

'Vicky.'

She was pleasant but hard work. OK, I'm lying; she was just plain hard work. She clearly had the socializing skills of a hermit with the plague.

'So how do you know Sara D?'

'I went to school with her.'

'Cool. Remind me, which one was that?'

'City of London, and it wasn't.'

I wasn't quite sure what else to say to her. *OK, I'm not Brad Pitt to look at, but make an effort*, I thought. Maybe she just didn't like me. But I had been friendly. I wasn't trying it on. *Oh God, she doesn't think I'm trying it on, does she?* Did I need to start talking to her about my girlfriend to put her at ease? I looked around to see if there was someone else we could drag into this house-on-fire dynamic, but there wasn't. I conveniently put my lips to my beer bottle and kept them there. The ball was now in her part of the court and she had no option but to smack it back.

'So, where are you from?' she asked while exhaling, clearly uninterested in the response.

'North-west London and a regular attendee and friend to the organizers of the Mark and Bert balls.'

She carried on looking over my shoulder so I looked over hers towards the possibility of ending this conversation by going to play on one of the Space Invader arcade tables that had become free.

'I work for Thames Water in the sewage department,' I said. I waited for a reaction. The look I got back said, *I thought as much*. It felt like her head was tilting back further by the minute as she looked down her nose at me. OK, now she was pissing me off. *Don't get snooty with me, girlfriend*, I thought with a RuPaul finger snap. Blood began to rush to my head and before I knew it I was talking, from the wrong hole.

'I was joking, I work at The Beat,' I said in as smug a way as possible.

The reaction was almost instantaneous. Her head started to tilt forward, she began to look me in the eyes and her body twisted towards me.

'*Really?*' she said, not sure whether to believe me.

'Yes, *really*,' I replied, feeling cocky now.

'What do you do there?'

'I'm a producer,' I lied.

Her eyes widened.

'Cool, for which show?'

'*Total BEATS*, and it is,' I said smugly. Without another word, I put my empty bottle on the table in front of us and walked off to the toilets. Even I thought I was a quant now. Either I pulled it off like John Wayne or I looked a right Charlie Chaplin.

84

To complete my campaign I returned via the bar with a bottle of champagne for Sara D. Could I afford it? Of course not, but bizarrely my ego had to show Vicky I was a 'baller'. Her transformation was remarkable as she listened to every word I said and even laughed at my jokes.

My charm was working to full effect as I got her number and an invite to go round to her place in Chelsea for a drink later that week. But it was most satisfying seeing the look on her face when I asked her what time Sophia and I should come over. I left her wondering if I was joking or suggesting a threesome.

I spent some more time catching up with the others before kissing Sara on the forehead and leaving. As I walked up the stairs to the exit, I wasn't sure when I'd next see them all. For now though, I was looking forward to going to meet my new buddies. My Beat buddies.

As I sat on the bus I checked my phone, which had been vibrating for the last thirty minutes with text messages from the other interns who were heading to the party. Sonya sent me one with directions to the address near Old Street, while the one from James III read:

Alright fella. Bring something to get us off our tits.

Arriving at the flat, the beers from the bar had started to kick in and I was in party mode. The lift chugged its way up to the apartment and as I got closer to the fifth floor, the music got louder and louder till finally the lift jerked to a halt. The doors opened into a small corridor, at the end of which was a sign reading 'PARTAY'. I didn't immediately recognize the tune in the lift, but now the streaks of red I could see coming from M-Beat and General Levy's 'Incredible' were bouncing off the walls and towards me in rapid motion.

The flat was dark and I couldn't make out any faces as I walked in. There were candles everywhere for mood lighting and the smell of a spliff was in the air. I felt someone pinch my arse but my excitement turned to disappointment when I saw James III grinning behind me.

'What did you bring, lad?' he asked, eyeing up the carrier bag in my hand.

'Not much . . .'

'Let's have a butcher's then, lad,' he said as he snatched it and dumped it on a coffee table, whistling 'Deck the Halls'. He stuck his hand in and rummaged around like it was a lucky dip. 'Right, a bottle of . . . cheap plonk . . . bread . . . peanuts . . . cheese . . . Pringles – and some Nutella.' He paused, then opened both containers and philosophized in a thick Yorkshire accent, 'I wonder what that tastes like?'

'So how is it?' I asked.

'It's tricky but it tastes OK,' he replied through a mouthful of hazelnut-smeared crisps.

'No, I meant the party.'

'Oh, it's a fair crack. There's some fine-looking lasses here. It's like being at a Woolworth's pick and mix counter.'

'So who's here?' I asked, checking the place out.

'Not sure. There's some hippidy-hoppidy girl called Estelle. Dunno who she is but I got an aunt called Estelle, so I can't go there. Know her?'

'Your aunt? No. The rapper? Yes. Been on the scene for a while, waiting to break through.'

'Well, with a name like that, it's no wonder.'

James III kept his plastic cup by his mouth, his teeth gripping the edge as his eyes shifted above at every move. 'Well, shall we go sharking?' he said, making a gesture of a fin above his head.

'Sharking?'

'Hunting. We swim gracefully through the fish and then make a move. But I can't shark alone. I need a Goose,' he said.

'Why are you talking in animal terms?' I asked, confused.

'Have you never seen *Top Gun*? I need a wingman.'

'Oh! That I can do,' I said, finally getting it.

We 'swam' around the apartment smiling and saying hello to people we did and didn't know. Once James III hooked a girl in, I went in search of the others. I spotted them dispersed around the party socializing. Or were they? I noticed Sonya was using her charms on one of the exec producers, as was Tola, who had a member of senior management hanging on her every word. Cara and Sam were at it too. I felt a faint panic rise in my stomach. Was I missing a trick or was this being overly competitive? I wanted to get in on the action as well but knew I was too drunk to make a good impression. I had to sober up first so went for the table in the kitchen that held an array of top-notch nibbles, from hummus and Italian bread to samosas and Thai spring rolls. *Thank God*, my stomach rumbled. As I scoffed another samosa, I felt a tap on my arse again.

'I take it you didn't score?' I said, turning round, expecting to see James III looking jilted. Instead it was one of the hosts, Alyssa, in a super-hot outfit. My eyes nearly fell out of their sockets.

'Hungry?' she said playfully.

'Oh no,' I responded nervously, wondering if I was eating all the food.

'Can I get you some wine?'

'Thanks, but I better not, I've already had quite a few.'

She ignored me, grabbed my hand and took me to the table of drinks, pouring us two. We spent the next half-hour talking about London, Milan and travelling across the world with a backpack. She was so much more fun and easier to talk to than Vicky the Trustafarian.

'Want to dance?' she said, suddenly getting in the mood.

'I'm not very good, plus I'm slightly drunk,' I warned as Montell Jordan's 'Get It on Tonite' played in the background.

She smiled flirtatiously. 'Don't worry, I'll take care of you.'

My guilt-radar kicked into action. Sophia would not be happy about this scene. 'OK . . . but I warn you I have two left feet,' I said nervously, wondering if I could escape without seeming rude.

'Really? That's nice.' She led me to the dance floor.

What am I doing?

But you're only dancing, said the voice inside my head. Tonight it was Mick Jagger.

Yeah, but I'm sure she's eyeing me up, I replied.

It's official, you are drunk and clearly deluded, said Mick. *She's a hot Italian, out of your league, clearly bored and just wants to dance.*

At first we danced a few feet apart until she got fed up with me being so awkward and grabbed me closer. She began laughing at the expense of the squirmy Englishman.

See, there's nothing to worry about, said Mick.

Yeah, I said, still unsure. *But is this a bad time to say she's really turning me on?*

So? Mick shrugged nonchalantly.

Is it cheating if you get a hard-on while dancing with someone other than your girlfriend? I asked.

No, of course not. You're not in charge of the fella downstairs, said Mick.

I'd never been in a position like this before and wasn't used to the attention, especially from an older woman. I was waiting for someone to represent my conscience and speak up to bring a halt to proceedings. But John Lennon was hooded, bound and gagged by the agents of Alcohol, Perfume and the words of Salt-N-Pepa's 'Push It'. The music tasted like tangy peaches.

Sophia, Sophia, Sophia. John Lennon had finally broken free and was telling me to get a grip. It was now a wrestling match between Mick and John for control. Mick was trying to pin John down using my senses, which could smell, see, touch, hear but not yet taste Alyssa. Mick was winning with DDTs, backbreakers and clotheslines to hush John as horny impulses continued travelling down south.

John decided it was time to play dirty. What would be the one thing that would work? Eureka! John readied his combination moves and let rip on Mick. *Pritz's feet. Pritz's extremely manky feet. Alyssa's feet. Alyssa having Pritz's manky feet.* As I looked down at her feet I imagined crusty soles, long dirty toenails, corns, bunions, athlete's foot and every other disgusting foot funk.

John had applied a reverse pin and won. The voices became faint as calm was restored in my Calvins.

'Hello there, lad,' said a real voice in my right ear. I turned round to see a pair of green eyes staring at me, eyebrows raised. 'Room in there for another?' It was big, bungling James the bloody third. How I could kiss him. He'd saved the Goose's goose.

'Plenty of room,' I said, disconnecting quicker than a sprinter from the blocks. 'I need to go to the bathroom and then I feel it might be good to order a cab home. I have a really important thing to do in the morning and laundry and cleaning and shopping and work stuff to prepare.' I was rabbiting.

Alyssa smiled but she wasn't giving up so easily. 'Well, the bathroom's that way and I can call you a cab if you like, or you can always sleep here on the spare bed?'

'Thank you. Um, maybe next time. Thank you, though. Thank you,' I said, walking backwards.

She carried on smirking, enjoying my discomfort. Even James III was smiling like a Cheshire cat. I turned and staggered to the hallway to find the toilet.

I stood in an orderly queue outside the bathroom, using the wall to help support me while I sobered up. What seemed like two poos, one piss and a tampon change later, I stood over the toilet trying my hardest to aim straight. Wow, I really had drunk a lot. I had to call for my uncle – Uncle Lee that is – to rescue me. It was time to find the emergency exits and ditch this party.

12
EVERY BREATH YOU TAKE

Hungover from the previous night, I sat in the flat with the TV on, staring at it but not watching anything. I had concert tickets but didn't want to move from this vegetative position. I'd already used up all my energy going home to see Mum for Sunday lunch, even though I could barely face eating anything.

Daylight was fading fast outside by the time Pritz returned from his parents' house, with freshly laundered washing, to see me looking glum.

'Listen to this, mate – this will make you laugh.' He tried his best to cheer me up with a story about attempting to explain to his mum why the back seat of her car had red marks on it. He'd told her it was Ribena, and it was in her best interests to believe him. With Pritz, ignorance was more than just bliss, it was keeping your sanity. I got the true story: all the sordid details of his fumble in the back seat with a childhood sweetheart from next door, who'd been home for the weekend too.

'I'm not sure what it was. Do you think I took her virginity?'

'Pritz,' I laughed, 'spare me the analysis. I don't want to

know!' But he'd successfully lifted my spirits. Now it was my turn to return one of many favours. 'I've got tickets to Puff Daddy at Wembley,' I boasted. 'Wanna come?'

'Pump Daddy? Why not? There will be loads of hot girls at that concert. All that "I'll be missing you" emotional drama, with hands in the air. I'm in.' He started chanting, 'Wem-b-leee Wem-b-leee', like a football hooligan, stuck his arms out like a plane and glided round the front room and into the shower, singing as many Puff Daddy songs as he knew – words all wrong – until he was ready to leave.

On the Tube we chatted about my Italian experience the night before. Pritz shook his head.

'Damn, Jay, that sounds like hot sex on a platter. You idiot!'

'I know, I know,' I admitted. 'But I couldn't do that to Sophia. I'm, you know . . .'

'In love?' He sighed exaggeratedly.

'I'm not you.'

He rolled his eyes. 'Yeah, well I love my mum, but the veg curry at Sakonis beats hers hands down. I just wouldn't think of telling her. Hear what I'm saying? Live the dream.'

I nodded but we were living in two different worlds. Pritz saw relationships like a deep-sea diver saw a lead weight: they just dragged you down.

We got off the train and headed down the famous Wembley walkway towards the stadium's two towers, a worldwide icon of football. It felt odd not to be wearing an England scarf, eating a hot dog and singing 'Inger-land, Inger-land, Inger-land'. Instead we were surrounded by girls dressed up to the nines with flashing bunny ears on their heads. Pritz tried chatting one of them up as we were hurriedly marshalled through the gates by stewards in bright yellow jackets. Some kids without tickets were readying to bum-rush in.

Our seats were awesome. We sat among VIPs, Pritz people-watching, his neck spinning nearly 360 degrees. As the lights dimmed and a big cheer went up, my phone began to vibrate in my pocket. It was a text message from Sophia.

> Where r u RV? U haven't returned my call from earlier. U ok?
> LV xxx

Everyone was standing up and screaming now as Puff Daddy came out from beneath the stage, a solitary beam of light focused on him.

> Yeah I'm ok. Recovering from hangover. Just with Pritz. How r u? X

The lighting show was in full effect, strobing and pulsating to the music as Puffy worked the stage.

> Why didn't you call me back babe? Where r u? I've packed so can we meet 2night? xxx

Pritz was still craning round looking for celebs. 'Isn't that what's-his-name, the Arsenal footballer sat next to the Spurs one? In fact I can see Liverpool and Man U players too.'

> Sorry. Went to see mum. Was monged out today. Watchin' Puff Daddy@Wembley. When do u fly? X

'The show's actually better than I thought it would be,' Pritz said, finally turning his attention to the concert.

'Yeah. It's not bad. He knows how to work the crowd,' I said, distracted by another new message.

U didn't tell me u were going? We still haven't watched ur first
show. I'm on my Easter holidays + I want to see you. Fly 2moro.

'Who you texting all the time?' Pritz asked, annoyed I wasn't
bird-watching with him. 'You're missing the show.'

'Sophia,' I said.

'Everything all right?'

'I don't know, she sounds a bit off.'

'Well, she's probably wondering why she isn't here with
you,' he suggested.

'I wasn't going to come till you got back to the flat.
Besides, I only had two tickets.'

'Did you ask her?' he replied.

'No, because I didn't think it was her thing,' I said dismissively.

'Yeah, but did you *ask* her?'

Could he not follow my logic? 'No, because I asked
you.'

'Well, there it is,' he said in conclusion. 'Even I know
girlfriends get first dibs.'

I sighed. My brain was too tired for this but I knew he
was right. I should have offered her first refusal, even with
the last-minute decision to go. Worse still was that I was
being taught the lesson by Pritz, a man as capable of holding
down a relationship as a bulimic with a BLT sandwich. I
texted her back with lashings of grovel thrown in.

I'm so sorry, babe. Wasn't going to come. Very last-minute.
Wanted to do s'thing for Pritz as he's been paying majority of
rent. Sorry. X

94

My phone vibrated in my hand immediately.

> Stop playing text tennis, put your phone away and enjoy the show. You've missed half of it already!

It was Max. I looked around to see where he was. I couldn't see him anywhere.

My phone vibrated again.

> Haha! Side of stage.

I peered at the stage and I couldn't believe it. There he was, standing with Hugh, Oli, a heap of other people and some hot-looking girls next to him. Bastard. I should have considered myself lucky to even have tickets, yet seeing where Max was made me feel like I was sat right at the back of the auditorium behind a supporting pillar, with a blindfold and headphones.

My eyes shifted back to my phone, waiting for Sophia to reply. Nothing came. She was clearly pissed off. My favourite track about Benjamins came on as I left my seat and went out to the concourse to call her. The merchandise stall was setting up for the end of the concert as I dialled her number. It rang several times and then eventually went to her voicemail.

'Hey babe, I'm sorry for being stupid. Honestly, I know I should have at least asked you first about the concert. I'm sorry. I'll make it up to you when you get back. Please don't be mad at me. Love you. Much-much.'

Back in the arena, I tried to enjoy the show but guilt was descending heavily on me. I was waiting for my phone to vibrate with at least a message. Puffy was now in his full glory and his finale was tinged with irony to me – it was his world-conquering 'I'll Be Missing You'. I felt like an atheist at the Vatican as everyone sang along beside me. Pritz grabbed me in a headlock and forced me to be a believer once more.

Back at the flat, and having devoured his lamb shish as quickly as possible, Pritz went straight to bed, ready for his early morning start at 'making rich people even richer'. I sat in the front room with the TV on mute and a VHS tape in my hand. The label read:

Defm8, TX Weds 21:00 – The Beat

My show. Sophia still hadn't called back as I put the tape into the VHS player and sat down to watch it. The light from the TV flickered and danced around in the dark room as PJ read his opening link.

I began to reflect on the events of the past week that had shot by so quickly. The Doc's speech; cycling around the office; filming in the studio; meeting Jay-Z and Puffy; Chinawhite; auditioning hot girls . . . and too many late nights. One week was under my belt and I had twenty-three more to go.

I was exhausted at the thought of the coming week and the one after that and the one after that. It was exciting doing all these things that most people would be envious of and I was living a dream I'd always wished for. But I still feared landing flat on my face, not wanting the dream to turn into a nightmare like it had for the captain of the *Titanic*.

As the end credits rolled a little ray of hope shone through. It suddenly made the thoughts of failure disappear to be replaced with a sense of pride, all achieved by four simple words on a TV screen.

Production Assistant – Jay Merchant

13
ALL NIGHT LONG

I was now almost a month into my internship, but every week was as hectic as the first. By day I was working like a dog, and by night I was with Sophia, who was back from skiing and spending the rest of the Easter holidays in London. I'd been busy saving up future stamps for her good books – some quality time together, a present from Selfridges, dinner dates and theatre tickets from the T.A.D. girls to see *The Lion King*. But now it was Me Time. Specifically, time to reap the benefits of my internship with my first Beat party. I'd never been to one as a punter because they were always sold out in advance. I'd grown up watching enticing adverts with beautiful people dancing and celebrity PAs in attendance. I was about to find out what the fuss was about.

We were driving into Middlesbrough from Manchester, where the night before we'd been treated to VIP tickets from Nike to see Max's team, Manchester United, play Real Madrid. Thankfully Max was so drunk from the free hospitality drinks that he didn't actually care what the score was by the end – his team lost.

By three p.m. we had checked into our hotel and were meeting Milly and Stuey in reception to go for a sound and lighting test at the club. Different producers and presenters took it in turn to film the parties each month, and this was April's dream team.

'So here's your crew room for your equipment and your rider, as requested,' said Alison Cooks, the party promoter. The woman was ballsy, delivering the line seemingly with a sense of pride about the snacks she'd laid on for us in a room that was stacked full of beer crates with a smell of damp.

'Smells lovely. Wow, a box of Quality Street, some crisps and a bowl of fruit too,' Max said with fake incredulity to Stuey. 'Now I know what it feels like having a Rolling Stone's rider.'

Max had filled me in on Alison and the parties on the drive up the M62 while we listened to the Black Eyed Peas trying to bridge the gap. She got the promoter gig at a chance meeting with a member of The Beat's senior management at a BRIT Awards afterparty, where a lot of business was conducted – usually badly and under the influence. Allegedly she wrote a contract on a napkin and got him to sign it while he was off his face. Max reckoned it wasn't so much the napkin that persuaded him to honour the contract but the pictures on her phone of him tonguing a male dancer. Nothing wrong with that – if only he didn't have a wife.

The in-house marketing team was too small to be able to do this role full-time, and only attended events to oversee what was going on and get drunk partying with the kids. The Beat covered most costs, and all Alison really had to do was a bit of on-the ground promotion to reap the benefits of the ticket fee. It was a nice little earner and explained her

Range Rover and two-bed flat in London's Little Venice. The Beat was turning over too many millions to be bothered by the comparative scraps from the parties.

The Beat banners made things official and were placed everywhere to remind people which church they'd come to worship at. As we reached the pulpit – the DJ booth at the back of the club – the ceiling dropped low, giving the place a really intimate feeling. If you were claustrophobic, this wasn't the place for you as later that night it would be packed with 1,000 people all gasping for The Beat experience.

'I've placed two big fans on either side of the stage to blow some cool air into the crowd as the manager tells me this place gets really hot,' said Alison.

'Don't they have any air-con?' asked Max.

'Apparently it broke last week.'

'We're trying to give the punters The Beat experience, not a sauna experience. You want kids passing out? Surely it's a health and safety issue,' he said.

'It'll be fine. Besides, won't it look cool to shoot them all hot and sweaty?' she suggested.

'Thanks for the directing tips, Alison, but I think we can handle that,' he snapped back.

'Just a suggestion, Max,' she said. 'I've done plenty of parties without air-con – trust me, they love a sweat-pit. Anyway, I have to finalize some things with the security team, so I'll see you later tonight.' She walked off with her assistant in tow.

Max rolled his eyes, thinking she'd cut corners again to keep her costs low and her profits high.

Back at the hotel after a quick pizza, we had some down-time to ourselves, which allowed me to play Nirvana's *Nevermind* really loudly as I shaved and got changed for the night ahead. By nine thirty p.m. we were sat in a taxi en route to the club. I was dressed up like I was ready for a date, thanks to Max's PR friends and the free designer label clothes. Now that I was on the team, he ensured I dressed like it. The rest of the team were bizarrely downbeat. They were dressed like they were off strawberry picking rather than heading to the coolest party in the country.

C'mon, it's a Beat party, I thought to myself. Clearly my first time was more exciting than their umpteenth time. I got a text from Sophia wishing me luck. Luck? I didn't need luck for this. I was ready to have fun; how hard could it be?

We arrived outside the club to see things had changed significantly. Each Beat party had a theme and tonight's was the Eighties. The queue of excited kids in outfits from big shoulder-padded dresses to Adidas break-dancing tracksuits stretched fifty metres down the street and round the corner. Scantily dressed PR girls from the club were handing out free lollipops as street performers kept the crowd entertained as they slowly ploughed into the club.

We all headed inside to the crew room where Max gave out the filming orders for the night while sipping on a JD and Coke and scoffing all the purple Quality Streets.

'Hopefully we'll be done by two a.m. Any questions?' Max asked, rubbing his hands together, clearly ready to go.

Milly shook her head. I had loads but I stayed silent, worried I'd ask something stupid. Then all of a sudden the three of them started ripping open bags and setting up the equipment. It was impressive to watch them in action, like a Transformer turning from a kettle into an awesome kick-ass robot. By the end of it they looked like commandos, locked and loaded with cameras, lights and mics instead of semi-automatics and batteries and spare tapes instead of ammo. Meanwhile I'd spent the same two minutes and fifty-four seconds trying to open the legs of the tripod, turning it over several times like it was a Rubik's Cube, looking for the opening latch.

Back outside, Milly pointed the camera at the queue as Max said, 'Lights.' In response I pressed the 'on' button of the powerful light in my hands and what was a dimly lit side street became flooded with light that bounced off the graffiti-covered brick walls. We filmed the mass of people in the queue as it snaked to the front of the club. Kids were waving, jumping up and down, blowing kisses and one or two girls flashed their boobs.

'Your mum will be proud,' Max teased them, but their eagerness to make their mark on camera overtook their dignity.

Even out on the street we could hear the music from inside the club, the warm-up DJ mixing and cutting, adding to the exhilaration of the crowd. The energy and anticipation was infectious and I felt the excitement rush around inside me.

We headed back to the crew room to ready ourselves to film the secret guest PA. It added to the mystery of the party and it was the luck of the draw if your city got Destiny's Child or Sweet Female Attitude.

Max was huddled in a corner with PJ, who had arrived to present for the night, discussing the talent on show. The club was now packed to capacity and we fought our way through the throngs of people. Stuey and Milly headed for the middle of the dance floor while Max and I took up our position on the stage. He handed me the camera and the burden of filming made it feel like a keg of beer. I looked down at the girls at the front of the stage. The sight of someone holding a Beat camera was enough to make them give out a little scream.

I turned to Max. 'Are you sure?' I asked with a big gulp.

'Yes, I'm sure,' he said. 'How else will you learn?'

I started to feel panicked and edgy. 'But what if I fuck it up?'

'You worry too much, kid. You won't fuck it up. The camera's been set up, just stop holding it like Shakin' Stevens on speed.'

'What?'

'Tuck your arms into your body to get a steadier shot,' he huffed as I didn't get the reference.

'Oh,' I said, immediately embarrassed. I wished the front-row girls weren't paying so much attention now as I got a paint-by-numbers lesson on the side of the stage.

All of a sudden the DJ stopped Sonique's 'It Feels So Good' and the crowd reacted in screams of anticipation. Moments later the lights on the stage were turned up and out came PJ to introduce the night. Once the crowd were worked up into a frenzy, Sisqó bounced on with his gyrating dancers in support. Everyone immediately went wild as he sang the 'Thong Song'. A girl at the front managed to take off her underwear and throw it on stage. It wasn't a thong but a pair of pants with cute teddy bears on it.

Wrong on so many levels, I thought. It took the dress code of 'dress to undress' to a new level.

Panic nearly set in when Sisqó threw one of his sweaty towels into the crowd and the girls in the third row spent the next two minutes fighting over who had dibs on it: the girl whose face it landed on, or the girl who leapt on her from behind nearly snapping her neck back? I never understood why people would fight over a towel an artist had thrown into the crowd. *You want their germ-infested piece of raggedy cloth? What were you going to do with it – take it home and frame it?*

Sisqó kissed the crowd goodbye and was ushered out of the back door into his people carrier where our cameras soon followed to film an interview with him and PJ. As we packed up to follow Sisqó, the DJ continued the musical orgasm with Moloko's 'Sing It Back', this time accompanied by a bongo drummer, to keep the girls in the mood. Right on cue, The Beat dancers jumped on to the stage to become the dance conductors for the night. Scantily dressed and in the best shape of their lives, they free-styled, switching from dance to hip-hop moves, wowing the audience.

Soon we were back in the crew room and taking in a few drinks and much-needed energy-giving chocolates. I was shocked at how knackered I was. It was much better than standing around on a shop floor waiting to sell trainers all day, but it was hard work and I couldn't honestly say I'd had fun yet. There was a lot to do and stay focused on. The night was going by in a blur.

Moments later Alison walked in with Isabel, who had been watching everything from the top floor with the marketing girls. Max introduced her to Stuey and Milly, who hadn't met her before but instantly liked her. How did she do it? As I ate some chocolate I smiled and asked, 'So, you ready?'

'Yes, especially as the girls have been plying me with alcohol.'

'Might be the best thing. This crowd isn't exactly sober.'

'What if I slur? Stay close by,' she said, laughing and grabbing my arm for support.

'Don't worry –'

'Right!' Max cut me off as he came back from the drinks table clutching a plastic cup filled to the brim with JD and Coke. 'Let's find the weird and wonderful.'

Isabel smiled and it was time to get started.

We fulfilled Max's request for weird immediately, finding lesbian vampires and a guy who decided to break up with his girlfriend on TV.

'I'm sure you're watching this at home, Lorraine. This is Diane.' (Kisses her.) 'I know you've been cheating on me with that muppet David from school. Well, guess what? Two can play that game.' (Continues kissing Diane, with more tongue.)

The vox-pops deteriorated like the polar ice caps as the night went on, prompting Max to wrap things up at two a.m. Everyone headed back to the crew room for a quick break and an opportunity to get some party action in. But not for me. I had to go and practise filming people dancing with my next teacher, Stuey.

'OK, Rudeboy,' he instructed. 'You need shots of pretty faces smiling to camera and remember, no bugly people make it on to The Beat. I need people dirty dancing up close, panty shots are a bonus as are bouncing breasts. Oh, and try to get some buff men – gotta keep it balanced for the girls. Safe?' he asked, switching to street terminology.

I took a deep breath and plunged into the crowd, following Stuey's notes to the tee while being pushed, shoved, groped and trampled on, and beer regularly dropped down the back of my T-shirt. I made it back on stage in time to film the podium dancers throwing a hundred Beat T-shirts to the revellers. It was mayhem as kids scuffled and played tug-of-war for a £3 'Made in China' T-shirt, just because there was a Beat logo on it.

The lights came on and three hundred of the faithful who had stayed to the bitter end waited to get their pictures and autographs with PJ. I could see Max smoking weed with Stuey and Milly at the back of the stage while the two back-up DJs were in the crowd looking for the quarter-to-three girls – any half-decent-looking girls who were left and fancied coming back to the hotel for an 'afterparty'.

I escaped to the crew room and sat squeezing my aching calf muscles, not having had a drop of alcohol, or even a sip of water for the last few hours. I was truly shattered and the fun part had officially escaped me. My clothes were wet and stank of beer and sweat, while my feet ached in what was a pair of crispy clean trainers five hours ago. They'd been trampled on hundred of times, and a few pointy heels had hit the mark and managed to stub me on the big toes. Lesson learnt: come as a strawberry picker next time. I felt strange – I was completely exhausted yet on a high and still smiling.

Back at the hotel the equipment was dropped into my room so I could pack it away properly while everyone headed to PJ's room to continue the party.

'Jay, can I help?' asked Isabel as bags were dumped in a heap.

'Oh that –'

'. . . won't be necessary,' said Max, interrupting. 'You've done your work for the night, this is ours now.' He placed his hand just above her butt and whisked her off, with a wink to me and a sparkle in his eyes. It was exactly the same look the wolf had before he gulped down two of the three little piggies.

Bastard, I thought, looking at the mess of tangled wires.

I packed everything up as quickly as I could, but by the time I had finished everyone was sleeping or 'entertaining'. Mainly the latter.

Back in my room I attempted to sleep but instead lay awake to the sound of buzzing in my ears, a memento of the loud music in the club. It wasn't the only noise I had to contend with, as the sound of doors opening and closing reverberated in the walls, followed swiftly by people giggling, talking and running through corridors.

I wanted to call Sophia and tell her about the night but it was six a.m. Instead I lay in the dark reflecting on the party, images flashing through my head. It had all the ingredients of a normal party – a club with music, a DJ, lots of people. Yet why was the sum of the parts so much more? It was another experience that left me buzzing with excitement at my new job. A stark contrast to where I'd been a few months ago: careerless, depressed and steadily going nowhere. It occurred to me that if there was one person who would have enjoyed the last twenty-four hours, it was Manchester United fan and party animal Pritz. I smiled to myself: finally I had something for him to be jealous of.

14
AICHA

I had been so busy at work I hadn't done any laundry, not even the dirty clothes from the Middlesbrough party last week. So today's visit to the laundrette round the corner from the flat was urgent; I needed clean socks and boxer shorts in preparation for Hugh and Oli's notorious 'Pimps and Hookers' party. The two came as a pair, like socks, and their annual jaunt had become an unofficial Beat-wide staff party.

Sanctuary can be found in many different places. A quiet park, a place of worship, a hedonistic club, on the toilet. Me, I found it in the laundrette. They had been a part of my life from day dot. As a child I recalled Mum lighting up a fag and reading a magazine while I played with my Optimus Prime, who had fifty minutes of a full wash to get from base camp at machine fifteen across various points of ambush to dryer number one, a.k.a. enemy base camp for Skeletor. I did homework and wrote my best essays for school and university with the whizz and hum of washing machines and dryers in the background.

I did keepie-uppies with a rolled-up ball of socks as I listened to Kelis's debut album. Max had seen me fiddling with a chewed-up tape on my first week and kindly upgraded me from cassette to CD with a hook-up from his friend at Sony PR. Barely a few songs in and I was pressing pause as I got a call from Sophia, who was at home packing to go back to university for her summer term. I was sad that it felt like she was leaving so soon. After laughing about being down to my last old, torn pair of boxer shorts the conversation changed for the worst when I mentioned the theme of tonight's party. It was met with a stony silence.

'You didn't tell me about it,' she said eventually.

'I'm a hundred per cent sure I did,' I said, checking my memory banks.

'No, you didn't,' she persisted, clearly trying not to sound pissed off.

Within seconds we were back and forth, trying to convince the other they were wrong, with both of us digging in our heels like a tug of war.

'Anyway, I thought you were going back today,' I said, trying to find an end to the fight.

'Only because I was getting a lift with Simon,' she said.

'Simon?' I asked awkwardly.

'The guy in my class . . . lives in Watford?'

'No, you didn't tell me he was taking you, but, see, I'm not flipping out.' Actually I was, but I was determined not to show it. I'd met Simon once during Sophia's Freshers' Week and it was enough for me to not like the vibe from him. He always seemed to be around her, and not in a best-gay-friend way.

'I'm not flipping out,' she said.

'Yes you are. So why don't you come with me? It's not a big deal, it's just some party.'

'I can't, you're telling me too late.' She exhaled with frustration.

'But you can finish packing tomorrow and go up on the train.'

'I can't say no to Simon now,' she said, like I'd suggested something ridiculous.

'Why not? I'm sure he'll understand.' I was slightly peeved he was a bigger consideration than I was as she continued to find reasons not to come. Softening up, I added, 'Look, babe, just come. It's not a big deal. I don't have a costume either.'

'It's not so bad for guys, girls have to make an effort,' she reasoned.

'Look, how about we don't dress up but just go in normal clothes?'

'Your friends from work can't see me in normal clothes. I remember how underdressed I felt in front of them at Puffy's party,' she said, seemingly astounded I'd even suggested it.

'Yes you can, and you weren't,' I said. 'Besides, I'd prefer you didn't make a lasting impression in a hooker's outfit anyway.'

'Well, it's too late,' she said stubbornly.

My 'OK' was met with another moment of silence. Then she asked, 'Are you gonna go?'

I paused, not expecting the question. The old man at the other end of the laundrette peered across at me momentarily before returning to staring at his spinning clothes. I spoke a bit quieter, 'Well, yeah, I have to.'

'You *have* to?' she said sarcastically.

'I told all my friends I'd be there –'

'With all the girls dressed as hookers.'

I felt my voice rising again. 'A minute ago *you* were contemplating going dressed as one.'

She ignored me. 'There's going to be scantily dressed, drunk women all around.'

'Listen, I'm going to hang out with my mates, nothing else.'

'And so you won't be drinking and flirting?'

'When you go out, do you drink and flirt?' I retorted.

Her voice raised in return, 'Answer the question.'

'You answer mine,' I said, in full combat mode.

Silence descended again at the end of what felt like the tenth round. We both paused to get our energy back and thoughts in order. No one was backing down on this one. Then suddenly I heard a click on my washing machine as the power light turned off.

'Listen, my machine's finished and I gotta throw them in the dryer. Can I call you back in a few minutes?'

Sophia put the phone down without saying goodbye. I used the sanctuary of the laundrette to get my head straight as I pulled the wet clothes out of the machine and threw them into a broken washing basket. I tried to rewind and slow down the conversation in my head to see where it had gone wrong, adamant Sophia was overreacting.

Maybe I should back down. Maybe I shouldn't go, I thought.

What? Why not? Because she's being insecure? said *NSYNC's Justin Timberlake.

Well, if it would make her uncomfortable . . .

So, doesn't she trust you? he said, taking the Socratic approach to debating.

Well . . .

You'd trust her in this situation, right? Justin went on.

Yeah, but . . .

Everyone from work will be there. Do you want to be the only person on Monday morning who's left out of the conversation? This is where you get people to like you for that permanent position. Why isn't she being supportive like a girlfriend's meant to be?

But I think –

So don't you think you should make a stand against it or she'll do it every time she feels insecure? he continued.

Well, I don't –

Don't get bullied by her. That's what she's doing, bullying you. Stand up for yourself for once.

Justin had convinced me that I was right and she was wrong. I put £1 into the machine and the wet clothes began to swirl around in the big dryer. I picked up the phone and called Sophia back to state my case and to once again offer her a way out – to come with me.

The phone rang and rang but she didn't pick it up. With every ring I could feel my blood pressure rising. Why wasn't she picking up? This was childish and unreasonable. OK, fine. I was trying to be grown up about it, but two can play that game. I will go to the party and what's more I'll get as drunk as I want and do what I want. I put my headphones back on and sat back, listening to Kelis's 'Caught Out There'. The hook said it all.

I turned my attention to the 'homework' I had been set by Max for next week's shows – listening to several yet-to-be released albums and reading *Blues & Soul* and *The Face* magazines.

I had spent years copying albums and CDs to tape that I'd borrowed off friends. When you're poor you don't think it's stealing and you certainly don't consider the morality that it's the artist's music and they deserve to get paid for it. Like crack to a fiend, you just want it, by any means necessary. Radio helped give me my fix too. I'd record from the aficionados such as David Rodigan on Kiss FM, Zane Lowe on Xfm, DJ Swing on Choice FM, Pete Tong on Radio 1 and Capital FM's Tim Westwood. My house was filled with 90-minute Sony and TDK tapes that I'd label and store meticulously in my bedroom.

Luckily I was now getting the music for free and legitimately. I was on all the major labels' mailing lists thanks to Max and was getting CDs by the bucketload. There was so much music and so little time to listen to it all – it was a dream come true.

As tastemakers and journalists that kids looked to, The Beat needed to know it all; it was expected from us. If we didn't, it would be like an economist not knowing what the current Bank of England base rate was. My passion had turned into the job and the job into the passion. Where to draw the line was confusing, but it was a win-win when it came to getting CDs for free.

As I listened to an advance copy of *The Marshall Mathers LP*, my thoughts turned back to tonight's party. I mentally flicked through my wardrobe for anything that could double up as a costume. There was a suit in my wardrobe, but it wasn't very pimpish, more wimpish. There was a dressing-gown *à la* Hugh Hefner but that would be as obvious as a seventies' afro and gold medallion.

My phone started flashing with Sophia's name on the screen. She'd grown up and wanted to talk.

Well, guess what? I'm not ready to talk to you, I thought.

I distracted myself and looked out of the window for inspiration. A dog ran up to a lamp post and cocked its leg against it, and people wandered into the corner shop. My eyes darted around and landed on a big red phone box that no one entered any more unless it was to take a piss or leave postcards that read '38FF Busty Blonde Massages' or 'Asian Whip Mistress'. Suddenly an imaginary lightbulb lit up above my head.

If I could get enough cards of women hiring out their services and some safety pins from the corner shop, I could pin the cards all over a black turtleneck and be the walking epitome of a pimp! I didn't quite have a golden goblet or walking stick like Archbishop Don 'Magic' Juan, but it wasn't bad with a few hours to go.

My fight with Sophia was pushed to the back of my mind. I got up off the bench and started jigging a celebratory dance at having found a solution. The old man looked across at me for a split second then went back to watching his machine. My sanctuary had come to the rescue.

15
PURPLE HAZE

JamMasterJay is online

SaraD is online

JamMasterJay: Sara D, what you doing you loafer? Long time no sprechen.

SaraD: Just back from Berlin weekend with the others from Uni. I've returned royally mashed up. You so should have come.

JamMasterJay: I wish. How's the gang?

SaraD: Good. You were sorely missed.

JamMasterJay: Had to work. Beat party in Liverpool.

SD: Oh I feel sooooo sorry for you. Boo hoo. What was the theme?

JamMasterJay: Pyjama party. Was v. funny. VIP footy players, TV soap stars and a few thousand screaming fans all in their PJs.

SaraD: Sounds like it was boring! How's Sophia?

JamMasterJay: Hmmm . . . There's been beef for a few weeks since I went to a party without her.

SaraD: Why?

JamMasterJay: Just arguing over small, stupid things!

SaraD: Sit down and talk it through. Long distance is hard. Mainly about insecurities.

JamMasterJay: Would love to but she's studying hard before her exams and I've got more working weekends coming up. Won't get a chance to see her for weeks now.

SaraD: Don't leave it too long & let things fester.

JamMasterJay: You're right. Just wanted a bit of support, that's all.

SaraD: Well, are you supporting her?

JamMasterJay: The only support you need as a fresher is a lamp post after a drunken night out . . . I think you'll remember!!

SaraD: I plead the fifth. Besides those days are behind me. I'm in the respectable world of PR now.

JamMasterJay: Respectable?

SaraD: ☺ Speaking of which, how is the new job?

JamMasterJay: In my memoirs this will be the chapter called 'The Week From Hell'.

SaraD: Memoirs? Haha.

JamMasterJay: Coming back from Liverpool, my bag gets stolen on the train.

JamMasterJay: Went to mum's place, my car's been broken into. Stereo nicked.

JamMasterJay: Go to mechanics to get quote, get snapped speeding. 3 points & a fine.

JamMasterJay: Garage wants £200 to fix car. Can't afford that.

SaraD: Wow. Bad week.

JamMasterJay: Then boss tells me last minute I can't go on an upcoming shoot to Denmark. Work can't afford my ticket. But he's taking his 2 mates from the department instead.

SaraD: ☹

JamMasterJay: Some bloke calls me at work and mouths off about me getting off with his gf at the Liverpool party. Kept talking about being in a gang. Blah blah.

SaraD: Loser.

JamMasterJay: Work's taken over majorly. There's not enough hours in the day. I get so much on my plate and I can't say no. That's what interns do.

SaraD: Really that bad? We were all talking about it in Berlin and thought it looked like a lot of fun.

JamMasterJay: It is. Just don't want you to think it's all a barrel of laughs! ☺

SaraD: OK, now you're really killing my Berlin buzz.

JamMasterJay: Lighter note. Made a new friend. Isabel, a party presenter we just hired.

SaraD: Oh yeah! Nudge, nudge ☺☺

JamMasterJay: Not like that. Besides boss has already moved in. We don't speak or meet, just play text tennis.

SaraD: Careful Jay, some cultures consider that adultery. Sophia might chop your balls off!

JamMasterJay: Haha . . . OK, what else . . . Sanderson Hotel opened, Ian Schrager & London's latest hotspot. Went to a movie premiere for Ewan McGregor's new film.

SaraD: Cool. Who did you see?

JamMasterJay: All the big celebs. Sat behind Jonathan Ross as he stuffed his face with popcorn! At least I think it was him. Kept letting off silent ones.

SaraD: LOL.

JamMasterJay: Another intern, James III, magic'd us into the BAFTA Awards afterparty at Grosvenor House.

SaraD: Haha. How was it?

JamMasterJay: Not bad. Boy George in full DJ mode entertaining *Royle Family, Eastenders* and *Corrie* casts plus me, while James III shared some Daz off a drinks menu in the women's toilets with an actress.

SaraD: James III – the good-looking guy you work with that you're going to introduce me to?

JamMasterJay: For the right price ☺

SaraD: Your presenter came in last week. PJ?

JamMasterJay: What for?

SaraD: The partner of the firm was giving him some clothes to wear on the show I think. We've got a load of brands that need exposure and presenters are our first port of call.

JamMasterJay: Oh really? He gets free clothes? I thought he bought them.

SaraD: Irony is he can probably afford to buy them but gets them free.

JamMasterJay: Lucky sod.

SaraD: Payment for getting snapped for papers & mags or seen on TV. Public wants to be like them and go buy that brand. Basically free advertising.

JamMasterJay: Walking ads. Genius. Better than the guy holding luminous 'Golf Sale' sign on Oxford Street.

SaraD: That reminds me, my boss said PJ wanted to give some PlayStations away on his show.

JamMasterJay: Yeah, defo.

SaraD: Brill. PS2's not out in the UK till end of this year but we've managed to get some for key tastemakers. Can you give them to the other presenters too?

JamMasterJay: Sure.

SaraD: Also gonna send you a football game with it called ISS Pro Evolution. Apparently it's the latest rage in Japan and the boys in our office are totally addicted.

JamMasterJay: Cool.

SaraD: So what music should I be buying right now?

JamMasterJay: Buying? Don't be silly. I'll put together a stack for
  you along with some tickets for the Jazz Cafe.

SaraD: OK, thanks. I'd better shoot. I have PR'ing to do.

JamMasterJay: ☺

SaraD: XXX

16
CHALO DILDAR CHALO

'Twenty-four hours a day, Sunrise Radio . . .' chimed the jingle as I stood next to the mechanic. Mr Rafi was a lovely 'ickle' old man who looked like the wind would blow him over any moment as he stood next to my car inspecting the damage through his thick-framed glasses. Someone at work had recommended him after my car got broken into a couple of weeks earlier, and his workshop was luckily a few streets away under the A40 flyover. The wrinkles on his face and his rough hands suggested he'd worked here nearly every day for the past thirty years. That, and the yellowing poster of a Page Three girl from the 1970s in his workshop. Having taught me about 'proper' music of his generation, from Lata Mangeshkar to Diana Ross, we haggled on a price. Content, I left as he began lighting a cigarette with a match that refused to ignite on the first few strikes. The overpowering smell of petrol and oil from his workshop made me walk that bit quicker.

The noise levels in the office were high on the decibel meter that morning as Milly sat by the tape-viewing machine in the middle of the department, surrounded by girls from all over the office. The boys looked on, trying to figure out what the huddle was for. On tiptoes at my desk I could see the screen: soul singer D'Angelo – naked. OK, naked from the pelvis upwards. Body covered in baby oil, ripped like an athlete and singing his heart out on the song 'Untitled'.

Most of the girls didn't know who he was but when his torso came on the screen there was a combined sigh that seemed to say, *Finally a video of a scantily dressed man we can ogle over, non-stop, for four minutes and twenty-six seconds.*

'That's disgusting. Leering at a man and judging his naked specimen not his vocal talent,' said Stuey with deliberate irony.

'If we sat here watching a woman singing totally naked you'd be on to HR in a jiffy,' said Hugh, backing him up.

'Like you don't have your choice of naked women to look at on the channel,' Milly retorted.

'Oh no,' said Lizzie Hudson, presenter for *iWant*, 'they get to do that filming up girls' skirts at Beat parties.'

'It's The Beat way. We don't like doing it,' said Oli with a serious face.

A communal groan came from the girls.

'Let's fight fire with fire,' said Stuey as he reached for an unmarked VHS tape in his rucksack. 'In the name of equal rights I play this,' he said in a Winston Churchill tone as he placed the tape into the video player.

The girls, intrigued by what he was going to show, elbowed their way past the boys to the front. As the fuzzy start on the tape turned to black, there was a heightened anticipation. The boys were hoping for porn and the girls expecting it. All of a sudden a man appeared on the screen.

'Right, it's the part of the season you've all been waiting

for, it's Goal of the Season time,' said sports presenter Gary Lineker.

As the girls groaned and barged their way out and back to their desks, Stuey quoted from *Gladiator*, 'Are you not entertained? Is this not why you are here?'

To this the boys shouted back, 'Stuuuey, Stuuuey, Stuuuey!'

Playtime for the girls was officially over. For the boys, this was better than porn and as each goal flew in, it was greeted with a chorus of orgasmic noises to goad the girls.

Lunchtime arrived and as the rest of the office emptied the other interns and I were all still sat at our desks, eating food and competing about who had it the worst: from who had been asked to do the crappiest job that week to who was most skint. All the while flicking through the papers and magazines, continuously researching for our shows. We had every print under the sun from music and fashion to cars and politics and everything in between, including *Playboy*. Anything that provided interesting insight into modern culture for our editorial. James III provided the soundtrack, whistling his repertoire of Christmas carols. I hit the US news websites next, hoping for a breaking newsflash, and came across the name Amadou Diallo.

'Did any of you guys see this thing about the guy who got shot forty-one times?' I enquired.

'Yeah, it was last year, but the family have just filed a lawsuit against the City of New York and the police officers involved. I can't believe this is still happening in this day and age,' said Tola.

'Hip hop needed to come together on this one. Barring Mos Def, why aren't there more voices on this?' said Sam.

'Hip hop lost its intellectual voice long ago with the demise of Public Enemy and KRS-One,' I replied. 'Now it's bling-bling, booty-booty and kill-kill. Anyway, music in general doesn't seem to have a voice.'

'Well, there's still Dead Prez isn't there, and what about Asian Dub Foundation?' said Cara as the conversation went back and forth across the small table dividers.

'Yeah, but they don't get any love, even The Beat doesn't play them much. Too busy showing naked women gyrating on the screen,' said Sam.

'Nothing wrong with that,' James III spoke up in all serious-ness. 'Us kids don't want to hear a political lecture. Gimme more dance. More dance, damn it! Music is meant to be fun. I don't want to slit my wrists or hear a preacher. There's some really good stuff out there from pop and rap to dance and –'

Cara interrupted. 'I totally disagree. We're not dumb. Anyway, it's about money and heavily marketed acts. Music used to be all about being lyrical and thought provoking not "Oops! . . . I did it again".'

'No, that's what pop music is and always has been. Besides it's called show "business" for a reason. Course they want to make money,' argued James III.

'These acts will only be successful if consumers like the stuff being put out,' I said, trying to keep the debate balanced.

'It's hard when as a consumer I don't have any choice in the music that's being given to me,' Cara argued. 'It's played over and over, pumped into people's heads till they're brain-washed into liking it.'

'You can choose not to listen to it by going elsewhere,' I offered.

'But even if you do go elsewhere they're all playing the same Britney or Christina song. No one's giving an alternative. As listeners we have no say in the variation and quality of playlists. Labels and music outlets are in bed with each other,' said Tola.

'Good point,' agreed Sam. 'How the hell is a playlist chosen? It's got to be political. It's not based on what us kids want to hear. If so, why the hell is poppy shite like S Club 7 on all the bloody time? Real music doesn't get a look in.'

'Leverage. You support their latest pet pop project in return for more access to their bigger acts,' said Tola.

'Surely it's not that blatant?' I said, disbelieving.

Tola raised an eyebrow. 'I'll-scratch-your-back-if-you-scratch-mine. The entire thing is manipulated.'

'Bah! All conspiracy theories. Next you'll say Armstrong didn't land on the moon,' said James III.

'Well, take magazines that depend on record labels advertising in their mags for survival. Do you think they don't know who their paymasters are? Same for TV and radio – advertising is a big source of revenue,' said Sam.

'That's far-fetched. So if they give Ricky Martin a bad review, labels will spend less?' I asked.

'I'd give Ricky Martin a bad review for free,' said James III. 'Look, it's all based on popular music. Programmers will play music that will rate. They can't do it based on favours. If it's a shit track it won't get put on. Money's got nothing to do with it,' he argued.

'C'mon, James. Don't tell me you're just cute looking?' said Cara ironically.

'You think I'm cute?' James III gave her a cheeky grin.

'I thought you knew. Would you like me to grab you down under and confirm?' Cara asked with equal cheek.

'Eww. Get a room!' Sam put her sandwich down in disgust.

By mid afternoon the department was dead quiet as people dispersed to studios or edits. I still had research to do for the show and it was going slower than traffic out of town on a Friday afternoon. All I could find was news about yet another rapper who'd been shot. Nine times on this occasion.

'Jay, you busy?' asked Oli, standing behind me holding a camera.

'No,' I admitted, having not written anything for over twenty minutes.

'Can you do a second camera for an interview? Stuey and Max are stuck in traffic in Oxford Street and the Minister's asked me to cover.'

'What about Tola? She's Stuey's intern,' I said, not wanting to step on her toes.

'I can't find her. I can ask someone else if you're busy . . .'

'It's no problem, I can do it,' I said, bouncing to my feet, not even bothering to ask who the interview was with.

It went smoothly, as Oli asked his questions unfazed by Britney Spears who was sat opposite him. After fifteen minutes of a flirtatious interview, we both took a couple of Polaroid pictures with her for posterity and turned to leave. But, as everyone was distracted by the changeover and sixty-second break for make-up, Oli quickly turned back to Britney and handed her his business card.

'Oh, and there's a party tonight at the Mayfair Club,' he said, his lisp in full effect. 'Fancy coming, love?'

The entourage of people from her management, the record label, hair and make-up and so on looked aghast at this dishevelled short stump trying it on. His stunt risked pissing off the head of T.A.D., Irishman Declan 'the Duke' Patricks, who'd notoriously once reduced a producer to tears for asking Madonna the 'wrong question'.

I stared at Oli, disbelief plastered across my face too. Had the blokes in the office dared him to ask her or had he gone rogue? Bagging an artist would make you legendary between these walls and only a few had managed to do it. When we got out of the dimly lit interview room and into the full glaring light of the Greenhouse, I could see the reality of the situation. His cheeks were red and the armpits of his T-shirt were as sweaty as someone pushing a trolley of Class A drugs through the 'nothing to declare' lane at Heathrow.

I got to my desk with Polaroid picture in hand, to see Tola at her desk in a sweat of her own. She had returned from the library with several bags of tapes to find out I had taken her chance to film Britney. She was none too pleased.

'Jay, you should have told me. That's sneaky,' she said, peeved off.

'It's not like that. Oli asked me and didn't know where you were.'

'Well, why didn't you just call my mobile?'

'You're right, but he was in a rush. I'm sorry.'

'Well, don't let it happen again,' she said firmly.

'OK, OK, I didn't realize you fancied Britney that much,' I said, trying to make a joke. She didn't laugh.

It was the end of a laborious day and Max still hadn't returned, deciding to stay in town for some ad-hoc meetings with Stuey – in a pub. I had one last thing to do before I left and that was to swing past Kate Smith's desk, the intern for T.A.D. She kindly donated a signed poster and CD of Britney's latest 'for my cousin' to save me the embarrassment of asking.

By the time I'd got out of work and back to the garage, Mr Rafi was standing by the gates of his workshop with a half-smoked cigarette hanging off his bottom lip like he was Clint Eastwood in a western.

'You're lucky, I was just about to lock up,' he said, heading back into the garage.

I followed him and waited in his workshop as he went to get my keys. Moments later, he returned singing in Hindi, and suddenly stopped in his tracks.

'What's that?' he asked, staring at me.

'It's a poster,' I said proudly.

'Yes, I can see that.'

'It's a poster of Britney Spears. I thought you might like it for your workshop. I even got her to sign it to you. See, *With all my love, Britney*. Oh, and I got a signed CD for one of your lucky grandkids.'

'Oh, that's lovely,' he said, his eyes sparkling behind his thick glasses. 'You're a good boy, Jay. This will make me more popular than their other grandfather.'

I was pleased I'd gone to the trouble. I jumped into my repaired car and reversed just beyond the gates. As I was about to pull out, Mr Rafi hurried over to me.

'One last thing. I know my grandkid's going to quiz me so I'd better know, who is this Britney?'

17
DON'T LOOK BACK IN ANGER

With Max gone to Denmark with Hugh and Oli to film a fashion special, the workload instantly halved as we aired pre-recorded specials. While the mouse was away the cat had to play. Max couldn't be having all the fun in Copenhagen, so I took up any gig offer on the table, ensuring I was out every night with the other interns or people from various departments. We either blagged official tickets or, if that failed, a small camera and a mic with The Beat logo usually got us in, then we filmed the stars in attendance for half an hour before joining them at the afterparty. The footage didn't go to waste as *The News Feed* would put it into their bulletins just so long as we got someone famous tumbling out drunk at three in the morning.

When the weekend finally arrived, all the interns decided to hang out on the Sunday as the following day was the last bank holiday in May. We'd made a plan of action including a Maharishi clothing sample sale in an abandoned warehouse in Old Street followed by a late lunch at Tayyabs in Whitechapel, then a quick visit home to change and back out again for a big night at Hanover Grand.

This would have been a great weekend for Sophia to be

in London but she was in exam mode and couldn't make it down. She had made her presence felt all week though, with snide comments via text about me being out every night and not having time to call her. I didn't like it, but I was trying to be supportive and understanding. She was stressed and wasn't enjoying revision while I was partying. I tried to explain this week was a one-off and that I just wanted to make the most of it, but it didn't get through. Like Mary Mary, I was starting to feel like I had shackles on my feet.

After lunch, I headed home to see my mum and to get some fresh clothes. I hadn't seen her for weeks so this would be the perfect time to catch up. We'd developed a dysfunctional relationship after my dad left. Instead of growing closer together, we grew further apart. She worked two jobs as I went from primary to secondary school and then to university, which meant I barely saw her. I respected her for it but before long we'd lost even the weak bond we had. Recently our contact had been reduced to the odd phone call during the week and Sunday lunch once a month, but I didn't allow myself time to feel sad about it.

As I walked down the high street in Finchley Central where I had grown up, it brought back a sense of normality considering how crazy life had been in recent weeks. I hadn't realized how slow and sleepy the place really was. Well, compared to Notting Hill, most places were.

I was in good spirits, with a bounce in my step, listening to Santana's 'Maria Maria' on my CD player. But suddenly my senses were tripped and adrenalin began rushing through me. I felt my legs turn to jelly as Biggie's words became prophetic; I honestly thought I *could* hear the sweat trickling down my cheek. I felt my mouth go dry and the sensation of impending vomit grab my throat. I looked for a place to hide but the high street seemed empty, as if a Western-style showdown was about to take place. It wasn't far from the truth, because I was about to come face-to-face with the meanest, ugliest outlaw in the West – well, the north-west. Michael 'Four Eyes' Gambler.

He was the neighbourhood bully and my nemesis from the time I joined secondary school in a crisp navy blue blazer till I left in an egg-and-flour-covered blazer. Michael Gambler didn't even go to my school – I wasn't sure if he went to one at all. One day he might see you, smile and nod as he walked past. Then on other days he'd jump out of a telephone box, grab you, drag you into it and smack you around aggressively if you didn't empty your pockets sharpish. He would take anything of value that could be sold, used or eaten, ranging from a calculator or weekly bus pass to half an egg and cress sandwich.

His nickname alluded to the fact that he wore glasses and was possibly the only bully on the planet who did. But myth and legend had caused the meaning to evolve over time, and led us to believe that he saw all and there was no escaping him. As a result, I chose different routes home every day of every week. I'd move down the street between vehicles as though I were in the SAS, taking cover and establishing vantage points, trying to get a sense of what lay ahead. For years I suffered psychological torture wondering if that would be the day he got me. If he didn't, the satisfaction of getting home safe was short-lived knowing it would start all over again the next day.

This guy was in my nightmares. And here he was again, the last person I expected or hoped to see, acknowledging me from across the street with a 'what's up' head nod. He bowled over to me like he was Liam Gallagher strolling up and down a stage.

'Yeah mate, what you sayin'?' he said, giving people at the nearby bus stop the impression we were friends.

'Cool,' I said, trying hard to look as if I were.

'I've been looking for you,' he said.

My body stiffened up as I stood in silence.

'What's your name?' he asked, trying to remember.

I hesitated, but then told him. It would be unwise to get beaten up over my name.

'That's it, Jay. Yeah, I knew I knew you,' he said, maintaining an emotionlessly straight face.

My brain was in overdrive trying to read him, to see which way he was going to go. Then he leant in and said, 'Listen, I need something from you.'

And there it is, ladies and gents, I thought to myself. Mr Crazy was in town and now my bag was gone with CD player and wallet to boot. I looked around to see if there were any exit strategies available, or if I could garner any help from the two old ladies at the bus stop. I really didn't fancy getting beaten up so resigned myself with a sigh to losing my bag.

'I saw you the other day,' he continued.

Oh God, he's tracked me to my flat in Angel. He's going to have a field day in Pritz's room with all the clothes and money lying around. Oh God, oh God, oh God . . .

'You work on that Beat show right – what's it called, *BEAT Total*?'

I nodded, not wanting to correct him. 'You saw me?'

'Yeah, you and PJ were talking about the new Common album.'

Wow, I barely came into shot during that discussion, how the hell did he see me? Hold on, he's not interested in the show or Pritz's flat; he wants me to help him ransack The Beat! I felt my cheeks fill with blood and my hands get clammy. I clenched my butt cheeks a little tighter.

Michael put his arm around me and began to walk me away from the bus stop while continuing to talk in my ear. I was in trouble. Deep trouble.

'I watch that shit religiously. Never miss a show. Bruv, I'm lookin' for a hook-up,' he said as the smell of weed from his clothes ran up my nose.

I stayed silent and stared at the pavement below.

'I need a favour,' he said, thinking I didn't understand his previous request.

I looked at him like I was watching a car in slow-motion as it skidded on ice, wondering if it would stop in time or crash.

'I got this demo,' he continued, pulling out several CDs from his jacket pocket.

My eyes widened from my wince. 'Okaaay,' I said slowly.

'Do you think you can get it to your boy PJ?'

I tried to stall. 'Er . . .'

'Listen, if you can get him to play this –'

'We can't play it,' I interjected. Michael's face sank and a voice inside me shouted, *Take cover*, as though a bomb was about to explode. 'Um . . . We can't play it when it's just a CD. PJ doesn't do radio and we only play music videos.'

134

He paused. 'But if he plays it in the background, talks us up and it gets big we'll make a video and then you can show it,' he said, like an excited child dreaming of playing for England, even though the child is thirty-five years old and has two blown knees and a beer belly.

'We only really play artists who are signed to major labels and indies, to be honest, but, hey, I'm sure if it gets big then we will.' I knew there was more chance of me being invited around to the Queen's for tea.

'I just want you to put it in his hand and tell him to listen to it,' he said quite simply.

I looked at the CD in his grubby hand, not totally sold on the deal.

Seeing this, Michael acted fast. 'Listen, I can hook you up in return. What do you need? Name it, I got it all: TVs, videos, camcorders and jewellery. My house is like Argos, you can come an' choose whatever you like.'

Maybe I should ask him if he still had my Nintendo Donkey Kong from 1990?

'So what do you reckon?'

'You know what, yes. I will do that for *you*, Michael. I will do *you* this favour. I'll even play it for all the bods at The Beat, as a *favour*. I'll even play it to the head honcho.'

'Wicked. Absolutely fuckin' wicked,' he said as he punched the air. I was just happy his fist wasn't anywhere near me.

'But you have to do me a favour in return,' I added.

'Whatever you want,' he said.

I contemplated what to say for a moment. Maybe I could ask him to move to another country forever. 'I want you to give us the first interview at The Beat when you make it,' I said with my tongue in my cheek.

'Yeah, of course, bruv,' he said, bumping fists with me. He was now looking at me in a way he'd never done for the seven years he terrorized me. With respect.

I smiled uncomfortably. 'Anyway, I really gotta go,' I said hurriedly, trying to get away just in case Mr Hyde came out to replace Doctor Jekyll.

'How will I know how it went?' he asked as I walked away slowly.

'You can call me,' I said over my shoulder.

'You got a card?' he shouted back.

'Nah, they're printing them. Call enquiries. It's piss easy,' I said, smiling. From experience I knew how hard that was and that he'd soon give up.

'Nice one, Mr Beat!' he shouted as I walked off.

I turned down a quiet side road a few turns from my mum's house. The warm sun signalled the coming of summer and as I dropped his CD into the nearest wheelie bin, I finally felt a lifetime's satisfaction at getting one over on him.

18
THREE LIONS

Having filmed some Adidas-sponsored stars talking about their love of music (and their new football boots) a few weeks earlier for the show, the return favour from the head of Marketing, Jessica, saw us attend the sportswear giant's celebrity-filled party in Amsterdam at the start of the Euro 2000 championships. Editorially, we were filming *Total BEATS* there to show 'the continuing love affair between the world of sports and music.' Personally, we were there to rub shoulders and get our pictures with the legendary football players of yesteryear who were in attendance.

But the real reason lay over sixty miles away from our current location: the Philips Stadion in Eindhoven, where a few days later we'd be sitting in VIP seats watching England v Portugal, courtesy of our hosts. Stuey and I were on the trip by default as Hugh and Oli couldn't get anyone to cover their shows. I didn't care. I was thrilled to be going to a football tournament for the first time.

On match day we headed for Eindhoven via a midday meeting in Brussels. Alison Cooks had asked us to meet a fellow party promoter who wanted to bring Beat-themed parties to Europe. The weather was hot and sticky and after getting stuck in several traffic jams we arrived in Brussels two hours late.

Luckily we found an understanding promoter in Benedict 'Benny' Paradis, who schmoozed us over coffee, showing us a reel on his laptop of all the parties he'd put on around Europe for celebrities and royalty alike. In his smooth French accent, he painted a picture of 'an event' with thousands of revellers, A-list artists, superstar DJs, female dancers in bunny outfits and chill-out areas with food, drink, shisha and every other little detail he could think of.

Eventually we pulled ourselves away from Benny's tractor-beam charm and the offer of a 'boys' night out', and headed through the Belgian and Dutch countryside to Eindhoven. The only problem was that somewhere along the way we took a wrong turn and ended up in the south instead of central Holland.

Everyone was getting slightly tetchy now as hunger pangs began to set in. As Max put the pedal to the metal, PJ became the in-car DJ, choosing which CDs were played on the car stereo, eventually getting sacked when he put on '7 Seconds' by Neneh Cherry and Youssou N'Dour for the sixth time in a row. Meanwhile, Stuey's bowels gave way and he began letting off lethal farts in the back. I pinched my nose and looked out of the window, bored, as I texted Sophia with travel updates.

Having hurtled down endless miles of tarmac, the fuel light eventually came on. We pulled up at the nearest petrol station, which doubled up with a McDonald's, and got out for a long stretch. It was late afternoon and the place was busy with school kids. We all stood silently in the queue, having exhausted all conversation. Suddenly, without warning, the mood of the place changed, from noisy and bustling to one of subdued conversations and darting looks. Had we jumped the queue? Then slowly some of the kids walked straight up to PJ, who was texting at the far end of the restaurant.

'Esscuush me, are you PJ from da Beat?' asked the Dutch equivalent of Britney in her school uniform.

PJ looked back at her, equally shocked. We were in what looked like a little village in the middle of the countryside and PJ had been spotted. We were used to it walking through the streets of London, but a McDonald's on the outskirts of Liège?

'Yeah, I'm PJ,' he said.

The girl instantly let out a shriek that spread infectiously to her friends, and led to the entire restaurant going up a notch in volume. Suddenly girls and boys were coming from all corners of the restaurant and shoving school exercise books, receipts, napkins, big brown McDonald's bags, their own arms and anything else they could get at PJ to sign.

The McDonald's manager saw the stampede and came over to usher the kids away. He led PJ to an unopened till and began taking his order, which we jumped in and added to. We sat down and tried to appreciate the VIP treatment, even if it was only McDonald's. Still, six trays came out with an assortment of burgers, chips, drinks and desserts. There was enough to feed a small army. We stuffed our faces as PJ continued signing autographs.

'Right, it's time to head out of this meet-and-greet,' said Max, finishing his food.

Stuey slapped his belly in contentment. 'Are you thinking what I'm thinking?'

'Tall and golden all over?' teased Max.

'Yes yes, Rrrrrude-a-boy,' replied Stuey.

There was one thing missing that McDonald's just could not provide, a desire they couldn't satisfy on a hot day like this. Cold beer. It was just what was needed to get us ready for the journey ahead and in a boisterous mood for the England game.

Before we left, the manager asked PJ to take some pictures with him and the staff on the Polaroid camera he had in his office. PJ signed one of the first pictures that developed and handed it to the manager. As he stood there looking at it, confusion spread across his face. Max picked up on it instantly.

'He thought PJ was someone else,' he said under his breath, still smiling.

I looked back at the manager as he tried to make sense of PJ's scribbled autograph.

Stuey started to snigger and had to look at the floor so as not to burst out laughing.

We eventually dragged PJ out of McDonald's on a high. Yes, he got emails from all over the world but to actually meet fans outside the UK had clearly got to him. Max navigated the route as we walked through the narrow streets in search of a bar while Stuey tried to deflate PJ's bubble.

'PJ, they were fifteen years old.'

'Yeah, but it goes to show how powerful our show is,' said PJ, still amazed.

'Mate, it's Europe, not some village in the backwaters of Mongolia,' said Stuey.

'Look, don't hate on us because your show isn't having this kind of impact,' PJ sniped back.

'Except my show beats yours regularly in the ratings. Men lie, women lie, figures don't,' said Stuey, laughing.

We were all talking over one another now, getting louder and louder, not realizing we had ended up in a square full of pubs, when suddenly we came to an abrupt stop.

We'd found the watering hole in the desert we'd been so desperate for but it seemed that lions were already drinking from it. German football-fan lions, to be precise. They'd been drinking all day and were waiting to go to their game against Romania, ten miles down the road at the stadium in Liège. They all turned to stare at us, but unlike McDonald's this time we felt *real* unease. The Germans continued drinking and talking but their eyes were fixed on us.

Max didn't care; he just wanted a cold beer. PJ was worried about his presenter's face being hurt, whereas I was worried because I wanted to live to see my next birthday. And Stuey, well, he was suddenly aware that he was wearing a 1966 England shirt in a square full of German football fans. 1966: the year England controversially beat the Germans in the World Cup final. It was like waving a red rag to a bull. We walked into the first pub we saw and ordered a quick round. It was the most uncomfortable and least pleasurable drink I'd ever had.

The German fans outside in the square were waving flags while the ones inside started to sing to the tune of 'The Animals Went in Two By Two'. Not knowing a word of German my mind hysterically translated: 'There's some English fans in this pub, yes there are, there are / There's some English tossers in this pub, yes there are, there are / Are we going to kick their heads in? Yes we are, we are . . .'

More fans were coming in from other pubs to see what the commotion was. Our exit had been cut off and we were behind enemy lines. Max was finally appreciating the seriousness of the situation we'd walked into and his earlier bravado was now replaced with an expression of worry. We all looked at one another trying to stay calm but realized we were well and truly screwed.

Max slowly began to walk to the back of the pub towards the toilets. We didn't question it but just quietly followed him into the gents. I walked as close to Stuey as possible to try to hide his shirt.

'What the hell are we going to do?' said PJ with a sense of urgency.

'I don't know, let me think,' Max replied.

'Stuey, do you rate your shirt as highly as you rate your show?' PJ asked sarcastically.

It wasn't Stuey's fault he was wearing an England shirt but he kept quiet.

'Why don't I go back out and speak to the landlord?' said Max, throwing out the only suggestion he could think of.

'Yeah, because he's really going to know what to do,' said Stuey, breaking his silence. 'I'm a Jew in a '66 England shirt surrounded by Nazis. Do you really think I'm going to risk going back out there?'

They started arguing among themselves when I noticed something.

'Look, a window!' I shouted, pointing above the cubicles.

'Don't be stupid,' Max snapped.

'Well, do you have a better suggestion?' I said.

Everyone looked at one another before Max climbed up and led the way. Scrambling unceremoniously through the window and landing in an alleyway at the back of the building, we scooted around like rats until we somehow managed to find our way back to the McDonald's and jump into the car.

Everyone was silent for the next twenty minutes until a fart from Stuey broke the silence.

'Is that you shitting yourself, pooey Stuey?' said Max. 'Oh no, that was earlier on in the pub.'

'Oh sure, blame the only patriotic fucker in this car for wearing his three lions with pride. If any one of us has balls, it's me! Faced down a whole pub of Germans,' he said in a cocky tone.

'You're lucky we got out of there before they got their hands on you and your red blouse!' said PJ.

'It would have been fans of your show that would have got to you first. They watch you in Germany too, you know,' said Stuey, bitching back.

The touchy silence that followed was finally broken by Max. '"*Look*, a window!",' he boomed, trying to mock me in a Superman voice.

I looked at him through the rear-view mirror. 'Don't even start on me,' I replied forcefully. 'I just saved your fucking lives.'

'Yeah, whatever, cub scout, you shat it the most,' said Max.

I knew that being the most junior member meant that they would now all gang up on me and stop biting into each other.

'*Look*, a car!' said Stuey, taking the piss.

'Er, hello, you girls didn't exactly have any bright ideas,' I said.

'*Look*, another car!' followed PJ.

'Oh sure, says the man worried about his pretty face.'

The more I protested, the more they continued.

'*Look*, I'm about to piss myself,' said Max, laughing his arse off as he drove down the motorway towards Eindhoven. We were hideously late.

This way of talking would now be attributed to me for the foreseeable future. I tried fighting back but it was like going against your older brothers. You'd never win, but you just hoped you could get some good shots off before you eventually got pummelled. Before I'd have stayed quiet but now I found a new voice coming from within and a thicker skin to take their verbal jabs. I'd need it in bundles if I was to survive this industry.

As we ran to the turnstiles, the steward who checked our tickets looked surprised to see people coming into the stadium as there were already trickles of people starting to walk out. We were determined to see something having come this far but the full-time whistle went before we'd even made it to our seats. Everyone looked pissed off and dejected and as hoards of people began to shuffle past us we looked up at the scoreboard and felt our misery compounded. England had been beaten by Portugal 3–2.

The drive back was sullen and it was approaching one a.m. when we got to the outskirts of Amsterdam. Hunger pangs got the better of us and Max stopped at the only place that looked open.

The manager tried explaining the kitchen was closed but Max and PJ begged him to serve us. Perversely it was only when Stuey stepped up from behind us that the moustachioed manager froze, looked at the three lions on his shirt and then offered us whatever he had left in the kitchen.

We lay with our heads on the table waiting, nearly falling asleep, when two trays were brought out from the kitchen. On them was the weirdest thing I had seen on a plate – the tongue of some poor creature covered in gravy and sandwiched between a bun.

'I can't, I just can't,' whispered Stuey, looking traumatized.

'We have to, we've made such a fuss. At least let's try it,' said Max, with his fork hovering above the plate, not sure where to start.

PJ just dived in and began eating. He wasn't even taking time to chew, swallowing mouthfuls straight down. Stuey ate the gravy-soaked bread and left the tongue while Max ate half of his and then realized what he was doing and stopped. I chopped mine up, separated it, mashed it down and made it look like I had attempted to eat it, but really I was too scared to even try.

We jumped back in the car and headed for our hotel. Trudging through the foyer, we took the lift to our floor and said goodbye to one another, slapping and clasping hands while simultaneously hugging like we were rappers.

We'd barely separated by a few footsteps when Max whispered back to us, 'What goes on tour, boys, eh?'

PJ and Stuey replied back, equally fed up, 'Yeah, what goes on tour.'

Max wasn't using the phrase in its usual debauched context, but it had an equal if not better use considering the day we'd had. This was one trip we wouldn't be boasting about to anyone.

19
PAID IN FULL

Lonyo's 'Summer of Love' played on the speakers of the pub as kids who'd finished their A-level exams jostled in the line to be served. The bar was also full of people from The Beat's other departments who I'd seen in the building and smiled at, but didn't yet know. We were all here to salute birds leaving the nest. It had come as a shock to us all, but Hugh was joining a production company that was making a show for Channel 4 called *Big Brother*, while Oli was leaving to work in advertising, wanting to push his creative skills.

Why would you want to leave The Beat? I thought as I stood waiting to be served. Suddenly my phone began to ring. I looked down and saw Sophia's name on the screen.

'Hello!' I shouted over the noise.

'Hi, babe,' she said faintly. 'What are you doing? You on a shoot?'

'It's really noisy in here, I can barely hear you!' I said with the phone pressed hard to one ear and my finger in the other.

'. . . see you . . . where are you? . . . exams finished . . . back for while now . . . hardly seen you.'

I couldn't make out her sentences. 'Listen, babe, I'll call you right back. I can't hear you through the noise . . . Mate, can I get a round in please?' I asked as the barman pointed at me among the throng.

With drinks in hand, I barged my way back through the people waiting to be served, packed tight like the floor at a Michael Jackson concert. I got back to the intern crew who were gasping for a drink in the corner. They grabbed at the glasses and bottles of beer that I had jammed together tightly in the clasp of my hands. After collectively moaning about our low pay and trying to outdo each other for the prize of poorest intern, Tola provided us with some office gossip.

'I was speaking to someone in Finance earlier, and they said there's going to be some cutbacks in the company.'

'Is that why Hugh and Oli are leaving?' I asked. 'Have they been pushed?'

'Nah, I know for a fact they're jumping,' said James III confidently.

Excited at the possible opportunity, Cara jumped into the conversation. 'So that leaves space for us lot to step up and fill some shoes.'

'Not sure about that,' said Tola grimly. 'Apparently departments are having budgets not just frozen but *cut*. No budgets, no shows.'

'So are people losing their jobs?' asked Sam, clearly concerned now.

'I think so. There's panic in the company. Haven't you noticed? Lots of meetings behind closed doors with HR apparently.'

'But we're safe, right? We've only got a short contract,' I said.

'No one's safe, Jay,' she replied bluntly.

I looked at everyone's faces: they were frozen at the prospect of losing their jobs.

Then Tola added something that made everyone's ears twitch. 'But apparently there will definitely be *one* permanent position for one of us interns. We're going to be cheaper than anyone else, I guess.'

The momentary silence was broken by Cara, who was the first to put her cards on the table. 'Well, I don't know about you lot, but I haven't come all the way across the world to go back home just yet.'

'Well, I'm sure everyone wants it,' Sam reasoned.

Sonya stayed quiet as usual. She looked worried.

'Ah, who cares?' said James III, swigging his beer.

Surely he's kidding, I thought to myself. I couldn't tell. *I care*. Maybe he'd been told he had it. Suddenly we were all like poker players around a table playing for high stakes.

'All right, you lot,' came a voice from outside the group. Hugh broke the weird vibe that had descended on our corner. 'What are you all talking about?' he asked.

'Holidays,' I said, reacting quickest. 'Where you going this year?'

'I have no plans till *Big Brother*'s finished. We go on till September,' he said, letting out a big sigh. 'What about you lot?'

None of the interns took the floor. We looked round at each other, as if taking a holiday was going to be a sign of weakness.

'I can't, there's too much to do,' said Tola.

And so it went from all of us. Was it true or was the new

rumour exerting some influence? Max had already baulked at me when talk of holidays had come up inadvertently.

'Well, make sure you take them. It's only TV! Life will go on.' Hugh grinned round at us all.

'Yeah, but we can't leave our producers alone,' Sam pointed out.

'Don't be guilted into it; that's what all employers want. Make sure you take 'em or lose 'em,' said Hugh.

I wasn't sure if there was sound reasoning to his way of thinking, considering what Tola had just told us, or if the Karl Marx in him was right.

'Do you want to know the secret to surviving in this or any other place?' Hugh offered. 'Don't get caught up in the Matrix.'

Sophia was ringing my mobile again but it was still too loud to talk and I was distracted by the thought of my hard work spiralling down the toilet pan before my eyes. I'd phone her as soon as I finished my drink.

'So why are *you* leaving?' asked Tola.

'Time to get paid,' he said, laughing and rubbing his fingers together. 'To be fair, I've been here a while now and you lot are making me feel old.'

James III grinned. 'That's right, you started in TV when it was in black and white.'

'Very funny, big man. Before I leave I'll make sure you get to log The Beat's archive library for the last few months of your internship,' said Hugh, stealing the last laugh.

Cara came back with a pint for Hugh as he held court, passing on words of wisdom, now with a slight slur. 'Look, kids. We all came here wanting to make documentaries, different format shows, short films . . . and in the brainstorming sessions we've all had golden ideas thrown on the floor in favour of rubbish or due to lack of resource and imagination. As a result, all the talent leaves and ends up on another broadcaster's payroll. All these years we should've been a creative hub making shows for the terrestrial channels. Instead, they're just copying us and doing it for themselves.'

'But surely it will change?' said Sonya optimistically.

'The management promise exciting projects but they never come around. Our budgets are tiny and we can't make anything of value or significance. Every year it's the same thing about shrinking budgets, yet we're told we're making bumper profits.'

'Why don't they put those profits back into the company then?' I asked.

'Simple. The more profit senior management send back to the parent company, the more performance-related bonuses they make,' he said.

My phone was vibrating again and this time it was a voicemail message. There was another missed call from Sophia. I wanted to break off and call her back but this was interesting stuff.

'For example,' Hugh continued, 'years ago The Beat made the precursor to *Big Brother* with *College Lives*, a show that intimately filmed students who shared a house. That's how ahead of the times we were. The Beat should be the ones making this type of show. It pains me to leave because I've put a lot of blood, sweat and tears into this place. Like everyone else around here,' he said with emotion in his voice.

No one had interjected in a while. We all looked glum. Not for us, but for him.

Hugh looked genuinely sad too. 'Look, I don't want to put a dampener on it for you. But The Beat's a sinking ship. Like the *Titanic*, it's just a matter of time.'

He painted a bleak future for us. For The Beat.

My phone vibrated in my pocket.

I thought you were calling me back???

Just as I was about to text Sophia back someone else joined the sermon.

'Sad to see you go too, Oli,' said Cara, giving him a hug.

'Yeah, very sad. Why are *you* leaving?' asked Sonya as Oli strolled into our circle like a bowling ball into a set of pins, a beer in one hand and a cigarette in the other.

'They caught me having it off with one of the interns,' he said, holding a straight face.

James III and I looked accusingly at the girls, who momentarily looked at each other. But when James III started to snigger the girls simultaneously looked at James III, accusing him right back.

'Look around the building, man,' said Oli. 'Too many old people are in charge. They're making decisions about youth culture that you and I should be doing. What do they know? They're all in their mid thirties, in cushy jobs without much pressure, and suffering from Peter Pan syndrome.'

'What do you mean?' asked James III.

'They don't want to grow up. They're holding on to their youth for as long as possible working here.'

Suddenly it dawned on me how many older people really

did work at The Beat. You didn't see them because the young minority – with their crazy haircuts, clothes and ability to make more noise – stood out. But they were almost certainly the quiet majority.

'Yeah, but you can't have kids in charge, surely?' said Tola.

'Why not? At least you'd make some programmes that our viewers want to watch, be a bit more ballsy and irreverent. That's how The Beat started out. Apparently Ali G was sent to us first but people here passed on him till he ended up on Channel 4.'

I looked around – everyone was aghast at this cardinal sin.

Oli continued uninterrupted. 'Tech companies like Google and Yahoo! are successful because they have young guys at the helm ready to think outside the box. The greater the risk, the higher the return. The Beat keep harping on about taking risks but they never do. They're about as rock 'n' roll as Ovaltine and grandad slippers.'

'You sound bitter,' said Hugh sarcastically, while looking at Oli.

'Me? Nah, it's only television,' said Oli casually.

'You mean Tel-Lie-Vision,' Hugh corrected him.

Increasingly I wasn't sure if this was real talk, bitter talk, revolutionary talk, conspiracy talk or just alcohol-fuelled talk. I knew Hugh and Oli had been drinking in the pub since three o'clock.

Even after hearing everything Hugh and Oli had said about The Beat, I still wanted in. And so did the others. I felt a competitive edge coming out in me. I wanted to go and call Sophia but after today's rumours I had to stay and charm the senior producers who'd showed up. Only they could turn my intern dream into a full-time job. I realized I had to be more than just me. I had to have the confidence of Cara, the smarts of Tola, the gift of the gab of James III, the raw talent of Sonya and the likeability of Sam. I was sure Sophia could wait a little longer for me to call her back. This was important for my career.

As the night wore on The Beat staff took over the entire pub. Max had invited Isabel, who had come from a modelling shoot and was endearing herself to everyone, and the older lot were telling stories – some true, some just embellished myths – about the good old days.

They had all worked closely together in the trenches, whether it was sitting in on someone else's edit until three a.m. because the other had a hot date, or trying to get a usable vox-pop from gurning pill heads in a small club in Blackpool. More importantly they had been there for one another personally, offering someone a couch to sleep on for a month because their partner had thrown them out or consoling someone whose father had died of cancer.

After leaving school and university I'd realized that no matter how sincerely anyone says 'we'll stay in touch', invariably paths do diverge. These last few months had brought this into sharp focus for me. Maybe that realization had also hit the older lot and was the reason this farewell was so sombre.

It was getting late and I still hadn't had a chance to call Sophia so I stepped out on to the pavement and away from the noise of the pub. Just as I was about to call, Hugh and Oli appeared.

'Oli and I are offski. Good luck, Jay, and keep *doin' it for the kids*,' Hugh said sarcastically.

'Where're you off to?' I said. 'The night is still young and these are *your* leaving drinks.'

'Glastonbury,' said Oli.

'You lucky fuckers! Bowie, Travis, Chemical Brothers, Moby.'

'Screw them, I'm going for the women and drugs,' replied Oli.

'Darth couldn't go,' said Hugh.

'You mean, doesn't *want* to go,' Oli corrected him. 'No place for an Armani suit.'

'Yeah, so better a free pair of Glastonbury tickets than a Pokémon as a goodbye present for five years of service,' said Hugh philosophically.

A few hugs later and they drunkenly hopped, skipped and shoved each other down the street and round the corner. Saddened at the sight of them riding off into the sunset, I put my phone in my pocket and walked back into the pub.

20
KARMA POLICE

I wasn't sure where I had put them but I knew they were here somewhere. I just couldn't remember where 'here' was. I retraced my steps and checked everywhere. I double-checked. I triple-checked. It wasn't the loss of the two tapes that had the Aaliyah interview on them that worried me particularly, but the Max factor – his reaction if he were to find out. He'd been in a particularly foul mood since Hugh and Oli left a few weeks earlier and this morning was no different. I'd collected his dry-cleaning and got his morning coffee yet he was already snapping at me from across the department and I didn't want to hear, 'Oi, birdbrain, where are my tapes?'

I hadn't asked anyone to help for fear word might slip out that I was a doofus. Maybe I was being paranoid. But with only two-and-a-half months left on our intern contracts, everyone was competing – discreetly or otherwise – for that one permanent job. Some were blatantly networking with senior management in the office or going for lunchtime yoga classes with them, while others volunteered for extra shoots or got drunk in the pub after work with the people they thought could influence the decision.

Lunchtime came and went as I searched. My mobile rang

as I sorted through piles of tapes from the drawers, stacking them on the floor next to me like I was playing Jenga. 'Mum Mobile' flashed on the screen.

I had missed her birthday last week because I was on a shoot that overran. Max's boss, Robert, had asked me personally to help, so I had to impress. Luckily I'd managed to make it up to her by getting some tickets from the girls in T.A.D. to see Tina Turner tonight. She was a big fan and had made her friends envious that I was taking her.

'Hi, Mum.' I tried not to sound impatient.

'I won't keep you, I just wanted to know what time to meet you tonight? I'm so excited, and when I told Jane next door she –'

'Ummm . . .' A tape suddenly crashed to the floor from my hand as I interjected, 'Oh for fuck's sake!' still holding several tapes in my hands as I balanced the phone between my tilted head and shoulder.

Putting the tapes down, I tried to explain my predicament.

'Have you asked around?' she offered, in stereotypical mum-advice style.

'Do you know how big this building is?' I baulked.

'OK, well, why don't you send an email? I'm sure some-one has seen it.'

'And highlight my incompetence to the entire company?'

'You're tired, Jay. These things will happen,' she said, as if I'd spilt orange juice on the carpet.

Nothing she was saying was helping. In fact it was making it worse.

'Mum, unless you know where the tapes are,' I said, clearly exasperated, 'you're not helping right now.'

'All I'm saying is stay calm. Panicking about it won't help.'

I finally snapped. 'For fuck's sake, Mum! Staying calm isn't going to magic the tapes back to me!'

The phone went silent. I couldn't even hear her breathing, just the sound of the TV set in the background.

I tried to get an even tone back in my voice. 'Look, this is a bad time. I'll call you later and arrange when to meet, OK? Right now Tina Turner isn't high up in my list of priorities,' I said.

'Sure. I hope you find your tape. Bye.' She hung up the phone.

'It's not *tape*, it's *tapes*,' I said to myself, still wound up. As I put my phone in my pocket, my foot nudged the pile on the floor. *Karma*, I thought to myself. The crashing noise made everyone stop and look round like I was a clumsy waiter who'd dropped a plate in a restaurant. Then the momentary lull was filled again with people talking against the noise of photocopiers, TVs and stereos. My agitated mood turned to one of embarrassment as I kicked into gear like I was the multi-armed Hindu god Ganesh. I grabbed the tapes and tried to restack them, all the while replaying the phone call in my head. Worse than talking like a spoilt brat was the horrible realization that I was starting to sound like Max. Slipping into a meeting room I tried calling Mum to apologize but the phone was engaged.

By mid afternoon I wasn't any closer to finding Aaliyah or doing the work that was piling up. I had to face the music but I needed to do it on my terms. I called Max's desk phone.

'Can you meet me in the Seventies room?' I asked.

'Sure,' he said, and I saw him jump up to follow me into the room behind my desk.

'You've lost the tapes?' he said. With his voice rising, he added, 'Lost?'

We sat opposite one another at the meeting-room table, my eyes looking downward like a naughty schoolboy. I may as well have stood with my nose in the corner.

'Well, kiddo, the edit is tomorrow morning, so you had better find them before then or you'll find yourself having to explain to Robert Johns and the record label. I can't help you then, it's out of my hands. I just hope the label don't ask you to pay for costs of the trip and the camera crew.'

My stomach lurched at news of the full extent of my mistake. 'So what shall I do?' I asked, hoping for some help and support.

'That's for you to figure out. I have other things on my plate right now. So *chop chop*, *di di mau*.' He got up and walked out.

I sat there shell-shocked. Would they really want me to pay them back? Max had said it with such conviction, I wasn't sure if he was serious or trying to scare the hell out of me. Either way I had seriously fucked up. Desperation quickly got the better of my ego.

To: All@NottingHill
Subject: URGENT – Missing Aaliyah tapes

Dear All,
Has anyone seen two digi beta tapes labelled 'Aaliyah interview'? Please can I ask you to keep an eye out for them?
Regards,

Jay Merchant
Intern, Total BEATS & Defm8

Moments later:

Better find that interview – she's a priority act for the channel. I don't want to have to explain your cock-up to the label.

Declan Patricks
Head of Talent & Artist Department

———

Happens all the time around here. I'll keep an eye out at the viewing stations.

Regards,
Marcus
ITC Legal

———

Well done. You've made us look like we don't know what the fuck we're doing.

Max
Producer, Total BEATS & Defm8

For the next few hours I stayed at my desk, not even risking going to the toilet or downstairs to the cafeteria, despite having only eaten a bowl of cornflakes all day. I kept an eye on my computer screen praying an email would ping in, and stared at my phone, willing it to ring with good news. Everyone around me offered to help, but I had to decline, knowing they had piles of work themselves. The search for Aaliyah was proving fruitless.

By the end of the day I was faced with a serious decision. Take my mum to the concert and piss off Max? Or stay, hopefully find the tapes, keep my job and let my mum down. Again.

Sorry Mum, can't go! Tapes still missing. Sending tickets with a car to pick you and a friend up at 6.30. Sorry. Have fun.]

I asked Uncle Lee for a VIP car as opposed to a people carrier to try and make it special for her, but I still felt as guilty as hell. '*Idiot!*' I cursed myself.

By eight p.m. everyone had left the building except for Max and me. He was watching me as I literally turned the place upside down for the umpteenth time. The words to Aaliyah's 'Try Again' were starting to wear thin. Eventually he came over with his rucksack slung over his shoulder. He looked as tired as I felt.

'Any luck?' he asked in the calmest tone he'd used all day.

'Nope.'

He sighed and rubbed his face and forehead with both hands. 'Listen, Jay . . .' he began, pulling up a chair and sitting next to me.

Oh God, he's about to start up again, I thought to myself. *Worse, he's about to fire me.* Before he could continue, I tried to see him off at the pass.

'Max, I'm looking everywhere. I'm sorry for embarrassing you. You know I work hard and I'm extremely meticulous in everything I do. I get here before all the other interns and I'm the last to leave. I work late nights and weekends. I don't see my girlfriend, my family or friends. It's all my fault, I know, but I will find the tapes.'

The verbal diarrhoea all came out in one go. I was starting

to feel maybe I wasn't right for the job. Perhaps someone less forgetful would be better. Doubt had taken a mere working day to grab hold of me and knock my confidence back to square one.

He looked perplexed at my outburst but continued from where he left off.

'Listen, Jay . . . this isn't about the tapes. I'm sure they will turn up eventually.' He paused for what seemed like ages. I felt my heart thumping on all pistons with nerves.

'I've got some stuff going on and I think . . . I may . . . have taken it out on you.'

I sat there as calm overcame me. The mighty Max was apologizing? Well, almost. Where were my witnesses?

'I won't go into it too much but . . . well, there it is,' he said, getting up to go.

'Is everything OK?' I asked.

He sat back down again and let out a deep breath, but said nothing.

'Is it work?' I prompted.

'Partly,' he admitted. 'I was promised a promotion months ago but now they're saying they can't do it because the company is cutting budgets.'

'But the show's doing really well in the ratings, right?'

'Yes, but that doesn't matter. Cuts are cuts,' he said dismissively.

I got a sinking feeling. I might not even make it to six months at this rate.

'And, to make matters worse, my relationship's on the rocks.'

I was surprised to hear Max admit that. He always kept

his cards close to his chest and barely spoke about his private life. The pressures must have been really bad. He candidly explained how his two-year relationship had hit the rocks for various reasons from her alcohol abuse to his infidelity. It was a weird yet welcome conversation.

'I can't handle her, an ex-wife and a kid,' he said, sounding exhausted.

'A kid?' I blurted out in shock. That was a left-field ball I wasn't expecting.

'Didn't you know? I thought everyone in this place knew. Can't keep a secret like that hidden here for long,' he said, genuinely surprised.

'I had no idea,' I replied. There was no framed picture on his desk, for a start.

'His name's Kayan,' he said, showing me a photo from his wallet. 'He's from my short-lived marriage. I hardly get time to see him. His mum and I don't get on.' He looked disappointed. 'Don't get divorced, Jay – child support ain't cheap.'

Eventually his mobile phone interrupted things before I could reveal my own relationship woes. He showed me the screen. 'Leila. She's probably drunk somewhere and wants to be picked up.' He pressed decline. 'I can't handle her right now.'

As he got to his feet, he paused. 'For the record, you're doing really well. People are impressed. But you've still got a long way to go.'

Oh my God, I hope the security cameras are picking this up, I thought. It was the first compliment he'd ever given me.

'Oh, and I have a camera by my desk and some DV tapes that need logging for tomorrow morning. And I want Aaliyah found. *Vamos, vamos*!' He turned and walked off towards the stairs.

The feel-good factor of bonding with him went away in an instant as Max switched back to being my boss. I put my headphones on and began logging the tapes while eating one Snickers bar after another from the vending machine in the cafeteria. By the time I was done it was midnight. I checked my phone – I'd been completely unaware of the several texts on my phone from Sophia wondering where I was, Pritz tempting me with a party, Isabel asking if I wanted to meet up for a drink and my mum thanking me for 'the greatest night out in ages'. The last took some guilt off my shoulders.

I kept pressing delete as I skimmed through emails I hadn't read since the end of the working day, propping my tired head in my left hand.

Moments later I paused as my mind caught up with an email from the Production manager, Gwyneth.

To: Merchant, Jay
Subject: URGENT – Please put Max's camera under my desk

Jay,
Please ensure the camera Max borrowed from me is placed under my desk as it's needed for a shoot first thing in the morning. Also your tapes are safely in my drawers. I only just saw them under a pile of folders in my in-tray before I left work. Also can you confirm your edits for next week . . .

I didn't read the rest as I jumped up and raced over to her desk. As I stood there holding the tapes in my hand, my memory came flooding back. When I got back from the interview in Paris, I had rushed back to the office to give Gwyneth our camera for someone else's shoot. In a hurry I had taken the tapes out and must have absent-mindedly put them in her in-tray as I checked the camera bag wasn't missing anything.

I got back to my desk and sent my final email for the day before heading home. I was exhausted but relieved I'd saved myself from a certain P45 form from HR.

To: All@NottingHill
Subject: URGENT – Missing Aaliyah tapes FOUND

Dear All,
Many thanks to Gwyneth for helping to track down Aaliyah. You win a signed CD of her new single. Everyone else can watch her on Total BEATS this Thursday at 9pm in her full glory. Don't miss it!

Jay
Intern, Total BEATS & Defm8

21
SUMMERTIME

Sorting out the shows each week was a Herculean task. Hunting down content from the latest gossip to exclusive videos and features, I had to beg, borrow and steal from people as Max just wouldn't accept excuses. We'd been snowed under with several shoots and edits this week and I hadn't had much time to prepare for tomorrow's recording.

Thankfully the gods were smiling on me and the shows were almost making themselves. In a single morning I'd managed to get a heap of exclusive music videos. Negotiations for these were normally tough and done between all the producers weeks in advance. Everything was up for swapsies like kids in a school playground trading Panini football cards. An exclusive spin of an Eminem video was always hard to come by and demanded a lot of mediocre artists' videos in return. In Panini terms it was like swapping the Manchester United team badge for the entire Tottenham Hotspurs squad.

The reason for all the goodwill was the much-famed Beat staff summer party. People were barely working as they counted down the clock, and it wasn't even lunchtime. Even the senior lot, who'd been there, seen it and got herpes from previous parties, were excited. Max had gone as far as giving himself the day off to prepare – drinking at Soho House with Stuey.

Before we could get to the fun, the walkways upstairs were busy as the management team ran around like they were interns getting mail. They were preparing for the arrival of Gibaidem Corporation's owners, who were in town to see how this corner of the empire was doing. It was bizarre to see the usually calm Darth Vader looking jumpy.

By twelve thirty p.m. the building was almost empty as people left for an indefinitely extended lunch to go shopping for outfits or get their hair done. I still had the show script to finish off but that could be done later and I slipped out to meet Sophia for lunch at Zilli Fish in Soho. The streets of central London had been taken over by kids now that schools and universities were closed for the summer.

'So, birthday girl, what can I get you today?' I asked as I sat stuffing my face with bread and olives.

Sophia laughed. 'My birthday's not for a few weeks.'

'Who cares, let's start early,' I said eagerly.

'In that case, just this is perfect.'

'What, bread?'

'No, you taking time out from work in the middle of the day to make me feel more important than your job.'

I cringed inwardly. I wasn't about to tell her the place was a ghost town in preparation for tonight. Anything that decreased our recent friction, due to my lack of attention since she returned from university, was welcome.

'Babe, of course you're more important.'

'Well, I haven't felt like it. I feel like a stalker – calling, texting and not getting a response.'

'You know what, you're right,' I said, raising my hands and taking the blame. 'I was drowning before but I'm getting to grips with things now.'

'Wow, I've never seen you so . . .'

I stuffed some olives into my mouth, making my cheeks bulge. 'Gluttonous?'

'Confident! What a difference four months has made.'

'I am and it's all because of work.' I thought back to my success that morning in securing the content for the show. People liked me. 'I feel like I'm an important cog in the machine and not just an intern. Like I'm actually valuable. In fact, why don't you come in one day and watch the show being filmed?' I was getting carried away and making blind promises. 'I was also thinking we should consider going away for a week. We deserve it.'

'Er, what about Max?' Sophia raised an eyebrow, recalling all the horror stories.

'What about him?' I said, dismissing him with a straight face. A few seconds later we both burst out laughing.

'Seriously, I promise hand-on-heart things will be much better. I've just got to sort out my work–life balance. Anyway, not another word about work. Let's talk about you,' I said, leaning in.

She paused as her ears twitched and her eyes lit up. I'd forgotten this was what she'd wanted all this time – to feel special. It made me feel good to get things right for once. Our lifestyles had been so out-of-sync lately that even *I'd* started to notice the lack of contact.

I continued being the attentive boyfriend after lunch as we criss-crossed between shops. We were tantric shopping

– looking around for hours and not buying anything. Until we got to Selfridges, that is. Gladiator sandals were the must-have for girls this summer so I pulled out the credit card. Luckily the sales offered me the chance to be a big cheese without breaking the bank. To top off the day, I got a nice thank you from Sophia in the men's changing room.

Spending the afternoon with Sophia after such a long time apart was like human photosynthesis. Energized, I eventually returned to the office at six p.m., in time for the massive school assembly that was Darth Vader's Europe-wide company speech. The tables in the Greenhouse were stacked with bottles of beer, wine and snacks to nibble on as Bon Jovi's 'It's My Life' played through the speakers. There were lots of new faces, not just from the Mayfair offices but also from Paris, Stockholm, Berlin, Madrid and everywhere in between. I grabbed a bottle and joined the rest of my department.

When he began it was clear Darth wasn't a very good communicator to large audiences. Monotone and stiff, he was smart enough to know this was his second-in-command's strength and let him take centre stage as soon as possible. When he did, the Doc was truly in his element, just as he'd been for our induction, which seemed a lifetime ago now. Each announcement of good news was met by rapturous applause from everyone in the building and a swig of their drinks. He namechecked outstanding work from each department, surprising Max and me with praise for the high ratings and fan base we were getting across Europe.

At the end, he played a showreel of the company's programmes, achievements and awards that would further whip up everyone's euphoria. Edited in The Beat way, with really fast cuts and a booming soundtrack that reverberated round the building, it came to an explosive end with the sound of a beating heart with words on a black background: THEMUTHAFRIKKINBEAT – DOIN' IT FOR THE KIDS.

Cue whoops as everyone applauded with a sense of communal pride that they were part of something that was truly awesome. As everyone upstairs clinked beer bottles and wine glasses together in celebration, I noticed a handful of people sat at their desks, refusing to get sucked in to it all. They'd have been the ones to point out the imminent budget cuts and sackings, no doubt.

'Your chariots await outside,' someone from HR instructed over the microphone.

Iconic London Routemaster buses had been hired to whisk us away to the secret venue, where a feast of food and entertainment lay ahead. People quickly finished getting ready in the toilets, the talent dressing rooms and anywhere they could score a quick line, pill or toke.

'Well, it looks like you're in pole position for that job, doesn't it, you jammy fuck,' said Cara as our bus wobbled its way around central London, leaving everyone guessing where we would end up.

'What? Why?' I said, glugging back yet another bottle of Stella.

'Er, hello, you and your boss just got a namecheck.'

I paused for a moment, not knowing what to say. Normally I'd try to play it down but for some reason on this occasion I didn't. 'That's cos we're the shit,' I said with a cheesy grin.

Cara rolled her eyes. 'You've been hanging around James III too long.'

Sam instantly backed her up. 'Like Public Enemy, "Don't believe the hype!"'

Were they happy for me and joking? Or was I being an obnoxious twat? For once I didn't over-analyse. I had a nice buzz running through me, and not just from the alcohol. The memory of the Doc singling us out suddenly made my chest grow ten times in size and I felt like I was Michael Jordan, walking on air.

22
PERFECT DAY

The wheels on the bus went round and round, accompanied by the impromptu singalong of anything from ABBA and MJ to Nina Simone and Led Zeppelin. Eventually we all clambered off and piled into a huge warehouse that was the venue for the party.

Tonight's festivities had avoided the new cost-cutting measures only because it had been organized and paid for months before. James III and I explored the venue to find several rooms each with a specific genre of music, with DJs and stages set up for performances. My eyes were running laps around the rooms, eyeing up all the talent.

James III soon realized my attention was elsewhere. 'Oh, I see you're tempted?'

'Tempted? No . . . just *admiring*,' I replied.

'Oh sure, bloody sure. I've seen that look before at a particular house party,' he said, rubbing his chin, unconvinced.

I ignored him as we continued to the chill-out area – filled with beanbags and scented candles – but quickly exited. Next to that was a games room, with table football, Scalextric track, karaoke machine, mini casino and a sumo-wrestling ring with matching inflatable suits, which we were soon climbing into.

James III was in Sherlock Holmes-mode by that point. 'C'mon, Merchant, who've you got the hots for?'

'There's definitely some nice women, I'm not blind. But . . . I mustn't,' I said, charging into him in my sumo suit.

'Mustn't?' He laughed, tripping and pinning me to the floor. 'Not even Kate in T.A.D.?'

I paused very briefly. 'No. I don't cheat.' I tried to push him off.

'But I thought your missus does your head in?'

'Yeah, occasionally. But on the whole she's good and I'm sure I'm not easy to be with right now.'

'No other creature on this planet has just one mate,' he said, teasing me.

'Not true, some creatures do.'

'Yeah, and then the black widow spider kills him!' he replied, quick off the mark.

I laughed at his persistence as we clambered out of the sumo suits.

Walking through the corridors, the smell of weed got stronger. We explored the final room, which was filled with a hot tub for the daring, several masseuses and a magician doing card tricks.

'And you're sure she isn't?' James III asked as a masseuse kung-fu chopped his back.

'Isn't what?' I responded as my shoulders were rubbed.

'I mean, there she is at university. Going to all those parties. Getting drunk. We know what that's like,' he said.

'Yeah, but she's not like that.'

'Can you say that one hundred per cent?'

I paused momentarily. 'Yes,' I said, but without conviction. James III smiled.

I looked back at him. 'No, yes!' I said with more gusto.

He pretended to be confused. 'No? Yes? Which one is it?' James III was the devil in disguise. 'You sure there's no one in the background for her?'

Maybe it was the copious amounts of alcohol and lack of food but it was working. He was riling me up. Massage over, we stepped outside into the car park and entered a massive marquee that housed all the catering and a cocktail bar. The mixologist was like Tom Cruise in *Cocktail*. He was the European champion and had been flown in especially, as had some of the DJs. The theme for the party was Musical Icons, and all the bar staff were dressed up: I could see Blondie, Janet Jackson, Bono and Prince. Even Elvis was manning the barbecue.

'Well, there is this one guy who gives her lifts to uni,' I admitted, pouring lots of ketchup on to my chips. 'Some twat called Simon.'

'Twat?' said James III, sensing he'd found my Achilles' heel. 'Why so touchy?'

'I just think he's after something,' I said. 'For a start, he lives outside London but comes back in to pick her up to drive to Manchester.'

'Really? You mean he goes *out of his way* to come *back* and pick her up?' he said with satisfaction.

Seeing what he was trying to do, I countered, 'He's clearly not like you.'

'Oh, they're all like us,' he said pointedly.

'*Us?*' I said defensively.

'Oh yes, *us*,' he laughed.

We joined the girls to exchange gossip, rumour and scandal before going around meeting the 'family' from overseas. Every time I passed Max he had a cheeky grin on his face and was dancing or drinking with a different woman.

As I took a break from it all outside by the barbecue, someone walked in that I wasn't expecting to see. As always, she looked hot.

'Are you here to do more vox-pops?' I asked Isabel.

'Thought I'd surprise you,' she said.

'I'm used to speaking to you on text these days. What do we do, hug or fist bump?' I asked. She smelt amazing as I leant in and put my arms around her. 'Wow, someone's made an effort. Here to see Max, are we?' I joked.

'Yeah, he invited me but he's not the reason why I came.'

Am I drunk or is she flirting with me? I wondered. There was definitely something there. 'Oh, I get it, you came to drink from the ice statue.'

'That's right, let's go.' She grabbed my hand and we did a few shots together while I told her who was who at the party.

I was thoroughly buzzing now. How much more euphoric could I get? Just as we were about to hit the dance floor, in swooped Max from nowhere.

'Good timing,' he said, kissing her cheeks. 'Let's go and party.'

'Cool, come on, Jay,' she said, grabbing my hand.

'Actually, Isabel, there are some execs I wanted to introduce you to first. I'm sure Jay won't mind,' said Max, leading the way.

I knew my place. 'Yeah, sure. Cool, cool, you go ahead, I'll catch you later.'

'Oh no, I promised Jay,' Isabel said, using her puppy-dog eyes to best effect. 'I'm sure I can meet them after we've danced.'

I wanted to shout out, 'Ha! Rejected! In your face, Max,' but held the words in the back of my throat. Instead I just started dancing in the middle of the bar area to the sound of a Mojito being mixed in the background.

'OK, well come and find me later,' said Max, not interested in a dance floor threesome.

We headed on over to the main room where Sam was DJing thanks to a hook-up from the Doc. The sea of music-hungry revellers turned to look at the hot girl dancing with the dweeb. I had my hands in the air as I danced to Wookie's 'Battle', absorbing the various shades of purple it was letting off thanks to my inbuilt Technicolor music sensor. *Wicked buzz. Wicked*, I thought.

I still wasn't sure if Isabel was interested in me or if she was just teasing. Would a super hot girl like her fancy me? Either way I had to stop this from taking off on so many levels. Max liked her – what if this pissed him off? I had a girlfriend – what if she was doing this with Simon? And to top it off, I had just told James III how I wasn't like him. I went to my phone and read a saved message from Sophia as we danced.

RV I Love You Much-much LV.

Simple, but it was enough to kill the mood.

'I've gotta go to the front door and get a mate in,' I said abruptly. 'Just got a text.'

'I'll come with you,' she offered.

'Oh . . . er, you'd better find Max. Those execs could get you more work.' She looked slightly rejected so I quickly smoothed things over. 'Keep an eye on your phone and I'll call you later to carry this on . . . I mean the dancing,' I said, fumbling and tumbling over my words and legs as I stumbled off.

I managed to find James III and escaped with him to the dance room as Rude Boy Rupert played his set. As I raved, James III tried to convince the bar staff dressed as Madonna and Beyoncé Knowles to stop serving drinks and come powder their noses in the toilets.

I didn't need a box of Jaffa Cakes to make friends any more as I hung out confidently with people from different departments. I even looked out for the Doc to pitch an idea I'd had: let the interns run The Beat and make a reality TV show about it. Fortunately for my future employment status, I couldn't find him. While James III and I were sidetracked, the girls were speaking to the people who counted. But I was relaxed – I'd had a shout-out from the Doc and was in pole position!

I was checking the time on my watch and correlating it with how hammered everyone was getting. At two thirty a.m. the head of HR began to dirty dance with the head of Marketing. By three a.m. all the presenters were in a circle doing the can-can to 'Come On Eileen' by Dexys Midnight Runners. And at three thirty a.m. the head of Music Scheduling ran around the party screaming 'Tube' (Totally Unnecessary Boob Examination) at the top of his voice when squeezing an unsuspecting bloke's nipples.

That signalled it was time for me to leave; I still had the script to write for tomorrow morning's recording. As I sat in the rear of the Uncle Lee on the way back to the office, I started reading the stream of text bulletins from Sam, the only non-drinker in the company I knew, and therefore a reliable spy on the night's goings-on.

Max left with 2 Norwegian girls!

James III trying 2 take waitresses home!!

Head of T.A.D. punched head of Music Scheduling!!!

Milly getting Stuey to strip!

Cara kissing Monica from The Beat Italy!!!

The DOC is DJ'ing!!

All the presenters are singing karaoke with Darth Vader!!

I sunk my head back into the headrest, half dozing off, reflecting on the night. A smile crossed my face. Perfect days didn't come by for me very often. In fact the last time I could remember was when I was eight: I got a gold star for writing the best story in my class and read it out in morning assembly; at lunch I had seconds of my favourite dessert, chocolate cake and chocolate custard; in the afternoon I won a trophy for the sprint relay race at sports day; that evening Mum made the most perfect spag bol; at day's end I went to sleep dreaming I kissed my teacher, Miss Dawson! Today wasn't quite there, but it was pretty damn close.

23
TOM'S DINER

The building was fairly empty, and not just because it was a Monday morning. Even Max hadn't come in yet to bark orders at me, instead sending a text to say he'd gone to give blood. Summer holidays meant people were taking time off or working at the music festivals. Only Sonya and I were in the office while the other interns were either in edits or on shoots. I had just returned from T.A.D. where I'd seen the new Madonna and Ali G video.

Sonya sat with her feet on her chair and knees tucked into her chest. 'How was your weekend?' she asked, while nibbling on a Danish pastry like a mouse.

'OK,' I said, staring at the computer screen. I was feeling tired before the week had even begun.

For the past fifteen minutes she'd been downloading music from Napster. Now bored, she turned her attention to me. 'C'mon, gimme some gossip,' she pleaded, bribing me with half of her Danish. 'What's up?'

'Nothing much,' I said, continuing to read emails.

'Jay?' she said inquisitively.

I kept looking at the screen.

'Ja-a-ay?' she repeated in the teasing tone of an annoying younger sister.

'Naaa-thing,' I replied, mimicking her.

'Can you lot keep the noise down? I just got an email from Ad Sales saying it's already too loud for a Monday morning.' It was Terry 'the Minister' Perkins, the head of Production. Everyone turned the volume levels down on their TVs. Satisfied, he turned and walked away, the cue for everyone to grab their remote control and put the volume back up again.

Sonya eventually convinced me to talk rather than research.

'I don't know if working here and being in a relationship is possible,' I confessed.

'Tough weekend?' she asked.

'You could say that. I had an interview with Mary J. Blige on Saturday morning that overran thanks to flight delays and traffic. I was late to meet Sophia – by six hours – for a barbecue that started at one o'clock. She was seriously pissed off.'

'Rightly so. If you were my boyfriend I'd be the same,' said Sonya.

'Even though it wasn't my fault?'

She laughed. 'You're a man, it's always your fault.'

'Anyway, we eventually got to this barbecue in Richmond at her friend Mia's place. Her parents were away on holiday. I was surrounded by Sophia's university mates and, oh dear Lord, I exaggerate not, how boring.' There was something about gossiping with girls that made men sound extremely camp. Or maybe it was just me. 'All they spoke about was 'university this, university that'. When they did engage with me it was the same questions: "Which famous people have you met?" and "Can you get me some concert tickets?" Then they annoyingly kept calling me "Mr Beat". No, you muppets, J-A-Y. I'm not a music channel.'

Sonya smiled. 'Well, at least she has some mates to hang round with while you're working dusk till dawn.'

'Yeah, well, I met her "mate" Simon again. Twat! He blatantly fancies her.'

'Really, how could you tell?' she asked.

'A man can smell another man from a mile off.'

She smiled. 'That's a little bit gay and a lot Neanderthal, isn't it?'

I couldn't see the funny side. 'Trust me, when you pick up on a vibe, you go with your instinct.'

'Did you talk to her about it?'

'Yes, but she just turned it back on me, saying *she* had more reason not to trust *me*, seeing as I was the one surrounded by pretty women at celeb parties.'

'Fair point.'

'All she had to do was just reassure me with a few choice words. But she didn't. The way she reacted was so over the top it just roused my suspicions. So then, just as we were about to get into the discussion, my phone rang. Max was calling to say the Mary J. Blige interview tapes had gone missing from the dubbing department.'

It was a typical scene for an intern. As the producer, Max was being harangued by all the calls but wanted me to fix it. The guy on the morning shift had left work and his mobile was off. Max kept sending me texts every half-hour asking for an update. At one point I had Max on my phone on one ear while I was talking to the dubbing department on Sophia's phone on the other.

'I bet that pissed her off even more,' said Sonya sympathetically.

'Yeah, but what could I do?'

'So what happened with the tapes?'

Even the memory of it exhausted me. 'Eventually they track down the guy and get the tapes.'

'What a needless headache.'

'Then I couldn't get into the spirit of things and drink because I was driving. And Sophia and her mates just got more and more hammered and immature.'

'Clearly you've forgotten what it's like to be a student, grandpa.'

'It gets worse,' I warned her.

Her eyes lit up. 'Juicy. Come on, tell me.'

'Well . . . I had her phone from when I was trying to find the tapes for Max and I . . . accidentally read her texts,' I said.

'What? Jay! *Accidentally!*' she exclaimed. 'Really?'

'Sure, like you wouldn't if you were suspicious,' I challenged her, purely to hide my embarrassment. 'Anyway, as I thought, there were lots of texts from that Simon guy,' I said, justified.

'So? He's her friend,' Sonya defended Sophia.

'Hard to believe when I saw they were flirting on text. *Flirting.*'

'Jay, are you sure your bias didn't convince you to read more into it?'

'Don't worry, I gave her the benefit of the doubt and said nothing. It was getting late and I just wanted to leave. But Sophia was drunk and wanted to stay. We eventually started arguing about that too. And that's when it happened.'

'What?' she asked, staring at me in anticipation.

'I shoved –'

'Sophia?!' she exclaimed.

'No, no – Simon,' I corrected her. 'What do you take me for?'

She laughed at jumping the gun. 'Sorry.'

I explained how Mr Slimy had come to Sophia's rescue as we argued and I got pissed off. The benefit of the doubt ran out and it ended up being like *The Jerry Springer Show*, with two guys pushing each other and a girl in the middle trying to stop it.

'We argued all the way home about me not being by her side all night, my "interfering fucking job" and her "poor mate" Simon. That pissed me off more so I asked about the messages on her phone. Then she got angrier that I'd invaded her privacy.'

'Well, you did!' said Sonya.

'So she grabbed my phone and found some texts from Isabel.'

'The presenter?'

'We're just work colleagues!' I protested.

'Like Simon and Sophia are just uni mates?' She raised her eyebrows. 'So how did it finish?'

'With nightmares,' I replied. 'I dreamt about missing tapes and Max calling. I kept waking up thinking I was late for the studio.'

'You're dreaming about your boss?'

'Seriously, I'm getting totally absorbed by this job. I can't seem to get the work and play balance right.'

'Maybe Sophia's right about this job being an interference,' she said.

'I just think I'm not meeting normal people any more. It's only everyone in the entertainment and media world. Other people, like Sophia's uni friends, are –'

'What?' Sonya interrupted.

'– boring in comparison?' I said, slowly feeling I'd said something wrong.

Sonya looked shocked but tried to empathize. 'Look, it's tough; no one's finding this internship easy. I'm working nearly every other weekend preparing the shows and specials. I haven't seen my family in ages and I don't have time for *any* kind of relationship. I don't know how you do it.'

'Problem is I don't think I *am* doing it,' I said, realizing the truth.

'What's more important to you?' she asked.

I stayed silent for a while, taking in the question. Shouldn't I have said Sophia instantly? I didn't. The silence became deafening before Sonya interjected.

'So, how did you leave it with Sophia?'

'She's just not getting things. It's the first time we've hit a major patch of turbulence. I saw a different side to her, a very difficult and slightly nasty side.'

She paused. 'Seems like it's time to deal with the reality and not just the fantasy. My mum always told me, some things in life are a blessing for you to keep forever. Some are short term and mere lessons to learn from.'

I hesitated before saying, 'Are you talking about Sophia or The Beat?' I laughed.

'What do you think?' She smiled.

Just then the Minister came back. 'I can still hear you lot!' he bellowed.

Us lot reached for our remotes once again, and as he stalked off a few people pointed theirs at his back. Shame they couldn't mute *him*.

24
YEHA-NOHA

The stresses at work were piling up and I needed time to chill out. A week had passed but Sophia and I were still annoyed with each other about the barbecue. Isabel was the antidote, our friendship the antithesis to my relationship with my girlfriend. She'd been inviting me round for dinner for weeks and I decided it would be rude to keep saying no, so I went to her place in Hackney. I wanted to tell Sophia I was going but it would have lead to the Spanish Inquisition and I wasn't in the mood. Besides if she had a 'friendship' with Simon why couldn't I have one with Isabel?

'OK, so what are you making?' I said, standing over the kitchen counter as my stomach grumbled.

'*We* are making roasted peppers with mushrooms and feta for starters, mint lamb chops and potatoes for main and a pear and blackberry crumble for dessert,' Isabel said.

'What? I thought you were cooking. So you've got me here under false pretences,' I joked.

'You could say that,' she replied with a wry smile.

I wasn't much of a cook but was happy to be the intern in the kitchen too. I sliced and chopped while Isabel marinated the lamb chops in mint sauce. *My Name Is Joe* played in the background as we prepared the food, drank some wine and talked about a variety of subjects, finally landing on work.

'So how's The Beat treating you?' she asked.

'You mean Max? I'm running around like his bitch. How's The Beat treating *you*?' I said with a cheeky grin.

'You mean Max?' she laughed back. 'I wouldn't say I'm his . . . lap dog!'

The combination of an empty stomach and wine brought out my forthright side. 'So what are you two, then?'

'Just friends.'

I probed again. 'Just friends like after the party in Middlesbrough?'

'Why, what's he said?' she asked, unflustered by my insinuation.

'Nothing, I just assumed . . .'

'Well, don't assume, or you make an ass out of u and me!' she retorted, slightly tipsy.

Isabel began to cook the mushrooms and chives in olive oil as I drained and sliced the boiled potatoes. The kitchen was starting to smell really nice as the conversation simmered alongside the meal.

'So tell me, how *did* you get the reporter's job?' I asked, over-emphasizing for effect.

'You were there,' she said.

'I suppose you *were* the most natural,' I admitted, remembering the day.

'Well, there you go!' she exclaimed.

'So you didn't know Max from before?'

Still unfazed she said, 'I'd met him at some music industry party a few weeks before and he asked me to audition.'

'So there was no "casting couch"?' I made speech marks in the air. I'd always assumed the myth was true about how actors, singers and the like got ahead behind the scenes.

'Jay! No! There definitely wasn't,' she said with a look of horror on her face.

I poured the mushroom mix over the halved peppers, crumbled the feta cheese on top and placed the dish in the oven as Isabel began to sear the lamb chops and potato slices on a griddle pan. As we set the table for dinner I continued my interrogation, my curiosity unsatisfied.

'So nothing happened?' I asked, laying out the cutlery.

'People will think what they think. If I put myself about a certain way, then I'm not helping my cause. But if I'm friendly with people, they'll help me.'

'How friendly? Flirting?' I asked.

'Talking to people isn't a crime. If they like you and you can work together, then all the better. You've got to develop relationships with people at work and hopefully they like you enough to give you a bump up when the time comes,' she said.

I shook my head. 'I'm no good at it. I'm self-conscious that I look fake and tactical.'

'Everyone does it, Jay. How do you expect to get ahead – by *just* being good at your job?' she reasoned, like she was a self-help guru.

'Well, I need to do something. There's not even two months left of the internship and there's one permanent job available at the end of it.'

'Like you told me when I came to the audition, just be yourself,' she said.

'That's what worries me,' I said, laughing.

'Well, your advice to me was spot on.'

I sat down as Isabel served up. I was dying to eat as I needed some food to go with the wine that was sloshing around my stomach.

'To friends,' I said, raising a toast boisterously. 'So,' I added, more quietly, 'are we friends or are you friendly with me?'

She laughed and gave me a look I couldn't figure out as she sipped her wine.

Time flew by as we finished dinner and dessert and moved to the sofa for more wine. Isabel was fun to talk to and, ironically, the more of a friend she became, the more I found myself attracted to her. She just . . . got it. I was enjoying her company and I couldn't help thinking, *Why can't Sophia be chilled out like this?*

At the end of another laughing fit I looked at the time. 'Dude, I'm getting very drunk.'

'Getting?' she asked before giggling.

'OK, I won't lie, I'm already there.' I looked at my watch again. 'The hands are telling me it's late. I gotta head out soon, I've got work in the morning.' I had sunk deeply and comfortably into the sofa and felt unable to move.

'You want to walk through Hackney at this time of night?'

'I'll be fine,' I said, although I was suddenly worried. Weaving around the streets might be as good as wearing a sign saying 'Mug me'.

'You can sleep on the couch if you like,' she offered.

'I knew you got me here under false pretences,' I joked. I fumbled around for my phone to call the fourth emergency service – Uncle Lee.

Isabel smiled, not saying anything, as usual, but pouring me another glass.

25
GOD IS A DJ

Mid August saw me leave London and head out to what had become the unofficial holiday camp for the company: Ibiza, a.k.a. the debauched 'Gomorrah of the Mediterranean'. Each department at The Beat actually started the year with a line in their budget for the party island. Everyone had a well-rehearsed 'business reason' for going out there at least once during summer. The only person I could think of who got left out was poor Noah in the post room.

Stuey had set up shop in a villa for the summer season, filming news bulletins and specials from a different club each week. Max and I had flown in to shoot an interview with Kylie Minogue and a Top Ten countdown, with Sam and Cara as extra hands.

Our Easyjet flight was virtually a party plane, filled with excitable kids, us included. We landed on Saturday morning and filmed Kylie, who was promoting her new single 'Spinning Around'. By midday we were enjoying downtime at a secluded *playa* catching some mid-August sun. With my top off I noticed that even though I wasn't hitting the gym, carrying filming equipment through the busy streets of W11 was making my arms Hulk-like.

Come the evening, all roads led to the best club on the island, Pacha, with rumours that George Clooney had sailed in from St Tropez to attend. Stuey had promised us a VIP experience – without having to lug a camera and mic cube to get us in. From his years of filming he knew almost everyone, from club owners and managers to the DJs and dance acts. But it also helped a little when 'someone' started a rumour that his cousin owned Ministry of Sound.

'So why does The Beat go goo-goo-ga-ga for Ibiza?' I asked Stuey as he drove us on the C-733 road towards Ibiza Town.

'Why not any other island in Europe? Kos, Crete, Tenerife?' added Cara.

'The footballer-infested Ayia Napa?' added Sam.

None of us had been to Ibiza before and although we'd heard the hype, we were yet to see it for ourselves.

'Homies, what Paris is to romance, Ibiza is to partying,' replied Stuey. 'Everyone who's anyone comes here for the annual pilgrimage. For artists, if their song breaks on this tiny island, it will break all over Europe.'

Fiddling with the stereo in the front, Max asked, 'Who have you caught up with from the UK party pack?'

'Noel Gallagher's villa's in the south and Jade Jagger's hidden retreat is in the north.' Stuey reached into the glove compartment and pulled out a personal invite from her on a purple card that simply read: '*Party, my place, Ibiza, join the commune.*'

Just a few days before I'd left, I'd emailed Pritz about the trip, hoping to make him a bit jealous. Instead he outflanked me, booking a flight and hotel room in between a trade of

Apple shares, and we'd arranged to meet inside the club. Max had met Pritz several times now and thought he was obnoxious, arrogant and rude. Just his kind of guy.

Arriving at Pacha, we were escorted straight to the owner's table where the drinks continued. Max and Stuey weren't dancing much but in a huddle most of the time with the club owner and then the mega rich he introduced them to. Their combined monthly wages couldn't have paid for a table with all those drinks. But dressed in linen like Crockett and Tubbs from *Miami Vice*, with cigars in their mouths, they played the part.

I searched the club for Pritz – among all the good-looking people I guessed he'd stick out like a sore thumb. The women were sexy as hell. During winter these same girls would be a six out of ten at best. But in Ibiza they added two points to their overall total with what was known as the 'two-point tan'.

I finally found Pritz on the dance floor in one of the smaller rooms, vertically dry-humping a confused-looking Italian girl to DJ Luck and MC Neat's 'With a Little Bit of Luck'. I grabbed him and we went back to the main room where a familiar face had joined the VIP table. It was Alison's party promoter friend, Benny from Brussels. He was puffing a cigar with Stuey and Max, surrounded by an entourage of tall leggy Brazilian girls.

This was the first time in ages that I'd felt happy and relaxed in a club. I was a normal punter again. I had begun to associate clubs with work and holding a bloody camera. Looking for places to shoot links, filming vox-pops and finding sexy people for dance montages. Being here was like remembering how to ride a bike – I could listen to the music and just enjoy it, rather than thinking about what album it was from or who did the remix.

All my anxieties, from work to relationships, disappeared. It was nice to just follow the pied piper as he controlled the endorphins in my body. It was bliss hearing a heavy bassline, making a gun using my thumb and first two fingers and firing off a shot when the beat dropped. But even better was the sound of the next track being mixed in subtly and teasingly by Morillo, raising the urge to shout 'tuuuuuune' in anticipation. I mentally snapped the Kodak moment to look back on and help me remember this feeling. Mr Time was moving too fast and before I knew it, my internship would be over.

I stood up to dance as the best sound system on the island sent colours streaming in different directions before me like an indoor fireworks display. I closed my eyes and tilted my head back to suck them into my nose, smelling them. Hands aloft in the air, the colours bristled past my fingertips like falling snow. As the euphoria built in the pit of my stomach, I gave it an escape route through my open mouth as I screamed. I stuck my tongue out to grab a taste. *So this is Ibiza*, I thought.

We didn't leave the VIP section until they threw us out at five a.m. The street outside was packed with people standing around, looking for the next party. Benny invited us back to the villa he was staying at, with his harem of hot women and rich friends, before we'd continue on to the early morning rave at a club called Space.

'Right, so we'll see you guys later at our villa,' said Max, jumping into the Jeep with Stuey and some hot-looking French twins they'd chatted up.

'You're not coming with us to Benny's place?' I asked, wondering why the team was splitting.

He looked at the girls and then back to me. 'Silly question, Jay,' he said. 'Here's some money for a cab. You guys have fun and don't come back too early!'

26
MAS QUE NADA

The four of us found space in the convoy of supercars that Benny and his friends drove at breakneck speed away from Pacha. Blur's 'Song 2' provided the soundtrack for several hair-raising Hollywood-style overtaking manoeuvres before we arrived at the villa, which had a view across the island towards Ibiza Town and the rising sun. Pulling up on the gravel driveway, people piled out of the cars, which were still blaring music as engines shut down and cooled from the short race.

We congregated around Benny's Range Rover. 'Everyone, this is everyone. Please introduce yourselves.'

Cue handshakes and kisses all round. There were the four Brazilian girls (Georgia, Gisele, Adriana, Alessandra), one American (Jennifer) and two Russians (Irka and Maria). Benny's other friends included the son of a shipping magnate (Yannis), whose villa we'd arrived at, a hedge-fund manager (Dutchy), an ambassador's son (KD) and a cowboy hat-wearing playboy (Andrei).

We walked through the plush garden, past the huge infinity swimming pool and beyond the smaller outhouses to the main building. We sat on sofas in the front room as Benny gave out further instructions. 'OK, we have pizzas in the freezer and the drinks cabinet is in the corner by the stereo.' He then plonked a bag of Daz on to the table, which the boys obligingly cut up for everyone to take.

Pritz dived right in like Jacques Cousteau, followed closely by Cara. Sam was new to it and looked at me, slightly petrified, belying her usually hard exterior. She didn't drink and I wasn't entirely sure why. Religion? Dodgy liver? Recovering alcoholic? The gaggle of hot girls tried to persuade her to try some of the offerings on the table. She attempted to hold her ground but the peer pressure broke her. A round of applause from everyone finally coaxed her into it as Azzido Da Bass's 'Dooms Night' blared from the speakers.

I had only tried cocaine once in my life, at university, and didn't like it. Instead of relaxing and enjoying myself, I became panicked, images of Zammo from *Grange Hill* over-dosing in the school toilets running through my head. So instead I asked Benny if he had any weed, and within moments he had rolled the most perfect-looking spliff and presented it to me dramatically like it was the key to the island! Roughly four minutes later I got the biggest hit I'd ever experienced. The room began to spin, my tongue became almost too heavy to talk with and my heart began to race.

'What the fuck was in that? That's not weed,' I gasped, as though I had been given a Filet-o-Fish instead of a Big Mac.

He laughed. 'It's Holland's finest – with an added kick, of course.'

I was totally freaking out. I was ready to send a postcard . . . from my trip! But I didn't want to look like a rookie. The more I tried to relax, the more the voices in my head were telling me to get control of myself. The trance music that was playing didn't help matters as it turned into dark colours bouncing off the walls. It tasted chalky. I opened a bottle of water, drank from it and then lay back like I was Snoop Dogg and monged out.

For the next few hours I lost track of time as everyone partied, drank, snorted, laughed, chatted, smoked and ate while waiting for Space to open. I kept coming in and out of a state of awareness as Sérgio Mendes played on the stereo. One minute Pritz was telling me he was going to screw one of the tall leggy Brazilians, the next Cara was playing papers-scissors-stones with the American girl as Sam stumbled off towards one of the outhouses.

I finally became compos mentis when I woke up on a lounger by the pool with my hand in a bowl of warm water. The villa and its surroundings were totally quiet and the music had been replaced by the sound of crickets. I reached for my phone to get my bearings. The time was eleven a.m. Time to round everyone up and head to Space.

The front door of the villa was locked. The windows were shut and the curtains were drawn. They couldn't have gone to Space as the cars were still there. My friends wouldn't leave me, would they? As I listened closely at the door I could hear muffled voices and chill-out music playing. I went round to the side of the villa to peer through a gap in the curtains but the bright light outside was casting my reflection on to the glass. I placed my hands over my eyebrows to block out the sun and pressed up to the window for a better look.

Yannis, Dutchy and KD were sat on the sofas snorting Daz and watching the American girl, Jennifer, and two of the Brazilians dancing on the coffee table. I couldn't make out which two they were as it was so dark. Jennifer was down to just her G-string while the shorter of the Brazilians was still in her skirt and a half-unbuttoned blouse that revealed her bra.

Jennifer was writhing as KD plied her with vodka straight from the bottle. Dutchy then placed some Daz on her breasts and tried to snort it before it fell to the floor. Yannis was filming everything on his camcorder with one hand and rummaging inside his trousers with the other.

I blinked several times and opened my eyes wider, wondering if I was still tripping. Had I stumbled across a porno shoot? I hadn't experienced any *Eyes Wide Shut* parties but I suppose this was the done thing in Ibiza. KD was trying to get the girl on the table to get down but she was hesitating. Her leggy compatriot helped to prop her up as KD then attempted to pour vodka into both their mouths. She pushed it away and began rubbing the side of her head and looked wobbly on the table. I got a clearer sight of her face for a moment and saw a look of total helplessness on it. Except it wasn't Georgia, Gisele, Adriana or Alessandra. It was Sam.

I quickly ran round to the front of the villa and banged as hard as I could on the door. The music stopped and I heard people moving around inside. My heart was pumping and my mind was trying to think what I should do next. It dawned on me that I didn't know any of these people from Adam. What if it got violent?

Yannis came to the door and opened it slightly, just showing a bit of his face. 'Wassup, bro?' He squinted as the bright light hit his eyes.

'I just wanted to know if you guys were coming to Space now,' I said, staying calm and trying to get in the door.

He stood his ground. 'You go ahead. Um, we'll join you down there.'

I put my hand on the door, pretending to lean on it, and tried to give it a push but his foot was jamming it closed. I paused as a plan emerged from my fuzzy grey matter. 'OK, I'm just going to get my mates as I've just had a call from our boss and we need to get to Space to film,' I said, maintaining my cool.

'Now?' he asked, sounding surprised.

'Yep. Right now.'

'You guys aren't in any state to . . .'

I pushed the door a little bit harder, this time using my legs to help propel the door open. The room filled with sunlight, causing the occupants to scowl momentarily like disturbed vampires. The guys looked like naughty school kids with their heads bowed. I walked over to Sam, grabbed her hand and helped her down off the table. The Brazilian girl stepped back and sat on the sofa, then lit up a cigarette nonchalantly. Jennifer began swigging from the bottle of Grey Goose.

As we headed to the door KD tried to fill the awkward silence. 'It's not what you think. We were only having fun.'

I didn't bother turning to look at him. I just wanted to get Sam out of there. Why weren't the other girls following us? Was the skunk making me paranoid?

'Are you OK?' I asked Sam as we got out of earshot.

'Yeah, I think so. Everything's spinning,' she said, slurring.

'What did you take?' I asked.

'Just some coke and alcohol.'

'You sure? Did they give you any pills or put anything in your drink?'

'I don't know . . . I . . . I can't remember,' she said, rubbing her temples, looking out of it.

Leaving the villa, we went over to the outhouses to find Benny talking to Cara and two of the Brazilians in the front room, indicating that Pritz was with the other Brazilian girl in the bedroom. The Russians were nowhere to be seen.

'Hey, Jay, we were wondering if we should wake you up but you seemed so comfy on the lounger,' Benny said, laughing.

I looked at him, wondering if he knew what had been going on.

'And where have you been hiding, Sam?' asked Cara, her voice heavily loaded with innuendo.

Her comment pricked a nerve and I could feel myself getting angry. Why hadn't Cara kept an eye on Sam? She'd allowed Benny's charms to let her forget her friend. I stood there trying to get my thoughts in order before I reacted. I decided this wasn't the time for post-mortems.

'I've just had a call from Max and we've got to meet him at Space to do some filming,' I said.

'Oh, OK,' said Benny. 'I'll get the others and we'll come with you –'

'No,' I said abruptly. Then, calmly, I continued, 'It's OK, I don't want to stop you guys from having your fun.'

Cara looked visibly confused but didn't question it. We prised a fully clothed, horny and severely peeved Pritz off his Brazilian girl, said our quick goodbyes and headed straight out.

I hailed a taxi that was driving past the villa and helped Sam into the back as the others jumped in. As I sat in the front seat, my mind was awash with questions. Had I leapt to conclusions? Maybe there was a reasonable explanation? Sam could have been a willing participant. I couldn't trust myself to figure it out and she was in no state to tell me what had really happened.

Pritz eventually broke the silence. 'I was just about to get lucky with her. Couldn't you leave me behind?'

'Well, you had hours, why did it take you that long?' I said, exasperated.

'We were talking for ages. These chicks love to chat!' Pritz said.

'About?' asked Cara.

'Oh, everything. Brazil. Modelling. Travelling. But, phenomenally, football.'

Cara laughed.

'What? Football's important to us men,' Pritz said.

She didn't reply.

Pritz turned and looked at her. 'Don't be jealous, it's attractive when a girl knows about football.'

'Oh no, I'm not jealous,' she said.

'Well, what then?' he asked.

'You don't actually know, do you?' she said to Pritz.

'Know what, drama queen?' he asked, getting more and more irritated.

'Oh, you boys are so naive!' she said, unable to hold her laughter any longer. 'They weren't girls, they were men. Post-op.'

Pritz's cockiness slipped away in a flash as he sat flabbergasted. I was in shock too. She was clearly pulling our legs. But then she began laying out the evidence: the Adam's apples, their freakishly tall height and their big feet. Silence held court for a moment until the image of the beautiful Brazilian babes shattered into a million pieces.

'Are we really going to Space to film now?' Cara asked me as Pritz sat beside her silently in shock.

'No, we're going home. It was getting late and we've got a flight back to London in a few hours,' I said.

'Good job anyway. I'm battered,' said Pritz, trying to get a normal conversation going again.

'From all the kissing you just did with your fella,' laughed Cara, not willing to let it go that easy.

Pritz looked increasingly distressed. 'I think I need to get to my hotel and sleep.'

'So you can dream about your time in the sack with your Brazilian beauty?'

I looked back at Sam and her eyes were closed as she rested on Cara's shoulder. It was probably going to be something neither of us would mention again, but I was pleased I'd got her out of there. As Cara ribbed Pritz all the way to his hotel drop-off, I decided that, for better and worse, Ibiza had well and truly lived up to its reputation.

27
HERE I COME
(BROADER THAN BROADWAY)

The bank holiday weekend at the end of August meant one thing in London: Notting Hill Carnival. In one square mile or so, musical styles changed from street to street, flitting between hip hop, R&B, reggae, dancehall, bashment, soca, garage, drum and bass and many more. Half of the Production department were here filming, and mainly partying, while the rest were at the festivals in Edinburgh, filming and mainly laughing.

Having covered the world of dance music a few weeks earlier in Ibiza, this time we were putting our finger on the pulse of the UK's 'urban' music scene – past, present and future. Especially as it was being played out locally on The Beat's doorstep. I'd have loved a long weekend off to see Sophia and my family and friends, but Max put a stop to that by taking on extra work to force his promotion. I didn't put up a huge fight as it was good for me to impress the execs too. Plus I wanted to cash in my chips for a bigger prize – time off to go to New York with Sophia for my birthday at the start of October.

I hadn't asked Max yet but this was as perfect a time as any, as he was in a good mood thanks to the Carnival's atmosphere. Sam was meant to film with us but had got Sonya to stand in at the last minute instead, claiming she was sick. I was worried she was still upset about what had happened in Ibiza but I wasn't sure if I should be the one to bring it up.

Sonya walked ahead with PJ through a throng of people waving colourful flags and blowing whistles. Jamaica had the biggest showing, but Trinidad, Barbados, St Lucia and Antigua weren't too far behind.

'So do you think I can go?' I asked loudly, to ensure I was heard.

'I'm not sure. Isn't that at the end of your internship?' he replied.

'Yeah, but . . .'

'Well, I might need you for a handover to your replacement,' he said.

The suggestion made my heart sink. I'd been hoping he'd give me some good news about getting the permanent position.

'It's just that I haven't had any time off in the last five months and . . . it's my birthday,' I said feebly, feeling about eight years old.

'You haven't?' he asked. He thought about it. 'Are you sure?' He was clearly bluffing.

'Yes, I'm sure,' I said.

'Hmmm. Well, I suppose you should –'

'Thanks, Max,' I said, cutting him off before any 'but'.

'. . . otherwise HR will give me shit. I can't ask for an increased role as a manager if it looks like I can't manage,' he said philosophically.

'So will you sign it off next week?' I asked enthusiastically.

He looked slightly offended. 'Isn't my word good enough?'

No, I thought. I wanted it in writing in case he cancelled it the day before because 'Something had come up'. I quickly thought on my feet. 'Course it is. I just thought maybe HR would want it?'

The plan for today was to shoot a package for next week's show and finish by filming at The Beat's carnival party. We started by following the trucks that pulled the floats on the official carnival route down Ladbroke Grove. Some consisted of just huge speakers blaring out music while others had steel bands playing calypso and soca as performers of all ages danced in bright, extravagant costumes.

We headed to the inner streets of the carnival to judge who had the best sound stage. The annual battle was between the radio stations, pirates and commercial alike. Size didn't matter. A small station like Irie FM had as good a chance as anyone to bring down a giant like Radio 1. It was all about how well the DJ and MC controlled the crowd. The winner would be judged on who could make the kids shack out, bounce and two-step to the year's anthems.

At the centre of the carnival there was a constant buzz, with an equally hyped-up crowd – musical aficionados of the highest calibre – who knew the words to every song and reacted to every 'puuuuuuullll uppppppp'. Filming in public with PJ was a headache at the best of times, but today it was much worse. As soon as he began his link, his name would be called out by some giddy girl or excited fan. He loved the attention and instantly stopped to acknowledge it. Kids were coming up to him begging to be on camera, asking for autographs and taking pictures.

'This is a bloody nightmare,' said Max, realizing we were way behind schedule.

'Maybe we should have used Isabel,' I said. She'd been texting me during the day, and was looking forward to filming at the party later and discussing her outfit.

He twitched as I suggested it. 'Why do you care so much?' he snapped back.

'I don't. I'm just saying she's fairly unknown and might not get this level of attention.'

He paused as my words ran through his head. 'That's not what I've heard.'

'What do you mean?' I said.

'Don't think I don't notice. I know what's going on.'

'Notice what?' I asked, wondering what he thought he knew.

He ignored my question. 'Well, she's a newbie like you, she wouldn't be able to deliver in this kind of crowd.'

I got defensive at the implied put-down of my skills. 'And PJ's doing that much better? We haven't filmed in the last fifteen minutes.' As soon as it left my mouth I realized I shouldn't have said it. It got his back up, majorly.

'Are you saying you know better than me?' he snapped again.

'No, of course not. I was –'

'Well, why don't you do something useful instead of being a know-it-all?'

'I didn't mean anything by it,' I said, trying to defuse his anger but sounding like a little mouse. Had I just kissed NYC goodbye?

Eventually, tired and succumbing to the intoxicating smell of food, we huddled in a quiet corner away from the crowds to eat. We all tucked into a huge plate each of jerk chicken and curried goat with rice and peas, with lashings of Encona sauce, from a stall we'd just filmed at. My tastebuds tingled with every delicious spoonful I wolfed down. We were standing near a small sound system banging out Shyne's new tune. As Barrington Levy dropped his famous ad-libs of 'Shiddddlydidddlyddiddlywiddddlydidddlywhoa-seen', big aerosol cans of hairspray were pressed and lighters set fire to the gases, sending out huge flames above the crowds that excited the boys but horrified the girls with large weaves.

'Wouldn't it be great if I could actually say what we're all thinking?' said PJ, referring to the footage we'd taken earlier of a slightly podgy twelve-year-old girl who'd sung 'Viva Forever' even better than the Spice Girls, showcasing her talent to camera.

'No, it wouldn't! You can't,' said Sonya in shock.

'That girl needs honest guidance from someone who knows what they're talking about. Fat singers on the whole don't make it big,' he said, laughing as he tucked into his chicken. 'These other wannabe performers need to hear the truth too.'

Max chimed in. 'I agree. So they don't waste their time.'

'Let's bloody do it . . . let's film it,' said PJ, laughing. 'I'm telling you, it's a ratings winner!' He licked his fingers in delight.

'Not sure people would stand for someone ridiculing a person for trying,' said Sonya.

'Don't underestimate the human gene for mean,' Max cut in, sipping on his bottle of Ting.

'There's lots of talented people out there but the fact is they don't know how to sell themselves or the timing isn't right for the marketplace,' added PJ as they began picking up each other's thought processes with ease, like they'd had this conversation before.

'But real talent will always make it,' said Sonya defiantly.

'Oh yeah?' said PJ. 'I can show you lots of backing vocalists who are better than the main act they support but can't be marketed or just don't have that star-quality X-factor.'

'But lots of artists were told they wouldn't make it and did,' she responded.

'True. Perhaps it was timing, luck, persistence . . .'

'Whatever you do, you just need to ensure you have an ROI in what you're doing,' said Max.

'ROI?' I asked, perplexed.

'Return on investment. You don't plant apple trees in the desert. In anything you do, you're investing your time and talent. So don't waste it, maximize it. Some aspiring artists realized they weren't going to be the big star but diversified their talents into other areas in the music business.'

'Or did they give up? You have to believe that cream rises to the top,' said Sonya, not conceding the point.

As the conversation continued, we found we had an audience around us listening. How long they'd been there was hard to know as we'd been so engrossed in ourselves.

'So how do I get a video on to The Beat then?' asked a kid from the crowd.

PJ laughed. 'I take cash,' he quipped.

'Before we go there, do you have a good song?' asked Max, also laughing.

'What do you mean by good song? Who makes a bad song?' asked another kid.

I nudged Sonya and signalled we should film the conversation. It was an authentic Q&A session that I thought could be useful. As the tag team of PJ and Max got ready to share their pearls of wisdom, Max agreed my plan with a nod.

'You'd be surprised. The successful tracks in UK garage, street music, or any genre for that matter, are the ones that make mainstream radio. It's about vocals, catchy choruses and melodies, not just what bumps on the pirates and in the club,' PJ said.

'But UK garage isn't for Capital Radio, it's for the man dem. We're keeping it real,' shouted another voice from the crowd.

Looking in the direction of where the heckle came from, Max countered, 'Yeah, real broke.' Chortles of laughter went round as he continued, 'The man dem aren't the ones who are going to buy it. This is a business. It's the wider public that need to like it, then buy it. So spitting sixteen bars of fast nonsense might impress your mates on road, but Bonnie in Scotland or Josie in Wales won't have a clue.'

'Which track do you think those two kids know the words to – Biggie's "Warning" or "Mo Money Mo Problems"?' asked PJ.

The crowd laughed.

'Biggie catered for the street, the clubs *and* the charts,' said Max.

Where we were standing increasingly resembled Speakers' Corner in Hyde Park as Max and PJ took turns to preach and teach. Even the two police officers standing by were listening intently. It felt like a painting-by-numbers session, but PJ was enjoying the spotlight far too much to stop and the crowd didn't want him to either.

'The good thing is that it doesn't cost money to write a good song. That's not the be-all and end-all but it puts you in pole position on the grid,' said PJ.

'So what you saying we should do?' said a mean-looking kid with googly eyes standing next to him.

'Are you a singer or rapper?' asked PJ.

'I'm a rapper, like my whole crew from East London,' he said, pointing to an assortment of boys in Starter caps, Nike hoodies and Evisu jeans behind him.

'Have a well-constructed album with both street and radio-friendly singles. You don't need expensive studio time when you can make it in your bedroom,' said PJ.

'Then what?'

'Get a following started through pirate radio, gigging and mix-tapes,' said Max. 'If you stand out, regional radio will pick up on your heat then the nationals will sit up and take notice. At the same time, learn how the industry works and ensure you don't get shafted. Get a good manager, preferably someone who's not trying to make it themselves.'

'What about videos?' the rapper said, as though his mind was a sponge for information.

Max laughed. 'OK, well, when the time is right make your

music video engaging, creative and *original* so people want to see it again and again. It doesn't have to be a big-money thing. It has to be a smart thing. Pharcyde's "Drop" video is a classic to this day even though it didn't have a huge budget,' said Max.

'So try and stay away from filming it on an estate or, if you're a band, in a darkened warehouse – been done to death,' said PJ, pretending to yawn.

'Lots of other things need to come into play, like timing and luck,' Max added, trying to bring everyone back to reality. 'But make sure you're prepared when your moment arrives.'

'That's us, you get me, blud,' said one of the kids.

'No bluds. Please, no bluds,' said Max immediately. 'You need to answer articulately for the nice man from the *Guardian*. Start speaking street slang for your radio interview at Capital FM and you'll be blowing your chances.'

PJ nodded. 'Be your charismatic self and have your answers prepared. Don't sit there umming and ahhing.' He pointed to one of the kids. 'What's your favourite colour?'

The startled kid look petrified and blurted out, 'Red.'

PJ frowned. Immediately the rapper kid beside him said, 'My favourite colour is red because it's the same as my favourite football team!'

PJ applauded. 'Great back reference, you made it interesting.'

'So when I get all that done, *then* will you play my video on *Total BEATS*?' the kid asked, with an enigmatic smile that suddenly made him look less threatening.

'Of course, I'll play it,' PJ said without flinching. 'But it better be good. Deal?' He shook hands with the kid.

'You saw this, yeah. You mans saw this!' shouted the rapper, looking round at his witnesses. 'He's gonna play my video on The Beat!'

'Brapp, brapp,' came more cries from the hyped-up crowd as a police helicopter soared above and the crowd eventually started to disperse.

With filming done, the four of us walked towards Royal Oak station where our Uncle Lee was waiting. First we were off to Nando's for a quick bite. After that we'd be on our way to The Beat carnival party at The Hippodrome in central London where we'd meet up with the rest of the Production department to film and party. My phone beeped with a text message as Max and I walked together.

'Isabel says she hasn't heard from you and wants to know what time you want her tonight,' I told Max, putting my phone back in my pocket.

He didn't respond. I was about to ask him again when he stopped me in my tracks. 'I don't think I'm going to need her.'

What? I thought. *You've decided this just a few hours away from the party?*

'Who's going to do the vox-pops?'

'I'm sure we'll find someone else,' he said calmly.

I felt defensive for her. 'But what's wrong with Isabel?'

'I don't need a reason, Jay,' he replied, still unsettlingly calm. 'Am I the boss or are you? If I were you, I'd spend less time worrying about Isabel's job and more time concentrating on your own.'

I stayed quiet as we took the long walk back through the crowd, my phone beeping with messages that I dared not answer in front of 'the boss'. Suddenly, not going to New York was the least of my worries.

28
YOU GOT ME

Max was in a rush as we left the studio for an important meeting in town and said he wouldn't be back. He didn't even bother coming upstairs to go through the big box of clothes that had arrived from Diesel for PJ, as was customary. He left me to cover, which meant I got first dibs on a leather jacket.

I'd kept a low profile with Max in recent weeks since Carnival. Isabel was constantly asking me to pass on her messages to him, but I just didn't want to get involved. Once I'd said that, our text tennis stopped. But what did she want me to do? I was hanging by a thread myself.

'What's the drama in the Eighties meeting room about?' I asked James III, seeing all the suits congregated in there.

I had interrupted him reading *Rolling Stone* and whistling 'Here Comes Santa Claus', with his feet up on his desk. 'Senior management are in there with some distressed mother,' he said.

'Why?'

'Her daughter tried to commit suicide after some kids in her class called her ugly.'

I raised my eyebrows. 'Wow, bit over the top, isn't it?'

'Well, she reckons they kept singing "U.G.L.Y." by Daphne and Celeste at her daughter and they did it so much that she cut her wrists in the school toilets with a scalpel. It made the news and all the talk-show hosts and tabloids are up in arms.'

'So, what's that got to do with us?' I could see how the mother would be distressed, but still wasn't making any links.

'Apparently it's on high rotation on the playlist and been playing over and over on the request show,' he explained.

'Er, well, that's unfortunate, but it's not our fault.'

'Well, she and her high-priced lawyer husband seem to think differently about The Beat's influence,' he said, licking his finger and flicking to the next page. 'Apparently the head of PR thought it would be good crisis management if the suits obliged them with a meeting and at least paid them lip service.'

James III switched to *MOJO* magazine, saying, 'It's this week's gripe. Next week it'll be an MP saying that rap videos are to blame for youth crime and after that some religious group will be claiming that semi-naked dance videos lead to under-age sex. The Beat is the cause of *all* our social ills.' Then he started humming the words to 'U.G.L.Y.' absent-mindedly.

The girls were all out on shoots (or in Sam's case at her grandmother's funeral in Scotland) so me and James III had the run of the place. I was standing at my desk organizing tapes as we listened to *The Dark Side of the Moon* when I felt someone watching me. I looked up. From across the department the head of Production, the Minister, was looking at me. He stood by the printer waiting for something, so I did what I did best when I wanted to make an impression: I panicked. My face went red and I half-heartedly stuck my hand up to acknowledge him, only for it to come across like I was hailing Adolf Hitler.

Embarrassed, I quickly sat down in my chair and picked up my phone, pretending someone had called. James III saw the whole thing and burst out laughing, filling the department with his chuckling. I looked up again and the Minister was gone.

'Shut up, you arse!' I said without opening my mouth, barely moving my lips.

'That was brilliant,' he choked as the laughter diminished in his throat.

'I can't help it, he makes me nervous,' I confessed.

'Nervous of what?' he asked. 'You worry too much, Merchant.'

James III and I were probably neck and neck for the permanent job, and I was full of admiration for his supreme confidence. Not to mention his popularity. He was a loveable rogue liked by the women – and the men – in the office. 'So who are you trying to sleep with this week to get to the top?' I asked, regaining my composure.

'I wish. Everyone senior here's a bloke and I don't live on that side of the Pennines.'

'Well, our internships are up in a few weeks. Who do you think's going to get the permanent job then?'

He looked at me confidently. 'Cara.'

'What?' I replied, immediately offended he hadn't said my name, but also disagreeing with him. 'No way.'

'The Doc loves her.'

'One plus one don't make eleven,' I said, poo-pooing his theory.

'She's the one to watch cos *you're* not a threat to me,' he said brazenly.

I gave him a half-smile. 'Gee, thanks!'

'Anyway,' he said, 'there are more important questions. Like, who would you rather . . . Wonder Woman or Catwoman?'

I couldn't help but smile. 'Wonder Woman, definitely.'

After exhausting a debate on whether it was wrong to fancy a comic-book character and then counting down the top five most shaggable cartoon women (Wonder Woman, Jessica, Wilma, Marge and Chun-Li), I left the office to spend some time with Sophia. We were going to book our trip to New York. Max hadn't signed it off, but I was trusting that his word really was good enough.

Sophia and I met outside her house of worship, Topshop, before we left to spend the day at mine. Even though we'd spoken on the phone and met up a few times since her friend's barbecue, the air hadn't been cleared and neither of us was willing to back down. But today we were doing a great job of pretending it had never happened and being civil, despite the huge elephant following us everywhere.

After booking our flights and a hotel, we sat on my bed and watched a DVD on my new widescreen Sony TV, which had come courtesy of Exposed PR, care of Max, who already had three. We ate junk food and drank bottle after bottle of Budweiser. It seemed like the elephant had left the room and we were getting on like old times.

'Look at all this *stuff*, Jay!' Sophia exclaimed, staring around my room.

CDs had piled up into stacks and it looked like a model

of the New York skyline. There were more goodies dotted around the place: VIP passes to concerts, crew lanyards for The Beat parties, pictures of me posing with famous people, free DVDs, piles of new clothes, boxes of fresh trainers and a heap of gadgets, half of which were still unopened. Soon I'd have to convert Pritz's room into my storage facility and move him into the bathroom.

'Yeah, pretty amazing, huh?' I felt like the previous months of my life were on display in front of us.

With not much else left to do, and under the influence of the *Who is Jill Scott?* album, we eventually did what we hadn't done in ages. It was awkward at first and lacked any real connection. But soon normality returned as we committed properly, signalling we'd both given in a little to the other.

It was late as we lay hungry, naked and exhausted. Goswell Road was quiet, the silence only interrupted by the sound of the occasional bus. As I twisted round from lying on my side to my back, I couldn't help but let off a fart.

'It was the beer!' I said, trying to cover my embarrassment and holding the quilt down to stop anything potent escaping.

Sophia tugged at the duvet. 'I've smelt them before, RV,' she said, laughing at my reaction.

'What?!' I exclaimed, turning my head round to her sharply.

'When you're asleep. Everyone lets rip then.'

'What? No, I don't! Do I?'

The look on Sophia's face told me she wasn't exaggerating.

'OK, so sleep is totally different. We've never farted in front of each other.'

'That's cos I'm a girl,' she said.

I laughed. 'Yeah, so what?'

'OK, well next time I'll fart on your belly then so you can feel it!'

My knee-jerk reaction was immediate. 'Urgh, that's disgusting!'

'What? You won't let me fart on your belly? I thought you loved me,' she said, knowing she'd successfully wound me up. Then she reached for some CDs from the nearest pile and began asking me about each album as she flicked through them. I impressed myself with how much I knew.

'So all you see, day in day out at your desk, are hot, naked women?' she said, looking back down at an album cover.

'No, I don't think HR would let the women walk around the office like that,' I joked, twisting round to face her.

'No, silly, I meant on The Beat.'

I immediately suspected a trap. I wasn't sure if it was one or not but I wanted to avoid any last-minute banana peels that could cause today to go horribly wrong. 'I don't know. I don't really watch it. It's just on in the background.'

'So when you watch videos of these women, do you compare them to me?' she asked quietly.

There it was. 'What? No,' I said automatically, not even taking time to ponder.

'So do I look as sexy as . . . Beyoncé?' she asked tentatively, knowing she was one of my favourites.

'Much more, LV, and you don't even have a personal trainer.'

We laughed, and I hoped I'd passed the test. Just then I heard the front door being opened carefully. Pritz was home.

I could hear him trying to tiptoe quietly past but, being drunk, he wasn't doing a great job of it.

'I can hear you. Do you have to be so loud?' I said sarcastically.

'Sorry,' he slurred.

'I might have a woman in here,' I said, and Sophia sniggered.

'That's OK, it can only be one of two.'

I froze. I hadn't really thought before I spoke, and now Pritz was about to start the Third World War.

'Is it Sophia or your mum?' he said as he burst in, holding a flat takeaway box, sending Sophia scrambling to pull up the duvet. 'Who wants pizza?'

As I grabbed a slice, I noticed the cartoon of a smiling cowboy on the front.

'You went to Fancy,' I said, laughing.

Fancy Pizza and Burgers was Pritz's version of Uncle Lee. When he'd spent all but £10 of his money at the strip club in Euston and couldn't find an ATM, he would trudge a few streets down to Fancy. Standing across the road, he'd hit '5' on his speed-dial and ask for a pizza to be delivered to our flat. Then, waiting outside the shop, he'd convince the Sri Lankan deliveryman to let him sit in the passenger seat and cadge a lift all the way home. 'We're all brothers, brother!' he'd cajole.

'I'm doing something to save our planet from unnecessary emissions,' he explained. 'Anyway, I'm going to leave you lovebirds alone. I've got to be up in four hours to work in front of six computer screens and keep the world rotating.' He gave us a drunken rendition of 'So Long, Farewell' from *The Sound of Music* as he slowly departed, doing the Robot.

As Sophia and I lay spooning in a tight embrace, I felt the need to say something important before we fell asleep. It had been a good day for both of us and it was like when we first started going out. Friendship with fun. I knew I had to make things work.

'Babe, I've been thinking,' I said, whispering into her ear.

'About what?' she asked, sounding like she was dozing off.

'About us. About why we're good together. The reason why you're my LV.'

She squeezed my arm but lay silently, waiting to hear what I was going to say. I couldn't see her reaction but didn't let that stop me.

'I want our relationship to grow. I want to commit to you like I've never committed to anyone before. I can't believe I'm about to say this, but . . .' I paused, took a deep breath, smiled and said, 'LV, you can fart on my belly any time.'

29
TOCCATA AND FUGUE

After months of disinterest by the public at large, and the usual rumours that the Olympic stadium wouldn't be ready in time, the Games of the XXVII Olympiad arrived in Sydney with a bang. It didn't have everyone in the office as enthralled as the football in June had, but it was nice to have something other than the usual Beat playlist on the TV for the next two weeks.

I'd started emailing people at The Beat in New York for advice on where to go while Sophia and I were there for my birthday. The responses were phenomenal. My mind boggled with the potential for future holidays when I saw the world-wide network of The Beat offices on the internal mailing list. 'The Family' covered every corner of the world, giving access to local knowledge and tips like a personal Rough Guide.

I turned my mind to some of the admin that had been piling up, finally handing in months' worth of unclaimed expenses to Gwyneth, the Production manager. After that, and more excitingly, I ordered kit for a shoot. But this wasn't just a shoot for some new hip-hop night at Cargo in Old Street. No, we were flying out to Miami in a few days to interview Will Smith. PJ had a good relationship with him and wanted an exclusive interview about his upcoming role in the Muhammad Ali biopic, and about the rumours that he wanted to be the first black President of America. The film studio were flying us over to give the film some pre-release exposure. Then, seeing as we were already there, we'd tagged on a trip to Las Vegas, courtesy of the MOBO Awards, to interview their host, Lisa 'Left Eye' Lopes, in advance of the event in London.

It was lunchtime when I got a call from Max asking me to join him at Osteria Basilico, the Italian restaurant a few roads away from The Beat. He'd been spending a lot of time out of the office recently in edits while I manned the ship, but why was he summoning me there?

A voice immediately popped into my head. It was a slightly anxious Dave Grohl.

Oh no, are we in trouble? he said.

No, I've done everything he's asked for, I replied calmly.

He's not going to tell you you can't go to Miami, is he? said Dave.

I thought back to the time earlier in the year when I was left behind on the Denmark trip in favour of Hugh and Oli.

It's too late – the tickets are booked and he needs me to film this time, I said. Then I started doubting myself. *Maybe he wasn't happy with the way I filmed at the last Beat party?*

No, it can't be that, he'd have shouted at you over the phone, said Dave, knowing Max well. *Are we going to get fired?*

Surely we'd be in a meeting room with HR instead of a restaurant, I replied, thinking it through calmly.

What could it be then? said Dave, running out of plausible suggestions.

I kept racking my brains.

Has he broken up with Leila? I wondered. *Hold on, I know what it could be,* I thought as a possibility grew in my head. *The permanent position!*

Oh yeah, that's it! said Dave, jumping around in my head like a hyperactive child who'd just solved a riddle. *It explains the restaurant. He's going to buy lunch to celebrate!*

I couldn't help but do an impression of Bill & Ted on my air guitar at the thought.

I hurled myself out of my seat, feeling the urge to vomit with excitement before I sprinted down the stairs and through the revolving doors. I ran up to the door of the restaurant, then slowed down, not wanting to seem too ruffled. Max waved me to join him at a table at the back of the restaurant, which was empty except for a teenage girl with a piercing above her lip and long flowing black hair by the front window arguing with her boyfriend.

'How was the edit?' I asked as I sat down.

Max stared at the menu. 'The editor is finishing it off, so I thought I'd meet you for lunch,' he said distractedly, as if we met up like this regularly.

'Oh, OK. I thought something was wrong,' I said, hoping I could lead him to reveal more.

'Everything's fine.'

I picked up my menu and concentrated on choosing something. Maybe he was saving the good news until we'd eaten.

We ordered our food and drinks and, bizarrely, made

small talk. When they brought our food I was barely able to eat, I was so filled with excitement. *Patience*, I told myself.

'So, Jay, there *is* a reason why I've called you here,' Max admitted as he took a sip from his post-meal espresso.

I knew it, Dave said, reappearing inside my head. *Here it comes. Be cool.*

'I didn't want to talk about it in the office because I felt it would be better somewhere private.'

I sat still, trying to hold a straight face but pinning back a smile that was dying to get out.

'I just want you to know I've appreciated how you've worked tremendously hard these last few months. You've put up with my shit and I know you've made plenty of sacrifices in your personal life to ensure we deliver the best we can. I've had glowing reports from everyone you've worked with, whether at The Beat or outside.'

Hearing him say those words was like reading a straight-A report card from school. At that moment I had more glow than Afro Sheen. All of a sudden the last five and a half months felt worth it. I had made it to the end of the marathon in first place and now I was about to do my final lap in the stadium to applause from the crowd!

'I have some news and I wanted you to hear it from me before you hear it from someone else. I'm leaving.'

The false-start gun went off in my head. My eyes bulged and my jaw dropped. 'What?' I said in a whispery voice as my throat went dry.

'Yeah. It's time for me to make like a bad cheque and bounce,' he said brazenly.

'Why are you . . . ? But why would you . . . ?' I was dazed and couldn't complete a sentence.

He smiled and let out a big sigh. 'There're so many reasons, Jay. Where do I begin? Shit pay. Been here since I left school. Broken promises. But, worst of all, the poli-tricks.'

'Poli-tricks?' I said, looking confused.

'Trust me, I shield you from it, but it's all around. You don't see it because you're just an intern. You don't see how shady these people are.'

Who are 'these people'? I thought. Was he just bitter about something or were things really as he said? I couldn't tell. Everyone in the office seemed so nice. Surely he was just frustrated and overworked.

'Why do you think Hugh and Oli left? The best people don't stay behind, just the backstabbers and brown-nosers. All these years and I'm only getting that now.'

'But why . . . ?'

'Because the Minister eventually wants to bring in his mates from outside, and he knows he can't do it while the old guard are here. He's just fucking power hungry,' Max finished with conviction.

The Minister? I thought as the plot thickened. 'So why are you going?' I asked, still trying to understand it all.

'I want a senior role but he's blocking me. I was promised it when you started in April. That's why I took on so much work, to prove something to them. I've slogged all this time and for nothing. Fuck that,' he said, his voice carrying to the arguing couple, who paused for a minute before contin-uing their own heated discussion.

'It's getting way too corporate because of these assholes, and The Beat's losing its edge. The *Titanic*'s sinking. I want to get into a lifeboat before it's too late.'

I was just about keeping up with him as he vented months of built-up frustration.

'So before they try and screw me without the Vaseline, I'm leaving. On my terms. With my head high. At least they'll respect me, even if nothing else,' he said with a sense of satisfaction.

My eyes were flitting about as my mind searched for the right questions.

'When are you leaving?' I asked.

'Today's my last day.'

'*What?*' More shocking news was coming out by the minute. 'You're leaving *today*?'

'I handed in my notice three weeks ago,' he said breezily.

Three weeks ago? Why hadn't he told me earlier? I thought we were friends.

'I had a few offers, but I'm going to Sky TV because, well, they listen.'

So that's why he'd had so many meetings in town recently. I'd thought he was editing.

'I have one week off, starting tomorrow, then I take up my new job. I can't live in Neverland any more, Jay. Especially now that the Lost Boys have gone,' he added, clearly disappointed that Hugh and Oli had left on top of everything else.

'What about Miami? What about Vegas?' I said in quick succession.

'Mate, those places aren't going anywhere and seeing

them isn't paying my bills. I've got a kid and that's got to be my priority.'

I sat in shock, trying to get answers from Max to the questions that kept popping out of my mouth like a jack-in-the-box. 'What about the shows?'

'Fuck the shows. That's the Minister's burden now.'

'But what about PJ?'

'He's a big boy. He can handle it,' he said.

We sat quietly as I ran out of questions.

After a period of calm, Max went on reflectively. 'You know what pisses me off? I've put so much into this place and for what? It's my own fault I got sucked in,' he said, staring down while running his finger around the rim of his espresso cup. 'That's why I'm telling you, at the next place you go to, work hard but don't get attached. Make your money, learn what you have to then move on to the next challenge. Football players aren't dumb.'

It was clearly an epiphany he'd seen in the rear-view mirror instead of the windscreen. I could see the hurt in his eyes. Even Max wasn't that good at hiding things. Then something suddenly occurred to me. 'But what about me?'

'Well, I assume you'll stay till the end of the month, then that's it – your contract's up. Time for you to head into the big bad world as well,' he said.

I felt like my Achilles tendon had snapped just metres from the finish line, and the pain was about to engulf me. I sat there stunned as I started thinking about my bleak future. I'd have to start looking for a new job and if I didn't get one I'd soon have to move back home. I couldn't go back to being a new graduate, unemployed for months at a time.

But worse than that was the let-down: I had honestly thought I had the permanent job in the bag.

'Look, it's not the end of the world,' Max continued, seeing the shock on my face.

I sat still, looking down at the pasta sauce that had soaked into the tablecloth.

After a long silence, Max left money on the table for the bill and got up to leave. 'What can I say, mate? Themutha-frikkinbeat.'

30
KEEP ON MOVIN'

I stood in the Virgin Atlantic check-in area at Heathrow, waiting for PJ who sauntered across the polished floor to me.

'You checked in yet, mate?' he asked, barely looking up while reading the text messages on his phone.

'No, I was waiting for you,' I said, like 'duhh'.

'What? You should have checked in – I'm going left when I get on the plane.'

I was puzzled. 'What do you mean?'

'Upper Class,' he said, like 'duhh'.

'And me?'

'You go right,' he said, stone cold like the wrestler Steve Austin.

I headed to the Economy check-in queue, which was long. PJ meanwhile went straight to the gorgeous check-in girl behind the Upper Class desk and within two minutes flat had his boarding pass in his hand. When I finally got to the front, I tried flirting with my check-in girl. She put me in 58A. Just 57 rows behind PJ with enough legroom to swing an ant.

Once through Security, I didn't even have a chance to explore the shops to buy a gift for Sophia as the line on the departures board for Miami started to flash 'BOARDING'. I ran towards the gate to find yet another queue of people waiting to board the plane. Ahead of me, PJ was walking past everyone to the fast-track boarding line, chatting away to a leggy model. As I stood at the back of the crowd, my phone started ringing.

'Hello, this is Terry Perkins.'

What did the head of Production want from me? 'Hi, er, Min . . . Terry . . . I'm just about to board my plane,' I stammered.

'You off on holiday?' he asked.

'No, I'm going on a shoot with PJ,' I replied. Did Max not tell him?

'I see. Where are you boys swanning off to this time?' he said in a disapproving tone.

'Miami,' I said anxiously. *Should I tell him about Vegas too?* I wondered, then decided better not.

'So it *is* a holiday then,' he said sarcastically.

I made a vain attempt to defend the trip. 'We have an exclusive interview with Will Smith.'

'Does he still make music?' he asked.

I was surprised. *You're leading a TV music channel and you don't know?* 'Er, yes, he released *Willennium* last year,' I said.

'Right. Very funny. Anyway, as I'm sure you know, Max has left the company. We're having a big restructure at The Beat to move the company forward and I'm going to be more hands-on. I'm looking to change strategy and focus by scrapping some shows, because, well, they just don't work for me.'

For you? But you're a forty-something-year-old unmarried man who walks with a freakishly long stride. You probably don't even know *any kids*, I thought.

'*Total BEATS* is going to be one of those shows,' he said before I could respond. He went on to explain that, now that Max had gone, without a producer on board the show wasn't viable any longer. Then he told me he wasn't sure what to do with PJ, who still had a hefty contract that would need to be bought out. I didn't know why he was telling me all this.

'What about the viewers?' I asked.

He laughed incredulously. 'Wake up, there's a ratings war going on. Besides, the viewers won't care so long as we give them some other crap to watch.'

'And me?' I asked tentatively.

'Well, your contract runs out at the end of the month,' he said without hesitation.

'What about the other interns?' I asked.

'That doesn't concern you,' he said, clearly irritated by my questions.

'*Last call for passengers on the Virgin flight to Miami*,' said a woman's voice over the tannoy.

'Sounds like you've got to go and so do I. We'll speak later.'

'OK, bye –' He'd already hung up the phone.

Boarding, I took my right turn, quickly walked to the back and collapsed in my seat. I couldn't believe how effectively the last twenty-four hours had knocked the stuffing out of me, with one shock after another. My world was crumbling. I couldn't even think of what to do next.

'Excuse me, sir, are you, Jay Merchant?' asked the stewardess, accompanied by a member of ground staff in a bright yellow vest.

'Yes,' I said, looking up and thinking, *Oh, what now?*

'Can you follow us please, sir?' she said in a serious tone.

I got up and a sea of heads turned to look at me. I went red in the face. Had the Minister managed to get me taken off the flight and sent back to the office?

'Do I need to bring my bags?' I asked.

'Yes, please, sir,' she said, turning and walking off.

I grabbed my stuff and marched behind her, but we didn't head out of the door. Instead we walked past everyone until I got to a grinning PJ in Upper Class.

'Jay, welcome to the left! Take a seat behind me. So glad you could join us. This is Christy,' he said, pointing to the woman sat next to him. 'She's on her way to a modelling shoot. And this lovely lady who's upgraded you is Lucy. She'll be joining us with the other stewardesses pool-side at the Delano.'

The recent bad news I'd received completely left my mind as I behaved like it was my first time on a plane, pressing seat buttons back and forth while sipping champagne. I guessed this would probably be my first, and last, flight in Upper Class. PJ, on the other hand, was a pro, regularly flown by record labels or film studios to see artists in concert or film premieres. He had more air miles than an astronaut.

A few episodes of *The Sopranos* later, PJ had got bored of trying to convince the model to join the mile-high club, so he came and sat next to me. As he flicked through *GQ*, I thought I'd ask him the obvious question.

'So I take it you know about Max's news?' I asked, eating my eleventh Ferrero Rocher of the flight.

'Yeah, I found out last week. I'm pissed at him for not telling me earlier, but I understand.'

I was shocked he was so calm. 'You do?'

'Yeah, they've treated him like shit in that place for years. He always threatened to leave, but it looks like the boy's finally grown some and done it.'

'What about the shows?' I asked.

'Well, that's what I wanted to talk to you about,' he said, unwrapping a chocolate. 'I think we should carry on producing them.'

'What?' I exclaimed. '*We*?'

'I'm game, so why not? You're young, ambitious and clearly very talented.'

It was weird hearing praise from PJ when I was used to being the butt of his jokes. I wasn't sure how to take it. Suddenly the phone call I'd had with the Minister came flooding back. Surely PJ already knew about the show being axed? He must have assumed that I didn't, and was trying to be nice.

'But I just spoke to the Minister before I got on the plane,' I said. 'It sounds like he's going to cancel the shows.'

PJ suddenly looked like he was experiencing cabin sickness. He clearly didn't know. He suddenly sank back into his chair deep in thought. After several moments he finally spoke.

'Bastard!' he said. 'This guy wants to take my show off? *My* show?'

'I think they want reality-lead stuff,' I said, recalling the rumours.

'Screw reality. What about the music? That's what The Beat's about.'

He continued to scatter rhetorical questions in my direction. The shock of it all was clearly getting to him. I stayed quiet and let him vent.

'And all this right now, just as I'm about to go for Radio 1,' he said, rubbing his temples. 'I'm speaking to my agent when we get to Miami. We'll see.'

He got up and went back to his seat. I watched him get out a pen and pad and start scribbling on it. The model next to him had suddenly lost her appeal.

I continued watching TV and eating chocolates, when he suddenly jumped back to join me half an hour later.

'You and I *can* do it together,' he said with more gusto than before.

I took off my headphones. 'What?'

'Look, I'll come into the office and write scripts with you. You can produce and direct the show,' he said.

'But I've never directed before,' I said fearfully.

'Come on, Jay, why did you join The Beat? To be an intern forever? Step up! This is what The Beat's all about: learning. You've just been given a ticket to the Fast Track,' he said unswervingly.

'But I'd be –'

'Exactly: paid to learn. Do you know how many people would kill to have your opportunity?' he asked with a serious look in his eyes.

'Yeah, but it's a lot –'

Quickly cutting me off he said, 'You're right, it is a lot to be in a job where we make the rules up as we go.'

'I don't want to fuck it up and let you down,' I said, clamming up.

'You won't,' he replied. 'Listen, Jay, they want us to fail. They want us off air. So let's prove to them we can do it. Prove to *yourself* that you can do this,' he added, knowing the argument would appeal.

But his plans didn't match mine. Was he mad? I couldn't produce two shows alone and make them *properly*. I was just an intern. What if all I did was embarrass myself? I'd never work in the industry again. But PJ made it sound so simple and easy, and I knew I'd be mad to just turn it down without serious thought.

'Will I get a pay increase?' I asked.

'I'm sure we can arrange that. But it's not about the money, Jay, it's about the opportunity. Are you gonna grab it with both hands or let it slip through your fingers and then regret it for the rest of your life? What are you going to do outside of The Beat – go and look for another job? How long will that take? You have the opportunity to make one for yourself here and now.'

He was very good. He was listing very good and reasonable points and he didn't need to read it off an autocue.

'Let me think about it, PJ. It's a lot of work. I don't want to let anyone down. Let *myself* down,' I said.

'Look, we owe it to a lot of people to keep this show going. These execs might not care but the kids at home will. We're doing it for them.'

I knew he was chatting me up like I was a Virgin stewardess but it seemed like I had something more to gain than just a quickie. My other options weren't good. In fact there were no other options on the table. This was the chance of a lifetime. But as we flew on towards Miami I became increasingly sceptical I could pull it off, as the voice in my head reminded me that if the last five and a half months had hurt, the next few weeks would be unbearable.

31
SWEET DREAMS
(ARE MADE OF THIS)

PJ and I spent the next few days enjoying South Beach, Miami. We were chilling by our luxurious pool at the Delano with the stewardesses by day, and clubbing by night. The day before we were due to fly out to Vegas we caught up with Will Smith. He was on great form with PJ and produced an entertaining and hilarious interview that the European regions would lap up when we got back. Things had gone so well, we were invited to eat dinner with him later that night.

This was my first time in Miami and, staring out of the window of the restaurant, I was like a spectator at a tennis match, watching beautiful women walk by. Here Mother Nature was like Ben and Jerry, mixing all the flavours together with jaw-dropping results. In comparison, ice cream back home was just chocolate, vanilla and strawberry.

Dinner was an out-of-body experience which I spent listening intently as PJ talked to Will and his manager. But I snapped back to reality as the food arrived. The manager of the restaurant was trying his hardest to impress, laying on a great feast of sushi and sashimi for Will, who'd said he wanted to increase the protein in his diet to bulk up for his role as Muhammad Ali.

Seafood: I didn't like looking at it let alone eating it. Just walking past the counter at Sainsbury's made me want to vomit. Everyone picked up their chopsticks to dig into the yellow-tail sashimi like it was as normal a meal as beans on toast. Seeing the tails on the prawn tempura alone had triggered a gagging reflex that I was doing well to hide.

'Try this, it's amazing,' said PJ, pointing to some pinky-purple slab of raw fish.

Your funeral, I thought. My fingers had fidgeted with the chopsticks enough. I had to dive in. So I went for the smallest piece I could find, decorated with a small jalapeño on top, and placed it calmly in my mouth while holding a glass of water to wash it all down in case of emergency.

As I began to chew, I realized that it didn't taste like, well, fish! Even more surprisingly I actually appreciated the texture. This wasn't like my experiences of fish I'd had as a child: puking after I was forced to eat mackerel, the feeling of which had stayed with me ever since. I was just happy it was staying down and not coming back out as projectile-vomit all over the Fresh Prince of Bel-Air.

After dinner, PJ and I went back to the hotel for a drink at the bar, realizing another night out clubbing would have us in bad shape for the next leg of our journey – Vegas. We'd enjoyed three great days in Miami for only half an hour of work.

'So how was tonight?' he asked.

I began counting the fingers on my right hand. 'Beautiful women, succulent sushi, great stories, getting merry off sake and meeting my childhood hero – what more can I say but fucking amazing!' I said, like a giddy teenager. 'Not bad for a geeky kid from Finchley.'

He smiled. 'This is how it could be all the time if we continue the show. Trips abroad, award ceremonies, movie premieres, concerts, sporting events, freeness, parties, women, meeting the stars. Miami is just the tip of the iceberg,' he went on, trying to entice me to take up the challenge.

I looked around at the people in the bar, who were almost glowing with VIP-status. 'I could get used to this lifestyle.'

'Damn right. These are things mere mortals don't get to see and do. Thanks to The Beat you're in the front row of life-changing events, meeting the icons of our time, with an access-all-areas pass. You're seeing it up close. This isn't a job, this is heaven. How many people have jobs like this? All this just for a few scripts, a day of filming and some editing,' he said, like a lawyer delivering their closing argument.

He made good points but I was still hesitant, aware of the pain that lay ahead. I couldn't even imagine the effect it would have on my relationship with Sophia.

'Don't you get a buzz from meeting these people? I do. Their aura is palpable. I get an energy boost from it. It's the best natural high in the world,' he said dramatically while inhaling through his nose. He was drunk!

I still didn't say anything as I was trying to figure out what was real and what was his sales speech.

'We get to influence people's thoughts and attitudes on a weekly basis,' PJ continued, increasingly slurring his words. 'Sure, some may say it's just music, but in today's terms, it's a religion. I bet there are more people singing songs from the charts than psalms right now. I get more spirituality from listening to music than a preachy sermon. Everyone looks to us now – we're at the pulpit with a congregation that spreads across the world.'

It was amazing he'd brought religion into this. Did he believe it?

Not getting much response from me he changed tack to be more direct. 'Look, Jay, I'm offering you everything –'

I interrupted him before he killed my buzz. 'Shut up. You had me at trips abroad.'

Barely five hours later, in my hotel room, I was woken up by my mobile ringing. I reached over and grabbed it as the clock next to me flashed 6.01 a.m.

'Hello, Jay, this is Terry Perkins again,' said the unforgiving voice at the end of the line.

I know your surname, you don't have to say it every time! I thought.

'Listen, I've spoken to people here and it's going to be more cost effective keeping the shows than getting rid of them. So I'm going to extend your internship – until December only,' he said, adding the last word quickly.

I figured PJ's agent had been on the phone in the intervening hours, making it crystal clear how cost ineffective it would be to get rid of him. I hesitated before I dared to ask, 'Will I get a pay increase?'

'Increase?' He laughed.

I took that to mean 'no'. 'I can't make both shows alone –'

He cut me off. 'All right, I don't want to hear any violins.

I'll get Tola to report to you two days a week, but she'll still be working on her own show with Stuey.'

'And the other interns?' I asked, wanting to know the fate of my friends.

'They're all on rolling monthly contracts till their show budgets run out or until December. Whichever comes first.'

I was slowly waking up as the conversation continued.

'Max's old boss, Robert Johns, will assist you to direct the shows for one week and after that, apparently, you can do it yourself,' he said.

Oh shit, what had PJ been saying?

'OK, yes. Um, thank you for the chance,' I said, trying to sound grateful rather than half asleep. 'Terry, I just remembered, can someone cover me next week? I'm going away to New York for my birthday,' I asked.

He spent less time thinking about it than Elvis choosing between a burger or a salad. 'I think you've had enough holidays recently, don't you? We don't have the manpower or the budget to cover that.'

I tried to figure out what my next move should be. We were playing cards and I'd thought I had a good hand but the dealer now seemed to be in control. There was only one conclusion. 'OK, I'll sort it out,' I said, already imagining how Sophia was going to react. My stomach churned.

The Minister suddenly took a headmaster's tone with me. 'Mister Merchant, do I have to remind you again, there's a ratings war going on. So if anything goes wrong in the coming weeks I'm holding you personally responsible and no amount of pushy agents or anyone else will be able to sweet-talk Doctor Hewson,' he said.

'Sure,' I said nervously, realizing I had inadvertently gone into his bad books.

'And, Jay, one last piece of advice. On my tenth birthday, after I'd cut my cake, my father put his hand on my shoulder and said, "Remember, my son, if you ever need a helping hand, you'll find one at the end of your arm".' He said it raw like Eddie Murphy and then he put the phone down.

I dropped my head back on to the pillow and looked up at the ceiling, reflecting on the conversation.

The hand I'd finally been dealt was even worse. The wage was still shit, the work double, help was short of the mark, my new boss hated me, I was about to cancel my birthday trip so I'd be out-of-pocket and out-of-favour with Sophia. What was I thinking?

With the odds stacked against me, it was stick or twist time, and it seemed that – despite everything – I had decided to twist. All I knew now was that I needed – and more importantly I still *wanted* – that permanent job.

32
HAPPY BIRTHDAY

As I touched back down into London and the autumn cold, I was suffering a combination of jet lag and exhaustion. I'd hardly slept in Miami, and in Vegas, well, it felt like time didn't exist. We were either at the casino gambling PJ's money away, drinking, attending a spectacular show, eating, gambling some more, clubbing or going to a strip club. PJ wouldn't allow me to sleep, suggesting it was best done on the plane back. It was so full-on we'd almost missed the MOBO interview we were there to do.

Walking into my flat, I felt as if I had no sense of direction, literally and metaphorically. For the last week I'd been swept away in the land of fantasy and I still wanted to escape the reality of what lay ahead. Not just getting everything ready for my very first show on my own, but also explaining to Sophia that I wasn't going to New York. We were meant to be flying out on Saturday, the day before my birthday, and today was Thursday. It was hard to figure out which I was least looking forward to.

I left my suitcase by the door and crashed on to the sofa. I wanted to sleep but couldn't. I flicked the TV on to try to get a grip of what had been going on in the world since I'd been gone. American news was just that, American. There was no international coverage, they were completely engrossed in every baby-kissing moment a presidential election year brings.

There was a 'breaking news' graphic on the BBC news channel. After a period of relative calm for the region, it looked as though it was kicking off again in the Middle East. The dysfunctional family of Abraham needed counselling once more. It was followed by news of UK fuel shortages that made me reach for the off-button.

There was no sense in delaying; I had to get the ball rolling on something. Sophia knew Max had left The Beat as I'd told her before I went to the States. But now I had to bring her up to speed with the 'since I've been gone' episodes. I dialled her number and waited for her to answer.

'Babe,' she said. 'You're back! How was it?'

'It was crazy, is all I can say!' I went on to explain the new deal with PJ.

Sophia was excited that I was still in a job, that I'd been given more responsibility and was seeing only the positives.

'It's not that straightforward. There's a lot for me to learn in the next few days before going to the studio. I'm going to have to spend most of my time in the office doing the usual day-to-day stuff, then spend the nights learning how to direct and produce both shows by looking back at old tapes,' I complained.

'Well, let's have fun on our trip and then you can roll up your sleeves and get going when we get back,' she said, still unaware.

I went silent. I wasn't sure how to say it. I opened my

mouth several times but nothing came out as my brain pulled the words back each time. Eventually I spoke.

'That's the thing: we can't go to New York. The Minister won't give me time off,' I said sheepishly, waiting for the backlash.

'What?' she said quietly, ahead of the eruption I knew was coming.

'If I go, I'm basically fired,' I said, trying to explain my reasoning.

'They can't do that!' she yelled.

'Its not they, it's *he*,' I said.

'So our money's wasted? The flights, the hotel, everything?'

'Look, I'm sorry. I'll pay you back for your share,' I said, trying to counter every negative she could think of.

There was an audible sigh at the end of the line. 'That's not the point, Jay. It's not the money.'

'I know, but what do you want me to do?' I asked.

'I've already told all my friends we're going as well,' she said, more to herself than me.

That got my back up. I needed her to see this from my perspective. 'What's that got to do with it? It's either a shitty little holiday to New York or my career!'

'Shitty little holiday?' she gasped.

I cursed inwardly. 'I'm sorry . . . I didn't mean it like that. You know what I mean. This is really important to me in the long run and New York's not going anywhere,' I pleaded.

'I've waited the entire summer to go away with you. I haven't been anywhere while you've swanned off to Holland, Ibiza, Miami, Vegas –'

'Hey, I was working –'

'And I was dying to celebrate your birthday with you,' she finished.

Exhausted, we both fell silent.

'What should I do?' I asked after a long pause. 'You tell me?'

'New York.'

'I'm sorry, babe, but I just can't. I'll make it up to you later in the year. Let things calm down for me. I'll get the Minister on side and get us a trip away somewhere hot and nice from one of my contacts,' I said, hoping that would make up for it.

'You've been promising me it will calm down all year. It doesn't. I'll be at uni and when I get back my parents are planning a family holiday for Christmas.'

'Look, we can figure something out. Just understand I'm really sorry, my hands are tied. I was looking forward to this too, remember? Please support me on this because it's really important to me. This is my dream.' Then with a whispered voice, I said, 'I really don't want to be unemployed again.'

She went quiet on the other end, still seething.

I wasn't sure what else I could say. I wanted to reach through the phone and hug her, as much for my own sake as hers. I didn't have the energy to be fighting the Minister *and* Sophia.

'Shall I call you later?' I asked.

'OK,' she said, sounding flat.

'I love you, much-much,' I added, trying to get a warm reaction.

'I know.' She put the phone down.

I felt so bad, I knew I wouldn't sleep even though I was exhausted from the jet lag. But I didn't have time to sit and wallow; there was work to do. I had to catch up on emails, log tapes from our trip and order previous episodes of the shows to start learning from. I grabbed my keys and headed back out the door.

As I got to the revolving doors at work, people were already leaving the office to go home. The department was empty and not just because Max wasn't there. Even all the televisions were off. For the first time the place seemed to lack any energy or vibe. Had Ad Sales and the Minister finally got their way? Max, Hugh and Oli's desks were already covered with tapes, boxes, magazines, newspapers and competition prizes, wiping away their existence. As I got to my desk and put my bag down I saw the recognizable figure, or should I say the comical stride, of the Minister. He was heading home and gave me a small nod.

Smug fuck, I thought.

I sat down to go through my emails but was constantly interrupted by the other interns. They came by one after the other on their way back from studio recordings and edit suites, busy with party footage from Freshers Week. I should have just written an email of everything that had happened and forwarded it on to all of them. Instead I had to relay every detail to each of them individually.

Eventually the others all left and I was alone at my desk, trying to fight off fatigue and my guilt for cancelling the New York trip. I had sent a couple of texts to Sophia but hadn't heard back yet. I got up to make a coffee in the staff kitchen and noticed I wasn't alone in the building. Pavel, one of the Music Programmers for the UK, was still at his desk, typing away furiously with his headphones on. I walked over towards his cubicle for a chat on the new music videos I'd missed while I was away.

Soon I was back at my computer with a spring in my step and it wasn't just from the coffee I had nearly burnt my tongue on. I started to fly through the backlog of emails and things began to fall into place. I'd have kept going all through the night if my phone hadn't rung at 11.13 p.m. It was Sophia, and by the sounds of it she was in a pub.

'Hey, babe, how are you?' I asked.

'I'm good, nookie monster. Much better,' she said with energy.

'Oh, that's good to hear. I've been feeling so guilty about New York.'

'You don't have to be, Mia's going to help –'

'Well, I have something to put a smile back on your face,' I said, interrupting her.

'Oh my God, are you coming to New York?' she screamed down the phone.

'No. I have a surprise for you on Sunday,' I said. Then my head kicked into gear. 'What do you mean Mia's going to help?' I asked.

She told me that her friend had suggested going in my place. They phoned the travel agent, who pulled some strings and changed our names over so I wouldn't be out of pocket.

'And apparently someone from uni is already out there and has access to his uncle's timeshare in the Hamptons!

The Hamptons, how cool is that?' she said, full of excitement.

What she was suggesting was the perfect solution to the problem. Yet there was a niggling thought in my head. 'But what about my birthday?' I said pitifully.

'I know, babe, I'm sorry. Look, I'll be gone for a bit and you'll be working anyway. We can celebrate when I get back,' she said logically.

'Sure,' I said.

'So you're cool?' she asked.

'Yes, I'm cool, I'm slightly jealous that's all.'

'Babe, you get to go to all these places and I never say anything,' she reminded me.

'Yes, but that's because it's –'

'Work! Yes, I know,' she said sarcastically.

I laughed.

'So what was the surprise?' she asked.

'Oh that, it was nothing. It can wait.'

'OK, let's speak later, RV, gotta go.'

I hung up and tried to get back the energy I'd had before she called. I was pleased that Sophia was getting her holiday but it was true what I'd said – I was a little bit jealous. With a deep sigh, thinking of what lay ahead, I turned back to my computer screen and started going through old scripts.

The next few days blurred one into each other like I was back in Vegas. But without the fun. I had very little time to get my first show ready and know my shit. Added to this was all of Max's work, including picking up his rerouted calls. Independent labels and artist managers would be desperate, and occasionally aggressive, to get their video on the show. Saying 'no' took up sixty per cent of the day.

People were counting on me to succeed. And one person in particular wanted me to fail. That was enough to have me working all hours even though I could barely keep my eyes open. I didn't make it to a London Fashion Week party on Friday night with the other interns and I missed the chance to see a DJ set from Trevor Nelson on Saturday night with my uni mates. But, worst of all, I missed out on Sunday afternoon's birthday roast at my mum's. As I dined alone on a soggy chicken burger, oily chips and flat Coke from KFC, I hoped my hard work was all worth it. *Happy birthday.*

When I needed extra motivation I called up the Minister's face in my mind, hoping he'd change his opinion about me and give me that permanent role. That 'Access All Areas' VIP pass PJ had described. Maybe that's why I was being extra anal. I didn't even ask Tola for help. I could have had some downtime that weekend but I didn't want to take it easy until I'd delivered my first show perfectly.

At 10.58 p.m. on Sunday night I leant back in my chair to watch The Beat at my desk. The surprise I had for Sophia would have to be enjoyed by me alone. I'd told Pavel about the New York debacle and, to try to make things up with Sophia, he had allowed me to choose all the videos for the 'Love 2 Love' slot on the channel. Sophia's favourite songs would be accompanied by messages at the bottom of the screen: 'I'm sorry for messing up. I love you much-much' and 'This one's for the most wonderful gf, from the most sorry bf . . . from RV to LV'. They were hardly poetic but I only had 120 characters to play with. It wasn't much but still more original than a bunch of flowers to say sorry.

As the videos played I tried calling her mobile but it went to answering machine. I hadn't heard from her that day except for a solitary text message saying: 'Happy Birthday, love Sophia xxx'.

As midnight approached the TV screen went to black and all that remained was the infinity icon in the top right corner accompanied by silence. The channel had momentarily frozen. I sat staring at my reflection on the screen. After what felt like an eternity, order was restored and a video began to play. It was now 2 October – no longer my birthday. It had sucked. The best thing about it was that it was over.

I still had lots of work to do but needed a power nap for a few hours so I could wake up at four a.m. and carry on. I headed for the First Aid room and the only bed on offer in the entire building. There was a used condom on the floor but I was too tired to find it disgusting. As I lay down on the blanket, which smelt like disinfectant, my mind was a jumble of videos, links and scripts before I fell fast asleep.

33
NEW YORK, NEW YORK

On the day of my first record without Max, I got into the office at six a.m. to check over both shows' scripts and every last-minute detail. I had barely slept a wink as my overactive mind played tricks on me. I'd dreamt I was late and that the Minister was waiting by my desk with a P45 form, laughing loudly with the other interns. Even now I was safely at work, panic would hit me every so often, thinking I'd forgotten something. I found myself constantly looking over to Max's desk, a habit that was hard to break. I was like a little kid, wobbly without my training wheels.

Whenever things got a bit crazy I'd take the *Sun* newspaper and head to the one place where I could get peace and tranquillity: the toilets. The shows weren't quite right and I was trying to get some clarity. But every time I tried to think of a solution I'd hear someone, well, straining. At first it was annoying but after a short while it became quite funny. After one particular groan and cough, I enquired softly, 'James?'

The cubicle went quiet. I wanted to laugh but didn't want to embarrass the guy. I wasn't getting much done so I pulled up my pants and went to wash my hands. As I did, the door of the other cubicle opened and my face dropped. It was Darth Vader. I quickly averted my gaze from him and began to wash my hands as though everything was normal. The smell from his cubicle started to waft out. I held my breath while looking relaxed and casual but scrubbing my hands furiously. The soap wouldn't wash off quickly enough. As I dried my hands and escaped outside I gulped the fresh air into my lungs and went back to my desk.

Once we got to studio, Tola was floor manager while I sat in the gallery next to Robert Johns, who was directing today's show. Next time it would be me. I watched him work with effortless ease as he commanded the gallery and studio staff like an orchestral conductor. I tried to make notes of what he was doing and saying as he went along but it was impossible to keep up. But it helped to distract me from my nerves and before long the shows were recorded.

Robert and PJ gave me a thumbs-up on the script and were impressed I'd managed to pull it all together. Hopefully the Minister would get a good report. But the proof would be in the pudding; I had to impress everyone with my edit.

After agonizing over a few shots and links I delivered the show at two a.m. and got back to the flat buzzing at the achievement. Thoughts ran around in my head like an athlete doing the 10,000 metres. I couldn't believe I'd made my first show. *I'd made my first show!!* The exhilaration slightly subsided at the thought I would have to go through it all over again the following week but with the added burden of directing. At that moment, not only did I appreciate Max for having done this week after week for all those years, but also how much he'd taught me in just a few months.

As I lay there, filled with a mixture of excitement, fear, joy and trepidation, my phone began to ring unexpectedly. I was almost too scared to look in case it was someone from The Beat. Had I forgotten to do something? If the show didn't get put into the system in time they'd take it off the schedule and note it as a 'failed delivery'. That's what the Minister would be looking for.

Thankfully the number on the screen began with a foreign dialling code: Sophia. It was great to hear her voice as she filled me in on the shopping trips and sightseeing as well as the nightlife. It sounded like I was missing out.

'So where are you now?' I asked.

'We caught up with some friends from uni and we're in the Hamptons.'

I heard a male voice in the background. 'C'mon, Soph.'

'Who's that?' I asked.

She paused and I could hear that she'd muffled the phone with her hand. Then, with a slightly hushed tone, she said, 'It's the guy whose uncle owns the time-share.'

'Oh yeah, of course. Have I met him?' I asked casually.

She paused again. 'It's Simon.'

What the fuck? That smarmy git! She's lied to me.

'Simon from the barbecue?' I asked, trying to stay calm.

'Yes, but –'

My voice steadily got angry. 'The one who gives you lifts to university? Sends you inappropriate texts? The one I told you I don't like?' I said firmly.

She got defensive. 'You can't tell me which friends I can and can't keep. I don't tell you.'

'Oh really, coming from the girl who didn't even want me to go to a work fancy-dress party?' I said.

'And remember how you told me I was being silly?' she replied defiantly.

'So why didn't you tell me you were going to New York to see *him*?' I asked.

'I wasn't coming to see him, I was coming to see New York.'

'So why didn't you tell me it was his uncle's place in the Hamptons?' I interrupted.

She paused for a moment. 'Because I knew you'd get funny about it,' she responded.

'But you did it anyway?'

Sophia tried to assure me it was just one night but I was hung up on the fact that she hadn't been honest with me – she'd lied. We went round and round on the technicalities until she began justifying their relationship.

'Look, Jay, he's helped me out a lot this year. Driving me to uni and back. He helped me move out of halls when you weren't around –'

'Oh, so I pushed you towards him?' I asked.

'No. No one pushed or pulled me anywhere. He's just my friend,' she said.

I heard him again in the background. 'Come on, Soph, we're getting late for dinner.'

'Jay, I gotta go,' she said.

'OK, fine,' I said, and hung up before she could reply. Voices took over my head and I was too tired to stop them.

There's something wrong here. It's dodgy, said Bobby Brown.

No, it's not, you're being unreasonable, said Whitney Houston.

Why did she lie? asked Bobby.

She didn't lie, you're making it out to be more than it is, replied Whitney.

Well, if she is lying and there's something going on, then you're the mug.

Stop dramatizing. Trust in your relationship. Sophia loves you and you love her, Whitney said, reasoning the situation.

Yeah, but I can sense something from this guy, said Bobby, increasingly paranoid.

Stop being such an alpha male.

Bobby wasn't giving up. *It's got nothing to do with that. It's a gut thing and you have to go with your gut.*

Why can't you go with reason and logic?

Bobby and Whitney kept debating as I tried to sleep. I had too much on my plate and didn't need this.

I'd barely closed my eyes to sleep when they were open again. I looked at my alarm clock as it sent beeping noises crashing against the walls in my room. Three hours had passed and it was time to get up for work.

34
SYMPATHY FOR THE DEVIL

As I sat at my desk drinking a Red Bull, I couldn't help but laugh. At the moment it really was pointless going back to the flat, given that I practically lived in the office. Worse still, my body was reacting badly to the lack of sleep and the artificial stimulants were messing with my mood.

The night before PJ had come good on one of his promises he'd made on the plane to take me places. With a suit from Armani's PR boys, I was at the MOBOs, sitting on one of the six tables paid for by Sony Records and watching Sade perform. Glass after glass of champagne rendered the ceremony a bit of a blur as the presenters and performers came on and off stage to sweeping camera cranes overhead. But I had just one thing on my mind – Sophia's betrayal.

'Shit, wherever she is, do you think *she's* stressing?' PJ asked, hazarding a guess from my glum face.

'No, she's probably having fun with –'

'Exactly,' he cut me off, 'having fun. There are people outside in the cold dying to be right here, right now. So c'mon.' He jumped to his feet. 'Before we go, don't forget the two-second rule.'

'Where are we going?' I asked, confused. 'What two-second rule?'

He looked surprised. 'I thought Max would have taught you this. He taught it to me. Anyway, listen, if I haven't introduced you to someone within two seconds it means I've forgotten their name,' he said.

It was the first thing to make me laugh all day.

'Laugh you may but do you know how many people I meet on a daily basis? I can't remember them all.'

'OK, OK,' I slurred, the alcohol kicking in.

'So, after two seconds you stick your hand out and tell them your name. There's a very strong chance they'll respond. Problem solved. But don't leave it for more than two seconds, otherwise it gets awkward and it's obvious I don't know what their name is.'

He took me around and introduced me to people from record labels, sponsors, artists and anyone who had bought a high-priced table near the front of the stage. I did as he said and Sophia was pushed to the back of my mind as I schmoozed and exchanged numbers with some of the most influential people in the business.

Soon enough we were at the afterparty and, thanks to the hobnobbing, I'd managed to get Pritz in too, who'd come straight from a work night out. Things warmed up as a summery vibe returned, everyone dancing to Shola Ama's garage mix of 'Imagine', a track that had been on heavy rotation in Ayia Napa earlier in the year.

As PJ drank with the other Beat presenters, Pritz and I stood gawping at all the hot women walking by, as if we were front row at a Victoria's Secret show.

'You know, as hot as some of these women are, none of them are worth it,' Pritz said.

'What do you mean?' I asked, too drunk to work him out.

'Well, if I was to ever retire from player-dom, the only woman I would fuck up my shit for would be Yasmin Le Bon,' he said.

'Eh?' It wasn't the obvious choice. I laughed. 'Well, the day you retire from player-dom is the same day you die, I bet. Back in a minute.' I was totally drunk now as I wove my way to the toilets while Pritz searched out some Yasmin lookalikes.

I stood with my eyes closed at the urinal, let out a big sigh and relaxed. PJ's philosophy for life was starting to make sense. I worked far too hard to waste opportunities. I had to be a bit more single-minded and selfish.

'So this is where you've been hiding all night?' said a voice next to me.

My eyes opened slowly and I turned to the right to see Max looking down into his urinal. I hadn't heard from him since he'd left and I certainly wasn't expecting to see him standing next to me.

'Hey, Max. I didn't know you were coming,' I said, all garbled.

'I still have a few friends here and there. I take it you went to the awards with PJ?' he asked.

'Yeah, he got me a ticket,' I said.

'I see. I thought he couldn't get any tickets.'

'It was literally last-minute. I even had to borrow this suit.' I looked down at my own urinal, feeling uncomfortable as Max seemed to be on the attack.

'So, I hear you're producing the show now?'

262

'Yeah,' I said timidly.

'Well, I suppose they couldn't let it go down the toilet. *Someone* had to do it.'

I kept quiet.

'Better it was kept in the *family*, I suppose,' he added.

Again I kept quiet, which only seemed to agitate him.

'I expected you, of all people, Jay, to do the right thing.'

'I thought I did,' I said, confused. 'Did you want your show to get pulled? Cos that's what the Minister –'

'You should have turned them down. They're just using you.'

'Yeah but . . .' I tried hard to recall PJ's rational words, but Max wasn't giving me a chance.

'You're just going to fuck it up. Everything that I've built,' he said.

'Look, I'm –'

'Don't you have any loyalty to me?' he asked.

I drunkenly raised an eyebrow, remembering that he was the person who told me 'There are no friends in this game'.

'I do . . .'

'Doesn't seem like it, Jay. You've stabbed me in the back. I believed in you when no one else did. And this is how you repay me?'

I couldn't believe that's how he felt. He was letting me have it with both barrels now, so I stood there and kept quiet like my older brother was telling me off.

'You've got some chutzpah, kid. You think you're a big shot now . . . Mr Beat?' He sounded like he wanted to thump me. 'OK, if that's how you want to play it . . .' He finished up and left.

I stood there, feeling my legs give way slightly. *Had I stabbed him in the back? What if I do balls-up the show? Am I being used?*

Once again someone was fucking with my head. This time it was enough to kill the night for me. I didn't want to bump into Max again for round two of psychological abuse so I went looking for Pritz to go home. When I found him, I wasn't the only one who needed to split. He was totally wasted, standing alone on the dance floor. I watched as he drank some beer only to puke it back into the glass. Moments later he started drinking from it again as his eyes shifted around the dance floor. I called a cab.

Pritz sat quietly in the Uncle Lee, leaning on the headrest as I looked at my phone. Sophia had sent text messages saying she wanting to talk. I didn't want to. She'd lied to me and I found myself not trusting her. I kept saying 'screw you' in my head as I deleted her texts one by one.

Once I'd got my composure back, I decided I'd had enough of being an emotional yo-yo. I wasn't going to let anyone mess with my head. Not Sophia, not Max, not the Minister or anyone else for that matter. I didn't need their blessing or co-operation. I could do it on my own.

Suddenly I was snapped out of my daze by the car's brakes being slammed on. Moments later, the driver had opened the back door and was standing on the street swearing at us. Pritz had puked in the back seat.

'That's it, get out! Get out, the both of you!' he shouted.

'Look, someone's spiked his cranberry juice. He's a Hindu-vegetarian. They don't even drink,' I said, trying to come up with something to keep us in the car. Clearly I was in no frame of mind to make sense.

'That's it, I'm calling my boss,' he said, diving back into the car for his radio control.

By now, Pritz was bent over on the side of the road puking some more as I patted his back.

'What the fuck, Pritz? How wasted are you?'

I continued whispering angrily in his ear as he slumped down further on to his hands and knees, preparing for the next hurl. Exhausted and desperate he said, 'Take it easy, dude, I'm futarcked. Can't you see I'm in trouble here?'

'You're not the only one.'

Before I could continue venting, the driver returned. 'Right, I've spoken to my boss and he said he's going to speak to your boss tomorrow.'

The Minister? No way. I can't get fired over this, I thought. I tried reasoning with the driver, but he wasn't having any of it. He had me by the short and curlies as he calculated the cleaning cost, our fare and his loss of wages to be £400.

'What?' I exclaimed.

'Look, you wanted to know the cost, mate. If you don't want to pay up, our bosses can sort it out tomorrow. Either way suits me,' he said.

If I argued, he'd leave us there and I'd be in a whole heap of shit tomorrow at work. It wasn't just Pritz who was bent over as I said, 'Take me to a cashpoint.'

Pritz had virtually paid for me to live in the flat with him so I had no choice but to be £400 out of pocket. After I'd paid up, the cab driver took us home as Pritz lay sleeping against the window, spit dribbling out the edge of his mouth. I couldn't believe Uncle Lee had turned on me too.

Home at last, I got Pritz to his room where he lay snoring as I went for a shower. As hard as I scrubbed myself, the stench of puke seemed to linger. Sophia had obviously given up on trying to get me to text back, and soon my phone began to ring. I stupidly decided to answer.

'Hello?'

'Why aren't you answering my texts?' she demanded with no pleasantries.

'Because you're a liar.' I knew it was going to annoy her but I didn't care.

We were soon having a full-scale argument with closed ears and closed hearts. Eventually exhaustion got the better of me, the night and the past few weeks catching up on me, and I fell asleep on her while she screamed about everything she hated about me, my job and my life.

When I finally woke up, it was ten thirty a.m. and production manager Gwyneth was on the end of the phone asking to talk, in person. Great, the cab driver had taken my money *and* grassed me up. I rushed into work, hoping that a chat with her would clear it up before it got back to the Minister.

I got to her desk and she took me to a meeting room. This was serious. She'd never looked so stern.

'Look, sorry I'm late in. It was the MOBOs last night and –'

She shook her head. 'It's not that. I've got some bad news. It's about your expenses,' she said.

'Expenses?'

'Terry Perkins says we can't pay them.'

'What? Why?' I exclaimed.

'He says we can't corroborate them and, as head of Production, the buck stops with him.'

'What?' I said again. It wasn't as if I was claiming for bottles of champagne or new clothes. The receipts were for miscellaneous costs like props, specialist magazines, spare tapes for shoots and anything Max had barked at me to get. They'd built up over the months in his in-tray, as had the dust. There was over £400 worth of receipts. I couldn't afford to lose that amount of money twice in twenty-four hours.

'But they've been seen and approved by Max,' I reasoned.

'He forgot to sign them off before he left. They'll need to be checked over again by someone else,' she said.

I knew it would be the Minister checking each line and following procedure down to the last letter. *When it rains, it really does pour*, I thought.

'Look, I'm sorry you'll be out of pocket,' she said, getting up to leave.

She left me in the room, dumbfounded.

Pritz had come home early that night but was locked away in his room, either still hungover or upset with me, I wasn't sure. Having worked a full tiring day after the MOBOs, I finally sat on the sofa and flicked through the channels. I distracted myself by eating two Pot Noodles until it was time to watch my first *Total BEATS* being transmitted. For a moment the pain seemed worth it as my name appeared on the end credits.

As the ads played, I got a text message from PJ.

Well done. Told you we'd do it. Fantastic job.

I felt proud, but I was out of pocket and way past the bread-line. I wasn't sure how I would make it through the next month, let alone to December, if my expenses didn't come through. Moments later my phone beeped again with another text message. It was Max.

Your show menus were too short.

I smiled. It was the biggest compliment I could have wished for.

35
FROZEN

Time: 10:13
To: Jay
From: Sophia
Subject: We need to talk with open hearts and minds

RV,

I think it's best we email to stop us from shouting over each other on the phone and not allowing each other to finish what we're saying. Firstly, I'm sorry about New York. I didn't think it would turn out like this. If I was really out to lie to you I wouldn't have told you it was Simon in the Hamptons. I could have used another person's name if something was really going on. Our problems have been building for a long time and they started when you began work at The Beat. Hate to say it, but we were fine before that. Your work is putting this pressure on our relationship, not anything else. We need to address that if we're to address our problems. I wish we'd met when I got back from New York and before I went to Manchester

as I don't know when I'll be back down next. I wish
you'd told me you loved me at least once during all
this. I wish this would go away.

LV

PS I hope you're not going to fall asleep while you read
this!

———

Time: 11:46
To: Sophia
From: Jay
Subject: RE: We need to talk with open hearts and
minds

LV,

I want to start by saying I love you . . . much-much,
despite everything recently. I don't want this drama in
my life. The bottom line is you lied to me. No matter
what my reaction would have been you should have
told me the truth. You clearly only said Simon's name
because I put you on the spot. If you'd had more time
perhaps you would have said another name. I don't
know but it's hard to give you the benefit of the doubt
right now. You know how stressful things are for me,
all I wanted was some support. Instead I find my
girlfriend has been away with someone else. I'm finding
it hard to get beyond that and nothing you've said has
made things better. You can't rest this on The Beat.

RV

PS I'm wide awake, thanks. I managed to get some sleep for the first time in ages instead of being on the phone in the early hours arguing!

———

Time: 11:59
To: Jay
From: Sophia
Subject: RE: RE: We need to talk with open hearts and minds

Jay,

You're not listening to me nor are you trusting me. I keep telling you nothing happened between Simon and me. I should have told you the truth before I left. That's my only mistake. But your reaction is way off. You've made yourself out to be the victim but you've forgotten how this year has been for me. I've started university and moved away from home for the first time in my life. Settling into Manchester has been really hard. You've not been here once since you started at The Beat. I'm totally neglected and usurped by your job and you're making me feel insecure. There's no time to speak to you. There's no time to see you. You've not realized that just as it's hard for you in London, it's hard for me here.

Sophia

PS Well, maybe I wouldn't have to call at stupid times of the day if you answered my texts or bothered to phone or visit!

———

Time: 13:36
To: Sophia
From: Jay
Subject: RE: RE: RE: We need to talk with open hearts and minds

Sophia,

What would you prefer, I sit and do nothing? I'm in a job. You have to put time in if you're going to make it. You'll realize this when you finish studying. Let's see if you feel the same when you leave uni. You keep blaming The Beat. It's got nothing to do with it and if anything that's a deflection from what you've done. I could be in another job, anywhere else and I'd have to work this hard to establish myself. I keep telling you I don't want to go back to being unemployed. That's why I'm working weekends and can't always come up to see you. It's down to us both to make time to meet and speak. It's not like you're sitting by the phone waiting for me to call. You're out partying in Manchester or when you're in London. When I can get time to speak to you, you're not around. When you're free to speak, I'm not around. You say I'm making you insecure.

Are you sure you're not making yourself insecure?
Regarding trusting you, I did, but you've broken my
trust and not done anything to rectify it. Make me a
believer, that's all I ask!

J

———

Time: 13:52
To: Jay
From: Sophia
Subject: RE: RE: RE: RE: We need to talk with open
hearts and minds

Jay,

What are you talking about? Of course I'm happy that
you're doing something you love. I'm very proud of
you, ask all my friends. I'm just saying that the
balance is all wrong. I'm not a part of your life. Why
aren't you taking me to any awards shows or parties?
I just don't feel you in my life any more. You've got
upset because you've realized Simon's doing the things
with me you should be doing. The Beat isn't a normal
job. It saps everything out of you. Going to all those
parties and surrounding yourself in that whole fake
celebrity circle. Those people don't care about you.
When did you last see your uni friends? You live with
Pritz but you barely see him. You're not Max. You're not
PJ. Don't try and be like them. Where's Jay gone?

Sophia

Time: 15:49
To: Sophia
From: Jay
Subject: RE: RE: RE: RE: RE: We need to talk with open hearts and minds

Sophia,

You keep mentioning my work. Are you jealous of it? You're acting as though The Beat's a woman. Would you rather I become an accountant in a boring office? I'm not absorbed in the lifestyle. I'm too busy working in the office to get involved. I don't always see my friends as they have jobs and are working hard too. That's the way it is. At least my friends don't badmouth you. You can deny it, but I know your 'friends' and slimy Simon are influencing you. No one complains when they're at the front row of a concert I've given you tickets to. But when I'm working at these parties, then it's all 'He's up to no good. How could he not be?' Oh, and if I could I'd take you to the awards but last time I checked I'm not a Vice President in senior management. Don't try and throw cheap shots – I'm not trying to be like someone else. I'm still me. Just under different pressures. And I don't care if Simon's doing things for you. In fact, good luck to the both of you.

J

Time: 16:03
To: Jay
From: Sophia
Subject: RE: RE: RE: RE: RE: RE: We need to talk with open hearts and minds

Jay,

That's right, I'm jealous of The Beat!! Like I give a fuck about that place. If you think it's more important than me, then fine. It's good to know. It's just a bloody job. There are other jobs out there. Do you think they give as much of a shit about you as you do about them? Enjoy yourself there but don't say I didn't warn you. It's weird – you think I'm being jealous and paranoid and I think you're being blind. You were a better person when you used to doubt yourself because at least you checked yourself. My friends don't say bad things about you. Besides, I'm smart enough to know the truth. All I wanted was for you to be a friend to me, that's all. You can be a friend to all these other people but not your own girlfriend. And thanks for your blessing. At least Simon knows how to be a friend to me. By asking me how I'm doing. Asking me if I need help.

Sophia

Time: 16:06
To: Sophia
From: Jay
Subject: RE: RE: RE: RE: RE: RE: RE: We need to talk with open hearts and minds

Sophia,

BECAUSE HE'S TRYING TO GET INTO YOUR PAAAAANTS!!!

J

36
ME AGAINST THE WORLD

A few weeks into my extended contract and I was wearily trudging down the stairs to the studio as if I was in the French Foreign Legion. I had work to do at my desk and so I wasn't looking forward to spending the morning with Year Eleven students from a secondary school. They were in for a tour to find out more about TV presenting and a career in the media. The kid's quiet excitement went up a few notches as soon as PJ walked in and they were given the chance to get in front of the camera and present. Two braved the challenge in front of their ready-to-laugh classmates.

'So, have you got any presenter positions going?' asked a cocky kid with big ears as he stood in front of the camera, deliberately smoothing his eyebrows with his fingers.

'Well, if you can read the link on the autocue and nail it on your first take, I'll give you my job,' said PJ, equally cocky.

As the kid stared down the camera lens his confidence deserted him and he became too aware of himself. Just a few words into the link he began making mistakes.

PJ stepped in to help. 'Rule one: chillax. Don't try to be someone else or what you think people want. Do I talk to you guys any differently from what you see on TV?'

'Noooo,' said a few like well-trained penguins.

'Just relax. Here's a tip. Flirt with the camera. Like it's a girl you really fancy and you're talking to her,' he said, stepping off behind the camera.

The kid tried again. When he got to the end of the link PJ asked, 'Have you got a girlfriend?'

'No.'

'No wonder. You call that flirting? There's some things you can't teach!'

Cue laughter and jeers. The girl with a blonde bob standing on the other side of PJ had a go, reading the lines from the autocue slowly and deliberately.

'Not bad, but it *looked* like you were reading. Pretend you're talking to a person, not reading from a script to camera. Rule two: don't read it, say it.'

He went back to the cocky kid. 'OK, I want you to read the link from this paper script, memorize it and then deliver it without any help.' A minute later he counted him in. 'Coming to you in 5, 4, 3, 2, 1 . . .'

The kid delivered it and then, to applause from his classmates, he stood brushing imaginary dirt from his shoulder.

'Not so fast, my friend,' said PJ. 'Yes, the delivery and look to camera was good but you got the name of the album wrong, you failed to namecheck Bono's bandmates and you didn't throw to the performance as the link says. Rule three: knowledge is power. What if that was live and you were introducing U2?'

'Oh, can I have another go, please?' he said, jumping up and down like he needed to pee.

'No, sorry – one take, remember!' PJ said.

Moments later the girl with the blonde bob was being critiqued, having interviewed PJ pretending to be Bono. 'Not bad but you kept talking over me. Count one second after the guest has finished speaking before asking the next question. Be attentive, listen to what they're saying and ask questions accordingly. A great interviewer is a friend who can get the guest to tell them things others can't. Rule four: be their mate to be great.' He rattled through some more rules and then opened it up for a Q&A.

'So what's your secret?' asked one kid.

'I'm not telling you,' said PJ, laughing.

'Go on, don't be stush,' he begged.

'OK, but it's real simple: I'm well read. It helps expand my knowledge and trains my mind. So, just as athletes work out, reading is my workout.'

For a few seconds they stayed silent taking it in. Moments later their teacher piped up. 'How did you make it?' she asked.

'I was in the right place at the right time.' He turned to the kids. 'But be ready for lots of rejection and feeling insecure about yourself. I haven't met a presenter who doesn't.'

'But it looks so glamorous and easy,' said one girl.

'It's not. You've seen today that your brain has got to be fully engaged while you're onscreen. You must be prepared. That's true of anything in life. Especially if your flirting face is like his!' he said, pointing to the cocky kid, making the rest of them laugh.

Later, in the Greenhouse, around a table of food and drinks, the kids looked up and around in amazement at the offices above.

'Wow, you're so lucky to work here,' one of them said to me.

'It's OK,' I replied flatly.

'I'd work here for free,' said another, biting into a pastry.

Not if you had bills to pay, I thought.

'You get to meet all the stars,' said another, knocking back a can of 7Up.

They don't pay my bills either.

I thought back to how, like them, I'd once thought this was Disneyland. Now it was anything but. I felt like the man inside a Mickey Mouse costume. He welcomed mesmerized kids to paradise, but the reality was a shift-work job requiring him to be extra jovial all day long, a pain-in-the-ass supervisor and a wife who'd just left him for the guy in the Goofy costume.

'It must be fun. Listening to music all the time?' asked another doey-eyed kid.

'It's the best thing about it. Music makes it all worthwhile,' I admitted. 'I'm not this passionate about anything else!' I stopped for a moment. It was the first time I'd realized how true that was.

Back at my desk, I turned my attention to the studio record with Ricky Martin tomorrow for *Defm8*. Tola had been working on PJ's scripts on and off for two days and had sent it to me to check over. Her previous week's scripts hadn't been up to par but I knew she was jumping between her work for Stuey and me. I'd given her some of the tips Max had passed on to me.

As I looked through, the links were in the wrong order and the script still wasn't written for PJ. It just wouldn't sound right coming out of his lips.

'Have you finished this script?' I asked Tola as she tapped at her keyboard in her seat across from me.

'Yeah, this morning. Why, is there a problem?' she asked with concern.

'Remember I said that you have to write it in PJ's words? Like he'd say it?'

'I did,' she replied defensively.

'Well, it still sounds like your voice. It's like method acting – just as an actor absorbs themselves in a role, we have to do method writing and absorb ourselves into the words for PJ,' I said dramatically.

'Right!' she said, clearly biting her tongue.

I asked about several pieces of footage. 'Where's the Coldplay gig at Shepherd's Bush Empire?'

'I was swamped, Jay. I was researching a *News Feed* special for Stuey at the same time.' She sat looking unmoved.

'For fuck's sake,' I mumbled under my breath. 'I'm going to have to find that and fix this script.'

'It won't take you long to write it,' she said, hearing me and snapping back.

'That's what I'm going to have to do, *for you*,' I said as our voices began to rise. 'I've got *Total BEATS* to write, like you don't know.'

She looked at me incredulously. 'Jay, if I'm honest, there's nothing wrong with that script. You're getting far too precious about it.'

'Look, Tola, I just want it to be right. People are watching the both of us,' I said, trying to raise a sense of camaraderie. 'We can't fail.'

'We're not performing brain surgery or saving lives. Chill

out. Don't get caught up in the Matrix, remember?' she said, echoing Hugh's advice.

'Look we have to take pride in our work –'

'Jay, it's *just* a bloody script!' she interrupted.

I looked at her as the walls of Jericho came tumbling down inside me. 'Well, if it's so easy then you should have nailed it first time. This is your fourth week and you still haven't got it. I may as well do it myself . . . Oh, wait, like I've been having to do!'

We were now loud enough for those near us to hear what was going on, but the sound of *NSYNC's 'Bye Bye Bye' prevented us from causing a scene in the wider department. James III kept reading his *Economist* as Sonya and Sam watched on helplessly, aware it wasn't wise to get involved.

'If I'm not good enough for you, then crack on yourself,' she said firmly.

'I'm working non-stop and in charge of two shows. One of which you report in to me for –'

'Whoa, whoa. Hold on, I don't *report* in to you. I'm just here to help you.'

'That's not what the Minister said.'

She shrugged her shoulders. 'Take it or leave it, Jay.'

'Well, I'll have to email him for clarity then,' I said, trying to recall his exact words.

This only incensed her further. 'Have you been reading *The 48 Laws*?' she said incredulously.

'What?' I said, not understanding the reference.

'You're just an intern, remember,' she said with contempt.

I couldn't understand her reaction. Then a thought fell

from nowhere into my mouth. 'Is all this because I filmed your Britney interview?'

She looked taken aback. 'Are you kidding? No! It's because you're acting like a right . . . a right . . . Qworn!'

I heard James III snigger, knowing she meant 'quant'. Tola turned to walk away but suddenly stopped in her stride, came back and said, 'A wise man once said, "All men can stand adversity, but if you want to test a man's character give him power." You could learn something from that.'

The others looked shocked as they turned to stare at their computers. I could feel rage rising inside me. I went back to staring at my own computer. But my head felt like it was buzzing with white noise. I needed somewhere to calm down.

I headed for one of the artists' changing rooms near the studios. I locked the door behind me and stood by a make-up mirror with lightbulbs that went all the way round the edge. Some were working and some weren't, a bit like the links in Tola's script. There was a residue of white powder on the table and I stood over it trying to calm myself down. I looked at myself in the mirror and my internal dialogue kicked in.

How dare she speak to you like that? asked Frank Sinatra.

Cos I'm being a twat, I replied.

Listen, she's meant to be working for you and not doing a half-arsed job.

Don't get all macho. She's got her own pressures, clearly.

Strap on a pair. Forget everyone else, you can do this alone, he said rousingly.

I reflected momentarily and then said, *I thought I was one of the good guys!*

Course you are, said Frank. *Don't question yourself, that's what they all want.*

I was silent again.

Have you come this far to fall on your face? Think of everything you've sacrificed. If you fail, no one's going to be there to help you up. Everyone's too busy looking after themselves. Who's got time for a loser without a job? This is your moment, don't let other people blow it for you now.

I sat for a while absorbing the pep talk. Eventually I stood up with a steely resolve and walked back to my desk. I had work to do.

37
BROWN PAPER BAG

Early the next morning I was in the empty office with just a few hours to get scripts done before we recorded the show with the boy formerly from Menudo. I went into my weekly ritual of getting into PJ's mind and began typing for him. I forgot everyone and everything else and enjoyed writing about the music I loved while it played in the background.

The only thing disturbing me was the constant drone of my work phone, which had been ringing for the last five minutes. Someone was really trying to get through.

'Hello?' I said, irritated. I looked at my watch. It was eight a.m.

'Jay? Hello, I've been trying to get a hold of you for weeks,' said the male voice.

'Well, you've got me. Who is this?'

'A mutual friend said you could help and gave me your number.'

'Which friend?'

'He said you're the man now and could spin a video for me.'

It was just another person trying to get a video on to the

show. I gave him one more chance before I put the phone down.

'What friend?' I said as my patience began to wear thin.

'Max.'

I paused. *OK, I'm listening*, I thought, not wanting to be rude just in case this guy really was Max's friend.

Flattering me at every turn, he introduced himself as Will Sturge and I immediately recognized his name from the numerous messages he'd left me in recent weeks. He explained about his unsigned new girl group, who he said were attracting attention from the major labels.

'Will, the thing is we only play signed artists,' I said.

'C'mon, you're Mr Beat. Sure you can bend the rules this once.'

'No, the company chooses what –'

'What will it cost?' he asked, interrupting me.

'Cost?' I repeated.

'I know someone's palm has to be blessed with some spice. I don't mind, I know it happens there all the time.'

'Look, I can't –'

'I've had this arrangement with Max before.'

What? I thought. *No way. He's bluffing.* 'Max has never played unsigned videos,' I said confidently.

'Sure he did, but maybe it was before your time. The video will make it on to The Beat soon. It just needs a gentle push. You get £2,000 and I get just one spin. More than enough exposure for me.'

I stayed quiet. *Was this test? The Minister?*

'It's a sweet deal and no one will ever find out. You'd be mad to turn it down.'

I was about to speak when he said, 'Think it over. The package is with your security people.' He put the phone down.

I went to Security and signed for the brown envelope he'd left for me. I took it upstairs and opened it under my desk, away from view. Sure enough, there was the tape and what looked like enough £50 notes to be £2,000.

My mind was buzzing with questions. Did Max really take money? Was this the done thing? But seeing so many lobster-pink bank notes was blocking out the questions and increasing my temptation by the minute. The money would help pay off my overdraft and then some. I watched the video on a viewing machine nearby and then quickly put it, with the money, into my drawer. It was so full of other junk that I had to keep violently banging it until it finally shut so I could lock it.

Just as it did, I felt a tap on my shoulder that made me jump. Stood behind me was the head of our website, Marianne Stevens, part of senior management. She was different from the other suits and not just because she wore Dolce & Gabbana. Unlike them, she didn't look like she worked for a law firm. I heard she had moved over from the New York offices a year earlier to be with her English husband.

She introduced herself. 'I've been trying to call but your phone was engaged.'

'Oh, sorry, it's studio time today and I'm just finishing off,' I said.

'Wow, you guys have all the fun,' she said playfully.

'Yeah, but none of the money,' I said, raising my eyebrows at her designer shoes.

Thankfully she laughed. 'Touché. Have you got a minute to talk?' she asked.

'Sure.'

I followed her to the Seventies room, wondering what on earth she could want. After massaging my ego with how she'd heard so much about me, like a smooth-talking Dolly Parton, she suddenly said, 'I'll cut to the chase. I'm not sure what you know about our plans but we're moving all our TV content online.'

'What, everything?' I said, thinking how arduous a task it would be.

'Eventually, yes. First I have to get kids coming to the website to make it viable in the long run. So I want to produce some exclusive content using A-list stars that will only be available on the website. It's called "Project Pied Piper" internally. We'll bring them to a virtual youth club that has chatrooms letting them watch programmes at the same time as other Beat viewers across the world while messaging each other.' With gesticulating hands she continued to describe her vision about providing huge discounts at top stores as an incentive, finishing by describing it as a global communication network for youth culture that would be bigger than the Scouts and Girl Guides.

'I see,' I said, thinking about my scripts while she painted her online fantasy.

'We've been given a worldwide exclusive to film at Usher's video shoot for his upcoming single "Pop Ya Collar". We want to do a behind-the-scenes show called *Lights, Camera, Action!*'

'Wow, that's great,' I said, looking at her like, *And?*

'The only problem is my team don't know how to film so I spoke to your boss, Terry, and he said you'd be free to do it.'

My shoulders sank. The Minister really was trying to break me.

Seeing my reaction, she added, 'Terry said you were one of the best in his team. Besides, I think you'll find this project is high up on the list of priorities for the company, especially at HQ.'

I suddenly sat up in my chair. 'So when is it?' I asked enthusiastically.

'Halloween,' she replied.

'But I've never made a show like this before,' I said, suddenly worried.

She grinned. 'But that's the opportunity! There's no elevator to success, just stairs. But sometimes you can take the escalator. I'll get a US producer to call and help you,' she said reassuringly. She reached out her hand. 'So do we have a deal?'

'Sure,' I said, shaking it with excitement. I should have stopped to consider it more but the euphoria of hearing 'HQ', 'Terry said' and 'one of the best in his team' got the better of me.

Soon I was back at my desk and finishing off my last link. Screw Tola. My hard work had been noticed. Screw Sophia. I was right to put everything in to work like I had been doing. As I sat there for a moment, I felt a trickle of doubt trying to worm its way into me but it was immediately swallowed up by a tsunami of excitement. As I basked in the warmth that radiated from my chest, the phone rang. It was Will Sturge again.

'Did you get the package?' he asked.

'Yes, I did,' I replied.

'Good. So we have a deal?' he said with confidence.

As tempting as all that money was, it wasn't worth risking all I'd worked for and could now almost touch. It didn't matter any more if the offer was real or a trap.

'Like I said before, we don't play unsigned acts,' I said.

He let out a sigh, frustrated. 'But this is win-win for you.'

'Please come and collect your package from Security,' I said, unmoved.

'It's OK, I want you to keep the spice,' he said, changing tack.

For a moment I contemplated the value of £2,000. 'No way,' I said firmly.

'Look, all I want is one spin,' he said with increased desperation.

'I'm sorry, Will, I've got to go. I'm recording in the studio soon.'

'Just one measly spin.'

'Listen, Will,' I said, finally getting annoyed. 'I wouldn't play that pile of shit if you paid me double. The video is awful. The song is tacky. And the group is bugly. Your package will be at Security for you to collect.'

The phone went silent for a moment before Will's voice changed. 'Who the fuck do you think you are? You don't even know who I am to be talking to me –'

I slammed the phone down. I was sick of people trying to tell me what I could or couldn't do.

38
COULD YOU BE LOVED

For the first time in ages I could enjoy the relative respite the coming weekend offered, as there were no interviews lined up or shoots abroad. I had been producing the show on my own for the past month, making me realize what Max had been going through for years. I considered going up to Manchester to sort stuff out with Sophia but my ego didn't feel like I should be the one who was making the effort, considering I hadn't done anything wrong. If she wanted to talk she should come to London.

My decision was made all the easier when I received a card at work on Friday, delivered by courier.

Dear Plonker,

Like Rama, I want you to come back from the wilderness and join me for an evening of belated Diwali festivities. Saturday we'll party like it's 2099. I propose a club crawl from the boujis to the grimey. Don't tell me about any edits or filming crap. That excuse might wash with Sophia, but it won't with me. Bring your crew along!

*I need back-ups just in case I don't chirps. Also I have a
game to try out on you losers.*

   Your gay lover

I hadn't seen Pritz that much lately, so it was the perfect
plan.

   The next evening, in the Met Bar on Park Lane, with Daft
Punk's 'One More Time' playing overhead, Pritz lined up
three beers and three shots and gathered me and James III
into a huddle.

   'All right, boys, time to make the night a bit more fun.'

   James III and I stood looking at him, wondering what
crazy idea he had in store.

   'Time to introduce you to "The Blind Trader",' he said
triumphantly.

   'OK. What are we trading, though?' asked James III,
intrigued.

   Pritz rolled his eyes. 'Women, of course!'

   'What? That's sexist, misogynistic and rude. I'm in,' said
James III, all perked up.

   'We basically buy and sell girls, blind. Walking down the
street, on pub or club crawls, restaurants, anywhere we find
them. Blind, as in poker, means you haven't seen their faces.
So I see a girl from behind, if I think she'll be hot I "buy"
her. If I think she won't be, I "sell" her. If I buy her and we
all agree she's hot, that was a good trade so I get a point. If
she's not, that's a bad trade and I lose a point. And it works
in reverse too, so if I sell her and she turns out to be hot, I
lose a point. If she turns out to be as ugly as Jay's first girl–'

   'Hey!' I interjected.

'. . . then I get a point. Get it?' he said, looking back and forth at both of our faces.

I looked at James III and he was looking at Pritz just like I was. He didn't get it either.

'Now my clients and I settle a bad trade using money or alcohol. But alcohol's more fun as a bad trade means you down a shot. Also, by the end of the night when you can't see straight, anything looks hot,' he said, laughing.

'So it's basically a guessing game,' I said.

'Yep. End of the night the most points wins and that person is crowned the Blind Trader and gets the losers to do a forfeit.' He swigged from his drink.

'Job's a good 'un,' said James III in agreement.

'OK, you see that tall leggy blonde with her back to us?' Pritz said, pointing at the far end of the bar. James and I nodded attentively. 'I think she's gonna be a looker when she turns round. So I'm buying her.'

'Er, OK, I'll buy that too,' James III said, like he'd put real money on it.

'I'm selling, her fat arse tells me she'll be ugly,' I said, craning my neck.

We drank our beers and waited patiently for her to turn round.

Seconds later Pritz was running round us with one arm in the air, *á la* Alan Shearer's goal celebration, a gesture he normally reserved for when he'd scored with a girl in bed. Instead this time he was high-fiving James III.

She was a stunner so I had to down a shot that burnt the back of my throat.

'We can go bigger too. Before I get somewhere, I can bet

on the entire place. If I think it's going to be full of bugly girls then I sell it for ten points,' Pritz went on.

'High risk, high return,' said James III, rubbing his hands with excitement. 'I like it.'

Armed with a new drinking game and with London's bars and clubs at our disposal, we left the Met Bar having lost a trade each. We walked behind a group of girls going clubbing on Oxford Street, trying to trade them. The famous 'Don't be a sinner, be a winner' preacher extolled the virtues of godliness with his megaphone to all the clubbers as we walked past the Tube station.

My phone went off in my pocket as James III and Pritz eyed up the next set of females to trade. I looked down to see a text from Sophia.

I'm in London for Reading Week and my parents have gone to Paris. I've got the place to myself. Can we please talk? X

I was satisfied that she had made the first move, but I wasn't going to reply immediately.

My Beat staff pass worked wonders in getting us straight into the VIP hotspots. The bar at MöMö had high-end tottie and we all ended even. Emporium didn't fare so well, surprisingly filled with buglies wall to wall. James III guessed wrong multiple times and took a pasting. After a drink, some handshakes with the manager and a 'promise' to throw a Beat party at the celeb-friendly 57 Jermyn Street, we left to meet up with Tola, Sonya, Cara and Sam at the Voodoo Lounge.

We stood at the bar and downed our first round of shots.

'So c'mon then, show us your moves, boys. I want to watch you crash and burn,' said Cara.

'Moves, I don't need moves, I just need my lucky shirt,' said Pritz, showing off the small badge on his chest which read '21 today' even though it wasn't actually his birthday.

James III explained the trading game we'd been playing all evening and was met with a collective 'You pigs!' from the girls.

'What? You can play it too!' he said, unsure what was so wrong.

'Well, we're not buying any of your stock,' said Tola, pointing at us.

'You *wish* you could buy our stock,' I said, trying to be funny and break the ice. Tola and I still hadn't cleared the air since our altercation and had barely spoken in the office.

She turned to speak to Sam without cracking a smile.

Fine, I thought. If she was going to be stubborn, then so was I.

Pritz was on fire, his lucky shirt working in tandem with his chat-up lines. He'd bump into a girl with a drink and say, 'So sorry. Hi, I'm Pritz. Red, Thai chicken, JD and Coke, Mr Burns, Manchester United and did I mention I'm a producer/camera man/head of talent . . . at The Beat?' It was cheesy but it started a conversation with every girl, particularly reeling in a very hot girl in a trucker's cap. To seal the deal with her, he cheekily gave his number on a fifty-pound note. I realized he was living life better than me at the moment. Was this a sign that I was meant to be single?

The girls joined in with the game at the Spoilt for Choice night at Rainforest Café. Pritz happily kept us all watered and pushed aside any offers from anyone else. 'Don't worry,

I'm not paying either. I'll claim these as expenses for taking "clients" out.'

A set from DJ Matt White later and we were on our way to Camden Palace for some garage and jungle courtesy of DJ EZ at Love Injection. Deep Blue's 'Helicopter' had us in a circle swaying. But the place truly went nuts when he mixed in Oasis's 'Wonderwall' and then, moments later, started scratching in the words 'Oh No' from So Solid Crew.

Everyone was enjoying the extra hour we had as the clocks were about to go back to signal the end of British Summer Time. I stood for a moment looking down at my phone and Sophia's text, weighing up what I should do. Suddenly I felt a pinch on my waist.

'I need a break,' said Sam, puffing air up on to her face from her upturned lips. 'As a proud Scot it pains me to say this but I defy anyone to find a city that has a more diverse sound on the radio, TV, clubs or in record stores than London.'

'Wow, if it's coming from you it must be true,' I said, laughing.

'You know what else is true? You need to sort things out with Tola,' she said, jumping right in with her thoughts. 'She might look hard on the outside, but she's not happy.'

'She shouldn't have been so rude and confrontational, then,' I said.

'Maybe you both were, huh, Jay?'

I shrugged my shoulders then changed the subject immediately before she killed my buzz. 'So how are things with you?'

She paused for a while. 'I quit!'

'What?' I said, suddenly standing up straight.

'Yeah, it's too much. I can't keep up. I'm giving far too much and I don't think it's going to be worth it at the end.'

'Course it is, you just have to stick with it. Don't quit now, we're so close.'

'Jay, there's one job between the six of us and I don't think I'm going to get it.'

'You don't know, they might make some extra roles for us. They haven't replaced the departures yet,' I said, trying to throw something that would stick.

'The execs barely know who I am and my show isn't high profile. On top of it all, I think our budget's about to be pulled by the Minister.'

'Bastard!' I said.

She smiled and nodded. 'It's not just that. I'm missing my friends and family. I don't get to see anyone,' she said, slightly welling up. 'I didn't get to see my grandmother before she died because I was on a shoot, and I nearly missed the funeral a few weeks back because I was waiting for tapes to arrive to send to an edit. To a bloody edit!' she exclaimed.

I stayed quiet, not sure what to say. 'This isn't to do with what happened in Ibiza, is it?' Neither of us had mentioned it since, but I could understand if it had affected her. 'Because if it is, I didn't tell any–'

'No, it's not that.' She sighed. 'Or maybe it is. I just don't feel like myself any more. I've become someone else. Haven't you?' she asked.

'I'm on top of it,' I said confidently. 'And you haven't –'

'It's too late. I'm going back to running my mag. I've got an investor who's interested in helping me grow it.'

'Wow,' I said. 'Well done.'

'If I'm going to work this hard, I may as well do it for myself.'

We were quiet momentarily until Sam said, 'I'm going to miss you guys. It's weird, I wanna go so desperately, but I'm still so sad. I can't explain it.'

'What have the others said?' I asked.

'I haven't told anyone just yet cos I don't want to make a big deal of it. I wanted to tell you because I won't be here when you get back from the US,' she said.

'What, you're done that quick?' I exclaimed.

'Yeah, I just want to get out.' She paused again. 'I've asked myself, over and over, why I've put myself through this. What's so important that my loved ones came second?'

While Pritz had shown me the case for being single, Sam was reminding me of the people who really mattered. Sophia was one of them. We stood there, not saying anything, as the crowd screamed at another dope mix being dropped.

Sam looked at the dance floor. 'What a great way to go out. All of us together.' We both headed back out into the sea of people to join our friends.

When the night eventually came to an end, everyone jumped into their Uncle Lees and went home. Pritz was crowned the Blind Trader, and instead of forfeits for us, he settled for a prize. A cream cheese and salmon bagel from Beigel Bake on Brick Lane on the way home. Pritz's phone had been beeping with text messages the entire time we were in the cab. I saw why as we pulled up outside the flat.

'This is Jay, my assistant producer at The Beat,' he said as he met the girl with the trucker's cap from the Voodoo

Lounge at our front door. I laughed heartily all the way inside.

Once upstairs, and before I could even blink, Pritz was walking her into my room and putting on the CD player. He led me into the kitchen before I could say anything and whispered, 'I can't exactly take her into my room, can I? It's hardly The Beat-esque. Yours is perfect with all the CDs, VIP passes and all that good stuff,' he said, flattering me.

'Mate, I don't care, I wanna get some sleep,' I said, sounding tired.

'C'mon dude, let this be my Diwali present.'

'You don't even believe in it,' I said, laughing.

'This isn't a "ting and fling". I think she might be the one,' he said, straight-faced.

We both laughed this time and, moments later, I gave in.

As I crashed on to Pritz's bed my mind turned to Sam's words and to Sophia. Doubts about her and our relationship had been growing like poison ivy for weeks, spreading roots across my mind. Perhaps I needed to pull them out and give us a chance.

The next morning I woke to Pritz singing in the shower while the stereo in my room played U2's 'Beautiful Day'. As the light filled the room, I could see it truly was; the only thing that seemed out of place was that Pritz wasn't following Bono. He was singing something we'd performed in school assembly when we were kids. '*Diwali avi chaay, Diwali avi chaay.*' It had indeed arrived for him, belatedly so.

After a long Tube ride and a pit stop at the florist, I was

walking through Fulham having decided I wouldn't be ruled by my ego. Sam's words had convinced me to pay Sophia a surprise visit to clear the air as I was flying out to LA for the website shoot in a few days.

As I got to Sophia's house, I could see that her parents' car was absent from the driveway but had been replaced by a silver Ford Fiesta. I knocked on the door but she didn't answer. I could hear the TV was on loud in the front room so I went to the window to get her attention.

At first I couldn't see through the net curtain, but as my eyes focused my heart fell to the floor. I saw Sophia's head on Simon's shoulder as they sat on the sofa watching TV. My pride wanted me to run away but weeks of fury that had built up took over in an instant as I banged hard on the window. They were both startled and jumped up in shock.

I banged on the front door and they both came to open it.

'What the hell's going on?' I asked, without waiting for explanations.

Sophia was red in the face. 'Simon was j-j-just dropping some notes over to me.'

'Oh, really? It didn't look like it from the window,' I blared back.

'We were watching TV. Don't be paranoid,' she said, still sounding shaky.

'With your head on his shoulder? You bitch, Sophia! How could you do this to me, and with *him* of all people?'

'Don't be a twat,' said Simon.

'Who's talking to you?' I said, eyeballing him.

He took the bait and started mouthing back. I was so

enraged I wanted to deck him. Sensing this, Sophia stood in the middle and tried to calm things down. But before I knew it, my left hand had taken it upon itself to hit Simon plumb in his eye.

'Jay!' screamed Sophia. 'What is *wrong* with you?' She turned to check on Simon.

'Fuck this, we're done,' I said, and turned and walked off.

As I got halfway down the road, I noticed she hadn't come after me and nor had he. I felt the adrenalin drain away and I sat down on a wall, clutching the flowers. Voices had taken over in my mind and I tried hard to clear them. Had I got it wrong?

Moments later I headed back, calmly, with the flowers in hand. I got to Simon's car and individually stuffed twenty-four long-stemmed lilies as far as they would go into his exhaust pipe. By the time I was done they were packed in deep and tight. No, I hadn't got it wrong.

39
WELCOME TO THE JUNGLE

Subject: Out of Office AutoReply

Thank you for your message. I am currently out of the office filming in LA. For anything urgent please call me on my US number: +001 310 202 2025. Otherwise I'll respond on my return.

Regards,
Jay Merchant
Intern, Total BEATS & Defm8

The memory of Sophia and Simon getting cosy was only a few days old but a trip abroad was the perfect antidote. Direct flights to Los Angeles were sold out weeks ago so I flew Virgin Atlantic into JFK and, after a long stopover, connected to LAX with American Airlines. Being back in economy sucked! However, looking at the in-flight map of the world, it reminded me that, thanks to The Beat, this year alone I'd been to more places than the previous twenty-one years combined.

By the time I landed and collected my baggage to head

to the celeb-filled Mondrian hotel, it was rush hour. The traffic was always murder as everyone scrambled home, but more so today as it was Halloween and the streets were lined with people in costumes heading out to celebrate. I flicked through the driver's *LA Times*, reading about Michael Jackson's controversial invitation to speak at the Oxford University Debating Society about child welfare.

I checked into my palatial room, threw my bags down and flopped face down into the big comfy bed. I stopped for a second to consider how spoilt I'd become. I was desperate to sleep as the jet lag began to make my muscles twitch with fatigue all on their own.

I got myself to reception at seven a.m. the next morning to meet Zoe from Usher's record label, who'd flown in from the UK. She was in her mid thirties but had the looks, body and energy of someone ten years younger.

Hiding behind her sunglasses, after some air kisses she asked, 'Where were you last night?'

'In my room, why?'

'Didn't you get my message on your mobile? Usher's dancers wanted to hit the town.'

'My personal mobile's been off. I'm using the work one,' I said.

'That would explain it.' She laughed.

'Sorry, the production manager didn't want me racking up my phone bill as usual. So what did you do?' I said, disappointed to have missed out.

'Oh nothing,' she said, trying to play it down. 'Just some food . . . drinks . . . and a club . . . or two.' She lifted her sunglasses momentarily and rubbed her eyes. It looked like it had been a great night.

We were on the road and at a school football field by nine a.m. where we met my camera crew. Gwyneth had ensured I got a crew that had done umpteen shoots of this kind for The Beat US so I didn't have to figure everything out on my own.

At first I was eager to see Usher and to get to watch a video being made but my excitement soon dissipated. The process was very technical and stop-start, taking time to set up all the various shots with Usher, the extras, Usher and the extras. It was primarily a waiting game between takes.

The sound guy, Sergei, an Oakland Raiders fan, and the cameraman, Larry, a San Diego Chargers fan, entertained us by goading each other about the other's team. It was like having Arsenal and Spurs fans working together. Zoe chipped in with salacious stories about her artists and the good old days when she and her entire department would go on a jolly on Concorde to see groups perform at Madison Square Gardens in New York.

I took my small camera around shooting some B-roll to avoid the boredom.

The college-girl models dressed in skimpy cheerleader outfits with perfect tanned bodies, smiles and racks were a timely distraction after recent weeks. I tried talking to them but, as cute as they were, the conversation ran dry like the Sahara. I tried talking to the blokes too, but they were equally boring, and not even sure where London was.

I continued to walk around until something caught my

attention. It was the front cover of a book I recognized but I was surprised to see it here.

'I see you're a fan of Eric Arthur Blair?'

The girl reading *1984* looked up and seemed equally taken aback.

Six out of ten and fairly pretty. OK, who are you trying to impress reading that? I thought.

'Yes, it's my father's. How do you know about him?' she asked.

And you don't speak like a Beckkkky or a Britnaaaay.

'Oh, he's staple reading back home,' I said, instantly sounding more English than before. 'I can tell you in the end –'

'Oh no, don't spoil it for me.'

'. . . reptiles appear from underground and take over the world. I'm sorry, I thought everyone knew that!' I laughed.

She giggled at my idiocy. 'Very funny. I'm Angela,' she said, reaching out a hand.

'Hi, I'm Jay. Sky blue, spag bol, vodka cranberry, Milhouse, Manchester City!' I fired out Pritz-style.

'What's that now?' she said.

'Favourite colour, food, drink, non-family *Simpsons* character and football – sorry, soccer – team,' I said.

'I see.' She smiled.

'And did I mention I work for The Beat?' I said, in a deliberately over-the-top way.

'Oh really? That's *so* impressive. Should I scream for you or for Usher?' she countered sarcastically, in an overly animated cheerleader way.

OK, funny and intelligent. Well done, LA, she's not a plastic Barbie.

I continued to cross-examine Angela and the more she spoke the more impressed I was. We spoke about the upcoming presidential elections, our favourite TV shows and her background, which was a quarter African American, a quarter German and half Native American Indian. Only in America! She was doing a lot of work as an extra to save money before leaving for Europe to study French at the Sorbonne in Paris.

Wow, was this girl for real? From the outside she was a loner reading *1984*, but I knew who I'd be hanging out with on set for the next few days.

The command from the First Assistant Director to stand by for scene three eventually made us go our separate ways. The rest of the day sped up as the light began to dim on the football pitch. I was now running around after Usher, then the director, asking them what they had done after each set-up. Once we got to eleven p.m., the yell of 'That's a wrap!' saw people shooting for the exits. I looked out for Angela but I couldn't see her.

The next few days were rained off but we were soon back filming, this time on something street and '5th'. Angela looked increasingly hot to me each time I saw her – today she was playing a businesswoman. We met again the following day, which required an intricate sequence of filming in a factory. We'd already spoken about the socio-economic rise of southern hip hop and the use or misuse of the N-word in music.

During one break I said, 'You know what's really lame is that you haven't once asked me for my number?' as if it was preposterous.

She laughed. 'Lame like that line?'

'What line? I come to your country and you still haven't shown me around.'

'We've been working,' she said.

'But otherwise you would have?'

'Would have what?' she said, playing dumb.

'Been my tour guide!' I pretended to do sign language. 'I tip well!'

'Maybe.' She smiled.

That smile was enough. Like Pritz, I went in for the kill. Yes, I was flirting and yes, it was working – I'd finally found something she succumbed to.

I gave her my call sheet to put her number on as I stood behind the Assistant Director, sending him vibes to shout 'Wrap'. Not just because I wanted to ask Angela to join me for dinner but because I'd also had enough. Having continuously heard the same song again and again on set, I had vowed never to wear a shirt so I wouldn't ever have reason to pop its bloody collar.

40
HOORAY FOR HOLLYWOOD

Zoe had seen me hanging around Angela, not filming a single vox-pop, and realized I was doing more than having a cultural exchange about our two countries. So she booked a table that night at some swanky LA restaurant called Linq, supposedly for the whole crew but, like a superb wing woman, then left it to the two of us. She sent me a text later saying, 'Thanks for your hard work – courtesy of the label.'

We had the whole night to ourselves with no pressure as the next, and final, day of shooting didn't start until nine p.m. Angela had already agreed to spend the next day showing me the sights, and I was looking forward to it. Over dinner, Angela and I became absorbed in conversation once more. It was exciting to flick from one subject to the next and then come back again. I felt a pinch of guilt, momentarily forgetting I had no reason to feel bad any more. It was OK to be enjoying my time with Angela. She was completely on my wavelength when it came to The Beat and how hard you had to work to make it in the industry. The only time my attention swayed was when Jennifer Aniston came into the restaurant.

'Oh my God, there's Rachel,' I said out loud, like a nerdy fan with my mouth gawping wide and my finger still pointing.

I quickly wiped the gormless look off my face and replaced it with a straight one. It was meant to be sexy, but I think it probably looked as if I was constipated.

'So do you . . . ?'

'Do *you*?' I asked back, not sure what she was asking but playing along.

She laughed. 'I see. You wanna see what I say before you say what you wanna say?'

'That's right,' I said, pretending to follow.

'No, I don't,' she said straight-faced. 'How about you?'

I finally got what she meant when I saw a suspicious look in her eyes. I went to respond about having a girlfriend but hesitated. 'Er . . . well . . .' I stuttered.

'Uh oh,' she said, laughing.

It was the last thing I wanted to discuss but I found myself telling her about my relationship with Sophia and how things had gone bad between us. Lack of time. Insecurities. Trust. Sophia cheating on me. Somehow it was easy to talk to a stranger about it all.

She didn't take sides, playing devil's advocate at every turn with 'Perhaps they were enjoying a lazy Sunday afternoon on the sofa?' and 'Maybe they were startled because of the knocking on the window.' But she did break her neutrality, laughing at my Eddie Murphy impression when I told her I'd left a surprise in Simon's exhaust pipe *à la Beverly Hills Cop*.

'So, where are you now with it?' she asked.

'She's been emailing and texting, wanting to talk, but what's there to talk about?' I said. 'It's over.'

'Clarification? Closure?' she offered.

'I suppose. I still can't come to terms with the fact that she made me doubt myself. My gut instinct. Even if it's all circumstantial, at what point do you believe in yourself and stop believing in the other person?'

She paused for a moment before responding. 'Good question. I've always believed in myself because that way, if the shit hits the fan, the mistakes are mine to make and not someone else's.'

I looked at her like she'd made a crucial point in a murder trial.

'The way you've been acting the last few days I'd never have thought there was something wrong. You seem so happy,' she said, perplexed.

'That's the thing with this job, it helps you mask things. You get so involved that you forget about your life. I think that's been the problem. On the one hand it's a gift, but on the other, it's a curse.'

Before Angela got in her cab to go home, she kissed me on both cheeks and hugged me as I stood looking confused, feeling the world's troubles back on my shoulders again. 'Jay, thanks for a great evening. It's been the most fun I've had in ages,' she said, smiling.

'Yes, all the talk about my ex must have been real fun,' I said apologetically.

'Look, I'm sure if it was the other way around you'd have been a friend to me,' she said reassuringly.

I rubbed my forehead. 'Thanks. I've not really had a chance to make sense of it in my head since it all happened. Anyway, I'll see you tomorrow for the sight-seeing trip.'

She opened the door to the cab. 'One thing I have to say,'

she started before she got in. 'If I was your girl, I wouldn't have had him round if he was the cause of the fight in New York. But that's just me.' Then she climbed inside and blew me a kiss from the window as the cab pulled away.

I slept for a few hours and woke up in time to go sightseeing with Angela. We drove around hitting as many spots as possible from Rodeo Drive to Venice Beach, picking up some cheesy gifts for the guys in the office along the way. We parted ways briefly only to reconvene at nine p.m. at the club, where she was dressed like a reveller in a sequined white top and tight white jeans.

It was the early hours of the morning when I got my final soundbite from Usher, followed by the Assistant Director shouting out, 'Thank you all from Usher Raymond, the king of R&B. This was "Pop Ya Collar" – put a fork in it, we're done!'

Everyone dispersed in different directions. Some went to find one of the few cabs that were around at that time of the morning, while others gathered around Usher's trailer, hoping for a wrap party. Zoe air-kissed us goodbye and went straight to the airport for an early flight.

Angela dragged me into a cab, saying, 'There's one last place you need to see before you go.'

She leant forward and whispered into the driver's ear and then covered my eyes with both her hands as we drove off. As we reached our destination, she removed her hands and it really was the best place to end the trip. I stepped out of the cab and marvelled at the view of the city below and the huge 'Hollywood' sign above us.

We sat on a bench to see the sunrise as I received another text from Sophia, asking to talk. I showed it to Angela.

'So, what are you going to say?' she asked.

I took in a deep breath and typed.

Sophia. I'm not sure what's left to discuss. I saw it all with my own eyes. You made your bed. Jay.

I pressed 'send'.

I looked down at the phone, wiped its memory back to factory settings so my messages wouldn't be on it for the next person who used it and then I shut it off.

And the next thing I knew, I was watching Angela as she kissed my lips. At first it felt weird, but soon a buzzing sensation was running through me. When we finally stopped, I said, 'So how was that?'

She put her hand horizontally in front of her and wiggled it saying, 'Nyaaa.'

Once back at my hotel, we shared one last long kiss before she headed home to sleep. I'd get mine on the plane, which I was now within a whisker of missing.

'Call me,' she said, blowing me a kiss through the cab's open window.

Meeting Angela had come at just the right time. Seeing Sophia with Simon had knocked my confidence, but Angela had fully reinstated it. There were plenty more fish in the sea and, bizarrely, some of them wanted to be caught by me.

I grabbed my gear and raced back out to a waiting cab. 'Airport, please, mate. And quick as you can.'

The traffic was awful and I felt myself getting tense as we crawled along the freeway towards the airport. I tried to distract myself with the newspaper and the inconclusive results of the presidential election, but it didn't help. I rushed to the check-in desk and was met by a middle-aged Hispanic lady who confirmed the worst. 'I'm sorry, sir, you've missed that flight.'

'But I have to make it, it's imperative that I do,' I said with a tone of desperation. *Imperative to my job, that is. The Minister will have my guts if he finds out I missed my flight.* I'd already been gone for longer than expected and earlier in the week he'd set a deadline for my return 'or I could stay out there permanently'.

'I'm sorry, sir, there's nothing we can do,' she said in a dismissive nasal tone that check-in staff seem to specialize in at times.

'Listen, you have no idea how important it is,' I pleaded, thinking of the huge sum I'd have to stump up for a new ticket.

'I'm sorry, sir, I told you there's nothing we can do.' She raised her voice as others started to look over at us.

I slumped on her desk, my passport, ticket, wallet, call sheet and the driver's newspaper, that I'd taken by mistake, all strewn on the desk looking as haphazard as I felt. I wanted to fling something at the woman's head when I suddenly felt something click in my own as I looked at the cover of the newspaper.

'You have to help me . . .' I said, peering down at her name badge, 'Gabrielle. It's vital I get to Washington ASAP.' Leaning into her slightly, and in a calm voice, I said, 'I have to interview the new President of the United States of America for The Beat in the UK.' I pulled out my ID card and showed her. 'If I don't go, I'll be fired,' I said, sounding as posh as I could.

'*You're* going to interview the new President?' she asked, looking like she didn't believe a word.

'Yes,' I said with unwavering conviction.

'Which one you interviewing?' she asked with a poker face.

'The winner, of course,' I replied, unsure quite what to say. She looked sceptical so I continued with more gusto. 'We reach a huge and influential young audience who love current affairs. I only have a limited window today in which to do the interview, and a very specific time-slot from the White House.'

Within moments, my bag was heading down the conveyor belt and she had booked me on a different plane to Washington that would then allow me to make my connecting flight to London.

'Bless you, bless America,' I said as I gathered all my stuff. 'LA truly is the City of Angels. It truly is.' I hammed it up as much as possible.

I hurriedly raced to the departure gate and as I finally made it to my seat on the plane, I checked my rucksack for all my important things. Passport, check. Wallet, check. Tapes from the shoot, check. But something was missing. I frantically looked through my bag. The horror inside me kept growing and growing. It dawned on me that I had left the newspaper at the check-in desk with my call sheet under it. The call sheet Angela had written her number on.

41
GENTLEMAN

A week back in London and I was feeling the LA blues. Tola and I walked into the office with bags of filming equipment over our shoulders, having interviewed Green Day at one of the pubs nearby. Communication between us was still at a bare minimum. As I looked around the Production department I realized there were lots of unfamiliar faces in the form of freelancers. Brought in to work on the Minister's new shows, no doubt.

There were people running back and forth from the gangway, near to where the heads of departments sat by the windows.

'Mate, the Minister wants to see you at his desk,' said James III, looking concerned as he came to deliver the message.

What now? I thought as my stomach rumbled for food.

I dropped my bags, quickly gobbled a half-eaten Twix from my drawer and went to see him. A small group were gathered around his office so I stood on the outside listening in.

'If this gets reported to the watchdog, we're in the crapper,' said one voice.

'I'll try and minimize any other fallout,' said another.

I suddenly felt like Tupac as all eyes were on me and silence gripped the group. They parted like the Red Sea, leaving a direct path to the Minister, who sat at his desk looking up at me with rage in his eyes.

'So you got my message then?' he said.

'I was at a shoot –'

'Sit down.' He pointed at the chair in front of his desk.

I scanned my brain for all the possible things I could have done wrong. It felt like seeing a police car in a rear-view mirror. I immediately felt guilty and panicky, although I didn't know why.

'So I'd like to congratulate you on getting the company in the shit,' he said.

'What?' I said, in total shock

'You write the links and choose the videos for *Defm8*, don't you?'

'Yes, I do.'

'So it's true then, this is our fault?' he said, leaning back in his chair.

Before I could say anything he began talking about a £100,000 fine and sending emails to HR. He sounded almost manic.

'The defamatory show that *you* produced had parents calling up to complain. You put a video in for Busta Rhymes called "Get Out!!". Is that true?'

'Yes, I did. Is there something wrong with that?' I asked, perplexed.

He looked down at a piece of paper and said, 'There is when it uses the words "motherfucker" twice, "fuck" seven times, "bitch" six times and "nigga" sixteen. I've had calls from parents wanting to know why their children have been watching this excuse for music.'

'Well, that's not the video I asked for. I asked for the clean one. I can prove it, I can send you my email instructions to the music programmers,' I said, defending my corner.

The Minister went quiet. 'Why did you put this video in anyway?' he asked.

'It's doing really well on radio and it's been in the charts.'

'Well, it shouldn't have been in there. After that whole "U.G.L.Y." song debacle you should know better. A proper producer would know this,' he said, clearly on the back foot and not knowing what else to come back at me with.

'Well, that's the criteria Max told me to follow.'

'You know what, I'm sure we can contain this,' said a voice from the group of people behind me, who it appeared had hung around to watch the fireworks.

'It's not as bad as a few years ago when we accidentally played "Smack My Bitch Up" at four o'clock just as the kids were getting home for their tea!' said another, laughing.

The Minister maintained a straight face as the others saw the funnier side of it.

'It's clearly human error and I'm sure the two parents who called in will understand. I'll send some flowers and tickets to a concert,' said another voice.

'But not to a Busta Rhymes gig.' They all laughed.

The Minister, who was still seething, said, 'Consider this a warning, Jay. You can get out now.' The others laughed even harder at his choice of words.

As I got to my desk, I forwarded the Minister my email

to the programmers in which I'd underlined the need to play the clean version. He didn't reply and my blood boiled like the passenger who runs to catch the bus only for the driver to close the doors in his face at the bus stop and drive off.

I'd spent the rest of the week at the edit house, cutting footage from the set of Usher's video shoot while contending with a barrage of phone calls from Sophia. I hadn't picked up at all since my return from LA as I didn't want to hear her voice or any of her excuses but I couldn't stop myself from reading some of the emails she'd sent imploring me to consider her side of things. Her words began to run around in my head, looking for a governor to sign a pardon. Doubt had led to the downfall of our relationship and was now playing the double agent, making me think I was making a mistake.

At home The Beat played in the background as I packed a travel bag. The next day I was flying to our annual awards show in Amsterdam. The mundane task allowed my head to flood with voices. It was time to hear closing arguments.

EMINEM: It's done. Jay's finished with her.

DIDO: Are you sure? Things weren't the best between them for most of this year and yes, they fought, but that's passion.

EMINEM: No, it wasn't. She's childish, immature and it's all a waste of energy.

DIDO: He was no better. The relationship wasn't perfect but when push comes to shove, she's his LV, his little Sophster.

EMINEM: Yeah, yeah, yeah. She cheated.

DIDO: Circumstantial. We don't know that for sure . . .

EMINEM: The text messages at the barbecue, lying about NYC

and then the two of them cuddled up on the sofa at hers. What more do you want, a signed confession?

DIDO: Jay's not been immune to the temptation of other women, remember?

EMINEM: Opportunity has come knocking but . . .

DIDO: Alyssa's party, The Beat parties . . .

EMINEM: OK, so he's guilty of flirting and enjoying the rush of getting attention. Is that a sin? Is it so bad to boost your confidence a little?

DIDO: And Isabel?

EMINEM: Look, we're straying off the point.

DIDO: Shall we point to his insane jealousy and paranoia?

EMINEM: Sophia's constant need for attention?

DIDO: His selfishness?

EMINEM: Her insecurities?

DIDO: What about his insecurities?! Look, we could argue all day about who screwed things up first. But look at the part he's played in this. Has he changed? Has he really been there for her? Surely he's not blameless?

Having finished packing, I grabbed a tennis ball and fell on to the bed. I lay on my back and began throwing it up to the ceiling and catching it until I totally misjudged it and it hit me right on the nose.

EMINEM: Perhaps Sophia needs to be single and enjoy university life too. Maybe that's why she continued to keep Simon in her life despite your concerns.

DIDO: Just as he'd decided to keep working all the time and neglect her? It's like R. Kelly warned about when a woman's fed up . . .

EMINEM: OK, so they both sabotaged the relationship. Clearly it's something that they both want, then?

DIDO: Is it?

EMINEM: Maybe he needs to be alone and enjoy this point in his life. Enjoy The Beat the way Pritz was doing at the Voodoo Lounge.

DIDO: That's your reason to break up? To play the field?

EMINEM: OK, what if there's someone even better out there for him? His experience is pretty thin! He's burnt right now, let it heal before stepping out.

I got up and went into the kitchen, looking for another distraction. It was in a mess and causing quite a stench. Pritz and I kept leaving it for the other person to clean, so empty Pot Noodle containers and pizza boxes were building up. I stood by the sink and waited for the hot water to come through the tap.

EMINEM: I won't deny it's going to be hard to let go of her, but in time it'll be all right.

DIDO: What if it won't? What if he's made a horrible mistake and the pain lasts much longer? Is he giving up someone truly special? Remember how he'd regularly sit and talk on the phone till the early hours of the morning?

EMINEM: That was just in the early romantic stages. Don't you remember how recently he'd been up until the early hours of the morning arguing?

DIDO: You think he can get this connection with anyone else? She knows his heart's thoughts before . . . before he knows himself. That's why she's his LV.

The kitchen was spotless. There was just the bathroom to go. *Pritz can do that*, I thought. I went to the front room and began flicking through the TV channels for something interesting, watching *X-Files* briefly until I landed back home on The Beat.

DIDO: OK, so explain why there's a pain in his chest right now? Is it because he knows it's a mistake?

EMINEM: That's understandable. This is someone he loves, not some squeeze. But he'll have to forget her. Throw himself into work.

DIDO: And thoughts of her won't come into his head when he's not working?

EMINEM: He'll just turn to music for help, like he's always done.

DIDO: That's not going to work. It's not working now. You don't get it – he wouldn't just be losing a girlfriend, Sophia's his best friend.

Was I scared to be alone? Was I just more concerned that she'd be with someone else after me? Simon? Someone she might love more? But surely fear wasn't a reason to stay in a relationship? I had to have faith. In karma, in God, the universe, the tooth fairy – in anything.

Coldplay's 'Trouble' played in the background as I sat there listening. The lyrics repeated until the song came to an end and the screen went black momentarily. I sat in silence staring into the TV.

42
STAN

We were in Amsterdam for The Beat Awards and, having checked into Hotel Okura the night before the ceremony, we'd already taken in the famous 'coffee shops' and some small private parties PJ had been invited to. They were the perfect warm-up to the excitement of the main event, but no one wanted to peak too soon. However, today *was* the main event. The Beat's chance to hold the biggest party saluting the best musical acts of the year and letting over a billion people worldwide share in it.

For PJ it was a chance to complete a lifelong mission to meet 'Her'. You could say he was a fan, bordering on a 'Stan'. Of Her music? Maybe. Of Her multi-faceted abilities? Likely. Or was it the fact that She was the only megastar still on his list that he hadn't interviewed? Definitely. He'd come close to meeting Her a few times in the UK but fate had always conspired against him. Now he had just twenty-four hours to complete his mission.

'I've assembled the best in the game. OK, the best I could find . . . at short notice . . . from what was left,' said PJ sarcastically.

We all groaned as we stood in the hotel lobby desperate to go for breakfast.

'Now I want us to stay focused. We all know what our M.O. is.'

'M.O.?' asked James III.

'Modus operandi,' said PJ, like it was obvious.

James III leant into me and whispered, 'I didn't know PJ could speak French,' with a genuine look of amazement. I shook my head.

'We're a well-oiled machine like U2. I'm gonna lead the front like Bono, Stuey you can be Edge, Jay and James III, you can be the other two,' he said.

Now just the two of us groaned. 'We know our target, troops,' he went on, pointing to the cover of a CD. 'Our mission is to track down and rendezvous with Her. Now some of you might not make it, but it was an honour serving with you all,' he finished dramatically.

We all stood facing each other and saluted as James III whistled the tune from *The Great Escape*. It was the first time I'd heard him whistle something other than a Christmas tune.

'What about me?' said Tola, standing on the outside of the group.

PJ stood in silence for a moment, thinking.

'You're the cheerleader,' he said, unable to think of anything better.

'Gee, thanks,' she said with a fake smile.

Having eaten and briefly pausing for James III to have his 'shit, shave and shower', we all went on the hunt together.

We started at Her hotel, from where the trail went hot and cold as we passed through boutique stores and various tourist sites. Conscious that he was in Amsterdam to work, PJ would stop at each location and film a link to camera, highlighting the great city then throwing to a music video. This would all be part of the show PJ had conceived – a 'behind the scenes' at the awards. The city had been covered in guerrilla marketing that had The Beat's infinity logo and today's date plastered everywhere. Finally we got a phone call: the final rehearsal for Her would be after lunch at the venue, Passenger Terminal Amsterdam.

Inside, it was a huge operation behind the scenes, with lots of staff, makeshift offices, stage rigging, cameras, cables and instruments all piled into a small space. The mood felt like The Beat staff summer party all over again, but on a grander scale as people attended from all the four corners. Although not everyone had been lucky enough to make it over to Amsterdam. Staff from different departments across the company had been flown in to work as talent escorts to all the celebrities attending. These positions had been decided by lottery, so even if you only worked in the tape library, it might just be you. One day you're sending out Madonna's music videos, the next you're leading Her around the awards venue screaming, 'Out of the way please, Madonna coming through!' Kate, the T.A.D. intern, had been the lucky lottery winner to escort Her, so she was acting as our woman on the inside.

By now it was lunchtime so we went to Crew Catering and grabbed some supplies. Just as I'd got some food, my phone rang. It was Kate telling me our target had arrived and was going straight to a closed rehearsal. Artists didn't like to give interviews during rehearsals as they were usually without make-up and we weren't sure She would like to either, but it was a gamble PJ was happy to take. We ran out, to the annoyance of James III who had carefully piled food on to two plates. He followed behind with a chicken wing in his mouth. We snuck in undetected with PJ at the helm.

'OK, you two take exit A at the left of stage and we'll take exit B at the right of stage,' he said, pointing at me to stick with him. 'Whichever side She comes off, try and hold Her there and call for back-up,' said PJ, moving and pointing like a general directing his troops.

As we sat in the empty seats, we realized She was performing just for us and the handful of cameramen who were rehearsing for the live show. PJ's wet dream had come true as She performed in front of us in living colour. One song and a heap of pyrotechnics later, the music and lights went off. We waited by our phones thinking that James III and Tola had cornered Her at Exit A as we'd had no movement at ours. My phone finally rang.

'Is that them? Where is She?' asked an enthusiastic PJ.

'Yes . . . aha . . . right . . . I see . . . OK . . . get me the extra large pizza and a Pepsi,' I said jokingly.

PJ wasn't in the mood for jokes.

'Sorry! That was Kate, Her escort. She left through the secret door in the middle of the stage. It's part of the routine!'

'Oh, I'll get Her. She's not getting away from me that easy,' he said defiantly.

We got back to Crew Catering to find our plates had been cleared away. Just as we were about to queue up again, I got a call from another informant telling me She had been seen heading to Artists' Catering on the other side of the building. Once again, with cameras in hand, we fled the scene, this time with a hot cross bun in James III's mouth. PJ lead the way. The wrong way.

Eventually we got back on the right track and managed to blag our way past the heavy security into Artists' Catering. We weren't meant to be in there but PJ wanted to film its opulence for a link to camera. The specially constructed area looked like the inside of a three-starred Michelin restaurant. A variety of food was being served, from roast beef and posh fish finger sandwiches to sushi and low fat snacks. There were even flamingos made entirely of fruit perched in every corner like statues, alongside chocolate fountains.

PJ went looking for Her as the rest of us stood waiting. James III's stomach began to rumble loudly at the sight of the food laid out. He sat down on a sofa nearby looking tired and hungry. But any thought of grabbing something to eat disappeared as the head of T.A.D., 'the Duke', walked in.

'What are you boys doing in here?' he asked like a headmaster.

'We're just waiting for PJ,' Stuey replied without flinching.

I panicked inwardly. The Duke was known for dishing out 'hairdryer' moments.

'What for? Even PJ shouldn't be in here,' he said firmly.

I clenched my butt cheeks a little tighter as his voice reverberated in my ears.

'Oh, we know, but he's saying hi to some of his, you know,

famous friends. Bloody annoying seeing as we have so many things to film,' Stuey said.

The Duke looked suspiciously at our cameras. 'Right. Well make sure you're not filming in here. I don't want to have anyone complaining.'

'Of course. You can trust us,' said Stuey, straight-faced.

PJ eventually returned, looking disappointed at not having found Her but nevertheless used the opportunity to try to get the Duke to organize a one-on-one interview.

'She's already given us a five-minute interview for all the regions to use. So don't try looking for another one. I don't want to get any complaints from Her management cos they'll eat my balls for breakfast.' But I could see that the more the Duke dissuaded us, the more it egged PJ on.

'Right, time we rolled out. People to see, filming to do,' said Stuey, leading the way out quickly.

We kept following the trail She had left, going to the artists' dressing rooms, the huge press and media rooms and everywhere else we received information from, but we didn't catch a break. As it got closer to show time the sense of anticipation grew as backstage filled with dancers and extras. But what really fuelled things were the rumours of celebrity strops, walkouts and fights.

By five p.m. we gave up and went back to our hotel to change and grab a bite to eat. PJ's spirit picked up after a plate of sushi and a glass of wine, and he was soon plotting again. I knew James III was back to his happy best, not just because he'd finally refuelled, but because he was whistling his Christmas carols again as we walked back to our chauffeured people carrier.

As we drove back to the venue, the illuminated infinity logo shooting into the sky on the blackened horizon was a beacon, alerting the people of Amsterdam that their city had been taken over. It was so bright I was sure the International Space Station would be picking up on it too. As I looked at the Batman-like beam, I turned to Stuey. 'Why are the awards in Amsterdam of all places?

'True say, there are a lot of factors, but I suppose whichever city puts in the highest bid helps,' he said.

'Oh, so they pay for the awards to be here?' I said, surprised.

'Putting on awards ain't cheap, homeboy. Consider the city as a sponsor, like some TV shows have. The money they pay gets recouped from all the PR the city receives across the world, not to mention the boost to the local economy.'

'That's some serious bragging rights,' said Tola.

Before I could ask about facts and figures we pulled up to the security gates. A huge crowd of kids had gathered in the freezing cold and welcomed us with deafening screams. James III quickly pressed his face flat to the window like he was squashed against it. Kids began to take pictures of him, not sure which celebrity it was inside the car.

Once inside, we waited for Her on the red carpet, interviewing famous guests in the meantime. Every major and minor news agency from across the globe had hustled for a spot, ready to quiz the celebrities on everything from scandalous gossip to who designed their outfit. Photographers screamed the stars' names as an orgasm of flashes went off and they posed for pictures.

Unsuccessful, we moved our search for Her into the

auditorium, which was packed to the rafters. Fans were sending round a Mexican wave to spread the energy before kick-off and we stood by the side of the stage, taking in the atmosphere that was building up. The VIP section of the audience housed strictly A-listers, including musicians, politicians, sportsmen, actors and a few members of organized crime who'd 'found' their way in.

'Didn't I tell you we'd have fun?' said PJ as we stood away from the others, glancing out on to the audience.

'Nothing's happened yet,' I said, playing it cool but giddy inside as Fatboy Slim's 'Right Here, Right Now' played prophetically on the speakers.

'Mmm, can you smell it?' he asked with his eyes shut. He tilted his head back and inhaled. 'Can you smell the aura? All these artists in one place. Tonight is my Christmas, Passover, Eid, Chinese New Year and Diwali all rolled into one.'

I remembered a similar speech from him at the bar at the Delano in Miami.

'They can smell it,' he said, pointing to the audience. 'All those kids are believers.'

I looked at all the keen faces of the kids who had waited several hours out in the cold just so they could get to the front of the stage. *Were they smelling it?* I wondered.

'Let's go, I just got word She's arrived,' said Stuey, coming and putting his arm round us both.

Backstage was now mayhem. Fully dressed and made-up dancers riddled the corridors along with their props as The Beat escorts rushed back and forth from the red carpet to the dressing rooms with their VIPs. Both new and old members of the musical family of the world had congregated together and were getting ready for one big party.

We went to Her dressing-room door to find a big burly bouncer standing guard, not allowing anyone inside. Not even PJ's charms worked on this guy; he wouldn't budge literally or metaphorically. PJ would have stood there the whole night if it weren't for the interview we had to do with The Spice Girls and Destiny's Child before the show started.

Once the show got under way it was a blur. One minute we were flashing our Access-All-Areas passes to go backstage and film, the next we were rushing front of house to catch a performance or a watch a guest presenter giving out an award. There was so much excitement it was hard not to get caught up in it all. Our base camp was outside Her dressing room and was where we set off from and came back to after smaller missions. When we weren't interviewing people, we'd be catching up with The Beat escorts to hear all the gossip: who'd thrown a tantrum, who didn't like who and bizarre goings-on in the dressing rooms.

*NSYNC were the next interview for us and Tola was left to stand guard with a camera outside Her door just in case She came out pre-show and we could scoop an exclusive. Tola stood next to the emotionless bouncer and tried to make polite conversation, hoping it might get us in, but he was well briefed in espionage.

PJ hadn't given up hope. He was still a believer. After our interview finished we stood by the stairs leading to the trapdoor on stage, patiently waiting as thunderous applause rang around the venue as She finished Her performance. Moments later we realized we'd been outmanoeuvred again and headed back to base camp to see the big bouncer gone. PJ rushed over and popped his head round the door to find an empty dressing room.

'Where is She?' he asked desperately.

'They've gone,' said Tola, shrugging her shoulders.

'Gone? Already?' I asked.

'I heard She was on a flight back to America tonight,' said Tola.

'What? Why didn't you call us?' said PJ.

'I tried but there was no reception. I explained the situation and tried to hold them as long as I could, but then they left.'

'Did you get anything, a manager's name, number, any sort of a lead?' he asked.

'I got a vox-pop,' she said.

'A vox-pop? A bloody vox-pop?' said PJ, astonished.

'Well, She was being rushed off, it was lucky that She had time to do even that. I had to beg Her management to let Her do it. They were being really protective,' said Tola exasperated.

We sat in Her empty room checking our kit as PJ sulked, watching Foo Fighters close the show on Her TV. Eventually he trudged off alone, talking on his phone. Our work for the night had just begun, but the main event, which had taken nine months to plan and pull off, had been a huge success. The Beat had once again connected all the global tribes finding a true common ground – the love of music. For us it was part two of our evening: the afterparty.

43
I WANT HER

We sat in our people carrier out back, preparing to go and film at the afterparty at the ballroom in Hotel Okura. Everyone from the awards was heading there, but not everyone was going to get in. All of a sudden the door slid open and in jumped PJ pulling behind him a massive sports bag with one hand while the other clutched on to a Beat Award.

'Drive! Drive!' he said as he slammed the door shut like he was Michael Caine in *The Italian Job*.

'What the hell is that?' asked Tola.

'That, my friends, is a swag bag,' said PJ, now all smiles as the taxi drove away.

'Which is?' I asked.

'It's the bag they give to the VIPs as a thank you,' explained Stuey. 'It's full of goodies.'

James III was peering over PJ's shoulder for a better look. 'Like what?'

'Well, let's have a look, shall we?' he said, unzipping the bag.

Out came everything Santa Claus had set aside for someone rich: a golden Motorola handset, a Viktor & Rolf diamond bracelet, Jo Malone candles, a magnum of Moët, dinner for two at Nobu (London and New York), a Gucci bag, DVDs, a PlayStation 2 with games, a weekend away at the luxury Half Moon resort in Jamaica, a track day at Silverstone. It was endless and PJ kept going until the bag was emptied out on the seat next to him.

'How did you manage to get that then?' asked Stuey.

'This smile gets me a long way. Jay, you can verify this,' said PJ, looking at me.

'So you stole it?' said Stuey, laughing.

'Stole? Such a dirty word. No, no.' PJ shook his head.

'And The Beat award?' Tola asked.

'That? Yes, I stole that,' he said unashamedly.

'Whose is it?' asked James III, still peering over from the back seat.

PJ turned it upside down and read the label. 'Dr Dre.'

Everyone laughed.

From the co-pilot's seat, Stuey blasted his favourite album of all time, *Born In The USA*, as the driver zipped through the streets of Amsterdam and deposited us on the red carpet outside the hotel. The party promoter was a friend of PJ's and had given us exclusive access to film inside. He led us to a cellar-cum-storage cupboard for alcohol where we could stash our kit.

As the others filmed around the party, PJ and I went to the velvet-roped VIP section to interview any celebs we could find who were not totally off their faces. PJ stood marvelling at his surroundings and inhaling the aura from the people in the room like it was a 1787 bottle of Château Lafite. People were already making power moves, forging new alliances that were both business and pleasure. The promoter had spared no expense in putting on a food and drink extravaganza for the guests. It was a party fit for King Louis XIV, the extravagant French monarch. The scene was set for an all-night lock-in. And I was there.

As we filmed in the far corner of the ballroom, the DJ went digging in his crates for everything from Black Legend 'You See the Trouble with Me' to Wu-Tang Clan's 'Gravel Pit'. Everyone was letting their hair down, some more than others, as celebrities jumped on to the small stage in front of the DJ booth and a guy began rapping like a drunken uncle at a birthday party.

'Stop filming, stop filming!' yelled PJ into his mic, which fed to my headphones.

'Why?' I said, wincing with earache.

'She's not on a plane to America, She's on the bloody stage over there!' he shouted, nudging past an out-of-costume Sacha Baron Cohen.

I craned my head to see if I could spot Her. Everyone was crowded round the tiny stage that held the stars, trying to get on. By the time we got there Security was forcing the crowd back, including us with our camera. We were being pushed further and further away with the tide. I had to take action: no one else would have this footage apart from our show, and it was the golden ticket all news outlets would want access to. I left PJ behind and pushed through the crowd, holding the camera above people's heads. I tried to film Her and the others dancing as people stepped on my feet, kicked my shins and elbowed me.

As I moved forward, two super-hot blondes sandwiched me and began dancing with me. The busty one behind me was squeezing my butt, while the big booty one at the front was 'backing that thang up' like Juvenile. It was the most fun I'd ever had filming. It was like being fed grapes and getting a massage from Gisele while you worked. The real rub though came moments later when one of the blondes began massaging my crotch. When I looked at her with shock she just smiled and carried on.

I eventually pulled myself away and fought through the crowd as She came off the stage because of the mayhem She was causing. PJ and I chased the mob all the way to the front door of the hotel and saw Her whisked away from the party. PJ looked like he wanted to throw The Beat mic on the floor and scream.

I dropped him off with the others on the Universal Records table to get drunk as I went to put the cameras away for the night. The door to the room that had our equipment in was held open by a fire extinguisher, allowing extra light into the dark room. I crouched down and started putting things away when I heard the sound of heels behind me. I got up and looked round to see Busty and Booty drunkenly walking towards me, knocking over empty champagne bottles, giggling and whispering.

'Hi, ladies, I'm just packing . . .' I said as they came into the room.

Without warning, Busty shoved her tongue in my mouth and began kissing me while Booty began biting at my neck. My eyes popped out of my head. I didn't have much control over things as the voice in my head was jumping for joy. After what felt like an age of kissing later, Busty asked, 'So what's your name?' in the sexiest broken English accent.

'Jay,' I said, gasping for air. My heart was thumping so

loudly with excitement, I was sure they could hear it too.

'So what do you do?' asked Booty, in an equally sexy voice.

I thought it was a trick question, seeing as they'd seen me filming.

'I work for The Beat,' I said.

They began whispering in a foreign language. My slightly drunken mind suddenly got paranoid, thinking, *Is this going to end like the urban myth, where one of my kidneys gets farmed out of me?*

'So where's the afterparty?' asked Busty, running her fingernails gently across my neck.

'This *is* the afterparty,' I said, trying to stay cool.

They began kissing me again, their hands running all over me and this time a hand went into my boxer shorts.

'No, the *after* afterparty,' asked Booty more sharply.

I was confused. 'The *after* afterparty?'

Did they want to go back to my hotel room? Had I just hit the jackpot? Was I having an out of body experience? Hold on, was I Pritz? Do as he does, I thought.

'I know the promoter so I'm sure he has something planned,' I said hurriedly. They began whispering again and then pushed me to the wall in the far corner of the room and unzipped my jeans.

'No promises, though,' I said, suddenly enjoying acting like Pritz for the first time in my life. As soon as I'd said that, they tried even harder to get a promise out of me. They did. Twice.

We agreed to meet by the bar as I began to put the kit away. They giggled drunkenly and left the room as they'd come into it, knocking over bottles, crates and the fire extinguisher. The door slammed behind them as I shoved things into any available space with the aim of keeping my buzz going and getting back out into the party. I wanted to see the look on everyone's faces as I walked up to the Universal table like a pimp, with a blonde on each arm.

As I got to the closed door and went to turn the door handle, I missed, causing me to lean forward and headbutt the door. I looked down at the door handle to find I wasn't that drunk – it actually wasn't there. I stood staring at the door as everything clicked into place.

The fire extinguisher that now lay by my feet was used to keep the door open so it didn't lock, not to let light in. This wasn't the type of lock-in I wanted to be a part of. I looked around for anything to open it. Nothing. I tried shouting over the loud music for help. Nothing. I looked at my phone to call the others. No reception.

I was itching to get out, not just because of the blondes and the amazing party but because I was enjoying the best buzz ever. It was time to blow the lid off the excitement that had been building up for days. It felt like I was beginning to taste the aura PJ was talking about, but it was hard to tell from behind a locked door.

In between swigs of vodka, I kept the pleas for help going. I refused to let the buzz die away. I even got up and danced in the room alone. But when I realized how pathetic the night had become, I collapsed in a heap, feeling miserable. There were now just fifteen minutes to go until the official end of the party and I was stuck in a damp-smelling storage room alone, wondering why my friends hadn't come to find me.

As I hugged my vodka bottle the door flung open and a

waiter looked at me with surprise. I didn't stop to thank him, I just raced past him to freedom. As I got out into the hall, the party was winding down and the standard of girls had dropped. I assumed all the pretty ones had been thrown over shoulders and taken away. The 'quarter to three' slim pickings were left. I raced to the bar, but Busty and Booty were gone. I ran to the VIP section to find the others where I'd left them, drinking.

'Where have you been?' asked Stuey as I ran up to them.

I was about to go into a long speech about how they'd left me locked in the storage room but suddenly thought better of it. 'So where's this after afterparty I've been hearing about?' I asked.

'It's upstairs in one of the big suites,' said PJ.

'So what are we doing here then?' I asked.

'Waiting for you. Leave no man behind, seen?' said Stuey.

'Where's Tola?' I asked.

'She's gone to her room slightly drunk. OK, very drunk,' said James III.

'OK, well let's go then,' I said, itching to party.

'What about the kit?' asked James III.

'It's safe. No one goes into that room,' I said.

Upstairs we entered a darkened suite, with the only light coming from behind the DJ booth. The choice crowd from the VIP section had been cut down so only the VVIPs had made it in. This was where the paparazzi would have had a field day. It was where the unreported juicy gossip happened and artists could really let their guard down. There were glass tables laid out with bottles of champagne and buckets of ice as the feel of a nightclub was brought into the suite.

We joined the promoter on one of his tables, ready to party till the early hours. It was surreal. There were celebrities two metres to my left, to my right and in front of me. The place was full of good-looking women who I was sure hadn't been downstairs, they were even better looking. I glanced around but Busty and Booty hadn't made the cut.

As the music bumped loud through the speakers I saw myriad colours enveloping those around me. Forget Miami, Vegas, the numerous Beat parties, the exclusive events we were invited to, the award ceremonies, the press junkets abroad and all the other things I'd experienced . . . this was it. There was no way Pritz or anyone else would believe it because even I didn't believe it. These were the moments PJ talked about being privileged to see, and here I was. Average Joe was sleeping in bed while we were living it up.

As we danced around our table PJ turned and spoke to me. 'So *now* can you smell it?' he asked, drinking straight from a bottle of Moët.

I laughed, then nodded towards the half Venezuelan, half Dutch girl he was dancing with. 'So I see you're not that upset about missing out on Her then?'

'Jay, the thing is, you have to continue to believe in tomorrow despite the setbacks.' He smiled and then joined in the screaming as Common's 'The Light' dropped.

We didn't get any sleep that morning, instead going straight to our rooms and then on to the airport with our luggage and some serious hangovers. As we all waited to board at the gate, we recognized most of the passengers as either Beat staff or artists. They had the same things in common

– an obvious lack of sleep, dark sunglasses and sore heads. At times you couldn't tell who was staff and who was a star. On the plane back to London, everyone was catching up on the gossip from the awards and the afterparty. Some of it was run-of-the-mill, like the woman from Online hooking up with the drummer of a band, but some was more salacious, like the member of senior management who was reportedly seen going into a hotel room with a teenager.

As we landed, the pilot came on to the tannoy system. 'This is Captain Curtis Jackson, I'd like to welcome you to London Heathrow. The time now is 11.56 a.m. As we taxi to the gate may I remind you to remain seated with your seat belts fastened until the seat belt sign is switched off . . . Finally a message from PJ to The Beat crew – well done on the awards last night. See you all next year.'

The plane erupted in applause and a communal 'Waaa-haaay!'

As everyone jumped into their Uncle Lee cabs home, I had to go straight to the edit and drop the tapes off to be readied for the next day. My work was just beginning, as Stuey and I had to deliver *Total BEATS* for a special one-off Sunday night transmission.

We began at seven a.m. in the Soho edit suites the following day. After working all day we continued through the night and the next day into Sunday evening. It seemed like a lot of time to make an hour-long show, but with all the footage we'd shot it wasn't. I'd already warned the broadcasting engineers we'd be cutting it really fine, delivering the tape for a transmission at eight p.m.

By seven thirty p.m. the show was finished and I jumped straight into a waiting Uncle Lee that took me to Notting Hill where the show was played live from the tape. It was close but we'd made it. I sat in the Greenhouse and watched the show go out on the huge TV screen, eating a packet of cheesy Doritos.

As the credits ran at the end of the show a now-familiar sense of pride jolted through me as my name came on for two seconds and the show eventually faded to black. Then one last vox-pop came on. It was Her.

'PJ. I'm sorry I kept missing you at the awards. I waited for you but you were nowhere to be seen. Maybe we can do it again when I'm next in London. Hopefully I'm worth the chase. [Blows kiss.]'

Moments later my phone rang. 'I knew it would be you,' I said, laughing.

'When did you get that?' he said like an excited child.

I laughed again. 'I didn't.'

'So who was it?' he asked.

'I found it when I was editing. Our cheerleader did well!'

'I owe her an apology. Tola deserves a promotion to three-star general for going beyond the call of duty.' He paused for a while, then added, 'You see, Jay, the man who persists in knocking will succeed in entering.'

44
RUN ON

'Come and sit down. I'm just waiting for someone to join us,' said the Minister in a serious tone, pointing at the chair in front of his desk. The last time I'd been sitting here, he was taking chunks out of me for something I didn't do.

The Beat's Sunday night schedule had been dedicated to the awards and the ratings had been the best for the year. Not only did *Total BEATS* lead the way but the show had been namechecked in the mainstream press for our exclusive footage of the afterparty.

People from different parts of the company had sent emails congratulating us all for a great show. I walked through the office like a star player instead of the sub from the bench.

But suddenly I felt uneasy in the Minister's presence. He wasn't exactly being warm, but then again when was he ever? Was he about to highlight a mistake, an oversight, a failure? Was the Duke about to come and tell me off for filming in Artists' Catering?

'I'm sorry I'm late, I was just on the phone,' said the Doc, dropping into the chair next to me.

'No problem, I was just sending an email,' said the Minister.

What is he doing here? I wondered, immediately even more worried.

'Jay, we'll get to the point,' said the Doc. 'It's about your show from the other night. Terry?' he said, letting my boss take the floor.

Oh no, here it comes . . .

'The Doc watched the show and he feels you're deserving of an on-the-spot bonus for your hard work,' the Minister said with a big smile.

'Thank you,' I responded, more shocked that the Minister was being so nice than about the bonus.

'Stuart Johns has also been acknowledged,' he added.

'The press coverage will go on for days. That's exactly what we need: people talking about what we do. The gossip, the drama, the controversy, it all makes us relevant,' said the Doc.

'This has really helped in the ratings war,' added the Minister.

I looked over at the Doc who beamed with pride as the Minister continued saying nice things about me. Was he finally seeing me as a valuable member of his team and not an annoyance? Had I turned him?

I sat feeling proud of the whole team but especially of myself. This was proof that all I had worked tirelessly for that year was worth it. The permanent position was now within reach and I was still in the race. I'd made the chequered-flag lap, albeit with a flat tyre, a smashed front wing and a burnt-out engine letting off flames. The championship that had started way back in April had turned out to be less Formula One, more 'Wacky Races'.

'Terry, you must be proud that this has come from your department. Well done to you for your vision, of course.'

'Yes, thank you, Doctor Hewson,' said the Minister, smiling.

Trust you to take all the glory, I thought to myself. *You didn't even know what we were doing out there.*

Soon the Doc was gliding down the walkway, meeting the troops on one of his regular 'walk and talks' that he said allowed him to feel the heartbeat of the company.

I sat there looking at the Minister. He looked uncomfortable but quickly brushed it aside. 'You can run on now.'

I got back to my desk and read two great emails. The first was from Marianne Stevens waxing lyrical about the Usher show I'd produced for the website. The second was from HR confirming my bonus – £1,000! Finally I could take back from Pritz some of the IOU slips I'd given him, signed on Monopoly money until I could pay him. What's more, I'd proved several people wrong and brought my boss on side.

'What you smiling about?' asked James III.

'Nothing,' I said. I didn't want the other interns to feel I was showing off. 'How about a rendition of "Joy to the World"?'

He gave me a strange look. 'You asking for that makes me worry for your state of mind,' he joked, then happily obliged.

I didn't have time to rejoice for long. I had to stay late to pull tapes, write scripts and prepare interviews for the next show. There was still a ratings war to win. Eventually, by ten thirty p.m., I couldn't go on any longer, feeling like a hamster running forever on a wheel. Pritz had texted me: he wanted to head out to a club and I felt I deserved to celebrate and rub his nose in my latest achievements. I grabbed my rucksack and left through the revolving doors on to the rain-soaked street.

With a spring in my step I headed towards the station. It was peacefully quiet except for the sound of a car door closing. I was just about to put my headphones on when the silence was broken again by two thuds. One was a punch to the back of my head and the other was my head smacking the bumper of a car as I crashed to the ground.

45
BEAT IT

I lay with my eyes shut, feeling exhausted and out of it. Which would have been acceptable if I was in bed. Unfortunately, I was lying on a rain-soaked street with my left ear pressed down flat in a puddle. I was sure I could hear the ocean. My right ear was ringing like it was four a.m. and I'd spent the night standing by a speaker at the Ministry of Sound. I could barely make out any other sounds except far-off traffic and what sounded like Charlie Brown's mumbling teacher standing over me.

I slowly opened my eyes to make sense of it, but everything was blurry and out of focus like a scene from a poncy French film. Water from the puddle filled my left eye while rain poured into the right one. As I squinted, all I could see was the deep darkness of the night sky and a streetlight nearby. A heavy-breathing dark shadow began to hover around me, occasionally blocking out the light. I blinked, trying to clear my vision again but everything remained out of focus. Despite my situation I was quite comfortable, like a drunkard on a street corner after a heavy night out. At least that's what I was thinking until I got kicked in my ging-gangs.

It was a direct connection – a full swing, the correct trajectory with controlled acceleration driving through to the tender point of contact. Kudos to the kicker. It was as sweet a connection as David Beckham famously lobbing the Wimbledon goalkeeper from the halfway line. Instantly I felt a heavily concentrated pain in my groin. My body collapsed inward as I went into the foetal position, both hands instinctively diving down to protect my crown jewels. The last time I felt it this bad was in primary school when a hard leather football did the damage and I'd slowly, yet hysterically, cried 'Mummy'. I barely suppressed the need to do it again now.

Adrenalin quickly spread through my veins as my body fell into deep shock. It was such a fierce blow, I could feel my pulse beating heavily in my groin. The pain shot straight up my torso but got lodged between my stomach and diaphragm as I tensed every muscle in my body to try and contain it there. If I didn't relax soon, I'd black out. The need for oxygen quickly took priority as I opened my mouth and gasped for air, except my lungs didn't respond. Instead my mouth filled with puddle water, grit, oil and possibly, almost definitely, canine and human excrement. My taste-buds reacted quickly to reject it, but in reflex I swallowed instead of spitting. The cold mix sloshed about inside me as I gagged repeatedly.

I felt more blows from a clenched fist and boot on my shin, chest, shoulder and head but the pain was nothing in comparison to the constant throbbing between my legs. Completely worn out, I made no noise as each swing connected. I just lay still, hoping my attacker would eventually give up too.

The blows finally stopped, along with the aggressive grunting with each effort. My normal hearing gradually started to return and I listened to the rainwater running into the street drain near my head. Moments later, it was replaced by a gravelly sound of someone clearing their nose and hawking in their throat, followed by a thick spitting noise. The warm phlegm landed directly on my cheek, accompanied by my attacker's parting words: 'Not such a big man now, are you, Mr Beat?'

46
BLOWIN' IN THE WIND

I felt wet when I regained consciousness. *Have I just pissed myself?* I thought. Instead I opened my eyes to see I was totally drenched by rain, lying in the street outside work.

I came round to the surreal sight of the members of the Fugees standing over me.

What the fuck, man? What the fuck? asked Wyclef, nearly hyperventilating while kneeling over my body in the street. *What happened?*

I was used to hearing imaginary conversations in my head but to see it acted out in front of me was a traumatic novelty; I hadn't experienced this in a while.

'Not sure,' I said, lifting my head off the floor like a boxer who'd been knocked upside down by a Mike Tyson punch. I felt cold, stiff but mainly achy all over, as though I'd been trampled by bulls on the run in Pamplona. Pras and Lauryn helped me get up painfully on to my elbows and knees and eventually my feet. I didn't have enough hands to clutch all the sore parts so my ribs and crotch got dibs. I needed to get inside, away from the cold wind that was blowing through my wet clothes.

They walked with me back to the office that was barely

twenty-five metres away, but it felt a lot further. I staggered past the security guard sleeping at his desk, up the stairs and into my chair. The bright lights shone painfully in my eyes as I sat down figuring out what I should do next. *Toilet. I really need to piss.*

I stood over the ceramic bowl, tilted my head upward and winced at the onset of more pain shooting from my groin. I flushed the dark orange urine and stood at the sink to wash my hands, finally seeing my face. I'd got away with it. Apart from a few scratches and some bumps, I was relatively unscathed. There would be nothing worse than bruises on my face and having to repeatedly explain what had happened. It didn't matter, anyway, as you were either a pussy who got his head kicked in or a pub-drunk troublemaker. No one ever believes you fell off your bike or it was a footballing accident.

Adding insult to injury was seeing a big splodge of phlegm on my cheek. I immediately washed it off.

Wyclef was pacing around by the urinals and broke the silence. *We should tell Security or call the police.*

The attacker's long gone and there's no security cameras beyond the gates, said Lauryn, sitting on the edge of the sink.

Eyewitnesses? suggested Wyclef.

At this time of night and on a side street? And pointless calling the police unless you're dead, said Pras, leaning against the toilet door.

I poked my ribs. The pain was real. I inspected the rest of my body: there were bruises on my legs, my front and my back.

Suddenly Wyclef spoke and sent a chill down my spine. *What if they come back?*

I'd never been jumped before and my body was starting to shake as fear ran through me, causing my heart to beat faster.

Splash some water on your face, get a grip, said Lauryn firmly.

I breathed in deeply, let out a sigh and repeated it several times until my heart calmed down.

Who did this? asked Lauryn.

As I stood looking at my reflection, Pras was first to speak. *Damn, it could be anyone.*

Max? He wasn't happy with you at the MOBOs, said Wyclef.

Simon? Now that you've split with Sophia, maybe it was payback for the barbecue? Pras suggested.

Or his car, his eye or how you've treated Sophia? said Lauryn, adding to the tally.

Michael 'Four Eyes'? He's probably pissed you haven't played his song, said Wyclef.

Will Sturge, for rejecting his video so insultingly? said Pras.

A jealous boyfriend of some girl you spoke to at a Beat party? said Lauryn.

An angry work colleague? suggested Wyclef.

OK, that's absurd, said Lauryn.

The Fugees went through the extensive list and started arguing over the odds of each suspect. I'd understood *what* had happened, figured out *who* could have done it and uncomfortably swallowed the *whys*. Whether through fault of my own or not, I'd pissed people off. Had I been a twat?

Did I deserve this? The Fugees kept firing out questions, answers and theories that I was too tired to consider. The rollercoaster of emotions I'd felt this year had come full circle. I was back to square one: a loser.

Embarrassed, and not wanting Pritz to know what had happened, I made my excuses for bailing on him. I spent the evening at the hospital checking nothing was broken, then a sleepless night in bed sifting through my thoughts and theories.

The next morning, I got in early to speak with the Minister, who normally came in before everyone else too. He cut a lonely figure, further highlighted by the lack of personal pictures on his desk. He just kept a very sanitized collection of work things on display.

'Terry, can I have a word?' I asked tentatively, standing by his coat stand.

'Be quick, I'm late for a meeting,' he said, not bothering to lift his head from his computer.

'Something happened last night that I think you should know.'

He still didn't flinch.

'I was . . .' Suddenly I lost my bottle, feeling embarrassed to say it out loud. But eventually the word fell out on its own: '. . . jumped.'

Head still, his eyes shifted on to me and then scanned me all over. 'What do you mean?' he said, disbelieving.

'Someone attacked me outside the office,' I said gingerly.

'When?' he asked.

'About ten thirty-ish. Whoever it was knew that I worked at The Beat, so –'

'Were you going on a shoot?' he cut in. 'Did you have a camera bag?'

'No,' I said.

He looked relieved that expensive equipment wasn't lost. 'Were there any witnesses?' he asked.

'I don't think so.'

He made some notes on his pad. 'Did you tell Security?'

'No, because I was out for a while and whoever did it was gone by the time I came round.'

'Did it happen on the actual premises?' he asked.

I could see where he was going. 'No, it was just down the street though.'

'But you look perfectly OK. There's no obvious signs of anything,' he said, clearly sceptical.

'I must have covered my face, I don't remember much. But I have bruising on my body.' I offered to lift my jumper.

'OK, OK, you don't need to start undressing,' he said, turning his head away in disgust. He paused, thought for a bit, then exhaled loudly and concluded, 'So what exactly do you want me to do about it?'

I looked at him, stunned. As my boss I was expecting some concern at the very least.

'You want me to file a report with HR? Nothing's going to get done. The police will come, they'll ask you questions because they have to be seen to be doing so in front of HR. Then they'll go back to their office and type out a report that will get lost because there's no leads to go on.'

But I might have leads, I thought. *If you bothered to ask me.*

'They'll assume, like I have, that it was a druggy from

353

the estates who got overly exuberant trying to take your wallet from you. My advice is don't put up a fight, just give them the damn thing.'

But it wasn't a druggy, the guy called me 'Mr Beat', I thought. I didn't say it out loud because I could see it was pointless. His mind was made up. I'd just begun to think I was a valuable member of his team. In reality, I was just another ant worker. But I suppose the Minister was right about one thing – there were no witnesses and no evidence.

'Look, all that will happen is you'll be part of office gossip for a day. Do you really want people talking behind your back?' he said, like he was doing me a favour.

'Well . . .'

'Do you want this trouble? I sure don't,' he said.

'No, I don't want to be a problem,' I said quickly.

'I'm sure it seems worse than it was, that's just the side-effect of shock. You can walk and talk, surely you're all right?'

I wanted to tell him about the constant pain in my ribs. 'Yes, I suppose –'

'Good. I won't forget your discretion with this,' he said, grabbing his diary and standing up. Then, back to his usual headmaster tone, 'We've got a lot on for the end-of-year shows. I need all hands on deck.' He held open the door so I could leave, then walked off in the opposite direction.

I stood outside his office for a moment, taking stock of the situation, then hobbled back to my hamster wheel.

47
POLICE OFFICER

A week on since being jumped, and I was still out of sorts. My confidence was low and my pride dented at the hands of the anonymous attacker. If I knew who it was I could try to reconcile things mentally and get over it. The not knowing was beginning to torture me. But I didn't have time to feel sorry for myself. I had to keep going as I was so close to the finishing line.

I was driving up to the last Beat party of the year in Manchester in the Mini Cooper PJ had lent me as part of the deal we had struck in Miami. I breezed up the M1 and M6 playing Green Day's 'Warning'. I was ridiculously late after a doctor's appointment and I began switching through the lanes, speeding effortlessly past all the lorries and slow drivers. Moments later, though, I was being lapped by them all as I stood on the side of the hard shoulder giving my details to the boys in blue.

'Will this take much longer? I have to get to Manchester to film tonight,' I asked as one of them checked my details in the patrol car and the other loomed over me.

'What are you filming?'

'I'm filming a Beat party,' I said.

'Oh, really?' he said, looking genuinely impressed.

I described the intricate details of what lay ahead and even offered to put him on to the guest list. It was worth a shot.

'Oh no, I'm way too old for that,' he said, laughing at the thought.

'You're only as old as the woman you feel,' I joked.

He chuckled. 'That's true, but the missus is a bit of an old mare now too!'

'Well, perhaps we can get you a younger upgrade?'

We continued the banter until the radio on his chest went off and his colleague confirmed that I was insured and able to drive the car.

I let out a sigh of relief. 'Thank you, officer,' I said, heading for my car, knowing I needed to get back on the road as soon as possible.

'Sorry, sir, one last thing before you go,' he said.

Haha, he does want the VIP tickets to the party! I thought.

'I've just got to give you your ticket,' he said.

'What for?' I asked.

'You were doing ninety-eight miles per hour. That carries a ninety-pound fine and three points on your licence,' he said.

I begged him to let me off and tried every last trick in the book. 'I'm truly sorry, but I was already late for the party. I have to interview Nelly in thirty minutes for The Beat.'

'Nelly?' he said.

Name-dropping had paid off. 'Yes,' I confirmed as he stopped writing.

'You're interviewing an elephant?' he said, perplexed.

'No, Nelly the US rapper,' I replied, astonished.

He paused and then said, 'Never heard of him,' as he continued writing the ticket.

So now I was ridiculously late and freezing too, having been stood on the side of the road for what felt like ages. As I slowly pulled away from the flashing blue lights, I began cursing everything from the police to the car I was in. Barely two minutes later and I was stuck in slow-moving traffic which then ground to a standstill due to an 'overturned lorry ahead'. I called Tola to tell her I'd be late and to ask her to take over filming duties. She'd gone to Manchester by train earlier in the day with Cara and Sonya.

I eventually arrived at eleven p.m. and there were still queues of agitated people waiting in the cold to get in. Some had tickets and some didn't. I put my Beat crew pass on and rushed in to catch up with the others. They'd filmed as much as they could without Marcus Fieldman, a thespian and one of The Beat's wilder presenters, who still hadn't arrived.

I walked around with my camera imagining I'd bump into Sophia, but she was nowhere to be seen. In fact, as I walked through the crowd in their themed beachwear outfits, there seemed to be more 'grown-ups' than students. The notoriety of the parties had clearly spread. I realized I'd come quite far since Middlesbrough where I was wracked with nerves and inexperience. That thought momentarily lifted my shattered confidence.

Midnight was fast approaching and panic was slowly setting in as Nelly needed to be introduced on stage. Alison came running up to Tola and me looking flustered, which could mean only one thing.

'OK, this party is turning from bad to worse,' she said.

'Why, what's wrong?' Tola asked.

'Marcus definitely isn't coming.'

'What?' I said.

'He's caught in traffic on the motorway. Why couldn't he just get on the train like the rest of us?' she said, annoyed.

I quickly realized the full impact of his absence. 'How do we film links without him?'

'I don't know, that's your department. I've got other things to worry about. I just caught one of the dancers having sex in one of the storage rooms with one of the punters.'

We couldn't help but laugh.

'Not that funny, he didn't go quietly – Security had to throw him out,' she said, like the roof was caving in.

As midnight struck, things momentarily fell into place. Nelly needed no introduction. The music stopped, he came on with his entourage and smashed it for fifteen minutes, teaching the crowd his 'Country Grammar'.

But straight afterwards unexpected little skirmishes began breaking out as people got increasingly drunk. It was mostly masked by the loud music and Security who were at hand to sort things out quickly. But this was now no longer a Beat party. Cara, Tola and I stood in the VIP section, overlooking the dance floor, enjoying a drink with an hour to go, when all of a sudden a loud deafening bang went off.

The crowd below dispersed in an instant, screaming for cover and running for the exits. Security in bright yellow bibs were running in different directions. The DJ was furiously playing around with the knobs in the booth as the sound of screams took over. Panic had hit everyone.

'Is Sonya back?' Cara asked, realizing we were missing someone.

'She must still be downstairs, filming,' said Tola.

Cara and I rushed to look for her and were swept into the wave of people scampering for the exit. We broke through the tide and found Sonya outside the cloakroom, sitting on the floor with a bruised head. She explained that she had gone to film vox-pops with kids who were leaving, saying how good the party had been, when she got knocked over and on to the floor in the mad rush. The bump on her forehead had already gone purple and she was shaking, on the verge of tears.

With our arms around her, we walked her back upstairs to the crew room only to find worried looks on the faces of Tola, Alison's staff, the three Beat dancers and the girls from Marketing. An inquisition was already under way.

'Does anyone know where the hell Alison is?' asked Shirley Orr, The Beat's Head of Events, raising her voice to be heard among all the muttered conversations.

'No,' said Tamsin, who worked for Alison. 'Her phone's just ringing through.'

'Well, where's the manager of the club? He should know what's happened.'

'He's downstairs talking to the police and trying to sort out people getting their coats from the cloakroom. It's bedlam down there,' I said.

'Does anyone know what the fuck happened?' Shirley asked the room.

Pieces of information from witnesses were being pieced together. One of the dancers who'd been on a podium had seen everyone rushing out and a big trail of blood on the dance floor. At that moment, everyone went silent. The worst had happened.

'I knew we shouldn't have done a party in Gunchester,' said Shirley, looking visibly upset and fidgety.

'The kids were saying this wasn't a uni crowd. Even I thought there was a rough element in there,' said Tola.

'This was the hottest ticket in town and it clearly attracted the wrong people,' said the dancer.

'Why would people in Bermuda shorts want to start something?' I asked.

'Plus we only advertised among the university crowd,' said Tamsin.

'I heard someone got beaten up and that his friends from Moss Side came looking for the guys who'd done it,' said Tola.

Shirley looked increasingly shocked. 'What?'

'No way,' said Tamsin, concerned Shirley was about to have an aneurism.

'I heard someone got beaten up too, and they went to their car to get a shooter,' said the dancer.

'I have to speak to my boss,' said Shirley, 'and I'm sure he won't like being woken up at three a.m. to this news. We need damage limitation to the brand. And we need to know exactly what happened.'

By now the Head of Press was involved, as the company's name was at risk and the negative headlines would not be received well at HQ. Alison would be held accountable if security hadn't been up to scratch. So far, though, no reporters had shown up, although it wouldn't take long as there were now several police cars with flashing lights outside the venue.

Half an hour after the club had shut down, Alison and

DJ Rage returned to the crew room. They were both covered in blood.

'Where the hell have you been?' asked Shirley, looking at the blood in shock.

'I was at the hospital,' Alison replied.

'Why weren't you picking up the phone?' asked Shirley, firing another question at her.

'What happened?' I asked, cutting straight to the point.

Alison sat down, clearly exhausted. 'I was in the front office talking to the manager when it kicked off. I got to the DJ booth and Rage was fiddling with the controls. One of the main speakers popped, which sounded like a gun had gone off. In the panic, a boy's wrist got slashed by broken glass, probably from a broken bottle. He was lying on the dance floor bleeding heavily. Rage came down and helped me take him through the fire escape straight to the hospital,' she said.

'Where was your phone?' asked Shirley.

'I left it in the front office as I rushed out,' she said. 'It was an emergency; there wasn't time to get it. He could have died!'

'So no one got shot?' the dancer asked.

'No,' she replied, like it was a ridiculous suggestion. 'If they had, don't you think the police would be in here asking you all questions?'

Shirley let out a sigh of relief and sat down in a chair, looking equally exhausted. Calm suddenly prevailed in the room as everyone went over to Alison to find out more.

Tola and I stood in a corner putting the kit away as Cara sat with a shaken-up Sonya.

'Jesus! Makes you wonder if these parties are worth it,' said Tola.

'We have to have them, it's what's expected,' I said, amazed she was talking to me again.

'What's the point? Look at tonight. It's lucky nothing serious happened. Imagine if it did?' said Tola.

I stopped packing and turned to her. 'Are you serious? We can't stop doing these parties.'

'All the goodwill be forgotten if one bad thing happens,' said Tola.

'Damned if we do, damned if we don't,' I said, and she nodded in agreement.

This was the longest conversation we'd had in weeks. With the communication channel clear, was this the time to apologize to her? I wanted to. Desperately. But my pride lodged in my throat, rendering my vocal cords useless. It had done it to my finger too, stopping me from pressing the call button when I'd wanted to speak to Sophia so many times over the last couple of weeks. It seemed like pride had got in the way a lot lately. For now, the most I could muster was a brief hug, but Tola seemed to appreciate it.

We left Shirley in the club to carry out the full post mortem with Alison and the manager. The mood in the taxi taking us back to the hotel was sombre. Michael Jackson's 'You Are Not Alone' played on Galaxy Radio as heads leant against windows, preparing for pillows. I sat in a trance staring out of the window, watching milk floats go by as Sonya's head rested on my shoulder. My phone beeped with a new text message.

Oh no, not the Minister. Not now, I thought. I wasn't in the mood to have my balls busted. I looked down and read it.

Heard the police were at The Beat party. Are you OK? Sophia

362

48
ARE YOU GONNA GO MY WAY

The enormous fir tree fell over several times in the Greenhouse before it was finally hoisted into place. One of the workmen putting it up had to go to the hospital with a broken nose as he bore the brunt of one fall. When it eventually went up and stayed up it looked a treat and signalled that Christmas had officially arrived.

The end-of-year party was always held in the first week of December to ensure everyone from the Europe offices could make it before people left for their extended vacations. Departments were a hive of activity as they sought to tie up loose ends. Meanwhile, James III was in his whistling element, Christmas carols on loop from his pursed lips.

Our fate as interns was going to be announced by the Minister today but no meeting request had arrived yet. Our extended contracts were up on Friday, which was just a few days away. To celebrate the end of the year, we took in a quick visit to the pub before returning to hear the senior management's speeches. We were all taking bets on who'd get the permanent position with everyone nominating each other, yet deep down inside feeling it had to be them.

We returned in time to see Darth Vader turn on the

Christmas tree lights to an ironic cheer from the drunken crowd. Once again the place was packed as he and the Doc gave glowing end-of-year reports, ending with another fast-cut The Beat reel.

With the Doc's bit done, he called on a few members of senior management to speak. One by one the suits spoke about their major plans for next year and then fielded questions. Finally the Minister took to the stage and read like a robot from a printout, making Darth Vader look like an orator of the highest calibre. Once he had finished, to bored applause, he waited briefly for questions. Just as he was about to go to his seat, someone shouted out.

'I've got a question.'

He scanned the crowd to see where it had come from, as did everyone else. I suddenly saw everyone looking in my direction, including the Minister. Had I somehow blurted something out without realizing? No, the voice had come from over my right shoulder and the breath was distinctly laced with alcohol.

'Why aren't there equal opportunities for women in Production?' asked Cara, slurring slightly.

Oh God, I thought. *What is she doing?*

'Why is there a tinge of macho homophobia? In fact, why aren't there more people of colour working here apart from in Security?' she added, like an investigative journalist, nudging forward to stand beside me. The needle had fallen off the record.

A handful of people awkwardly applauded in different parts of the audience. The rest of the crowd froze as the entire Greenhouse lost its drunken buzz. The Minister stood still, not sure how to respond. The answers didn't lie on his printout no matter how many times he looked down at it. The silence seemed to last for ages. Soon he dispatched a freestyle ramble and quickly went back to his seat, afraid of a follow-up question. He'd sidestepped answering the question like he was walking down a path full of dog shit. The Doc leant into the mic and bravely asked, 'Any more questions?'

There was a long silence as everyone braced themselves.

'Yeah, I've got one,' said another voice, this time from over my left shoulder.

Oh no, it was James III. Was he going to ask if he could whistle 'Jingle Bells' for everyone? Going to the pub early was looking like a mistake.

'Out of the two BMWs in the forecourt, in a race, whose would be faster, yours or your boss's?' he said in a serious tone.

The Greenhouse burst into laughter and the buzz returned. James III had placed the needle back on the record and it was time for mistletoe and wine once again.

It wasn't long till we were all on the party bus singing Christmas carols, led by James III, on our way to Ministry of Sound in Elephant and Castle.

Inside, the venue was more Christmassy than the jolly fat man in red himself. The waiters were dressed up as elves and the waitresses, well, sexier versions of elves in short skirts. Those taking time out from the dancing could keep themselves entertained on the bouncy castle, the stripper's pole and the karaoke booth.

It was funny seeing heads of departments being coy as

they asked younger employees for drugs. I still marvelled at how commonplace drugs were in The Beat's world. I almost forgot they were illegal sometimes. The laser light show in the main room would look spectacular for those soon to be off their tits. Mistletoe was hung everywhere for those who felt shy – and to give some of the Technology Support guys a bit of a fighting chance.

'So, who's pulled who so far then?' I asked as I communed with Cara, Sonya and Tola for a gossip session. We were stood by the bar, watching the presenters make a circle in the middle of the dance floor, enticing everyone to drunkenly breakdance.

'Well, I heard the pretty woman from Legal was with the tall guy from Scheduling,' said Tola.

'But they're both married,' I said.

'Yeah, well I also heard she's filing for divorce. Walked in on her husband . . . with two other men.'

'What? But they've just had a kid,' said Sonya.

'Post-natal blues . . . for her husband, maybe?' suggested Tola.

'I heard two guys who work in the studios had a fight in the pub over one of the make-up girls a few weeks back,' said Cara.

'That's nothing, I heard one of the last interns here, a nineteen-year-old, had an affair with a married woman in the On-Air department and she left her husband for him,' said Sonya.

As the revelations came thick and fast, I looked around and noticed the people I'd worked with in a new light. They were paired off laughing, talking, dancing and kissing in the corners. The office was rife with rumours of who was doing who: it seemed almost inevitable that people hooked up with someone else from The Beat. There'd be no surprises over the lifestyle, I figured.

We all had more in common than simply the love of music: empathy for the hard slog. I realized that, thanks to The Beat, I had made some really good friends. We'd shared long stressful hours and had spent more time with each other than our family, friends or partners. There was a price to pay for being in Neverland. There should have been a skull and crossbones sign on top of the entrance: WARNING: MAY BE HAZARDOUS TO RELATIONSHIPS.

All of a sudden James III joined us, trying to catch his breath. The Minister had told him to round us up in the chill-out room. As questionable as the timing and location were for this meeting, we knew the time had come for us all.

We walked in to see the Minister sitting in a circle of beanbags, sipping a cocktail. Once we were seated he began.

'Thank you all for joining me. I wanted to do this in the office but time ran out. Firstly, I want to commend you for your hard work and efforts this year.' He sounded slightly drunk, which explained his good mood. He went through the group praising everyone and passing on all the good feedback he'd received.

As everyone was praised they sent out nervous signals like a contestant waiting for the answer to the last question on *Who Wants to Be a Millionaire?* The Minister ended on me as my foot tapped anxiously. 'Jay, you gave us a ratings peak during The Beat awards, making the sponsors sign a big deal for next year,' he said and I mentally punched the air.

We were fixated on him like he had a bogey at the end of his nose. He continued to speak for the next five minutes about his plans for next year, keeping us squirming on the edge of our seats. He eventually stood up, raised his glass and said, 'Thank you for your efforts. Enjoy the party and good luck in your future endeavours.'

He turned and left the room, taking all the air out with him. The man lacked IQ as well as EQ. Everyone sat there in silence.

But not for long. Cara reacted first, accompanied by a look of disgust. 'Fucker! Took my show ideas and I won't be here to make them?'

James III's usual cockiness had also disappeared. 'So was this permanent job even real or just a ruse to make us work harder?'

Sonya hugged Tola. 'Well, it would have been hard for them to choose one person among us all, ay,' she said. 'We've all been pretty awesome.'

'I thought this was all Jay's. That's why I got Talent to help me get a job with Universal Records,' said James III. 'It's true what they say that your network determines your net worth.'

I looked at him in shock.

'Good for you. Stuey helped me get a job at a production company called Endemol,' added Cara.

My head spun round to her on my right.

'Well, seeing as we're all sharing, I got a job at the Prince's Trust,' admitted Tola.

'I'm going to go back to my old job but as an edit

assistant. No more making cups of tea!' said Sonya, smiling.

With my head swinging back and forth like I was a spectator at the Wimbledon finals, it was 'Game, set and match' from the voice keeping score in my mind.

'What about you, Jay?' asked Cara.

Me? I've royally screwed it up, I thought. 'I've got a couple of offers I'm weighing up,' I said. If there was one thing I'd learnt from the Minister, it was how to conceal your true thoughts and keep smiling. On the inside I felt like my bones were all broken and my body wanted to collapse in on itself.

'Here's to the future, it's bright like Orange,' said James III, raising his bottle of beer for us all to clink.

Everyone sat laughing and joking about the year gone by while I felt sick to my stomach. I was the only intern to have not seen this coming. Had I refused to see it? Had my own ego convinced me I was a dead cert? I felt embarrassed and humiliated inside. A smart-alec voice in my mind that I hadn't heard in a while kept saying, 'I knew this would happen' repeatedly and making me feel even worse. I felt depressed at leaving the job I loved doing and the realization that the prince was turning back into a frog.

The longer I stayed, the more I suffered. Finally, when I couldn't stand it any more, I said my goodbyes to the others. Luckily they knew I still had the end-of-year show to write back at the office so I had an alibi to leave. I embraced them all long and hard, camouflaging the hugs under the guise of a drunken goodbye when really I needed the human contact for other reasons. As I walked down the stairs to a waiting Uncle Lee, I suddenly felt lonelier and lonelier with each step. No girlfriend, no job and no hope.

49
UNFINISHED SYMPATHY

The nostalgia about our experiences as interns was exactly what I needed to write the sentimental end-of-year special for *Total BEATS*. The best moments of the show were invariably my best moments here. Knowing I was leaving the job that had been my life for most of the year helped me write PJ's final link to the viewers for 2000.

During my final record in the studio the next day, the Doc came to watch from the gallery. Luckily his attendance didn't stop the swearing and banter. As the final shot dipped to black, everyone stayed behind for some champagne in the gallery courtesy of the studio manager. Even PJ, who normally had to rush off for something else, stayed around for a drink or two.

Just before the Doc left he took me to the empty studio floor and had a quiet word. I knew he'd done this with the other intern's last records and was saying goodbye the way he'd said hello: with real class.

'Jay, before I shoot off I just want to say thank you for your efforts. I hope you learnt as much from the experience as you gave us,' he said, putting his hand on my shoulder.

'Yes, I did. Thank you for the chance,' I said.

'It's sad we can't keep your talents here but I'm sure our loss will be someone else's huge gain.' He paused and then leant in. 'Us oldies have a secret. We can't do it without you youngsters. Neither revolution nor evolution can happen without you. You bring the energy that keeps us all inspired, young and fighting to keep up. We feed off that energy and drive. So, on a personal note, thank you.'

I nodded. I wanted to say, *Well, give me a job then*. But he'd already gone, leaving me standing in the empty studio.

Back at my desk, I grabbed my tapes for the edit and went for the stairs, but was cut off by Gwyneth. She lead me into the Eighties room and said, 'It's about your expenses –'

'It's OK, I've written them off,' I said, cutting her off before I had to hear her deliver the bad news.

'Well, you'll be pleased to know the money will be in your account before Christmas.'

'What? How?' I exclaimed.

'My boss accidentally signed them off thinking they were mine,' she said with a poker face.

I wanted to jump on her and hug her to me like a bearskin jacket. 'Gwyneth, thank you so much. I can't thank you enough. I really appreciate . . .' I was rambling.

She laughed. 'Jay, it's fine. I know they were genuine and, frankly, it makes me feel good to know that the right thing has been done.'

As I left the meeting room the good news gave me a small spring in my step as I headed for the final edit. Although I was upset not to be staying, I wanted to make sure I left on a good note.

The Christmas spirit was getting hold of everyone as PJ

joined me. He never attended edits as they lasted ages but this time he hung out for eight hours, eating, drinking and looking back at another year of service to music completed.

'You know, I don't know when this merry-go-round is going to end. They could cut it off tomorrow,' he said as we stood on the roof of the building, smoking one of the editor's spliffs.

'Well, the ride's over for me and I'm not quite sure what to do now,' I said. 'But it was fun while it lasted. Thanks, PJ,' I finished, with genuine appreciation. He'd put his neck on the line for me, and I could probably never repay him for that trust.

'You gotta find another ride,' he said slowly, exhaling smoke from his lungs.

'I honestly thought this was it,' I said, staring down at the people walking on the streets below. Why did I think I was going to get a full-time job? All the hours I'd put in? The sacrifices I'd made? The ill-placed bravado, thinking that I was the best intern? I was slowly starting to realize I'd worked hard, but not smart. I'd become addicted to the job and lost sight of the endgame. Robert Johns had warned me that this was just a stepping stone.

'You thought this was going to last forever?' said PJ in shock.

'Not forever, but I thought this was just the beginning,' I admitted. I coughed up a lung and sat down on the chair next to him, passing back the spliff. I put my head in my hands and rested my elbows on my thighs. Everything was spinning.

We sat in silence on the garden furniture for a moment, enjoying the buzz.

'You got a taste for it, didn't you?' he said, commiserating with me. 'You poor bastard.'

I didn't come back to the office for the next two days as the edit took time to complete after the computer crashed several times. It took so long I even ended up missing out on my own leaving drinks with the other interns. It was probably a good thing as it would have been as emotional as the last episode of your favourite sitcom. I didn't make it to the office until one thirty a.m., when I handed the tapes to the guys in Transmission and went upstairs to clear my desk away.

As I got to the intern area, I was met by empty bottles of champagne, plastic cups, Quality Street wrappers, popped party poppers and paper plates with the crumbed remains of chocolate cake from Patisserie Valerie. Suddenly I was sad I'd missed the big farewell. What a moron I was, I hadn't even had the chance to say goodbye to anyone. I sat at my desk and saw a small, unopened bottle of Moët by my computer screen with a Post-it note signed 'With Love' from the others. It stood on top of a David LaChapelle signed copy of *Hot House* that contained his photographs of celebs and artists from *Rolling Stone* magazine shoots.

Next to it, though, was the thing I would cherish forever, more than the pictures of me standing next to the stars, the record plaques from artists for 'helping to achieve high album sales', the signed Paul McCartney guitar and all the other memorabilia I'd collected over nine months at The Beat. I had proof I'd been here. It was a farewell card from everyone in the office signed to 'Jay', 'Jam Master Jay' and

'Wanker'. Lump after lump filled my throat as I read the kind words. I was feeling emotional and lucky to be smelling the flowers after I was gone.

I took in the department for one last time as images from my internship ran through my mind like a montage. The desks where Max and the managers had sat singing songs; the Pillar of Fame with everyone's mugshots from papers and magazines; the viewing machine where we'd gather round to watch new videos; and the area where I had taken a drop on the BMX bike. I'd been living the fast life like a music video. It had finally come to an end and was fading to black.

I walked down the steps towards the exit with a heavy heart. I was meant to hand my ID card to Security on my way out, but I decided to keep it as a memento. I got to the revolving door that had invited me in on my first day in spring and stared briefly at my reflection in it. I'd entered with unassuming clothes and was leaving with more designer labels than you could throw at a boy band. My face looked haggard and the bags under my eyes told a story all of their own. The person looking back at me was strange to comprehend.

Before I could have a full-on Dorian Gray moment, I quickly walked out. But as I did, the door got stuck in the middle of a turn. I tried to push it with one hand but it wouldn't budge. It needed a two-handed effort to get it going again and it finally spat me back out into the big bad world.

50
LOSING MY RELIGION

During my first week away from The Beat I realized I was still attached to the umbilical cord. I couldn't sleep without dreaming I was still at work, late for a studio record or that I'd forgotten to turn up at an interview with an artist. When I was awake my mind was whizzing but had nothing to do. It was a bit like a Ferrari in neutral but with the accelerator down, revs way up and the engine roaring. My body twitched at the inactivity.

As the US courts went about trying to settle the outcome of 7 November, my mind considered the outgoing American president, Bill Clinton. What was it like giving up the best job in the world? What must it be like going from being the President of America to the ex-President of America? Being the most powerful human in the world to just holding the title in an honorary capacity. Like Superman without his powers. What happens to you when you realize you don't get to influence the world any more? Would you forget what a ringing phone sounds like? Worse still, when it's over comes the question – did I have any real friends? Did Gorbachev call Reagan to see if he wanted to grab a beer? Sure you can open a library named after you or try to continue life in the public eye by lecturing, but that's like giving a drug addict a cigarette as a hit.

I was still connected to The Beat in the real world as my phone kept ringing with calls from the office. Each time I looked down to see 'The Beat' calling I hoped it was the Minister calling to ask me to come back. Instead it was always someone asking for a videotape that was out in my name from the library. Eventually I stopped answering. The following week the calls stopped altogether.

My low self-esteem and feeling of humiliation ensured I didn't go out or speak to anyone. I couldn't even turn to music to lift my spirits as it just rubbed salt into my wounds. I stayed in my room with the blinds down, blocking out the world. Soon my paranoia was asking if I was ignoring the world or if it was ignoring me. My phone lay silent, just like the people who'd once called to invite me to their party or event.

Pritz knocked on my door every day, but I lay still and quiet, successfully avoiding him. Other than staring at the TV and sleeping, the only constructive thing I did was try to raise money to make the rent and pay the bills by selling off the free stuff I'd got on eBay. Even the signed copy of *Hot House*, my leaving present, had to be auctioned along with anything else that was autographed and worth something. It added to my glum state but I had no choice.

As the second week rolled on, I spent time flicking through my tattered work diary, looking back on the end of a remarkable year. Full of notes, to-do lists, doodles, phone numbers and graffiti from week 14 to 50, the last weeks of December were now looking threadbare. Was the depression making me inactive or the lack of structure making me depressed? Nothing 'to do' apart from a job interview at the BBC PJ had put me on to and a visit to the job centre.

The latter was a morbid place containing others inflicted with the same unemployment disease, and we all smelt the same. For any of us to get out of this, we needed someone else to believe in us again. I had a degree and had worked at a global media giant. But the only believers appeared to be shops wanting part-time shelf-stackers. I needed the money but how could I go from interviewing A-list stars to stacking shelves? I only went through the humiliation of going to the job centre to sign on because I needed any scrap of money.

The 'employment advisor' spent the time asking me to tell her my celebrity stories from the year. Apparently it was necessary to 'identify skills' I'd picked up. I willingly obliged. Initially it was a buzz that made me feel happy for the first time in days, but I ended up leaving there feeling even worse, having relived every small detail of the life I'd left behind. This was yet another reminder that I'd been living a fantasy, like Harry Potter. With the spell broken, reality loomed large.

Mum had already gone to Essex to spend Christmas with her sister's family. I wasn't looking forward to joining her as they'd want me to repeat my Beat adventure and that would depress me all over again.

The night before the BBC interview, I sat alone in the flat. *The Beach* was playing on the TV on mute. The lights in my room were off as Track 13 on Moby's old CD repeated on a loop. There was trouble in my own paradise and I was feeling lost. Christmas is a time for celebration and joy for most people. But for those who have nothing, it's not. I may have had a roof over my head, but my soul felt homeless. I needed someone or something to help me get out of this.

I sat at the edge of my bed, rocking back and forth as my mind filled with voices. I wanted to call my friends but I wasn't sure who they were any more. There were ten times as many numbers in my phone now than when I began at The Beat but I still felt alone. As I scrolled through my contacts list, not one name jumped out to me. Like everyone else, Pritz was probably having a good time at some work Christmas party. I wanted to turn to him in my hour of need, but who wanted to hear from a downer like me? Sophia and I had sent each other the odd friendly text since the Manchester party and now my finger hovered over the 'call' button. But pride still stopped me.

I'd lost touch with Sara D and my uni mates and it felt awkward to call in this state. I hadn't heard from the other interns either. Were they feeling withdrawal symptoms like me or was I the only one? I stopped looking for names. I had to try and find some inner strength but all the things that gave it to me were gone. My confidence was linked to the love from Sophia, my family and friends, being in my dream job. The Beat had given me a sense of purpose, belonging and a reason to get up and be something. It was my *raison d'être*. I'd lost it all and it was my fault. My eyes began to fill with the pain as my mind went into a haze.

A voice came to the fore. *Not everything enjoyed is good.*

The voices kept coming and I couldn't recognize them. *You were hooked on it and enjoyed the addiction.*

I blocked the voices out in a panic. Fear had gripped me

and I felt like I was wandering in the dark. Would this ever lift?

Was Sophia right, would I regret letting The Beat take control of me?

Deal with it, it's over. Whatever you do, don't panic. Everything will work out, said a returning voice.

Will it? I asked. *My only worry is I'll never change. I'm used to the high speed.*

That won't be any trouble. Parachutes will help you to land softly.

So everything's not lost? I asked.

No. *Life is for living. But you have to rip it all down and start again.*

I decided to trust the voices. I took down all memories from the wall, CDs from the shelves and everything else, throwing them into black bin bags and into the back of my cupboard.

I busied myself by getting my suit ready for the interview the next day. But soon my doubts returned and I realized hiding things away wasn't going to solve my problems. How could I get away from the biggest reminder of all? I couldn't run from it forever. My world revolved around it like a whirling dervish. Even if I escaped to the quietest place on the planet, my heart would continue to create a beat for music.

51

BITTER SWEET SYMPHONY

'Ndugu Bwana, you there?' said Pritz, outside my door.

It was eight a.m. and I lay awake, having barely slept a wink.

'I'm coming in, so cover up your knackers.'

'What's up, dude?' I said, sitting up.

Standing by my doorway he asked, 'You OK? You haven't responded to my texts or calls.' He looked around the room. 'Where's all your stuff?'

'Early spring clean,' I said.

Behind him was a red suitcase that reminded me he was going home for Christmas and then to Rio de Janeiro on Boxing Day for a week with his banker mates. He'd offered to spot me, but I was already too indebted.

As he said his goodbyes we spoke about everything except the cloud that was clearly over me, but that was our dynamic. We didn't talk about feelings with each other; that's what women were for. Whenever either of us got close to it, it would be met by an elongated 'Don't get eeeeeeeeemotional'.

Before leaving he said, 'Listen, you big, prancing, dancing gaylord, I'm out. If you change your mind, the Bank of Pritz can sponsor you to Brazil.' With a quick high-five he was gone.

I'd reflected on a lot these last few weeks and now it was time to get my house in order, from getting a new job to reconnecting with friends like Sara D and Isabel. But there was one person in particular with whom I needed to build a bridge. I sent Sophia a text to see if she was up for a chat over coffee. She agreed to meet me in a Notting Hill coffee shop later that morning.

Having been hugged by Mary Schmich's wise words via Baz Luhrmann as I got ready, I took the Tube to the BBC in White City, almost getting off at Notting Hill as a force of habit. During the journey the *Metro* was quick to remind me of the world I'd left behind with gossip about the stars.

This new job would be in the children's TV department as a researcher. I was worried at the thought of perma-smily-faced presenters, puppets and gunk tanks, but was in no position to be choosey. However, my trepidations were ill-founded and it seemed like a nice place, if a bit quiet. There weren't any people throwing frisbees, pinging rubber bands, riding BMX bikes or playing music really loud. I'd be a minnow worker with about as much responsibility as Baldrick from *Blackadder*, but it was the return to the real world I needed.

It went well, especially as the interviewer had studied at my university. I wasn't offered the job on the spot but was happy to be in the half pile of CVs that didn't get thrown in the bin as he gave me a big hint that it was mine. But I wasn't falling for that again. I'd wait for the call.

As I left the BBC I took a right and walked down Wood Lane past a huge construction site on the left and on to

Shepherd's Bush Green. From there I walked up to Notting Hill Gate to meet Sophia.

I entered the quiet coffee shop and saw her in the corner reading *Hello!* We didn't hug or embrace but it was clear all defences were lowered.

I filled her in on what I'd been doing, but kept some of the more depressing details to myself.

'Sounds like your new job will be a step forward. Now you've got the BBC to conquer,' she said, smiling.

'Haven't got it yet. But I will handle things differently, I suspect.'

She hugged me with her smile.

'So, plans for Christmas?' she asked.

'I was dreading it, but I think time with the family is in need. Going to get a train there tomorrow. How about you?'

'Same. Dad's taking us on a skiing holiday.'

After small talk about the contents of her magazine, we finally addressed the real issue. Refreshingly, neither of us were blaming the other but ourselves for not communicating properly, point scoring and making bad judgements. We didn't go into it any further as it was water under the bridge now and wasn't going to help bring us back together. But the *entente cordiale* was signed.

I wanted to put it all on the table and apologize for my behaviour. The job, my pride and the bad decisions I'd made. The words wanted to come out but they weren't ready just yet. It seemed like Sophia wanted to do the same but our confessions stopped short. Maybe for another day? Perhaps there was hope for the future. Even so, there were signs we'd salvaged a friendship from this car crash.

As we got up to leave, I hesitated before hugging her. The human photosynthesis she always offered me gave me the strength to finally apologize. 'I'm –'

'Me too,' she said, cutting in while squeezing me back.

I could have gone home on the Tube but had a Forrest Gump moment and decided to walk instead. I blocked out an entire city of people with each step and gathered my thoughts. I had pressed the 'reset to factory settings' button and was ready to start afresh. Doubt could only be defeated in a duel by belief and so I had to believe in myself once more. Like Biggie, there would be life after death.

I went past Marble Arch and Oxford Circus, the arching Christmas streetlights of Oxford Street above my head. I continued till I got to Holborn and took a diagonal left past a shop with a lit Hanukkah menorah in the window. Soon I was on Goswell Road outside my flat, watching as Kemal, the kebab shop owner, and his co-workers broke their fasts with dates.

As I entered the flat, the streetlight outside the kitchen window made turning the hall lights on pointless. I threw the mail and newspaper I'd collected on to the table and opened the fridge door, scanning the shelves for something exciting to eat. The only thing that looked remotely edible was the milk – just. On tonight's menu would be a bowl of Kellogg's Corn Flakes that I placed into the microwave for two and a half minutes.

Exhausted, I sat and scanned the newspaper in the dim light for its happiness and goodwill messages. The last mail drop hadn't brought much Christmas cheer as I held up bill after bill, pizza leaflet after pizza leaflet and, right at the end, a postcard. Clearly just another marketing gimmick by a travel agent asking why I was still in the UK and persuading me that it wasn't too late to be in Thailand. Idle curiosity to see the offer got the better of me. I turned it over.

J, Whatttup? Hope you're enjoying London weather! Been trying to call you, but you haven't picked up. Wanted to speak to you on the phone but I figured a postcard would be best as the Internet cafe is six miles away from my beach hut. Good news, got a call from the Doc and he wants me to come back for something big. With my own team. The beat goes on like Sonny & Cher. 2001, we bring the roof down. I don't need to ask you if you're in, do I? M

The microwave pinged. The house had dealt a new hand.